THE PENGUIN BOOK
OF GERMAN STORIES

The Penguin Book of German Stories

EDITED BY
F. J. LAMPORT

PENGUIN BOOKS

Penguin Books Ltd, Harmondsworth, Middlesex, England
Penguin Books Inc., 7110 Ambassador Road, Baltimore, Maryland 21207, U.S.A.
Penguin Books Australia Ltd, Ringwood, Victoria, Australia
Penguin Books Canada Ltd, 41 Steelcase Road West, Markham, Ontario, Canada
Penguin Books (N.Z.) Ltd, 182–190 Wairau Road, Auckland 10, New Zealand

—

First published 1974
This collection copyright © Penguin Books, 1974

—

Made and printed in Great Britain by
Richard Clay (The Chaucer Press) Ltd
Bungay, Suffolk
Set in Monotype Garamond

—

CONTENTS

PREFACE

A FORM long established in Romance literatures, the short story did not appear in German until the end of the eighteenth century. Indeed, some critics would maintain that the short story (*Kurzgeschichte*) as such did not appear until the twentieth; and that the characteristic German form of shorter prose narrative, the novella (*Novelle*), is quite distinct. Whatever may be its distinguishing formal features – and there has been a great deal of theorizing on this point – the typical German story is, at all events, of substantial length. This presents problems for the anthologist with a limited space at his disposal. I have tried to get in as many writers as possible; this has meant choosing shorter and less familiar pieces to represent some well-known authors, but others, including a number of major nineteenth-century prose-writers, had still to be left out altogether. In trying to present a picture of a literary tradition, I have also perhaps unduly neglected the more varied experiments in story-telling of the twentieth century, though I have sought to show how writers still discernibly related to that tradition have dealt in their fiction with the experience of modern times.

The *Novelle* was introduced into Germany by Goethe with his *Conversations of German Émigrés* (1794): a collection of tales within an overall narrative framework, modelled on such early Romance examples as Boccaccio's *Decameron* or the *Heptameron* of Marguerite de Navarre. At the beginning of Goethe's collection, and thus at the beginning of the history of the German *Novelle*, stands the tale of Madame Antonelli and her faithful ghost-lover which opens the present volume. It appears little more than an extended, or amplified, anecdote, but its simplicity is deceptive. Two features were to prove particularly characteristic of the form as it developed in Germany: its concentration upon mysterious, inexplicable events, and its self-conscious narrative manner. Here the story-teller with quizzical self-irony disparages the artistic

form of his own story and thus alludes to the problematic
relationship between his art and the reality which it mirrors.
Fantastic, extraordinary occurrences and characters, and the
self-preoccupation of the artist, are both key elements in
German Romanticism, here represented by its greatest and
most influential story-teller, E. T. A. Hoffmann. His contemporary Kleist, however, prefers to narrate his extraordinary
tale more directly, thereby relating its events more forcefully,
even brutally, to the world of our everyday experience. For
the Romantic, on the other hand, the world of mystery and
art, though it holds its own terrors, still offers an escape from
the philistine constrictions of mundane reality. Moving on
further into the nineteenth century, we find a similar contrast
between the searing honesty of Büchner's realism and the
more self-consciously artistic filtering of reality by the 'poetic
realists' Storm, Keller, and Heyse. Yet Büchner too is a self-
conscious artist: almost like a Romantic, he takes a deranged
artist-figure as the protagonist of his story, and puts his own
(albeit totally un-Romantic) artistic credo into his hero's
mouth. The Holsteiner Storm and the Swiss Keller typify
much nineteenth-century prose-writing in their concentration on the landscape, character, history, and manners of
their own respective corners of the German-speaking world.
Paradoxically, while the political fragmentation of eighteenth-
century Germany had led to the creation of something of a
united republic of letters, the nineteenth century's strivings
for political unity were accompanied by the growth of region-
alism in literature.* Some writers turned to historical or
exotic settings: Heyse's story was conceived, he claimed, in
Sorrento, where it is set. Its local colour is perhaps superficial compared with Storm's, but Heyse's effective shaping
of a simple human encounter provides an elegant example of
the story-teller's craft. Such elegance was, however, viewed

---

*Particular mention should perhaps be made of Adalbert Stifter
(1805–68), the 'poetic realist' of Austrian Bohemia, with his rapt evoca-
tion of a rural tranquillity far from the turbulent world of cities, politics,
industrialization, and progress. He is still much admired – indeed, there
has been something of a Stifter cult in certain quarters: witness the
ironic reference in Böll's story, p. 345.

with disfavour by the Naturalists of the eighteen-eighties.
Naturalism sought to portray man and social phenomena with
scientific objectivity, and not to shirk life's more sordid
scenes: Hauptmann depicts the suffering of a humble member
of society in the setting of his job and his natural and human
environment. Schnitzler, on the other hand, with a deadly
accuracy sharpened by wit, depicts an entire fabric of social
relations, attitudes, and values through the internal mono-
logue of a single representative figure. With Thomas Mann
we return to the artist concerned above all with his art,
though his little vignette of 'decadent' *fin de siècle* Munich
has its social resonances too. The elements of satirical fantasy and the grotesque, hinted at here and in much of Mann's
work, are a vital part of the tradition of the German story,
tracing their descent back through Keller and Hoffmann;
they make their most deeply disturbing appearance in Kafka,
and have recurred in much German fiction dealing with the
experience of the great wars of the twentieth century and
their aftermath – experience which it so often seems a more
straightforward realism can hardly grasp, let alone convey.
Gaiser treats the theme of war and occupation – here from the
occupier's point of view – in a comparatively direct manner,
but his story recalls the nineteenth-century *Novelle* in its
scale and in its careful artistic structuring. In Böll's portrait of
post-war West German affluence satirical fantasy and realism
blend once more.

The present anthology thus offers, I hope, a representative
selection of German stories from the inception of the genre
to the present day: a characteristic mixture of realism and
fantasy, of tragedy and comedy, of concern with man and
with nature, with reality and with art.

I should like to thank all those who have had any part in
the preparation of this anthology, for their contributions,
their advice, their help, their patience. I should particularly
like to record with gratitude the encouragement I received in
the early stages of this work from the late Robert Baldick, who
as Editor of the Penguin Classics did so much to introduce the
literatures of modern Europe to English readers.

ACKNOWLEDGEMENTS

FOR permission to reprint the stories specified we are indebted to the following:

Blackie & Son Ltd for Hoffmann's 'Krespel the Lawyer' from *Tales of Hoffmann*, translated by James Kirkup

Max Hueber Verlag and Verlag Ullstein GmbH for Gerhart Hauptmann's 'Thiel the Crossing-Keeper', translated by John Bednall

Eric Glass Ltd on behalf of the Schnitzler Estate and Sheila Stern for Arthur Schnitzler's 'Lieutenant Gustl', translated by Sheila Stern

Martin Secker & Warburg Ltd and Alfred A. Knopf Inc. (copyright 1936) for Thomas Mann's 'The Infant Prodigy' from *Stories of Three Decades*, translated by H. T. Lowe-Porter

Martin Secker & Warburg and Schocken Books Inc. (copyright 1946, 1948) for Franz Kafka's 'The Village School-teacher' ('The Giant Mole') from *In the Penal Colony* (U.S. title *The Great Wall of China*), translated by Willa and Edwin Muir

Carl Hanser Verlag, München, and Faber & Faber Ltd for Gerd Gaiser's 'Aniela' from *Modern German Stories*, translated by Lionel and Doris Thomas

George Weidenfeld & Nicolson Ltd for Heinrich Böll's 'Murke's Collection of Silences' from *Absent Without Leave and Other Stories*, translated by Leila Vennewitz (copyright 1966 by Heinrich Böll)

Johann Wolfgang von Goethe

THE FAITHFUL GHOST

Translated by F. J. Lamport

Johann Wolfgang von Goethe

GOETHE, the dominating figure of German literature, was
born in Frankfurt-on-Main in 1749 and died in Weimar in
1832. He contributed to all the major literary genres: poetry
and drama, novel and story. The collection which the present
story (untitled in the original) opens dates from 1794, and
the setting is topical: a group of German aristocrats, driven
from their houses west of the Rhine by the advancing armies
of revolutionary France, distract themselves from their present misfortunes by story-telling.

THE FAITHFUL GHOST

AFTER supper that evening, when the Baroness had retired early to her room, the others remained together and discussed various items of news just received and various rumours which were circulating. As is usually the case at such times, there was some doubt as to what one ought to believe and what should be discounted.

The old clergyman said: 'I always think it is best for us to believe what is agreeable to us, to dismiss out of hand what would be disagreeable to us, and, apart from that, to allow the truth of anything that seems possible.'

It was observed that this was indeed what people usually did, and by and by the conversation turned to man's powerful inclination to believe in the miraculous. Romantic adventures and ghost-stories were mentioned, and, when the old man promised to tell some good tales of this kind one day, Louise replied, 'It would be very kind, and we should appreciate it very much, if you would tell us one of those tales now, as we are all together and just in the right mood; you would be assured of our attention and our thanks.'

Their old friend needed little persuasion, and began in the following words.

'Once, when I was in Naples, a series of events occurred which aroused great attention and caused considerable argument. Some said the whole story was a fabrication; others said it was true, but there was some trick behind it. Within the latter party there was further disagreement: they argued about who could have been playing such a trick. Others again claimed that it was by no means proven that spiritual entities could not influence physical substances and objects, and that it should not be immediately concluded that every miraculous event must be either a lie or a deception. Now for the story!

'In my day a singer called Signorina Antonelli was the favourite of the Neapolitan public. At the height of her youth,

her beauty, her talents, she lacked none of those feminine
charms which enchant and allure the masses and give delight
and happiness to a small circle of friends. She was not un-
appreciative of admiration and affection; but, temperate and
shrewd by nature, she knew how to enjoy the pleasures of
both without losing the composure which was so necessary
to her in her situation. All the fine, rich young people
crowded round her, but only a few were admitted to her
society; and if in bestowing her favours she mostly followed
the dictates of her eyes and her heart, yet in all her little
adventures she showed a firmness and sureness of character
which was bound to win any keen observer to her side. I had
the opportunity of seeing her for some time, as one of her
favourites was a close associate of mine. Several years had
passed, she had made the acquaintance of many men; and
fools enough there were, weak and unreliable creatures,
among them. So she came to the conclusion that a lover,
though in a certain sense he is everything to a woman, is
usually of no use at all at those moments when she has most
need of help, in everyday affairs, domestic matters, quick
decisions; indeed, by thinking only of himself, he may even
harm the woman he loves, and out of concern for his own
interests feel himself compelled to offer her bad advice, and
lead her to take the most terrible risks.

'In most of her previous associations her mind had been
little occupied; now it demanded sustenance. At last she
felt the need of a friend; and scarcely had she become aware
of this, when there appeared amongst those who sought her
attention a young man in whom she put her trust, and who
appeared to deserve it in every way.

'He came from Genoa, and was in Naples at this time on
some important family business. He was highly favoured by
nature and had enjoyed the most careful upbringing. His
accomplishments were many, his mind as well as his body
brought to perfection; his manners were exemplary, those of
a man who never forgets himself, yet seems always to think
of others first. He had the commercial spirit of his native city;
he took a broad view of everything he had to do. And yet his

situation was not of the most favourable: his family had engaged in some extremely hazardous speculations and become involved in risky legal proceedings. As time went on his affairs became more and more confused, and the anxiety he felt about them gave him an air of sadness which was most becoming to him and encouraged our young lady to seek his friendship, because her intuition seemed to tell her that he needed a woman's friendship himself.

'Previously he had only seen her occasionally and in public, but now on his first approach she admitted him to her house, indeed she invited him most pressingly, and he did not fail to appear.

'She lost no time in revealing her confidence in him and her desire. He was surprised and delighted by her offer. She earnestly requested him to remain her friend and not to claim any of the rights of a lover. She disclosed to him an embarrassing situation in which she found herself just at that moment, and in which he, by virtue of his extensive acquaintance, was able to give her the best possible advice and to turn things very quickly to her advantage. He for his part confided the state of his affairs to her, and, as she was able to cheer and console him, as in her presence he realized many things that he might not otherwise have noticed so soon, so she seemed to be his counsellor too, and in a short while mutual respect and dependence, of the noblest and most beautiful kind, had led to firm friendship. But unfortunately, in agreeing to conditions, we do not always stop to consider whether they are practicable. He had promised to be no more than a friend, to make no claim to be regarded as a lover, and yet he had to admit to himself that he resented the presence of her favoured lovers most deeply, indeed that he found them quite insupportable. In particular he found it most painful to hear his lady-friend cheerfully discussing the good and bad qualities of one of these men, seeming to know all the faults of the man to whom she granted her favours, while yet perhaps the very same night, as if to mock her worthy and esteemed friend, she would be lying in the wretch's arms.

'Fortunately, or unfortunately, it soon happened that the

fair signorina's heart became free again. Her friend observed
this with satisfaction and tried to persuade her that he had
first claim to the vacated place. Not without resistance and
reluctance she acceded to his wishes. "I am afraid", she said,
"that in giving way like this I am losing the most precious
thing in the world: a friend." Her prophecy was soon fulfilled;
for he had only functioned a short while in his dual capacity,
when his moods began to be more difficult: as a friend he
demanded all her respect; as her lover, all her affection; and
as an intelligent and agreeable man, her constant conversation.
This, however, was by no means to the taste of the lively
young lady; she was not prepared to make any sacrifices and
was not at all inclined to grant anyone such exclusive rights.
She therefore tried in a tactful way to cut down his visits
little by little, to see him less often, and to make it plain to
him that she would not surrender her freedom for anything
in the whole world.

'As soon as he realized this, he felt that the greatest possible
misfortune had come upon him, and, sad to say, it did not
come alone: his private affairs began to take a very bad turn.
Here he had to admit to himself that ever since he was a very
young man he had regarded his fortune as inexhaustible, and
that he had neglected his business affairs for the sake of travelling and of cutting a finer and more opulent figure in the
great world than his birth and income could justify. The law-
suits on which he had pinned his hopes were a slow and costly
business. He had to go to Palermo a number of times on
account of this, and while he was away for the last time the
clever young lady took steps to change her domestic arrangements and to remove him gradually from her side. He returned
and found her in different apartments, some distance from his
own, and saw the Marquis of S—, who at that time was a
very important man in the theatre and the world of public
entertainments, visiting her and enjoying her confidence. This
was more than he could bear, and he fell seriously ill. When
the news of this reached his friend she hurried to his side,
cared for him, arranged for him to be nursed, and, as she could
not fail to realize that his financial situation was far from

healthy, left behind for him a considerable sum of money, which satisfied his needs for some time.

'By his presumption in trying to limit her freedom, her friend had already sunk a great deal in her estimation; as her affection for him had declined, so she had become more observant of his ways; and finally, the discovery that he had so foolishly mismanaged his own affairs had given her a far from favourable view of his character and his capacities. He in the meanwhile did not notice the great change which had come over her; rather, her anxiety for his recovery, the constancy with which she would sit often half the day long by his bedside, seemed more to betoken friendship and love than mere pity, and he hoped that on his recovery he would be fully restored to his rights.

'How wrong he was! The more he returned to health and renewed vigour, the less sympathy and affection was apparent in her; indeed it seemed that she found his company as burdensome as she had once found it agreeable. He too, although he did not realize it himself, had grown bitter and ill-tempered during the course of these events; any responsibility which he might bear for his own fate he laid at others' doors, and found excuses for himself in everything. He regarded himself purely as the innocent victim of persecution and injury, and hoped to be fully compensated for all his wrongs and sufferings by the perfect devotion of the woman he loved.

'Armed with these demands, he appeared before her as soon as ever he was able to go out visiting again. He asked for nothing less than that she should devote herself entirely to him, dismiss her other friends and acquaintances, retire from the stage, and live apart, with him and for him alone. She tried to make him see the impossibility of granting his demands, first jokingly and then in earnest, and at last was unhappily obliged to tell him the sad truth that their relationship could continue no longer. He went away and never saw her again.

'He lived for a number of years after this in a very small circle of acquaintances, or rather indeed in the sole company of a pious old lady, who shared a house with him and kept herself on a small income. During this time he won one law-suit after the other; but his health had been undermined, and the joy was gone out of his life. Upon a trivial infection he fell seriously ill once more; the doctor told him that he was a dying man. He heard his sentence with indifference, except that he wished to see his beautiful friend again. He sent his servant, who in more fortunate times had often returned with a favourable answer from her. He asked her to come; she declined. He sent a second time and implored her; still she refused. Finally, it was already far into the night, he sent a third time; she was moved and confided her embarrassment to me, as I happened to be dining with the Marquis and a few other friends at her apartments. I advised her and asked her to perform love's last service for her friend; she seemed hesitant, but after a little thought her mind was made up. She sent the servant away with a cold answer, and he did not come again.

'After dinner we were carrying on an intimate conversation, and were all cheerful and good-humoured. It was about mid-night when suddenly we heard a plaintive, penetrating, anxious and long-drawn sound, as of a voice. We started, looked at each other, and looked about us, wondering what was going to happen. The voice seemed to fade away at the walls, just as it had sprung up in the middle of the room. The Marquis rose to his feet and hurried to the window, and we others busied ourselves with the signorina, who had fallen in a faint. She took some time to recover. The jealous and hot-blooded Italian had scarcely seen her open her eyes again when he broke out into bitter reproaches. "If you must arrange signs with your friends," he said, "then make them less violent and obvious." She replied, with her customary presence of mind, that since she was entitled to see anyone she liked and at whatever time, it was hardly likely that she would choose such doleful and frightening noises to herald an agreeable hour.

'And indeed, there was something horrible beyond belief about that sound. Its long-echoing reverberations had re-mained with us all, in our ears, yes, in our bones. She was pale, her features distorted, constantly on the verge of fainting;

we had to stay with her for half the night. Nothing more was heard. The following evening the same company, not so cheerful as on the previous day, but resolute enough – and at the same hour the same violent and fearful sound.

'In the meantime we had expressed innumerable opinions about the cry, and our speculations had exhausted themselves. There is no need to prolong the story. Every time she dined at home it was heard, at the very same hour; sometimes it seemed to be louder, sometimes less powerful. All Naples was talking of the affair. All the household, all her friends and acquaintances expressed the keenest interest, and the police were even informed. Spies and observers were posted. For in the street it seemed that the noise sprang out of the empty air, and in the room it sounded close at hand in just the same way. Whenever she dined out, there was nothing to be heard; whenever she was at home, the sound rang out.

'But even away from home she was not completely free of her malicious escort. Her charm had opened the houses of the best families to her. Her agreeable company was welcomed everywhere, and in order to escape her malicious visitor she had made it her custom not to be at home in the evenings.

'A man respected by virtue of his age and position was taking her home one evening in his carriage. As she takes leave of him, before her door, the noise rings out between them, and the man, who knew the story as well as a thousand other people, had to be lifted into his carriage more dead than alive.

'On another occasion a young tenor, of whom she was rather fond, was driving through the town with her to visit a friend. He had heard people discussing this strange phenomenon and, being a bright young man, did not believe in prodigies like this. They were talking about it. "I should like to hear your invisible escort's voice too," he said; "will you not call him up? As there are two of us, we need not be afraid!" Thoughtlessness or bravado could do anything, I suppose; at all events, she calls upon the spirit, and in that moment it rings out, there in the middle of the carriage, that shattering noise, three times in rapid succession, and fades away with a timid echo. When they reached the house, their friend found the two of them unconscious in the carriage; only with difficulty could they be revived to tell what had happened to them.

'The signorina took some time to recover. This ever-recurring terror weakened her health, and the noisy ghost seemed to grant her some respite; indeed she hoped, as it had not been heard again for a long time, that she was now at last completely free of it. But this hope was premature.

'When the carnival was over, she went on a little excursion with a friend and a servant-girl. She wanted to visit someone in the country; it was dark before the three women could reach their goal, and as something was amiss with their carriage as well, they were obliged to spend the night in a poor inn, where they had to dispose themselves as best they could.

'The friend had already retired, and the maid, after lighting their candle, was just about to join her mistress in the other bed when the signorina jokingly said to her, "We are at the end of the world here, and the weather is dreadful; do you think he could find us here?" That very moment the noise sounded, louder and more terrible than ever before. The signorina's friend thought for all the world that hell was let loose in the room; she leapt out of bed, ran downstairs just as she was, and roused the whole house. No one enjoyed a wink of sleep that night. But it was in fact the last time that the sound was ever heard. Unfortunately, however, the uninvited guest soon found another and more tiresome way of announcing his presence.

'He had held his peace for some time, when suddenly one evening at the usual time, as she sat at table with company, a shot rang through the window, as if from a rifle or a heavily-charged pistol. Everyone heard the report, everyone saw the flash, but when the window-pane was examined not the slightest damage could be found. Despite this the company took the matter very seriously, and everyone was convinced that an attempt had been made on the signorina's life. They run for the police, they investigate the neighbouring houses, and as they can find nothing suspicious, they mount guard there the next day from top to bottom. They search the house in which she is living most carefully, they post spies along the street.

'But all these precautions were in vain. For three months, at the same moment, the shot came through the same window-frame, without damaging the glass, and, strangely enough, always on the stroke of the hour before midnight; although in Naples they usually count the hours according to the Italian system, so that midnight is of no particular significance.

'At last people became accustomed to this manifestation as they had to the previous one, and gave the ghost no great credit for his harmless prank. Sometimes the shot did not even frighten the company or interrupt their conversation.

'One evening after a very warm day the signorina, without thinking of the time, opened the window in question and stepped out onto the balcony with the Marquis. They had scarcely been standing out there a minute or two when the shot rent the air between them and hurled them both violently backwards into the room, where they collapsed unconscious on the floor. When they had recovered, each felt – he on his left cheek, but she on her right – the smart of a powerful blow; and as they found that no further harm had been done, the incident occasioned all kinds of witty comments.

'From that moment the sound was no longer heard in the house, and now at last she believed that she had shaken off her invisible tormentor, when one evening on the way to visit a lady-friend she was once more terrified by an unexpected adventure. Her way took her along the Chiaia, where once her beloved Genoese friend had lived. The moon was shining brightly. A lady who was sitting beside her asked, "Is that not the house where Signor — died?" "It is one of those two, I believe," replied the signorina; and in that moment the shot, fired from one of those two houses, rent the air of the carriage. The coachman thought he was being attacked and drove on as fast as he possibly could. When they reached their destination the two ladies were lifted from the carriage in a dead faint.

'But this fright was also the last. The invisible companion

changed his methods, and some evenings later the noise of loud applause resounded before her windows. As a favourite singer and actress, this was a sound she was more accustomed to. There was nothing frightening about it, and it could rather be attributed to some admirer or other. She paid little attention to it; her friends were more vigilant and posted sentries as on the previous occasion. They heard the sound, but saw no one, any more than they had done before, and most people were now hoping that these manifestations would soon come to an end.

'After some time this noise too faded away and turned into more agreeable sounds. They were not exactly melodious, but unbelievably sweet and agreeable. The most accurate observers judged them to come from the opposite street corners, to float across the empty air until they reached the window-sill and then to fade gently away there. It was as if a heavenly spirit were playing a beautiful prelude to announce a melody which he was about to sing. But this sound too was finally heard no more, after the whole strange business had gone on for about eighteen months.'

As the narrator paused, the company began to make their thoughts and doubts about this story heard, wondering what truth there might possibly be in it.

The old man maintained that it must be true if it were to be of any interest; for if it was an invented story then it was not a very good one. Upon this, somebody observed that it was strange that no one had inquired about the signorina's departed friend and the circumstances of his death, since after all something might have been discovered to cast a little more light on the story.

'Yes, it was,' replied the old man; 'I myself was curious enough to call at his house immediately after the first occurrence, and to find some pretext for visiting the lady who at the last had tended him like a mother. She told me that her friend had cherished an unbelievable passion for the lady, that towards the end of his life she had been almost the sole subject of his conversation, and that he had described her sometimes as an angel, sometimes as a devil.

'When his illness had finally overcome him, he had had no wish but to see her once more before his end, probably in the hope of pressing from her just one more tender word, a regret or some other sign of love and friendship. All the more terrible to him had been her persistent refusal, and it was plain to see how that last cold rejection had hastened his end. In desperation he had cried out, "No, it shall not avail her! She shuns me; but even after my death she shall have no peace from me!" With these violent words he died, and we afterwards learnt all too well that even beyond the grave one can keep one's word.'

E. T. A. Hoffmann

KRESPEL THE LAWYER

Translated by James Kirkup

E. T. A. Hoffmann

ERNST THEODOR WILHELM HOFFMANN was born in Königsberg, East Prussia, in 1776 and died in Berlin in 1822. He had some success in three careers – as a lawyer, a writer, and a musician: he changed his third name to Amadeus in homage to Mozart. The fascinating, at times demonic, power of music, and the mesmeric control of one human mind by another, are frequent themes of his fantastic tales, and strange, eccentric characters abound. *Krespel the Lawyer* was written in 1816; those who know Offenbach's *Tales of Hoffmann* will recognize it as the basis of Act III of the opera.

KRESPEL THE LAWYER

KRESPEL was one of the most remarkable men I ever encountered in all my life. When I went to H— to take up residence there for a while, the whole town was talking about him, because just around that time one of his most lunatic projects was in full swing. Krespel was celebrated as a learned, skilful lawyer and a clever negotiator. A ruling German prince – not one of the first rank by any means – had called upon Krespel for the drafting of a memorandum which was to press the prince's legal claims to a certain territory, and which he was intending to submit to the Imperial Court.

This plan was carried out with all possible success, and, as Krespel had once complained that he had never been able to find a house to his liking, the prince, as a reward for the memorandum, undertook to pay for the construction of any dwelling Krespel cared to build in accordance with his own desires. The prince said he would also purchase for Krespel whatever piece of land he required to build his house on. However, Krespel did not accept this offer; instead, he stipulated that the house should be built in the most beautiful district, at the main gate of the prince's beautifully laid-out garden.

Then he started buying all kinds of materials and had them transported to the site. There he could be seen, day in, day out, in a peculiar garb which he himself had fashioned according to certain principles of his own, slaking lime, riddling sand, putting the stones for the walls in orderly piles, and so on. He had consulted no architect, and drawn up no plans.

One fine day he went to a very reliable master builder in H— and asked him if he could come to the garden next morning, at daybreak, together with his assistants, apprentices, labourers, and so on, and build his house. The builder naturally asked to see the plans, and was not a little taken aback when Krespel replied that no plans were necessary, that everything would just fall into place in its own way.

When the master builder and his men arrived at the site early next morning, he found that trenches had been dug round a large rectangle. Krespel said: 'This is where my house's foundations are to be set: after that, kindly continue building the four walls upwards until I tell you when they're high enough.'

'No windows and doors, no inner walls?' the builder burst out, apparently shocked to the core by Krespel's mad idea. 'Just do as I told you, my good man,' Krespel answered very composedly. 'The rest will follow naturally.'

Only when he was promised a rich reward could the builder be persuaded to undertake the crazy construction job. But no building had ever been worked upon with greater enjoyment; the task was accompanied by the ceaseless laughter of the builders, who never left the work-site, for they were regaled there with food and drink. So the four walls rose with incredible rapidity, until one day Krespel shouted: 'Stop!'

Then trowels and hammers fell silent, the workmen climbed down from the scaffolding, and, standing around Krespel, inquired with broadly grinning faces: 'What's the next step?'

'Stand aside!' Krespel cried, ran to one end of the garden and then slowly paced back towards his rectangular structure until he came right up to the wall. Then he shook his head testily, ran to the other end of the garden, again strode slowly towards his edifice and did the same as before. He repeated this performance several times, until finally, running his sharp nose-end right against the wall, he shouted: 'Here, men, here! Knock me out a door, here, knock me out a door here!'

He gave the precise measurements for its width and height, and his command was carried out. Then he stepped into the house and smiled politely when the builder pointed out that the walls had exactly the height of a regular two-storeyed house. Krespel paced meditatively up and down, followed by the masons with their hammers and picks, and whenever he cried: 'A window here, six feet high, four feet wide – a small window up there, three feet high, two feet wide –' the apertures were immediately knocked out.

It was just while this operation was being carried out that I arrived in H—, and it was vastly entertaining to observe the hundreds of spectators standing about in the garden, suddenly all shouting triumphantly at the tops of their voices whenever the stones flew out and a new window was made where it had been least expected. Krespel adopted the same technique in the construction of the rest of the house and all the necessary installations; everything had to be done just so, there and then, according to the whim of the moment.

The ludicrous nature of the entire proceedings, the growing realization that in the end everything was turning out better than had been expected, and above all Krespel's liberality – which after all cost him nothing – kept everyone in a good humour. Thus the difficulties entailed by such a quixotic mode of construction were overcome, and in less than no time there stood a fully equipped house whose exterior had the crankiest appearance, for none of the windows were of the same size, and so on, but whose interior appointments were conducive to a sense of quite unusual wellbeing. Everyone who visited it proclaimed this fact, and I myself was conscious of its truth when, on our becoming better acquainted, Krespel invited me there.

But so far I had not yet spoken to this extraordinary man: he was so busy with his building that not once did he put in an appearance for lunch on Tuesdays at Professor M—'s, as had been his custom. When the Professor sent him a special invitation, he sent word that he would not stir outside his new dwelling before the house-warming party. All his friends and acquaintances were looking forward to a great feast: but Krespel invited only the builders, masons, apprentices, and labourers who had worked on his house. He regaled them with the finest dishes: mason's apprentices tucked into partridge pies with riotous abandon, carpenter's lads gleefully planed off slices of roast pheasant, and famished hod-carriers treated themselves to the choicest morsels from the truffle fricassee. In the evening their wives and daughters came and there was a great ball. Krespel waltzed a little with the builders' wives, but then joined the town orchestra, took a fiddle, and led the dance music until daybreak.

The Tuesday after the banquet, which had made Krespel

the idol of the people, I finally found him, to my great delight, at Professor M—'s. Nothing more eccentric than Krespel's behaviour could be imagined. Stiff and uncoordinated in his movements, one was constantly afraid that he was going to bump into something, do some damage; yet nothing of the sort happened, and from the serene expression on the face of the lady of the house, when he strode heavily round the table laid with the finest china-ware, when he jerked his way over to the floor-length mirror, when he even seized a flower-vase of exquisitely painted porcelain and swung it in the air as if to let us appreciate the play of colours, one realized nothing was going to happen. Moreover, before lunch was served Krespel examined everything in the Professor's room very closely, and he even went as far as to climb on a velvet-cushioned chair and take down a picture which he then hung up again. He spoke throughout volubly and passionately; first (this became most noticeable at table) he would jump from one subject to another, then he would be incapable of abandoning an idea: returning to it again and again, he would become entangled in all sorts of curious side issues and be unable to find his way back to the point; and then some other notion would strike him. His voice would sometimes be rough, loud, and vehement, at other times soft, liquid, and musical, but whatever tone Krespel used, it was never appropriate to what he was saying. If the conversation was about music, and they were praising a new composer, then Krespel would smile and say in his soft, mellifluous voice: 'I would that black-pinioned Satan might send the wretched note-twister spinning ten thousand million fathoms deep into the darkest pits of hell!' Then he would say, in a wild, violent manner: 'She is an angel from heaven, purely and simply an embodiment of perfect sound and tone dedicated to the glory of God! The sun, moon and stars of all song!' And as he said this, there would be tears in his eyes.

Here it is necessary to recall that about an hour beforehand the talk had centred on a celebrated woman singer. We were enjoying some roast hare, and I noticed that Krespel carefully cleaned every bit of flesh from the bones on his plate, and made detailed inquiries about the hare's paws which the

Professor's five-year-old daughter brought to him with a very amiable smile. During the meal the children had indeed been casting very friendly looks at the lawyer; now they got down from their chairs and, shy and awestruck, moved towards him, though only taking two or three steps. 'What's going to happen now?' I thought to myself. The dessert was served. Then the lawyer took out of his pocket a little box in which lay a tiny steel lathe which he straightway screwed on the edge of the table and, with unbelievable skill and speed, using the hare bones, turned little boxes and circular containers and tiny balls which the children received with rapture.

As we were getting up from the table the Professor's niece asked: 'And how is our dear Antonia, sir?' Krespel pulled a funny face, as if he had bitten into a sour pomegranate but wanted to give the impression it was sweet. But soon this expression changed and became a horrifying mask which projected a really bitter, ferocious, and, it seemed to me, devilish contempt.

'Our? Our dear Antonia?' he inquired, in his soft, liquid, mellifluous tones. The Professor hastily intervened; in the withering glance he cast at his niece, I saw that she had plucked a chord that would produce unpleasant dissonances in Krespel. 'How are the violins getting on?' the Professor asked with great affability, seizing both the lawyer's hands. At that, Krespel's face brightened, and he replied in a loud voice: 'Excellently, Professor. You remember the magnificent Amati fiddle I was telling you about recently – what a stroke of luck it was brought that my way! – well, today, this very morning, I cut it up. I hope Antonia will have carefully dissected the remains.'

'Antonia's a fine girl,' the Professor said. 'Yes, indeed she is!' the lawyer cried, suddenly turning on his heels, grabbing hat and stick, and dashing out of the door. I glimpsed his face, reflected in the mirror, and saw that his eyes were brimming with tears.

As soon as the lawyer had left, I pressed the Professor to tell me what all the fuss had been concerning the violins, and particularly begged him to tell me about Antonia.

'Oh,' said the Professor. 'Although Krespel is a quite remarkable man, he goes about making violins in the craziest way.' 'Making violins?' I asked, quite astonished. 'Yes,' the Professor went on. 'Connoisseurs claim that Krespel creates the finest violins to be found in modern times; once he used to let others play on those he had been particularly successful with, but that was some time ago. Now, if Krespel makes a violin, he himself plays on it for an hour or so, and that with the utmost mastery, with ravishing expression, but then he hangs it up with the others without ever touching it again, or letting others touch it. Whenever there is any old master violin to be obtained, the lawyer will buy it up at any price he is asked for. However, just as with his own fiddles, he plays on it only once, then takes it to pieces in order to examine closely the interior structure; if, in his opinion, he does not find what he is looking for, he tosses the pieces angrily into a big chest which is already filled to overflowing with the remnants of dismembered violins.'

'But what about Antonia?' I broke in, eagerly.

'Now *that*,' the Professor went on, 'that is a matter which might well have aroused in me the greatest detestation for our lawyer friend, if I were not convinced that there is something here which must play a very special and mysterious part in the lawyer's character, one which is fundamentally benevolent to a fault. Several years ago, when Krespel first came to H—, he lived like a hermit with an old housekeeper in a gloomy house on — Street. Soon his outlandish way of life attracted the curiosity of the neighbours, and as soon as he noticed this he sought out, and found, acquaintances. Just as in my own home, everywhere people got so used to seeing him that he became indispensable. Overlooking his rebarbative exterior, the children all loved him, though without overwhelming him with their affection, because in spite of their friendliness they retained a certain awed respect that preserved him from any forwardness on their part. You saw today how he wins children's hearts, with all kinds of playful tricks. We all took him for a confirmed bachelor, and he did nothing to make us alter that opinion. After he had been living here for a while, he went away, no one knows where, and returned a few months later. The evening after Krespel's return his windows were all illuminated – most unusual for him – and this alone was enough to draw the neighbours' attention. Soon they heard a most glorious voice, a woman's, accompanied by a piano. Then the notes of a violin were heard, and they engaged in a passionate contest with the voice. Everyone knew at once that it was Krespel playing. I myself mingled with the vast throng which the marvellous concert had attracted outside the lawyer's house, and I must confess that in comparison with that voice, that unknown singer's performance, penetrating to the depths of my being, the voices of the most famous artists I have ever heard seemed to me dull and expressionless. Never before had I heard anything approaching those long-sustained notes, those nightingale trills, those leaps from high to low, that *crescendo* to an organ-like fullness, that *diminuendo* to the faintest whisper. All, without exception, were enthralled by the voice's sweet witchery, and only soft sighs rose through the profound stillness when the singer fell silent. It must have been past midnight when Krespel could be heard talking loudly: another man's voice answered, and, judging from its intonations, seemed to be reproaching him with something; and from time to time a girl could be heard uttering broken lamentations. The lawyer shouted louder and louder, until finally he fell into that mellifluous, singing tone of voice you are familiar with. The girl interrupted him with a scream, then all was deathly still until someone could be heard stumbling down the stairs; a young man, sobbing, dashed out, threw himself into a waiting post-chaise and drove rapidly away.

'The next morning Krespel seemed in very good spirits, and no one had the nerve to ask him about what had happened during the night. However, the housekeeper, when questioned, said that the lawyer had brought home with him a very young and extraordinarily beautiful girl whom he addressed as Antonia, and who had sung so gloriously. She said a young man had also come with them, who had treated Antonia with great tenderness and might well be her betrothed.

But on the lawyer's express orders he had had to make a sudden departure.

'The relationship between Antonia and the lawyer still remains a mystery, but this much is certain: he treats the poor girl in the most despicably tyrannical way. He keeps watch over her just as Dr Bartolo in *The Barber of Seville* does over his ward: she can hardly even cast a glance out of the window. If, after pressing invitations, he is persuaded to bring her into society, he guards her with Argus eyes and will not countenance her hearing a single note of music, much less permit Antonia to sing; in any case, she is not even allowed to sing in his own house any more. And so among the general public Antonia's performance that night has taken on the proportions of a most miraculous legend, exciting both the imagination and the emotions; even those people who did not happen to hear her are wont to say, when some female singer performs in these parts: "What sort of caterwauling is this? – She can't hold a candle to Antonia."'

As you know, I'm quite obsessed by such fantastic situations, and you may well imagine how important I felt it was to make Antonia's acquaintance. I myself had already, many a time, heard people talking about the wonder of Antonia's voice, but I had never realized that the divine singer lived here in Krespel's lunatic clutches, as if in thrall to some tyrannical magician. Naturally, that very night I seemed to hear Antonia's wonderful singing in my dreams, and when she appeared most movingly to implore me, in a magnificent *adagio* (strangely enough, it was as if I myself had composed it), to come to her rescue, I made up my mind at once to gain entry into Krespel's house, like a second Astolfo breaking into Alcinea's enchanted castle, and to free the queen of song from her humiliating bondage.

What actually happened was quite different from what I had imagined; for hardly had I spoken a couple of times to Krespel, entering into eager discussion with him over the best methods of constructing fiddles, than he himself invited me to visit him at his house.

I went, and he showed me his treasury of violins. There

must have been thirty of them at least hanging in a special cabinet. Among them was one which stood out from the rest: it displayed signs of the greatest antiquity (carved lion's head and so on) and seemed, hung higher than the others, and adorned with a floral wreath, to reign over its neighbours like a queen.

'This violin,' Krespel said, after I had asked him about it, 'this violin is a very remarkable and admirable piece of work by an unknown master, probably belonging to Tartini's period. I'm quite certain that the inner framework has some very special feature, and that if I took the instrument to pieces it would reveal a secret I have long been trying to discover. But – and you may laugh at me if you wish – this dead thing, which only I myself can gift with life and voice, often speaks to me of its own accord, in the most miraculous way, and it seemed to me, when I played upon it for the first time, as though I were merely a mesmerist exerting his influence on a sleepwalker who automatically expresses her own inner feelings. Now I don't want you to get the notion that I'm so giddy-pated as to attach the slightest importance to such fantastic conceits; yet it is peculiar that I have never been able to bring myself to cut up that stupid, lifeless thing. Now I wish that I had done so, for ever since Antonia has been here I have played her something on this fiddle from time to time. Antonia is fond of hearing it – much too fond.'

The lawyer spoke these words with evident emotion, which prompted me to come out with: 'Oh, sir, if only you would do so when I'm here!' But Krespel pulled his bitter-sweet smile at this and spoke in his smooth, singing tone: 'No, my dear Herr Studiosus!' And that was that. Then he would have me view all kinds of somewhat childish curiosities: finally he fished out of a chest a piece of folded paper that he pressed into my hand, saying with great solemnity: 'You are a friend of the arts: take this present as a precious memento which you must cherish above all else.' Whereupon he shoved me very gently towards the door and on the threshold put his arm round my shoulder. But he was actually, in a symbolical manner, throwing me out. I found a piece, about one-eighth of an inch long, of violin string when I unfolded the paper, on which was inscribed: 'A piece of the tenor string the blessed Stamitz used on his violin when he played his last concert.'

That brusque dismissal when I mentioned Antonia seemed to indicate that I should never have a chance of seeing her. But this was not so: for when I visited Krespel the second time, I found Antonia in the room, helping him to put a violin together. Antonia's appearance at first sight made no very strong impression, but soon I was unable to stop staring at the blue eyes and rosy lips in her uncommonly delicate and charming countenance. She was very pale, but if something witty or amusing was said, a sweet smile would make her cheeks glow a fiery crimson that nevertheless soon died to a pale rosy flush.

I spoke quite freely with Antonia and was aware of no side-glances from the Argus-eyed Krespel, as the Professor had dubbed him; in fact, he remained quite calm and collected, and indeed even seemed to approve of my conversation with Antonia.

So it came about that I began visiting the lawyer more and more often, and as we became more accustomed to one another there developed a wonderfully easy relationship between the members of our little group, something really heart-warming. The lawyer, with his very peculiarly scurrilous tongue I found a constant source of entertainment; and yet it was really Antonia who attracted me with an irresistible enchantment, and helped me to bear much that, impetuous as I was in those days, I should otherwise have avoided like the plague. For the lawyer's odd and unique personality displayed far too often tasteless and boring facets. Particularly irritating to me, however, was the attitude he took as soon as I spoke about music, especially singing, when, with his diabolical smile and his repulsively mellifluous tone of voice, he would change the conversation, introducing something quite irrelevant and usually rather coarse. From the deep distress which would shadow Antonia's countenance at such moments I soon realized that he behaved in this way simply in order to prevent

me from making any request for her to sing. I did not give up.
The more the lawyer put difficulties in my way, the more I
determined to overcome them: I had to hear Antonia sing,
in order not to let her singing melt away into the sphere of
dreams and increasingly vague memories.

One evening Krespel was in a particularly good mood;
he had anatomized an old Cremona violin and discovered
that the soundpost was slanted a little more than usual. This
discovery would be of the utmost importance, he said, enrich-
ing as it did our knowledge of violin construction. I managed
to get him worked up about the art of true violin-playing.
Krespel spoke about the technique of the old masters studied
by truly great singers; this led naturally to the remark that in
these days, on the contrary, singing was a feeble imitation of
the affected leaps and runs of instrumentalists. 'What could be
more idiotic,' I cried, jumping up from my chair and running to
the pianoforte and throwing open the lid, 'what could be
more idiotic than such confounded mannerisms which, instead
of being music, sound more like dried peas being dropped
on the floor!' Whereupon I sang many of the modern arias
that dash hither and thither and rattle along like some demented humming-top, striking a few dissonant chords as
accompaniment. Krespel laughed loud and long, and shouted:
'Ha-ha! I seem to hear our German Italians or our Italian
Germans straining at an aria by Pucitta or Portogallo or some
other *Maestro di Capella* or rather *Schiavo d'un primo uomo* –
slave of a leading male singer!'

'Now,' thought I, 'now's the moment.' Turning to
Antonia, I declared. 'I'm sure Antonia has nothing to do with
this kind of screeching!' And immediately I began singing a
magnificent, soul-stirring song by Leonardo Leo. Then
Antonia's cheeks glowed, a heavenly radiance sparkled from
her enraptured eyes, she flew to the piano – opened her lips
– but at that very instant Krespel forced her away from the
instrument, seized me by the shoulders and screamed, in his
harsh tenor: 'Laddie, laddie, laddie!' But immediately he
continued, crooning very softly and courteously bowing as
he took my hand: 'My most honourable Herr Studiosus, it

would indeed be contrary to all etiquette and contrary to all good manners if I were quite plainly and simply to express the wish that here, on this very spot, hellish Satan with red-hot claws might grab you by the scruff of the neck and, so to speak, make short work of your miserable person. But setting that aside, you must admit, my dear fellow, that it's getting quite dark, and as there is no lamp outside today, you might very well, even were I not to throw you immediately down-stairs, do some damage to your dear, precious limbs. Now go quietly home and think in the friendliest way of your true friend, even if you never again – d'you follow me? – never again come to visit him at his house.'

Thereupon he put his arm round my shoulders, and, hold-ing me very tightly, turned round and walked me slowly out of the door, so that I was unable to give Antonia one last look. You must admit that I was in no position to give Krespel a thrashing, which is what I really should have done.

The Professor laughed in my face and assured me that I had now put my foot in it for good and all with Krespel. Antonia was too precious to me, I may even say too sacred, for me to play the love-crossed adventurer or the languishing *amoroso* gazing up at her window. Wrung to the depths of my being, I left H—, but as is usually the case in this life the dazzling colours of my imaginary portrait gradually paled, while Antonia's singing yes, even that singing which I had never heard – often illumined my profoundest soul with a soft, comforting, rosy glow.

Two years later, while I was employed in B—, I went on a trip to southern Germany. In the misty rays of the setting sun rose the distant towers of H—; as I drew nearer the town, I was overwhelmed by an indescribable sensation of the most painful anguish; it lay on my breast like a heavy burden, and I could hardly breathe. I had to get out of the coach and ride on the top, in the open air. But my oppression developed into acute physical pain. Soon I seemed to be hearing the chords of some solemn chorale drifting on the air – the notes became clearer, and I could make out men's voices chanting a sacred melody. 'What can it be? What can it be?' I cried, and at the same time felt as if my breast had been pierced by a red-hot dagger! 'Don't you see,' the postilion, who was riding beside me, replied, 'don't you see? Over there in the grave-yard they are burying someone.'

Indeed, we were in the vicinity of the churchyard and I made out a ring of people in black standing round a grave which was at that very moment being filled in. Tears suddenly dimmed my eyes; it was as if all happiness, all joy in life were being buried there. We descended a hill at top speed, I could no longer see into the churchyard, the chorale faded away and I noticed, not far from the gate, people dressed in black returning from the funeral. The Professor with his niece on his arm, both in deep mourning, were walking close by the road, but failed to notice me. The niece had a handkerchief pressed to her eyes and was sobbing bitterly. It was impos-sible for me to enter the town; I sent on my servant with the coach to the inn I knew so well, and started walking in that familiar neighbourhood, trying to rid myself of a mood that perhaps had only physical causes, overheating during the journey and so on.

When I reached the avenue leading to an amusement park, I was the spectator of the most extraordinary performance. Krespel was being conducted by two male mourners, from whom he appeared to be wanting to escape, for he was making all kinds of jerking movements. As always, he was dressed in his very unusual grey coat, created by himself; but from the small three-cornered hat that he wore in martial fashion tilted over one ear, a very long, narrow, black crêpe ribbon hung and fluttered in the breeze. He had buckled round his waist a black scabbard, but instead of a sword it contained a violin bow. An icy tremor ran through me: 'He's mad,' I thought, following slowly behind. The men led the lawyer to his house, and there he laid his arms round their shoulders, laughing loudly. They left him, and then his gaze fell upon me, for I was standing quite close to him. For a long while he stood staring at me, then he called out in a hollow voice: 'Welcome, Herr Studiosus! So you've guessed what has happened.'

Thereupon he seized me by the arm and dragged me after him into the house – up the stairs to the room in which the violins were hung. All of them were draped with black crêpe; missing was the old master violin: in its place hung a cypress wreath. Then I knew what had happened: 'Antonia! Antonia!' I shrieked, in inconsolable grief. The lawyer stood beside me, with folded arms, as if frozen to the spot. I pointed to the cypress wreath. 'When she died,' the lawyer said in a deep, solemn voice, 'when she died, the soundpost in that violin broke with a rending groan and the sounding-board split asunder. The old faithful could live only with her, in her. Now it is lying with her, in her coffin: it was buried with her.'

Shattered to the depths of my soul, I collapsed into a chair, but the lawyer began to sing a merry song in a rough sort of voice, and it was really horrible to see him jigging round the room on one foot (he still had his hat on) with his crêpe ribbon fluttering across the violins. Yes, I could not help uttering a frenzied scream of alarm when, the lawyer making a sudden turn, the crêpe came trailing over me: it was as if he wanted to drag me, veiled with crêpe, down into the frightful black abyss of dementia.

Then Krespel suddenly stood still and said, in his melli-fluous tones: 'Laddie – laddie – why do you scream so? Have you glimpsed the angel of death? That always happens *before* the funeral!' Then he strode into the middle of the room, wrenched the violin bow from the scabbard, held it over his head in both hands and broke it again and again, snapping it into several pieces. Laughing loudly, Krespel yelled: 'Now is the rod broken over my head, is it not, laddie? Is it not? Not at all, not at all, now I'm free – free – free – Hurrah! Free! – Now I shall make no more fiddles – no more fiddles – Hurrah! – no more fiddles!'

The lawyer chanted these mad phrases to a horribly jaunty air, at the same time beginning to hop about again on one foot. Overcome with terror, I wanted to make a run for the door, but the lawyer held me tight, speaking very composedly: 'Don't go, Herr Studiosus! Don't take this outburst, caused by an anguish that martyrs me to death, for insanity. This all comes of trying to create for myself, some time ago, a night-shirt that would make me look like Fate or God!'

The lawyer rattled off all kinds of deluded, terrifying nonsense until he collapsed, exhausted. I called the old housekeeper, and I was thankful when I found myself outside again. Not for one moment did I doubt that Krespel had gone raving mad; yet the Professor disagreed with me.

'There are certain men,' he declared, 'from whom nature or some peculiar destiny snatches away the covering under which the rest of us are able to lead our insane existences unnoticed. They are like those insects with paper-thin skins which appear to be deformed in the visible action of their muscular structure, yet which soon adjust themselves to the norm. What for us remains merely in the realm of imagination is translated, in Krespel, into direct action. Krespel acts out in crazy gestures and clever inconsequentialities that bitter contempt which a frustrated spirit resorts to in its dealings with worldly matters. It is simply his lightning-conductor. What comes out of the earth he thus returns to the earth, but he is able to retain the element of the divine; and so, I believe, despite the acts of apparent madness that keep breaking out, he feels quite easy in his conscience. Antonia's sudden death may well lie heavy upon him, but I'm ready to wager that by tomorrow our lawyer friend will be acting the fool in his accustomed manner.'

It came about almost exactly as the Professor had predicted. The next day, Krespel seemed his old self again, except that he claimed he would never construct another violin and never wished to play on one again. And I learnt later that he stuck to his resolve.

The Professor's remarks strengthened my inner conviction that the intimate, so carefully screened relationship between Antonia and Krespel and her death itself might have aroused in him a heavy sense of guilt that could not be expiated. I did not want to leave H— without charging him with what I suspected had been a criminal offence; I wanted to shake him to the core and thus force him to a complete confession of his horrifying deed. The more I thought about the matter, the clearer it seemed to me that Krespel must be a villain, and this made the tirade I was preparing all the more fiery and forceful; indeed, it seemed to me to be developing of its own accord into a real masterpiece of denunciatory rhetoric. Thus forearmed, and in a great passion, I ran to the lawyer's house.

I found him at his lathe, turning toys with smiling composure. 'But how,' I flew at him, 'how can you find peace in your soul for one moment when the thought of your fearful deed must be stinging you with viperish remorse?' The lawyer gazed at me in astonishment, laying his tools aside. 'Whatever do you mean, my dear fellow?' he asked, adding: 'Kindly take a seat.'

But I went on determinedly, growing more and more heated as I roundly accused him of having murdered Antonia and threatened him with retribution in the highest courts. Indeed, as a professional jurist who had only recently taken silk, and very full of my own importance, I went so far as to assure him that I would employ every means in my power to bring the case into the open and to deliver him into the hands of his earthly judge.

I was somewhat at a loss when, at the close of my aggressive, pompous address the lawyer, without saying a word, gazed at me very calmly, as if he were expecting me to continue. Indeed I tried to do so, but then everything sounded so wrong, so silly, in fact, that I again fell silent. Krespel gloated over my confusion, and a malicious, ironical smile flitted over his face. But then he became very serious, and spoke in solemn tones: 'Young man! You may well think me foolish, indeed insane; I can forgive you that, as we are both confined to the same madhouse of a world, and you are only abusing me for fancying I am God the Father because you yourself imagine you are the Son of God. But how can you presume to force your way into the secret, and try to seize the most mysterious springs of a life that were always, and always will be, beyond your comprehension? She is gone, and the mystery is solved!' Krespel paused, stood up and strode about the room for a while. I ventured to ask for an explanation. He stared at me, took me by the hand and led me to the window, opening both panes wide. Supporting himself on his arms, he leaned out, and, gazing down into the garden, told me the story of his life. When he had finished, I went away feeling deeply moved, deeply ashamed.

This is how it had all started. Twenty years before, the absolutely fanatical passion he had for seeking out and buying up the best violins of the old masters took the lawyer to Italy. At that period he was not constructing any himself and therefore he also refrained from dismembering these old fiddles. In Venice he heard the celebrated singer Angela —i, who in those days shone in all the leading roles at the Teatro di S. Benedetto. His enthusiasm was aroused, not only for her art, which Signora Angela did indeed exercise in the most wonderful way, but also for her perfectly angelic beauty. Krespel cultivated Angela's acquaintance and despite all his uncouthness he succeeded in completely winning her affections through his dashing and yet highly expressive violin playing.

Their very intimate relationship led, within a few weeks, to marriage, which was kept secret because Angela did not want to abandon either the theatre or her famous singer's name; nor did she wish to tack the harsh-sounding 'Krespel' on to it.

With the sharpest irony, Krespel described the very special way in which, as soon as she had become his wife, Signora Angela oppressed and martyred him. In Krespel's opinion, all the moods and whims and tantrums of every great female singer had been incorporated in Angela's tiny figure. If he ever ventured to speak out in self-defence, Angela would send to plague him a whole host of *maestri* and academics who, ignorant of their true relationship, would berate him as the most intolerable, discourteous lover, one totally unable to appreciate the Signora's charming moods.

Immediately after one such stormy scene, Krespel had fled to Angela's country house, where, improvising on his Cremona violin, he forgot the miseries of this life. But it was not long before the Signora, who had quickly followed the lawyer, strode into the room. It so happened that she was in the mood to play the gracious lady; she embraced Krespel, giving him sweet, melting glances, laying her head on his shoulder. But the lawyer, lost in the realms of harmony, played on, making the rafters ring, and it so happened that he knocked the Signora somewhat urgently with his arm and bow. She jumped back, filled with rage, shrieking: '*Bestia tedesca* – German beast!' She tore the fiddle out of the lawyer's hands and smashed it into a thousand fragments on the marble table.

Krespel stood rooted to the spot, but then, as if roused from a dream, grabbed the Signora with a giant's strength, threw her out of the window of her own country house, and fled, without bothering to see what had happened to her, back to Venice, and thence to Germany again.

Only after some time did he fully realize what he had done: although he knew that the window had been scarcely five feet above ground, and that, given the circumstances, the necessity of throwing the Signora out of the window had seemed quite plain, he felt haunted by a certain uneasiness, all the more so as the Signora had given him clearly to understand that she was 'in an interesting condition'. He hardly dared make inquiries about her, and he was not a little astonished when, after about eight months, he received a charming missive from his beloved spouse, in which she made no reference at all to the episode at the country house, and regaled him with the news that she had been delivered of the darlingest wee daughter, adding a most earnest request that the *marito amato e padre felicissimo* – beloved husband and blessed father – should journey at once to Venice. This Krespel did not do; instead, he made more detailed inquiries through an intimate friend and learnt that the Signora had dropped lightly as a cat into the soft grass, and that her fall had had absolutely no physical after-effects. But after Krespel's heroic action, the Signora had seemed to be completely changed: no more moods, ludicrous notions or any kind of bad temper were to be found in her and the *maestro*, who was busy with his compositions for the next carnival, was the happiest man under the sun, because the Signora was willing to sing his new arias without insisting on the numberless alterations which he had usually to put up with. Moreover, the friend added, it was of the utmost importance to keep quite secret the manner in which Angela had been cured of her tantrums, otherwise *prime donne* would be flying out of windows all day long!

Krespel was not a little excited by this news; he ordered horses and got into the carriage. 'Stop!' he suddenly cried. 'How do I know,' he muttered to himself, 'that as soon as she sets eyes on me again the evil spirit won't regain his power over Angela? If such a thing were to happen, what on earth could I do? I've already thrown her out of a window. What more could I do?'

He got out of the carriage again, wrote a tender letter to his convalescent wife, in which he politely mentioned how sweet it was of her to spread the news that their little daughter had, just like himself, a little mole behind the ear, and – remained in Germany. A lively exchange of letters went on. Protestations of love – invitations – reproaches about the loved one's absence – hopes deceived – desires unfulfilled and so on, flew back and forth from Venice to H— and from H— to Venice.

Finally Angela came to Germany and, as is well known, scored a triumph as *prima donna* at the great opera house in F—. Despite the fact that she was no longer young, she won the hearts of all with the irresistible magic of her magnificent singing. In those days her voice had not lost any of its glory. Meanwhile, Antonia had grown up, and her mother's letters to Krespel were full of how his daughter was blossoming out as a singer of the first rank.

Indeed, this information was substantiated by friends of Krespel in F—, who implored him to visit the city just once, there to marvel at the unique phenomenon of two quite sublime sopranos. They had no inkling of the close relationship between the pair and Krespel. The latter would have liked more than anything in the world to see with his own eyes the daughter who was part of his flesh and blood and who often appeared to him in his dreams. But as soon as he bethought himself of his wife, a very peculiar sensation came over him, so he stayed at home among his dismembered fiddles.

You will have heard of the promising young composer B— in F—; he suddenly disappeared, no one knows how or where (or perhaps you knew him personally?). This young man fell deeply in love with Antonia, and, as his love was returned in full measure, he requested her mother to give her approval to an early marriage that would be hallowed by the Muses. Angela had no objections, and Krespel gave his consent all the more willingly as the young artist's compositions had already been greeted with favour by his sternly critical judgement.

Krespel thought he would be receiving news of the consummation of the marriage, but instead there came a black-bordered letter written in an unknown hand. Dr. R— had the sorrow to inform the lawyer that Angela, in consequence of a severe cold caught at the theatre, had fallen seriously ill and had died the very night before Antonia's wedding-day. Angela had revealed to the doctor that she was Krespel's wife and Antonia his daughter; the lawyer was requested therefore to proceed to F— with all speed and take custody of the motherless girl.

However deeply shaken the lawyer felt at Angela's decease, nevertheless he soon began to feel that a dreadfully disturbing element had been removed from his life, and now he could really breathe freely again. That very day he departed for F—. You cannot imagine how vividly and movingly the lawyer depicted to me the moment when he first saw Antonia. Even in his most bizarre expressions there lay a wonderful power of description which I am quite unable even to hint at. Angela's every grace and charm had been embodied in Antonia, who was nevertheless quite untouched by the obverse side of Angela's nature. There was no ambiguous cloven hoof threatening to appear from time to time.

The young fiancé made his appearance, and Antonia, her delicate perceptiveness correctly sensing her queer father's deepest feelings, sang one of those motets by old Padre Martini which she knew Angela used constantly to sing to the lawyer in the springtime of their love. The lawyer wept floods of tears; he had never heard Angela sing like this. The timbre of Antonia's voice was quite individual and strange, resembling now the sigh of an Aeolian harp, now the passionate throb of a nightingale. It seemed hardly possible that such exquisite tones could issue from a human breast. Antonia, radiant with joy and love, sang and sang – all her most beautiful songs, and in between B— played with that inspiration that only ecstatic joy can produce.

At first, Krespel listened enraptured, but then he turned thoughtful and fell silent. Finally he jumped up, pressed Antonia to his heart and begged her, in a very gentle, quiet voice: 'If you love me, don't sing any more – it breaks my heart – the anguish – the anguish – don't sing any more.'

'No,' the lawyer said next day to Doctor R—. 'When, during her singing, that flush contracted to two deep red patches on her pale cheeks, it was not just a case of family resemblance; it was something else – something I had always been afraid of.' The doctor, whose face during this speech had shown deep distress, replied: 'It may be that it is caused by the strain of singing at too early an age; or if nature is at fault, then Antonia is quite simply suffering from an organic defect in her chest, the very thing that gives her voice its wonderful power and strange, vibrant timbre which we can say is far beyond the bounds of human singing. But it can also bring about her early death; for if she goes on singing, I give her six months at the very most.'

Krespel felt as if a hundred sharp swords were being driven through his body. He felt as if some beautiful tree had borne the most glorious blossoms for the first time in the barren garden of his life, and now had to be sawn down at the roots so that it could never bud and flourish again.

But he had made his decision. He told Antonia everything. He gave her the choice of either marrying B— and giving herself over to the allurements of worldly success, thus bringing about her premature death; or of giving her father in his old age the peace and happiness he had never known, thus extending her life by many years.

Antonia fell sobbing into her father's arms, and he, sensing only too well the rending anguish the next few moments would bring, required no more explicit answer. He spoke to her fiancé, but though the latter assured him that not another note should pass Antonia's lips, the lawyer well knew that

even B— would not be able to resist the temptation to hear
Antonia sing at least those arias composed by himself. The
world too, the musical public, even if it were informed of
Antonia's malady, would certainly not give up its demands,
for music-loving people, when it is a question of their own
pleasure, can be selfish and cruel.

The lawyer vanished from F— with Antonia and returned
to H—. When he heard of their departure, B— became desperate. He followed them, caught up with Krespel and so
reached H— at the same time as he did.

'Let me see him just once again, then let me die,' Antonia
begged. 'Die? Die?' the lawyer cried, in a tempest of rage, an
icy shiver thrilling down his spine. His daughter, the one
creature in all the world who had fired him with bliss such as
he had never known in his life before, who alone had recon-
ciled him to existence, tore herself violently from his arms, and
he finally allowed the terrible thing to happen. B— had to sit
down at the piano, Antonia sang, and Krespel played merrily
on his fiddle until those red patches appeared on Antonia's
cheeks.

Then he gave the order to stop: but as B— was taking
leave of Antonia, she suddenly gave a piercing scream and
collapsed. 'I thought,' Krespel told me, 'I thought she was
then, as I had predicted, really and truly dead, and remained
very calm and collected, for I had reached the sublimest
heights. I seized B— by the shoulders – in his stupefaction
he looked quite sheepishly silly – and said' (here the lawyer
adopted his singing tone): '"Because you, our highly respected
Herr Virtuoso Pianist, have actually murdered your bride-to-
be, as you well and truly desired to do, and can now quietly
take your leave, you will be kind enough to wait a little longer
and allow me to run my bare hunting-blade through your heart,
so that my daughter, who, as you see, is rather pale, may regain
her colour with your own blood. You can take to your heels,
but I could easily throw a knife after you." I must have looked
somewhat fearsome as I spoke these words, for with a cry of
the utmost terror he wrenched himself away from me and
leaped through the door and down the stairs.'

Now, after B— had run away, as the lawyer was trying to raise Antonia, who lay lifeless on the floor, she sighed deeply and opened her eyes, only to close them again, apparently in death. Then Krespel broke out into a loud, despairing lamentation. The doctor, called by the house-keeper, declared that Antonia's state was the result of an unhappy, but by no means dangerous mischance, and in fact she recovered quicker than the lawyer had dared to hope. She now clung to Krespel with the tenderest, most childlike devotion; she encouraged him in his favourite occupations, humoured his maddest moods and whims. She helped him to dissect old fiddles and to construct new ones. 'I don't want to sing any more, I only want to live for you,' she would often say smilingly to her father, whenever someone had invited her to sing and she had refused. Yet the lawyer spared her such decisions whenever possible, and so it came about that he seldom went into society with her, and carefully avoided all musical occasions. He well knew how painful it must be to Antonia to renounce completely the art which she had prac-tised to such a pitch of perfection. When the lawyer had pur-chased the wondrous violin he later buried with Antonia, he wanted to take it to pieces, but Antonia looked at him very wistfully and spoke in a gently pleading voice: 'This one too?'

The lawyer himself could not say what strange power had compelled him to leave the fiddle intact, and to play upon it. Hardly had he bowed the first notes when Antonia cried joyfully: 'Why, that's me – oh, I'm really singing again!' And indeed the instrument's silvery bell-tones had something quite unique and wonderful in them, and seemed like sounds created by a human organ. Krespel was stirred to the depths of his being, and played more magnificently than ever, and when, in the boldest passages, he leaped from high to low notes with great power and profound expressiveness, Antonia clapped her hands and cried, enraptured: 'Oh, I used to do that! I used to sing like that too!'

Thereafter a great peace and gladness entered her life. She often said to Krespel: 'I should so much like to sing some-thing, father!' Then Krespel would take the violin down from the wall and play Antonia's favourite songs, filling her heart with delight.

One night, shortly before my arrival, the lawyer thought he heard someone playing the piano in the next room, and soon he realized that it was B— improvising in his own inimitable way. He wanted to get up, but a heavy burden seemed to be weighing upon him, and, as if fettered by heavy chains, he was incapable of movement.

Then he heard Antonia joining in, with soft, lightly breathed notes that gradually increased in tone to a rousing fortissimo. Then the wondrous sounds became the deeply touching song which B— had once composed for Antonia in the hallowed style of the old masters. Krespel said the state he found himself in then was inexplicable, because his frightful anguish was accompanied by a bliss never before experienced.

Suddenly he was illuminated by a blinding radiance, and at that instant he perceived B— and Antonia, in one another's arms, gazing at each other with rapturous delight. The notes of the song and the pianoforte accompaniment continued, though Antonia was apparently not singing and B— was not touching the piano.

Then Krespel fell into a deep faint, and the vision and the sounds died away. When he awoke, he still felt the dream's fearful anguish in his soul. He rushed to Antonia's room. She was lying on the sofa with closed eyes, an ecstatic smile on her lips, her hands reverently folded; she seemed to be sleeping, dreaming of heavenly joys and blisses. But she was dead.

Heinrich von Kleist

THE EARTHQUAKE IN CHILE

Translated by Nigel Reeves

Heinrich von Kleist

KLEIST was born in Frankfurt-on-Oder in 1777 and committed suicide on the shores of the Wannsee, near Berlin, in 1811, evidently no longer able to bear the chaotic vision of life to which his plays and stories bear eloquent witness. Though contemporary with the German Classics and Romantics, he fits into neither category. His works reflect a shattering of the eighteenth century's confidence in the goodness and rationality of man and of the natural order; his protagonists are confronted by a world of savage violence and baffling paradox, which his language reproduces with fierce objective precision.

THE EARTHQUAKE IN CHILE

IN Santiago, the capital of the Kingdom of Chile, at the very moment of the great earthquake of 1647, in which many thousands perished, a young Spaniard called *Jeronimo Rugera*, who had been arrested on a criminal charge, was standing beside a pillar in the cell to which he had been confined, with the intention of hanging himself. About a year before, *Don Henrico Asteron*, one of the richest noblemen of the city, by whom he had been employed as a tutor, had dismissed him from his residence on account of the intimate nature of his relationship with *Donna Josephe*, the nobleman's only daughter. Having expressly warned his daughter, the aged Don was so perturbed when his proud son's crafty vigilance revealed a secret rendezvous to him, that he sent her away to the Carmelite nunnery of Our Lady of the Mountain.

By a stroke of good fortune Jeronimo had managed to establish fresh contact there, and one quiet night the nunnery garden witnessed the consummation of his desire. It was on Corpus Christi Day and the solemn procession of nuns, followed by the novices, was just commencing when, at the sound of the bells, the unfortunate Josephe collapsed on the steps of the cathedral in the labours of childbirth.

This incident caused an extraordinary sensation; the young sinner was immediately imprisoned without consideration for her condition, and her confinement was hardly over before she was placed on severest trial by order of the archbishop. In the city the anger aroused by this scandal was so great, and the entire nunnery in which it had occurred so harshly criticized, that neither the intercession of the Asteron family nor even the personal wishes of the abbess herself, whose affection the girl had won through her otherwise impeccable behaviour, could mitigate the severity of the sentence passed on her by monastic law. All that could be achieved was for her sentence to be commuted by decree of the Viceroy, much to the indignation of the womenfolk of Santiago, both young and old, from death at the stake to death on the headsman's block.

In those streets through which the condemned woman was to pass to her place of execution the windows were rented out, the roofs of the houses were dismantled, and the pious daughters of the city invited their female acquaintances to attend this spectacle, which was provided for the purposes of divine vengeance, by their sides in sisterly union.

When Jeronimo, who in the meantime had also been imprisoned, heard of the monstrous turn that events had taken, he was almost driven out of his mind. All thoughts of escape proved futile; no matter where his boldest ideas carried him, he encountered bolts and barriers, and an attempt to file through the bars of his window which was discovered, resulted only in still closer confinement. He threw himself to the ground before the image of Our Lady and prayed to her with infinite fervour as the sole source of possible salvation.

But the dreaded day arrived and with it the inward conviction that his situation was entirely without hope. The bells accompanying Josephe to the place of execution were tolling, and he was overwhelmed by despair. He found his life odious, and determined to put an end to it with the aid of a length of rope that chance happened to provide. As has been related, he was standing beside a pillar, just securing to an iron spike set into the cornice the rope that was to snatch him away from this world of misery, when suddenly, with a roar as loud as if the very firmament were disintegrating, the greater part of the town crashed to the ground, smothering every living creature beneath its ruins. Jeronimo Rugera was paralysed with fear, and, as if his mind had been bludgeoned into oblivion, in order not to be thrown over he now clung to the very pillar from which he had hoped to hang. The ground shuddered beneath his feet, the walls of his prison were shattered, and, as the whole edifice gradually began to topple towards the street, only the collapse of the building opposite, which happened to fall against it, forming an archway, prevented the structure from caving in entirely. Trembling, with his hair standing on end and his legs barely able to support him,

Jeronimo slid across the steeply sloping floor to the breach that the impact of the two buildings had opened up in the front wall of his prison.

No sooner had he reached the open air than a second tremor caused the already severely shaken street to collapse completely. Without any notion of how he might escape from the overall destruction and assailed on every side by death, he rushed towards the nearest city-gate across a rubble of stone and timbers. There another house subsided, hurling masonry in all directions and driving him into a side-street; here flames, breaking through clouds of smoke, were already licking round the gables of the houses and, terrified, he hurried into another street; there the Mapocho river, which had burst its banks, came surging and roaring down upon him, tossing him into a third street. Here lay a heap of dead, there a voice was still moaning from beneath the rubble, here people were screaming down from burning roofs, there men and animals were battling with the waves, here a man was bravely attempting to help, there another, as pale as death, was standing speechless with his trembling hands outstretched towards heaven. When Jeronimo had reached the gate and climbed a hill beyond, he fell into a swoon.

It must have been for a quarter of an hour that he lay in a state of the deepest unconsciousness before finally awaking, and, with his back to the city, he partly pulled himself up from the ground. He felt his forehead and chest, not knowing what to make of his condition, and, as a westerly breeze from off the sea caressed him back to life and his eyes scanned the verdant surroundings of Santiago, an indescribable feeling of rapture came over him. Only the bewildered crowds to be seen everywhere about made him at all anxious; he could not grasp what had brought them and him to this spot, and it was not until he turned and saw the ruins of the city behind him that he recollected his terrifying experience. Bowing his head to the very ground he gave thanks to God for his miraculous escape and, as if the one horrific impression that had stamped itself upon his mind had driven out all others, he wept for joy that dear life in all its wealth and variety had not deserted him.

Then, noticing a ring on his finger, he suddenly remembered Josephe and his prison, the bells that he had heard while there and the moment before the building had collapsed. Once again his heart was filled with sadness. He began to repent his prayer, and the Being who reigns above the clouds seemed monstrous to him. He wandered among the people, who were everywhere hurrying out of the gates busily salvaging their property, and he plucked up enough courage to inquire about Asteron's daughter and whether she had been executed. But no one could give him any detailed information. One woman who was passing by, almost bent double by the vast load of baggage on her shoulders, and with two children hanging at her breast, told him, as if she had herself been an eye-witness, that Josephe had been beheaded. Jeronimo turned back, and, once he had worked out the time involved, he could no longer doubt either that the execution had taken place. Sitting down in a solitary wood, he gave way to total despair. He wished that the ravaging fury of nature would unleash itself on him again. In his misery he clamoured for death and could not understand why he had fled from it when it had appeared on all sides, offering salvation. He determined not to waver even if at this moment the oak-trees were to be uprooted and their tops were to come crashing down upon him. Then, when he could weep no more and hope had again emerged from amid the hottest tears, he stood up and scoured the whole area. He went to every hill-top where people were gathered. He set out to meet the fugitives on every path along which they were still fleeing; his feet took him wherever he saw a woman's dress fluttering in the wind, and yet not one was worn by Asteron's daughter. The sun was setting and with it his hopes were again declining, when he came to the edge of a precipice, from which he could see into a broad valley that had been reached by only a few. He hurried past the various groups, not knowing what he should do, and was about to turn back when suddenly he glimpsed a young woman washing a child in the waters of a spring that flowed into the ravine. And his heart leapt at the sight; eager with expectation he ran down over the stony slope and, crying out 'O holy mother of God!', recognized Josephe as she timidly looked round at the noise. With what joy it was that this unfortunate couple, who had been saved by a divine miracle, embraced one another!

On her road to death, Josephe had nearly reached the place of execution when suddenly the whole procession had been scattered by the roar of collapsing buildings. Her first horrified steps took her straight to the nearest gate, but, rapidly gaining mastery over herself, she hastened back to the nunnery where her tiny, helpless boy had remained. She found the whole building already in flames, and the abbess, who, during those moments intended to be Josephe's last, had promised to take care of the baby, was standing in front of the entrance, screaming for someone to rescue him. Fearlessly Josephe plunged through the billowing smoke into the building, which was already caving in on all sides, and, as if protected by all the angels of heaven, she emerged again from the doorway with him unharmed. The abbess placed her hands in blessing on the novice's head, and Josephe was about to throw herself into her arms, when, together with almost all the nuns, she was cruelly killed by a falling gable. Josephe recoiled at this shocking sight; she hastily closed the abbess's eyes and, filled with horror, fled in order to rescue from the destruction the dear child whom heaven had returned to her.

She had gone but a few steps when she saw the mutilated corpse of the archbishop just being removed from the ruins of the cathedral. The Viceroy's palace had been razed to the ground, the court of law, in which sentence had been passed on her, was in flames, and the site of her father's house was covered with a seething pool from which reddish vapours were rising. Josephe did her utmost to keep her composure. Mastering her despair, she courageously strode on from street to street with her prize and had nearly reached the gate when she also saw that the prison in which Jeronimo had pined lay in ruins. Wavering at the sight, she felt as if she were about to collapse on the street-corner when a building, which had already been weakened by the earthquake, toppled to the ground behind her, and, strengthened by her terror, she leapt

up once more. She kissed the child, wiped the tears from her
eyes and, ignoring the horror around them, reached the gate.
Once she was outside the town she realized that not all the
inhabitants of the destroyed buildings had necessarily been
crushed beneath them.

At the next crossroads she stopped and waited to see whether
the dearest person in the world to her after little Philip would
appear. As no one came and the crowds began to swell, she
went on and then turned round again and waited once more.
Weeping copiously she slipped into a dark valley, shaded by
pine trees, to pray for his soul, which she believed had departed
this life; and it was in this valley that she found her lover and
such bliss that it seemed like the Garden of Eden.

She related this all to Jeronimo with great feeling and,
when she had finished, she handed him the little boy to kiss.
Jeronimo took him, fondled him with all the indescribable
joy of a father, and, when he began to cry at the sight of his
unfamiliar face, he closed his lips in a rain of kisses. In the
meantime the loveliest of nights had fallen, scented, wonderfully mild, and as silvery and still as only a poet could imagine.
All along the streamside people had settled down in the shimmering moonlight and were making soft beds from moss and
leafy branches where they could rest from the agonies of the
day. And, because poor people were still moaning that they
had lost their houses, or their wives, or their children, or
everything, Jeronimo and Josephe crept into a thicket so
that no one would be saddened by the secret jubilation of their
own hearts. They found a magnificent pomegranate-tree,
whose widely spreading branches were heavy with fruit
and in whose top a nightingale was piping its sensual song.
Jeronimo sat down by the trunk, and, with Josephe in his lap
and Philip in hers, they rested beneath the cover of his cloak.
The shadow of the tree with its scattered points of light moved
across them, and the moon was already growing pale as dawn
approached before they fell asleep. For there was no end to
what they had to tell each other of the nunnery garden, of their
prisons and of what they had suffered for one another, and
they were filled with grief when they thought of how much

misery had had to come upon the world for them to be happy.

They decided that as soon as the earthquake was over they would go to La Conception where a close friend of Josephe's lived, and that, with the aid of a small sum which they hoped to borrow from her, they would take a boat from there to Spain, where Jeronimo's relatives on his mother's side lived. Here they would be able to live happily to the end of their days. Then, kissing each other over and over again, they finally fell asleep.

When they awoke, the sun was already high and they noticed several families nearby, busy making themselves a light breakfast at a fire. Jeronimo was just wondering how he should obtain some food for his own family when a well-dressed young man with a child in his arms came up to Josephe and humbly asked whether she could let the poor little creature, whose mother was lying injured under the trees, feed at her breast for a while. Josephe was rather taken aback when she saw that he was an acquaintance, but when he added, misinterpreting her confusion, 'It is only for a few moments, Donna Josephe, and the child has had no nourishment since the time of the disaster that has afflicted us all,' she replied, 'It was not for that reason that I did not answer you, Don Fernando; in these terrible times nobody refuses to share what he has.' And, taking the little stranger, she gave her own child to its father, and held him to her breast. Don Fernando was very grateful for her kindness and asked whether they would like to come and join the group that was making some breakfast at the fire. Josephe said that she would gladly accept his offer and, as Jeronimo did not object, followed him to his family, where she was received most warmly and tenderly by Don Fernando's two sisters-in-law, whom she knew to be very estimable young women.

When Donna Elvire, Don Fernando's wife, who was lying on the ground with her feet seriously injured, saw her hollow-cheeked boy at Josephe's breast, she drew Josephe down beside her. Don Pedro, his father-in-law, whose shoulder was injured, also nodded amicably to her.

Strange thoughts were passing through Jeronimo's and

Josephe's minds. When they saw themselves treated with such familiarity and kindness they did not know what to think of the past, the place of execution, the prison and the bell: perhaps they had only dreamt it all? It was as if, after the terrible blow that everyone had received, any feelings of hostility had vanished. Their memories could go no further back than to the time of the disaster. Only Donna Elisabeth, who had been invited to come to the spectacle of the previous morning by a female acquaintance but had declined, now and then gazed dreamily at Josephe, but the tale of some new horror dragged her mind back to the present before it had scarcely left it.

They heard how, immediately after the first of the main tremors, the town had been filled with women who had suffered the pangs of child-birth before the very eyes of the men, how the monks had rushed hither and thither, crucifix in hand, screaming that the end of the world had come, how a guard, acting on the Viceroy's orders to clear a church, had been told that the Viceroy of Chile no longer existed, how during the most frightful of moments the Viceroy had been forced to erect gallows to bring thieving to a stop, and how one innocent man, who had managed to escape through the rear of a burning house, had rashly been seized by the owner and hanged on the spot. At a moment when the tales were at their most furious, Donna Elvire, whose injuries Josephe was busily tending, took the opportunity of asking what had happened to her on the terrible day. And, as Josephe fearfully traced its main events, she had the pleasure of seeing the noblewoman's eyes fill with tears. Donna Elvire took her hand, squeezed it, and gave a sign that she should keep silent. Josephe felt as if she were in heaven. She could not suppress the feeling that the previous day was a blessing such as God had never granted her before, no matter how great the misery that it had brought to the world. And indeed it seemed as if, in the midst of those frightful moments when all men's earthly possessions were being destroyed and the whole of nature was in imminent danger of devastation, the human spirit were bursting into blossom like some beautiful flower.

In the fields, as far as the eye could see, men of all stations were lying beside one another, princes and beggars, the wives of patricians and of peasants, officials and labourers, monks and nuns, offering one another sympathy and mutual assistance and gladly sharing whatever they had saved to keep themselves alive, as if the general calamity had made all who escaped it members of a single family.

The meaningless chatter usually offered by society at its tea-tables was replaced by tales of remarkable achievement: people whom the world had scarcely noticed before had shown the stature of heroes of old. There were examples to spare of fearlessness, of joyous contempt for danger, of self-denial and saintly self-sacrifice, of lives thrown away unhesitatingly as if they could be recovered a moment later like the most worthless of possessions. Indeed, as there was no one that day who had not experienced some touching moment or who had himself not performed some great deed, joy so mingled with their grief that she thought it impossible to judge whether the sum total of common good had not benefited in one way as much as it had suffered in another.

Their silent reflections over, Jeronimo took Josephe by the arm, and in a state of inexpressible gaiety they strolled together beneath the shady boughs of the pomegranate grove. He told her that, because people's moods had changed and the old order of things had been overthrown, he had abandoned his plan to go to Europe; that if the Viceroy, who had always shown a favourable attitude towards his case, were still alive, he would venture to make a personal appeal for pardon to him; and added, with a kiss, that he hoped to stay with her in Chile. Josephe replied that similar thoughts had been running through her mind and that if her father were still alive she could undoubtedly make up their quarrel; but that instead of appearing in person before the Viceroy it would be better to go to La Conception and seek pardon in writing from there. They would then in any case be close to the port and yet still be in easy reach of Santiago, should they be fortunate enough to succeed in their plan. Reflecting for a moment, Jeronimo soon admitted the wisdom of this strategy and, dreaming of the happiness in store for them, they strolled a little longer among the trees before returning to the company.

By now it was afternoon and the teeming crowds of fugitives had no sooner begun to grow a little calmer, now that the tremors had abated, than the news came that in the Dominican Abbey, the only church to have been spared by the earthquake, the prelate of the monastery himself would say a solemn mass to implore heaven for protection from any further catastrophe.

Everywhere the crowds were soon breaking camp and streaming into the city. In Don Fernando's party the question was raised whether they, too, should take part in the ceremony and join the procession. With some anguish Donna Elisabeth reminded them all of the terrible event that had occurred in the church the day before, and that there would be other thanksgiving services in the future at which they could show their devotion with greater calm and cheerfulness because the danger would be further behind them. Springing up at once with some enthusiasm, Josephe declared that she had never been more eager to prostrate herself before her Maker than now when His incomprehensible and sublime power was so manifest. Donna Elvire energetically supported Josephe's view. She insisted that they should attend the mass and called on Don Fernando to head the party, whereupon they all rose to their feet, including Donna Elisabeth. But, because of the latter's obvious agitation and the hesitancy with which she made the few preparations needed for leaving, they asked her whether anything was amiss. When she replied that she felt some inexplicable sense of foreboding, Donna Elvire reassured her and suggested that she should stay behind with her sick father and herself. Josephe asked her whether, in that case, she would kindly take the little darling who, as she could see, had already found his way to her again. 'Certainly,' replied Donna Elisabeth, and was just about to take hold of him when he started to cry plaintively at being treated so unfairly and struggled to escape. And so, with a smile, Josephe said that she would keep him and kissed him till he was quiet. Impressed by the whole nobility and grace of her manner, Don Fernando then offered her his arm; Jeronimo, carrying little Philip, accompanied Donna Constanze, and, with the others who had joined the party following, the procession set off in this order for the city.

In the meantime Donna Elisabeth had been conversing heatedly on her own with Donna Elvire, and the party had barely gone fifty yards before they heard her call out, 'Don Fernando!' and saw her anxiously hurrying after the procession. Don Fernando stopped, turned round and without releasing Josephe's arm, waited for her to come. When she stopped some distance away, as if expecting him to come to her, he asked what she wanted. Donna Elisabeth now went up to him, though unwillingly it seemed, and whispered a few words into his ear so that Josephe, however, could not hear. 'Why then?' asked Don Fernando, 'What misfortune can come of that?' Donna Elisabeth went on whispering to him with an expression of agitation on her face. Don Fernando flushed with annoyance and, replying 'Very well then! Tell Donna Elvire she need have no fears,' he led his lady on.

When they reached the Dominican Abbey the organ could already be heard playing in all its magnificence, and inside a vast crowd had gathered. The throng stretched far beyond the porch out on to the forecourt, and high up on the walls boys were perching in the picture-frames, expectantly clutching their caps in their hands. Light streamed down from all the chandeliers, the columns threw mysterious shadows in the growing dusk, the great stained-glass rose window glowed in the distant background like the very sunset illuminating it, and when the organ fell silent such quiet reigned among the whole congregation that it was as if their very hearts had stopped beating. Never did such a flame of fervour rise towards heaven from a Christian cathedral as on that day from the Dominican Abbey in Santiago; and no human hearts lent it more fuel than Jeronimo's and Josephe's!

The service began with a sermon delivered from the pulpit by one of the most senior of the canons, dressed in his ceremonial robes. Raising his trembling hands towards heaven from beneath the long folds of his surplice, he began with praise, glorification, and thanksgiving that people in this devastated corner of the earth were still capable of crying out to God. He described what had happened at the behest of the Almighty. The Day of Judgement could not be more horrific; and when, pointing at a crack sustained by the cathedral, he called the earthquake a mere harbinger of that Last Day, a shudder ran through the whole congregation. Then, with flowing priestly rhetoric, he moved to the depravity of the city; he accused it of abominations unknown even to Sodom and Gomorrah and ascribed it to God's infinite patience alone that the city had not been wiped entirely from the face of the earth.

But our two unfortunate friends, whom the sermon had already rendered utterly distraught, were cut to the quick when the canon proceeded to expound in detail on the crime that had been committed in the garden of the Carmelite nunnery, to condemn the indulgence that it had received on earth as godless and, in an aside, to curse the souls of the guilty and literally to surrender them to the princes of Hell! Tugging at Jeronimo's arm, Donna Constanze called to Don Fernando. But he replied with as much emphasis and yet as little fuss as it was possible to combine, 'Keep silent, Madam, do not so much as move your eyes and make it appear as if you were swooning. We shall then leave the church.' But, before Donna Constanze could carry out this shrewd plan of campaign, a voice shrieked out, loudly interrupting the canon's sermon, 'Stand back, citizens of Santiago, the godless creatures are here!' And when another terrified voice asked where, and the terror spread to those all around, a third retorted, 'Here!' and with fanatic frenzy dragged Josephe down by the hair until only Don Fernando's arm prevented her from tumbling to the ground together with his son. 'Are you quite insane?' cried the young man, throwing his arm around Josephe, 'I am Don Fernando Ormez, son of the city commander, who is well-known to you all.' 'Don Fernando Ormez?' shouted a cobbler, standing immediately in front of him, a man who had worked for Josephe and knew her at least as well as her tiny feet. 'Who is the father of this child?' he demanded, turning with defiant insolence upon Asteron's daughter. At this question Don Fernando, now glancing timidly at Jeronimo, now seeking someone in the congregation who might recognize him, turned pale. Faced with such a terrifying situation, Josephe cried, 'This is not my child as you think, Master Pedrillo,' and, looking at Don Fernando in extreme anguish, added, 'This young gentleman is Don Fernando Ormez, son of the city commander, who is well-known to you all!' The cobbler asked, 'Is there any citizen who knows this young man?' and several of those standing nearby repeated, 'Let anyone who knows Jeronimo Rugera come forward!' At just this moment, frightened by the uproar, little Juan started to try and struggle away from Josephe into Don Fernando's arms. Then 'He *is* the father!' a voice screamed out, and 'He *is* Jeronimo Rugera,' another, and 'They *are* those blasphemous wretches,' a third, and 'Stone them! Stone them!' the whole body of Christendom assembled in the House of the Lord. Then Jeronimo cried, 'Stop, you monsters! If you are looking for Jeronimo Rugera, here he is! Release that innocent man!'

The incensed mob, bewildered by Jeronimo's words, stopped short; several hands loosened their grip on Don Fernando, and as a naval officer of considerable rank hurried up at the same moment and, forcing his way through the crowd, asked, 'Don Fernando Ormez! What has happened to you?' the latter, now completely released, replied with truly heroic composure: 'Just look at these assassins, Don Alonzo. I should have been lost if this worthy gentleman had not pretended to be Jeronimo Rugera to calm the crowd's rage. Take him into custody, if you would, and this young lady, too, for the sake of their own safety,' and seizing hold of Master Pedrillo, 'and this good-for-nothing, who started the whole trouble.' The cobbler shouted, 'Don Alonzo Onoreja, I ask you upon your conscience, is this girl Josephe Asteron or not?' As Don Alonzo, who knew Josephe very well, hesitated before replying and several voices, inflamed to fresh fury, cried out, 'It is! It is!' and, 'Put her to death!' Josephe placed little Philip, who had so far been carried by Jeronimo, together with little Juan into Don Fernando's arms and said, 'Go, Don Fernando, save your two children and leave us to our fate!'

Don Fernando took the children and said that he would rather perish than allow any harm to come to his party. After asking the naval officer for his sword, he offered Josephe his arm and told the second couple to follow him. Thanks to this arrangement they were in fact shown sufficient respect to be let out of the church and they thought that they were saved. But scarcely had they reached the forecourt, which was similarly thronging with people, when a voice shouted out from amongst the raging mob that had pursued them, 'This *is* Jeronimo Rugera, citizens, for I am his father,' and felled him with a monstrous cudgel blow as he stood at Donna Constanze's side. 'Jesus, Maria!' cried Donna Constanze and fled to her brother-in-law, but, 'Nunnery whore!' came the cry again and a second blow from a different direction threw her down lifeless beside Jeronimo. 'Monsters!' bellowed a stranger, 'That was Donna Constanze Xares!' 'Why did they lie to us then?' retorted the cobbler, 'Look for the right one and kill her!' When Don Fernando saw Donna Constanze's corpse he was filled with rage; drawing his sword, he lashed out so violently that, if the fanatical assassin who had caused all this horror had not managed to avoid the blow by leaping to one side, he would have been cleft in two. But as he could not overpower the mob surging around him, Josephe cried out, 'Farewell, Don Fernando, farewell, children! Here I am, murder me, you bloodthirsty tigers!' and rushed of her own free will in amongst them to put an end to the struggle. Master Pedrillo struck her down with his cudgel. Then, drenched with her blood, he shrieked, 'Send her bastard to hell with her!' and pressed forward again, his lust for slaughter still unsatiated.

With godlike heroism Don Fernando was now standing with his back against the church, holding the children in his left hand and his sword in his right. With every blow he felled an adversary; a lion could not have defended itself better. Seven of the vicious curs lay dead before him and the prince of this satanic pack was himself wounded. But Master Pedrillo did not stop until he had ripped one of the children by the leg from out of Don Fernando's grip and, swinging it in a circle high above his head, had dashed it against the edge of one of the church columns. Then all fell silent and everyone moved away. When Don Fernando saw his little child, Juan, lying in front of him with his brains oozing from his skull, he lifted his eyes to heaven, filled with indescribable anguish.

The naval officer made his way to him again, tried to console him and assured him that he profoundly regretted his own failure to act, though there had been many reasons for doing nothing. But Don Fernando said that he had nothing to reproach himself with and only asked him to help take away the corpses. In the darkness of oncoming night they were all carried to Don Alonzo's house, to which Don Fernando followed them, bent over little Philip's face, weeping bitterly. That night he stayed at Don Alonzo's home and, under various pretexts, delayed telling his wife the full extent of the disaster for some time, partly because she was ill, and also partly because he was not sure how she would judge the way in which he had behaved in the situation. But a short time afterwards, when this fine lady chanced to hear of all that had happened from an acquaintance who visited her, she wept for her child in solitude until she could weep no more; and then one morning she embraced him, and, with the remains of a tear glistening in her eye, gave him a kiss. Don Fernando and Donna Elvire then took the little stranger as their foster-son, and, when Don Fernando compared little Philip with Juan and the ways in which they had both come to him, he almost felt as if he should be happy.

Georg Büchner

LENZ

Translated by F. J. Lamport

Georg Büchner

GEORG BÜCHNER was born in Goddelau, near Darmstadt, in 1813. As a medical student he became involved in radical politics and had to flee his native Hesse to escape arrest; he completed his studies in Strasbourg, and had embarked upon an academic career in Zürich when he died in a typhus epidemic in 1837. *Lenz*, like the fragmentary drama *Woyzeck*, left unfinished at his death (the basis of Berg's opera), exhibits both a scientific and a passionately humane interest in a mind at the end of its tether. The events of the story are closely based on fact: J. M. R. Lenz (1751–92) was the author of dramas of social realism which profoundly influenced Büchner's own work.

LENZ

On the twentieth, Lenz was making his way through the
mountains. The peaks and high plateaux under snow, down
the valleys grey stones, green fields, rocks, and fir-trees. It
was cold and wet; the water trickled down the rocks and leapt
across his path. The branches of the fir-trees hung down heavy
in the damp air. Grey clouds were drifting across the sky, but
all so thick – and then the mist came swirling up and creeping
damp and heavy through the thickets, so slow, so clumsy.
He went on indifferently, he did not care which path he took,
now uphill, now down. He did not feel tired in the least, he
only regretted sometimes that he could not walk on his head.
At first he felt a surging within his breast when the stones
leapt away like that, the grey forest shook itself beneath him
and the mist now enveloped the shapes, now half unveiled
those mighty limbs; he felt a surging within, he was looking
for something, as if for a forgotten dream, but he found
nothing. Everything seemed so little to him, so near, so wet,
he would have liked to put the earth behind the stove, he
could not understand that it took him so long to descend a
slope, to reach a distant point; he thought he should be able
to pace out the whole world in a few steps. Only occasionally
when the storm-wind hurled the clouds into the valleys and
the vapours swirled up along the trees, and the voices awoke
on the rocks and came resounding first like distant thunder
and then with a mighty clamour, as if to sing to the earth in
wild jubilation, and the clouds came bounding like wild,
whinnying horses, and the sun shone suddenly between them
and was gone again, drawing its flashing sword on the snow-
covered surfaces, so that a bright, blinding light cut across the
peaks into the valleys; or when the storm-wind drove the
clouds downwards and tore open a lake of shining blue, and
then the gusts echoed away and came murmuring from far
below in the gorges, from the crests of the fir-trees below
like a lullaby, like church-bells ringing, and the deep blue was

flushed with pink, and tiny clouds scurried by on silver wings, and all the mountain-tops, sharply etched and firm, shone out and glittered over the whole landscape – then it tore his breath away, he stood panting, his body leaning forward, eyes and mouth wide open, he felt he had to draw the storm into himself, comprehend everything within himself, he stretched himself out and covered the earth, he burrowed himself into the universe, the joy of it was painful to him; or he stood still and laid his head upon the moss and half closed his eyes, and then he was far away, the earth shrank away beneath him, it became as small as a wandering star and plunged into a raging torrent whose clear waters swept by beneath him. But it was only for a moment; and then he would get up soberly, calm and collected, as if a shadow-play had passed before his eyes, everything was forgotten. Towards evening he reached the crest of the range, the snowfield, from where one could descend again westwards into the plain, up there he sat down. Westwards the sky was calmer now; the clouds lay densely packed and motionless; as far as the eye could see, nothing but peaks with broad slopes sweeping away from them, and everything so still, grey, darkling; he felt a terrible loneliness, he was alone, quite alone; he tried to talk to himself, but he could not, he scarcely dared to breathe, when he turned his foot it sounded like thunder beneath him, he had to sit down; a nameless dread seized him in this nothingness, he was in the void, he tore himself away and flew down the hillside. It had grown dark, earth and sky had melted into one. He felt as if there were something following him, and as if something terrible must surely come upon him, something no man could bear, as if madness were hunting him down on horseback. At last he heard voices, he saw lights, he felt easier, they told him there was another half-hour's journey to Waldbach. He went through the village. There were lights shining through the windows, he looked in as he went past: children at table, old women, girls, everyone with peace and calm in their faces, it seemed as if the light must be shining out of them, he felt at ease, soon he had reached the pastor's house at Waldbach. They were at table, in he went; his fair hair hung about his pale face, there was a quiver in his eyes, and about his lips, his clothes were tattered. Oberlin welcomed him, he thought he was a workman: 'You are very welcome, although I do not know you.' 'I am a friend of Kaufmann's, and he asked me to bring you his best wishes.' 'Your name, if I may ask?' 'Lenz.' 'Aha, have I not seen you in print? Have I not read some plays they say were written by a gentleman of that name?' 'Yes, but I hope you will not judge me by them.' They talked more, he groped for words and told his story quickly, but on the rack; by and by he grew calm, the homely room and the quiet faces emerging from the shadows, the child's bright face, on which all the light seemed to rest, looking up inquiring and truthful, to the mother sitting quietly like an angel back in the shadows. He began to talk to them, about where he came from; he drew them all the costumes, they pressed about him, their interest aroused, he felt immediately at home, his pale child's face, smiling now, his vivid story-telling; he was calmer, it seemed as if familiar figures, long-forgotten faces were emerging from the darkness, old songs were revived, he was far, far away. At last it was time to go. They took him across the street, the pastor's house was too small, they gave him a room in the schoolhouse. He went upstairs, it was cold there, a big room, empty, a tall bed at the far end, he put his light down on the table and walked up and down, turned the day over in his mind, how he had come here, the place he was in, the room in the pastor's house with its lights and friendly faces, it seemed to him a shadow, a dream, and he felt the emptiness again, as he had on the mountain, but he had nothing left to fill it with, his light had gone out, the darkness swallowed all; an unnameable dread seized him, he leapt up, he ran through the room, down the stairs, out in front of the house; but it was useless, all dark, nothing – he seemed a dream himself, stray thoughts flashed through his mind, he seized upon them, he felt he had to say 'Our Father' again and again, he no longer knew where he was, he felt a dark instinctive urge to save himself, he kicked the stones, he tore at himself with his fingernails, with the pain his consciousness began to return, he jumped into the trough at the pump, but the water was not deep, he splashed about in it. People came, they had heard it, they shouted at him. Oberlin came running; Lenz had come to himself again, he saw clearly where he was, he felt at ease again, now he was ashamed and upset that he had frightened these kind people, he told them he was in the habit of taking cold baths, and went upstairs again; at last he fell asleep from exhaustion.

The next day it was all right. With Oberlin on horseback through the valley; broad mountain-slopes falling from a great height into a narrow, winding valley, that led up into the mountains twisting this way and that, great rocky masses spreading downwards, few trees, but everything tinged grave and grey, a view to the west out into the country and to the chain of mountains running directly north and south, whose peaks stood mighty, grave, or dumbly silent, like a darkling dream. Great masses of light, sometimes swelling from the valleys like a mighty stream of gold, then cloud again, lying on the highest peak, then slowly descending along the forest's edge into the valley or sinking and then rising in the flashes of sunlight like a silver aerial web; not a sound, not a movement, not a bird, nothing but the wind that blew now near, now far away. Then, too, spots appeared, skeletons of hovels, planks roofed with straw, black and grave in colour. The people, silent and grave, as if they did not dare disturb the calm of their valley, greeted them calmly as they rode by. In the hovels there was life, they pressed about Oberlin, he admonished, gave advice, comforted; everywhere a trusting gaze, a prayer. The people told of dreams, forebodings. Then quickly to the practical things of life: making roads, digging dikes, going to school. Oberlin was tireless, Lenz his constant companion, now in conversation, now eager and busy, now absorbed in nature. Everything helped to calm and soothe him, often he had to look Oberlin in the face, and the great calm that comes upon us in the peace of nature, in the depths of the forest, in bright melting moonlit summer nights, seemed to him even nearer in those calm eyes, this grave, venerable face. He was shy, but he made remarks, he spoke,

Oberlin enjoyed his conversation, and Lenz's charming childlike face was a great delight to him. But only for as long as the light lay in the valley could he bear it; towards evening a strange dread came upon him, he would have liked to run after the sun; as the features of the landscape gradually became more shadowy, everything seemed so dreamlike, so horrible, dread fell upon him as it does on children sleeping in the dark; it seemed as if he were blind; now it grew, the hobgoblin of madness was sitting at his feet, the desperate thought that it was all a dream opened up before him, he clung to all the objects he could find, shapes passed quickly by him, he pressed himself upon them, they were shadows, the life left his body and his limbs were rigid. He spoke, he sang, he recited passages of Shakespeare, he clutched at everything which in the past had made his blood flow faster, he tried everything, but cold, cold. He had to go out into the open, the dim light that filtered through the night, when his eyes had grown accustomed to the darkness, made him feel better, he threw himself beneath the pump, the harsh shock of the water made him feel better, secretly too he hoped he might fall ill, he took his bath less noisily now. But the more he lived himself to life, the calmer he became, he helped Oberlin, drew, read the Bible; old, forgotten hopes revealed themselves to him, when he read the New Testament . . . Oberlin told him how an invisible hand had held him on the bridge, how on the hilltops a bright light had dazzled his eyes, how he had heard a voice, how it had spoken to him in the night, and how God had so entered into him, that like a child he had drawn lots from his pocket to see what he should do — this faith, this heaven everlasting in his earthly life, this being in God; now at last the scriptures were revealed to him. How nature came to touch men so closely, all in heavenly mysteries; but not with might and majesty, but intimately! — One morning he went out, snow had fallen in the night, the valley lay in bright sunshine, but farther off the landscape half veiled in mist. He soon left the path, and up a gentle slope, no longer any trace of footprints, beside a fir-wood, the sunlight sparkled crystalline, the snow lay lightly in flakes, here and there the track of deer lightly in the snow leading into the mountains. No motion in the air but a gentle soughing, but the fluttering of a bird shaking the flakes lightly from its tail. Everything so silent, and the trees far off with nodding white plumes in the deep blue sky. By and by he felt at home, the simple, mighty lines and masses, that sometimes seemed to be speaking to him in mighty tones, were veiled, he began to feel as if he were at home, as if it were Christmas, and sometimes he thought his mother was just coming out from behind a tree, tall, to tell him that she had given him all these things; as he descended, he saw that round his shadow a rainbow of beams was forming, he felt as if something had touched his brow, it spoke to him. He came down. Oberlin was in the room, Lenz approached him cheerfully and said that he would like to preach one day. 'Have you studied theology?' 'Yes!' 'Good, next Sunday, then.'

Lenz went to his room, pleased, pondered a text for his sermon and fell to meditating, and his nights were calmer. The Sunday morning came, a thaw had set in. Scudding clouds, blue sky between; the church lay near by up the hill, on a projecting plateau, the churchyard round about it. Lenz stood above as the bell rang and the church-goers, the women and girls in grave black dresses, their white, folded handkerchiefs on their hymn-books and their sprigs of rosemary, came up and down the narrow paths between the rocks on this side and on that. Sometimes a ray of sunlight lit up the valley, the warm air slowly stirred, the landscape swam in a haze, distant bells, it seemed as if everything were dissolved in a wave of harmony.

In the little churchyard the snow was gone, dark moss beneath the black crosses, a late spray of roses grew against the churchyard wall, late flowers too from beneath the moss, sometimes sun, then dark again. Church began, human voices joined in a pure bright sound; a sensation like looking into a pure, clear mountain stream. The singing died away, Lenz spoke, he was shy, with the music his tense anxiety had melted, all his pain awoke now, and filled his heart. A sweet feeling of infinite wellbeing crept over him. He spoke simply to the people, they all shared his suffering, and it was a consolation to him if he could bring sleep to eyes tired with weeping and calm to tormented hearts, if beyond this existence tormented by material wants he could help these inarticulate sufferings find their way to Heaven. He had become firmer when he finished – then the voices began again.

> Let this sacred grief and pain
> Swell the springs within my heart,
> Suffering be my reward,
> Suffering my gift to Thee.

The surging within him, the music, the pain, overwhelmed him. He saw the whole creation seared with wounds; he felt a pain, deep and unnameable. Now, another being, divine lips bent quivering over him and pressed themselves to his lips; he went to his lonely room. He was alone, alone! Then he heard the spring, streams burst from his eyes, he shrank into himself, his limbs quivered, he felt he must be dissolving, he could find no end to this ecstasy; finally it was twilight within him, he felt a profound gentle pity for himself, he wept at himself, his head dropped upon his breast, he fell asleep, the full moon stood in the sky, the locks of his hair dropped over his forehead and his face, the tears hung in his lashes and dried upon his cheeks, there he lay alone, and all was calm and quiet and cold, and the moon shone the whole night and stood above the mountain-tops.

The next morning he came down and told Oberlin, quite calmly, how in the night his mother had appeared to him; she had stepped out of the dark churchyard wall, in a white dress, and was wearing a white and a red rose at her breast; then she had sunk out of sight in a corner, and the roses had grown up slowly over her, surely she was dead; he could bear it quite calmly. So Oberlin told him how, when his father had died, he had been alone in the fields and he had then heard a voice, so that he knew his father was dead; and when he arrived home, it was true. This led them further, Oberlin went on to speak of the people in the mountains, of young girls who could sense water and metals under the earth, of

men who on many mountain-tops felt themselves seized and
had to struggle with spirits; he told him too how once in the
mountains when he had looked into a deep empty mountain
pool he had been plunged into a kind of somnambulistic
state. Lenz said that the spirit of the water had come upon
him, so that he had felt something of its strange being. He
went on: the simplest and purest were closest to elemental
nature, the more refined man's spiritual life and feelings were,
the duller this elemental sense became; he did not regard it
as an exalted state, it was not self-sufficient enough, but he
thought it must give a feeling of infinite bliss to be touched in
this way by the individual life of every form, to have a soul
sensitive to rocks, metals, water, and plants, to breathe every
natural thing into oneself as in a dream, like flowers with the
waxing and the waning of the moon.

He went on expounding his views: how in everything
there lay an inexpressible harmony, a keynote, a blessedness,
which in higher forms had more organs to express it, to echo
it and take it up again, but which thereby became more deeply
modified, how in the lower forms everything was much more
repressed, more limited, but their calm self-containment all the
greater. He pursued this further. Oberlin broke off the discussion, it was leading him too far from his simple ways.
Another time Oberlin showed him colour-cards, he showed
him what the connections were between the various colours
and men, he took out twelve apostles, each one represented
by a colour. Lenz absorbed all this, brooded on the matter, fell
into anxious dreams, and began like Stilling to read the Book
of Revelation, and read the Bible a great deal.

About this time Kaufmann came to the Steintal with his
fiancée. At first their arrival was unwelcome to Lenz; he had
found a cosy place for himself, the calm was so precious to
him, and now someone was coming to remind him of so many
things, someone he would have to speak to, to talk to, someone who knew about him. Oberlin knew nothing; he had taken
him in and looked after him; he saw it as a dispensation from
God, who had sent this poor unfortunate to him, he bestowed
his love on him. Everybody needed him there too, he was

one of them, as if he had been there a long time, and no one asked where he had come from or where he was going. At table Lenz was cheerful again, they were talking about literature, he was in his element; the period of idealism was just beginning, Kaufmann was one of its supporters, Lenz was violently against it. He said: The writers who, they say, give us reality have no idea what it is like, but even so they are more bearable than the ones who want to transfigure reality. He said: The good Lord must have made the world the way it is supposed to be, and surely we can't turn out anything better; all we should attempt to do is follow in His footsteps a little. What I ask in everything is – life, something that could exist, and that is good enough; we have no business to ask whether it is beautiful or ugly, the feeling that you have created something, that it is alive, is higher than either of these, and is the only criterion in artistic matters. It is a rare occurrence too, we find it in Shakespeare, and we hear it all the time in folk-songs, sometimes in Goethe; all the rest you can throw on the fire. Those fellows couldn't draw a dog-kennel. Idealized characters they are after, but all I can see in them is wooden dummies. This idealism is the most shameful contempt for human nature. Try it some time, steep yourself in the humblest man's life and reproduce it in a quiver, a hint, in all the subtle, scarcely noticed variations of a facial expression; that was the kind of thing he had been trying to do in *The Private Tutor* and *The Soldiers*. They are the most prosaic characters under the sun; but the vein of feeling runs the same in almost all people, only the veil it has to break through is more or less thick. You must just have an eye and an ear for it. Yesterday, when I went up here by the valley, I saw two girls sitting on a stone; the one was tying up her hair, the other was helping her; and her golden hair hung down so, and a grave, pale face, and yet so young, and the black dress, and the other one so serious about her task. The most beautiful, the most deeply felt pictures of the old German school could scarcely give an idea of it. Sometimes you feel you would like to be a Medusa's head, which could turn a group like that into stone, and call out to them. They stood up, the beautiful

group was gone; but then when they got down, between
the rocks it made another picture. The most beautiful pictures,
the most stirring sounds come together, then dissolve. Only
one thing remains: one unending beauty, changing from one
form to another, eternally blossoming and renewed, of course
you can't always catch hold of it and put it into a museum or
print it on a stave, and then send for young and old and let
the boys and old men chatter and go into ecstasies over it.
You must love humanity, to be able to penetrate each man's
individual being; you must not regard anyone as too humble,
anyone as too ugly, for it is only then you can understand
them; the most insignificant face will make a deeper impression than any mere sensation of beauty, and you can let the
figures step out of themselves, without copying anything into
them from outside because there is no life, no muscle, no
pulse swelling and beating for you to see. Kaufmann objected
that he was not going to find any figures like the Apollo
Belvedere or Raphael's Madonna in reality. What does that
matter, he answered; I must confess they make me feel very
dead. If I work in myself, I can get some feeling out of them,
but the best is my own doing. The poet and artist I like the
most is the one who gives me nature most truthfully, so that
I can *feel*, through and past his representation; anything else
distracts me. I like the Dutch painters better than the Italians,
they are the only solid ones; I can think of only two pictures,
both by Dutchmen, that have made the kind of impression on
me that the New Testament does; one is, I don't know who
painted it, Christ and the disciples at Emmaus. When you
read how the disciples went out there, it is as if the whole of
nature is there in those few words. It is a dull evening,
twilight, a plain streak of red on the horizon, half dark in
the street, someone they do not know comes to join them,
they talk, he breaks bread, then they recognize him, simply,
as men, and the divine suffering in his face speaks clearly to
them, and they are afraid, for it is grown dark, and something incomprehensible has come into their lives, but it is
not a ghostly fear; it is as if someone you loved but who
is dead were coming to meet you in the twilight just as he used

to be, and the picture is just like that, with a plain, brownish colour all over, the dull, quiet evening. Then another. A woman is sitting in her room, her prayerbook in her hand. Everything bright and clean for Sunday, fresh sand strewn, so homely, so pure and warm. The woman has not been able to go to church, and she is saying her prayers at home, the window is open, she is sitting turned towards it, and it is as if the sound of the village bells were wafted in through the window across the broad level landscape and you could hear the singing of the congregation from the church near by, and the woman is following in her book. He went on in this vein, they listened, there was a great deal in it, he had become flushed with talking, and now smiling, now gravely he shook his fair hair. He had quite forgotten himself. After dinner Kaufmann took him on one side. He had had letters from Lenz's father, he wanted his son to go back and support him. Kaufmann told him that he was wasting his time here, throwing it away for nothing, he ought to set himself some aim in life, and more of that kind of thing. Lenz attacked him: 'Away, away from here? home? Go mad back there? You know I cannot bear it anywhere except here in this neighbourhood; if I couldn't climb a mountain sometimes and look out over the neighbourhood, and then come down again into the house and through the garden and look in at the window – I should go mad! mad! Why won't you leave me in peace? A little peace, now, just when I am beginning to feel well! Go away? I don't understand it, those two words and the world is ruined for me. Everyone has some need or other; if he can find rest, what more can he want! Always climbing and struggling and throwing away for all eternity everything that the present gives, always languishing for the sake of a moment's pleasure; thirsting while clear spring water leaps across one's path. I can bear it now, and so I want to stay here. Why? why? Because I feel well; what does my father want? Has he more to offer? Impossible! Leave me in peace!' – He became violent; Kaufmann went away, Lenz had lost his composure.

The next day Kaufmann wanted to leave. He persuaded Oberlin to go to Switzerland with him. His desire for a personal meeting with Lavater, with whom he was already in correspondence, tipped the balance. He agreed. They had to wait another day on account of the preparations. Lenz was heavy-hearted, he had clutched anxiously at everything to be rid of his endless torment; in isolated moments he felt deeply how he was only arranging everything to suit himself; he treated himself like a sick child, it cost him the greatest dread to be rid of many thoughts and powerful feelings, then it pressed upon him again with infinite force, he trembled, his hair almost stood on end, till he had borne it out in the most terrible strain. He took refuge in a figure that he always saw in his mind's eye, and in Oberlin; his words, the sight of his face were an infinite blessing to him. So he dreaded the day when he would be leaving.

Lenz felt uneasy at being left alone in the house. The weather had turned mild, he decided to follow Oberlin, into the mountains. On the far side, where the valleys ran out into the plain, they parted. He went back alone. He wandered through the mountains, first in one direction, then in another. Wide slopes swept down into the valleys, few trees, nothing but the mighty lines and further off the broad plain with smoke rising, a mighty rushing in the air, nowhere any trace of people but here and there an abandoned hovel, where the shepherds spent the summer, leant against the hillside. He became silent, perhaps almost dreaming, everything melted before him into a single line, like a wave rising and falling, between earth and sky, it seemed to him as if he were lying by an endless sea, its waves moving gently up and down. Sometimes he sat still, then he went on, but slowly, dreaming. He was not looking for any path. It was late and dark when he came to a hovel where people were living, on the slopes towards the Steintal. The door was shut, he went to the window, through which a light shimmered. A lamp lit scarcely more than a single spot: its beam fell on the pale face of a girl sitting resting behind it, her eyes half open, softly moving her lips, further off in the darkness an old woman was sitting, singing in a

croaking voice out of a hymn book. After he had knocked for
a long time, she opened the door; she was half deaf, she gave
Lenz some food and showed him where he might sleep,
singing on all the time. The girl had not stirred. A little while
later a man came in, he was tall and lean, hair flecked with
grey, with a restless, disturbed expression on his face. He
went up to the girl, she started and became restless. He took
a dried herb from the wall and laid the leaves upon her hand,
so that she became calmer and spoke words one could understand, in long-drawn-out, piercing tones. He told how he had
heard a voice in the mountains and then seen lightning flash
above the valleys, and how it had seized upon him and he had
wrestled with it like Jacob. He threw himself down and prayed
softly but fervently, while the sick girl sang in long-drawn-
out, softly echoing tones. Then he lay down to rest.

Lenz fell dreamily asleep, and then in his sleep he heard the
clock ticking. Above the girl's singing and the old woman's
voice he heard the roaring of the wind, now nearer, now farther
off, and the moon, now bright, now veiled, cast its fitful light
into the room as in a dream. Suddenly the sounds became
louder, the girl spoke clearly and distinctly, she said there
was a church standing opposite on the cliff. Lenz looked up,
and she was sitting with wide-open eyes, upright at the table,
and the moon cast its quiet light upon her features, that seemed
to shine with a strange glow, meanwhile the old woman
croaked on, and with the fitfulness and failing of the light, the
sounds and the voices, Lenz at last fell sound asleep.

He awoke early. In the twilit room all were asleep, the girl
had become calm too. She lay leaning back, her left cheek
resting on her clasped hands; the ghostly look was gone from
her face, now she wore an expression of indescribable suffering. He went to the window and opened it, the cold morning
air buffeted his face. The house lay at the end of a deep,
narrow valley, opening to the east; ruddy beams were streaming through the grey morning sky into the twilit valley that
lay wreathed in white vapour, and sparkled on the grey rocks
and pierced the windows of the hovels. The man awoke, his
glance fell upon a picture lit up on the wall, he fixed his eyes

firmly upon it, now he began to move his lips, and prayed softly, then aloud and louder still. Meanwhile people came into the hovel, they threw themselves down silently. The girl lay quivering, the old woman croaked her song and gossiped with the neighbours. The people told Lenz that the man had come into the district a long time ago, no one knew where from; he had the reputation of a saint, he could see water under the earth and could summon spirits, and people made pilgrimages to him. Lenz learnt too that he had wandered further from the Steintal, he went off with some woodcutters who were going in that direction. He was glad of their company; he felt uneasy now with the mighty man, who sometimes seemed to him to be speaking in a fearful voice. He was afraid of himself in the loneliness too.

He came home. But the past night had made a fearful impression on him. The world had been transparent to him, and he felt a stirring within him, a milling towards an abyss, to which he was drawn by some inexorable power. He burrowed within himself. He ate little; often half the night in prayer and feverish dreams. A powerful surging, and then thrown back in exhaustion; he lay in scalding tears, and then suddenly he would feel strong, and rise cold and impassive, then he felt his tears like ice, he had to laugh. The greater the height to which he tore himself, the greater the depths to which he plunged. Everything flooded together again. Intimations of his old state quivered through him and cast flashes of light into the chaos and devastation of his spirit. During the day he usually sat downstairs, Oberlin's wife went to and fro, he drew, painted, read, snatched at any kind of diversion, always hurrying on from one to the next. But he attached himself particularly to Oberlin's wife when she sat there like that, the black hymn-book in front of her, beside her a plant she had grown in the room, the youngest of the children between her knees, he amused himself with the child a great deal too. Then once when he was sitting there, an anxious feeling came upon him, he leapt up, strode up and down. The door half open, then he heard the maid singing, at first he could not understand, then came the words.

In this world I have no joy,
My lover's far away —

It fell upon him, he almost swooned beneath those sounds. Oberlin's wife looked at him. He took heart, he could be silent no longer, he had to talk about it. 'Dear Madame Oberlin, can you not tell me what has happened to that girl, whose fate lies so heavy like a weight upon my heart?' 'But Mr Lenz, I know nothing about it.'

He was silent again then and paced rapidly up and down the room; then he began again: 'Look, I will go; in God's name, you are the only people with whom I could bear it, and yet — yet I must go, to *her* — but I cannot, I must not.' He was in great agitation and went out.

Towards evening Lenz came back, it was growing dark in the room; he sat down beside Madame Oberlin, 'Look,' he began again, 'when she went through the room like that singing half to herself alone, and every step was music, there was such bliss in her, and it poured over into me, I was always at peace when I could look at her or when she leant her head against me so — and oh, God! God! it was so long since I was at peace . . . Just a child; it seemed the world was too big for her, she drew back into herself, she sought out the tiniest corner in the whole house, and there she sat, as if all her happiness were gathered in one small spot, and then I felt so too; I could have played then like a child. And now I feel so shut in, so shut in, you see, I sometimes feel as if I were touching the sky with my hands; oh, I shall be stifled! Then I often feel as if I were in physical pain, here in my left side, in the arm I used to hold her with. And yet I can't remember what she looked like, her image runs away from me, and that tortures me; only when I can sometimes see everything quite clearly, then I feel quite well again.' He went on talking about it to Oberlin's wife from time to time, but mostly in disconnected phrases; she could think of little to say in reply, but it did him good.

Meanwhile his religious torments continued. The emptier, the colder, the nearer death he felt within, the more he felt a surging desire to awaken some fire inside himself; there came recollections of the times when everything was surging within him, when he was panting beneath all his emotions. And now so dead. He despaired in himself, then he threw himself down, he wrung his hands, he stirred up everything within him; but dead! dead! Then he prayed that God might perform a sign by him, then he burrowed in himself, fasted, lay dreaming upon the floor. On the third of February he heard that a child called Friederike had died in Fouday, he seized upon it like an obsession. He went to his room and spent a day fasting. On the fourth he suddenly appeared downstairs in front of Oberlin's wife, he had smeared his face with ashes, and asked for an old sack; it frightened her, he got what he had asked for. He wrapped the sack around him, like a penitent, and set out for Fouday. The people in the valley were already used to him; they told all kinds of strange stories about him. He came to the house where the child lay. The people were going about their business impassively; they showed him a room, the child lay in her shift on straw, on a wooden table.

Lenz shuddered as he touched the cold limbs and saw the glazed, half-open eyes. The child seemed so abandoned, and he himself so lonely and alone; he flung himself down upon the body; death frightened him, a violent pain seized him, these features, this peaceful face were to decay, he flung himself down, he prayed with all the grief of despair, that he was so weak and wretched, that God might give a sign by him and bring the child to life; then he sank into himself and burrowed all his will-power into a single spot, he sat motionless for a long time. Then he arose and took hold of the child's hand and spoke loud and clear; 'Stand up and walk!' But the walls echoed the sound drily back to him, as if to mock him, and the body remained cold. Then he threw himself down half mad, then he fled, up and away into the mountains. Clouds were scudding across the moon; now all was dark, now they revealed the misty dissolving landscape in the moonlight. He dashed this way and that. In his bosom rang hell's triumphant shout. The wind roared like a song of Titans, he felt as

if he could clench a huge fist up in heaven and tear down God
and drag him between the clouds; as if he could crunch the
whole world between his teeth and spit it into the Creator's
face; he cursed, he uttered blasphemies. So he came to the
crest of the ridge, and the uncertain light spread itself down
there, where the white masses of stone lay, and the sky was a
silly blue eye, and the moon in it looked so ridiculous, stupid.
Lenz had to laugh out loud, and as he laughed, atheism seized
him and took hold of him, quite firm and sure. He could no
longer think what had moved him so much before, he was
freezing, he thought he would go to bed now, and he walked
coldly and implacably through the uneasy darkness – all
seemed empty and hollow, he had to run, and went to bed.

The next day he was seized with a great horror at the state
he had been in that day. Now he stood before the abyss, into
which a mad desire drove him again and again to peer down,
to feel this torment yet again. Then his dread grew, the sin
against the Holy Ghost stood before him.

A few days later Oberlin returned from Switzerland, much
sooner than expected. Lenz was taken aback. But he grew
cheerful when Oberlin told him what his friends in Alsace
were doing. Oberlin went to and fro in the room as he did so,
unpacking and putting away. He talked about Pfeffel, extolling
the happy life of a country clergyman. As he did so he urged
him to submit to his father's wishes, to live in accordance
with his vocation, to go back home. He said to him: 'Honour
thy father and mother!' and more of that kind of thing. Their
talk plunged Lenz into violent agitation; he sighed deeply,
tears started from his eyes, he spoke haltingly. 'Yes, but I
cannot bear it; are you going to send me away? Only you
hold the way to God. But I am finished! I am apostate, I am
damned to all eternity, I am the Wandering Jew.' Oberlin
told him that it was on account of this that Jesus had died;
let him turn to Him with fervent desire, and he should partake
of His grace.

Lenz raised his head, wrung his hands, and said, 'Oh! Oh!
heavenly comfort.' Then suddenly he asked amiably what had
happened to the girl. Oberlin said he knew nothing, but

he would help and advise him all he could; but he must tell him the place, the circumstances, and the person. He answered nothing but a few broken words: 'Oh, she is dead! Is she still alive? The angel! She loved me – I loved her, she deserved it so – oh, angel! Damned jealousy, I sacrificed her – there was another she loved – I loved her, she deserved it so – oh, kind mother, she loved me too – I am a murderer!' Oberlin replied: perhaps all these people were still alive, perhaps happy; be that as it might be, still God, if he would only turn to Him, could and would grant such blessings to these people for his prayers and tears, that the benefit he should thus have brought them would perhaps outweigh the harm that he had done them. At this he gradually grew calmer and returned to his painting.

In the afternoon he came back. Over his left shoulder he had a piece of fur and in his hand a bundle of sticks, which Oberlin had been given together with a letter for Lenz. He gave Oberlin the sticks, with the request that he should beat him with them. Oberlin took the sticks from his hand, pressed a number of kisses upon his lips, and said: these were the blows that he had to give him; he should be calm, should settle his affairs with God alone, all the blows in the world would not purge a single one of his sins; this Jesus had provided for, let him turn to Him. He left him.

At supper he was as usual rather deep in thought. And yet he spoke of all kinds of things, but with anxious haste. At midnight Oberlin was awakened by a noise. Lenz was running about in the yard, crying out in a harsh, hollow voice the name Friederike, pronounced with the greatest speed, confusion and desperation, then he flung himself into the water-trough, splashed in it, out again and up to his room, down again into the trough, and the same a few times more, at last he was quiet. The maids who slept in the nursery below his room said that they had often heard, but particularly that same night, a buzzing noise, like nothing they could think of but the drumming of a snipe. Perhaps it was his moaning, in a hollow, terrible, despairing voice.

The next morning Lenz did not appear for a long time. At

last Oberlin went up to his room; he lay in bed, calm and still. Oberlin had to keep asking for a long time before he received any answer; at last he said, 'Yes, pastor, you see, boredom! boredom! oh, so boring! I can't think of anything more to say; I have already drawn every figure I could think of on the wall.' Oberlin told him he should turn to God; at that he laughed and said, 'Yes, if I were as lucky as you, to have found such a comfortable pastime, yes, then one could fill out the time like that. All out of idleness. For most people pray out of boredom, others fall in love out of boredom, some are virtuous, some wicked, and I nothing, nothing at all, I can't even be bothered to kill myself; it's too boring!

> O God! in these Thy waves of light,
> Thy glowing noonday sun so bright,
> My eyes are wounded with the glare,
> Will never Night again be here?'

Oberlin looked at him disapprovingly and made as if to go. Lenz scurried after him, and looking at him with a strange expression in his eyes, 'Look, I have thought of something now, if I could only decide if I was awake or dreaming; it's very important, you see, we must try to find out' – then he scurried back to bed. That afternoon Oberlin wanted to go visiting in the neighbourhood; his wife had already left; he was just on his way, when there was a knock at his door and Lenz came in with his body bent forward, his head hanging down, his whole face and, here and there his clothes, smeared with ashes, holding his left arm with his right hand. He asked Oberlin to pull his arm, he had put it out of joint, he had jumped out of the window, but as no one had seen him he didn't want to tell anyone. This frightened Oberlin very much, but he did not say anything, he did what Lenz asked, at the same time he wrote to Sebastian Scheidecker, the schoolmaster at Bellefosse, asking him to come over, and gave him instructions. Then he rode off. The man came. Lenz had seen him a number of times already and had attached himself to him. He pretended that he had wanted to talk to Oberlin, then said he must go. Lenz asked him to stay, and so they stayed

together. Lenz proposed they should take a walk to Fouday
again. He went to see the grave of the child he had wanted to
raise, knelt down time and time again, kissed the earth on
the grave, seemed to be praying, yet in great confusion, pulled
something from the flower on the grave as a keepsake, walked
back again to Waldbach, turned back again, and Sebastian
with him. Now he walked slowly and complained of a great
weakness in his limbs, then he walked at a desperate speed,
the landscape made him feel anxious, it was so narrow that
he was afraid of bumping into everything. An indescribable
feeling of unease came upon him, at last he tired of his companion, perhaps too he guessed why he had come and tried
means of escaping from him. Sebastian pretended to let him
have his way, but secretly found means of informing his
brother of the danger, and now Lenz had two guardians
instead of one. He led them farther afield, at last he went
back towards Waldbach, and, when they were nearly at the
village, he turned round again like lightning and galloped
back fleet as a stag towards Fouday. The men set out after
him. As they were hunting for him in Fouday, two shop-
keepers came and told them that in one of the houses they had
a stranger tied up, who gave himself out to be a murderer,
but who surely could not be a murderer. They ran to that house
and found it was so. A young man had tied him up, in terror,
at his insistent urging. They untied him and managed to take
him back to Waldbach, where meanwhile Oberlin had returned
home with his wife. He looked confused, but, when he saw
how kind and friendly they were to him, his spirits quickened,
they saw a change for the better in his face, he thanked his
two companions with a gentle, friendly word, and the evening passed peacefully. Oberlin asked him urgently not to
bathe any more, to stay peacefully in bed at night, and if he
could not sleep to hold converse with God. He promised he
would, and did so the night that followed, the maids heard him
praying almost the whole night through. – The following
morning he came to Oberlin's room with a contented expression. After they had talked about various things, he said in
an unusually amiable way, 'My dear pastor, the girl I was

telling you about is dead, yes, dead, – the angel!' – 'How do you know?' – 'Hieroglyphs, hieroglyphs!' and then looked up to heaven and again, 'Yes, dead – hieroglyphs!' Then nothing more could be got out of him. He sat down and wrote a few letters, then gave them to Oberlin, asking him to add a few lines.

Meanwhile his condition had become more and more disconsolate, all the peace he had drawn from Oberlin's company and from the calm of the valley was gone; the world he had tried to make some use of had a great rent in it, he felt no hatred, no love, no hope, a terrible emptiness and yet a torturing anxiety to fill it. He had *nothing*. He was aware of what he was doing, and yet an instinct within him drove him on. When he was alone, he felt such a hideous loneliness that he constantly talked to himself out loud, cried out, and then he took fright again and it seemed as if a strange voice had spoken to him. When they were talking he would often stop, an indescribable dread assailed him, he had lost the end of his sentence; then he felt he must keep hold of the last word that had been spoken and say it again and again, it cost him great efforts to suppress these desires. The good people were deeply grieved when sometimes he was sitting with them in moments of calm, talking without embarrassment, and then he stopped and an inexpressible dread was mirrored in his features, he clutched convulsively at the arms of those sitting next to him, and only gradually came to himself again. If he was alone or was reading, it was still worse, all the workings of his mind would sometimes stick fast upon a single thought; if he was thinking about some stranger, or if he pictured him vividly to himself, then he would feel as if he was that person; he grew totally confused, and then he felt an infinite desire to play capricious tricks in his imagination on everything about him; nature, people, Oberlin excepted, all like a dream, cold; he amused himself turning the houses upside-down, dressing and undressing the people, thinking up the maddest pranks. Sometimes he felt an irresistible urge to carry out whatever he had in his mind at the moment, and then he would pull hideous grimaces. Once he was sitting beside

Oberlin, the cat was lying opposite him on a chair. Suddenly his eyes took on a glassy stare, he fixed them unswervingly on the animal, then slowly he slid down from his chair, the cat too, it was as if his gaze had cast a spell on her, she was terrified, her fur stood on end with fright, Lenz in the same tone, his face horribly contorted, as if in desperation the two flew at each other, then at last Oberlin's wife rose to separate them. Then he felt deeply ashamed again. The incidents at night grew to fearful proportions. Only with the greatest difficulty could he fall asleep, while up till then he had still been trying to fill that fearful emptiness. Then between sleeping and waking he found himself in a state of terror; he came up against something hideous, terrible, madness seized him, he leapt up screaming horribly, bathed in sweat, and only gradually came to his senses. Then he had to start with the simplest things before he could be himself again. Really it was not he who was doing it, but a powerful instinct of self-preservation, it seemed as if there were two of him, and the one was trying to save the other and crying out to itself; he told stories, he recited poems, shuddering with dread, until he felt himself again.

In the daytime too he had these attacks, then they were even more terrible; for previously the brightness had saved him from them. Then it seemed as if only he existed, as if the world were only a figment of his imagination, as if there were nothing but himself, he was a thing damned to eternity, Satan, alone with the imaginings that tortured him. He tore through his life at a mad gallop, and then he said, 'Consistent, consistent'; if anyone said anything, 'Inconsistent, inconsistent' – it was the gulf of irretrievable madness, a madness to all eternity. The instinct to preserve his sanity spurred him on: he flung himself into Oberlin's arms, he clung to him as if he would surge right through him, he was the only creature alive for him, the only one in whom life was revealed to him again. Gradually then Oberlin's words would bring him to his senses; he lay on his knees in front of Oberlin, his hands in Oberlin's hands, his face streaming with cold sweat, on the other's lap, his whole body shaking and trembling. Oberlin

felt infinite compassion for him, the family lay on their knees
and prayed for the wretched man, the maids fled and thought
him one possessed. And when he grew calmer, it was like the
grief of a child, he sobbed, he felt profoundly sorry for himself; these were his happiest moments too. Oberlin talked to
him about God. Lenz calmly disengaged himself and looked
at him with an expression of infinite suffering, and said at
last, 'But I, if I were omnipotent, you see, if I were, I could
not bear the suffering, I should save them, save them, you
know all I want is peace, peace, just a little peace, so that I
can sleep.' Oberlin said this was blasphemy. Lenz shook his
head disconsolately. The half-hearted suicide attempts which
he went on making were not really serious. It was not so
much the wish for death, for him there could be no peace and
hope in death; it was rather an attempt, in moments of the
most terrible dread or of a dull calm bordering on non-
existence, to find himself again by means of physical pain.
Moments when his spirit seemed to be possessed by some mad
idea or other were the happiest that remained. It was a little
peace, after all, and his distraught gaze was not so terrible as
the dread thirsting for deliverance, the eternal torment of agitation! Often he would beat his head against the wall, or inflict
some other violent physical pain upon himself.

On the morning of the eighth he stayed in bed, Oberlin went
up; he was lying in his bed almost naked and was violently
disturbed. Oberlin wanted to cover him up, but he complained
bitterly how heavy everything was, so heavy, he did not think
he would ever be able to move, at last he could feel the colossal
weight of the air. Oberlin tried to cheer him. But he stayed in
the same condition and stayed like it for the greater part of the
day, nor did he have anything to eat. Towards evening Oberlin
was called to Bellefosse where someone lay sick. It was mild
weather and moonlight. On the way back he met Lenz. He
seemed quite rational and spoke calmly and amiably with
Oberlin. The latter asked him not to go too far away; he
promised. As he was going on, he suddenly turned round and
came quite close to Oberlin again and said quickly, 'You
see, pastor, if only I didn't have to listen to that any more,

I should feel better.' – 'What, my dear fellow?' – 'Why, can't you hear anything? don't you hear that terrible voice shouting all round the horizon, the sound people usually call silence? Since I have been in this quiet valley I have heard it all the time. I can't sleep for it; oh, pastor, yes, if only I could sleep once more!' Then he went on his way, shaking his head. Oberlin went back to Waldbach and was going to send someone after him, when he heard him going up the stairs to his room. A moment later something crashed into the yard with such a resounding noise that Oberlin felt it could not possibly be caused by a man's fall. Then the nursemaid came as pale as death and trembling all over . . .

He sat in the carriage with cold resignation as they drove westwards along the valley. It was all one to him where they were taking him. Several times, when the road was so bad that the carriage was in danger, he stayed sitting still quite calmly; he was completely indifferent. In this condition he travelled through the mountains. Towards evening they were in the Rhine valley. Gradually they drew away from the mountains, that now rose like a deep blue crystal wave in the ruddy flow of the evening, on its warm rolling surface the ruddy beams of evening playing; away over the plain at the foot of the mountain range span a shimmering bluish haze. It grew dark, the closer they came to Strasbourg; full moon high in the sky, all the distant features dark, only the mountain beside them drawing a sharp line; the earth was like a golden bowl, overbrimming with the foaming golden waves of moonlight. Lenz looked out calmly with a fixed stare, no intimations, no urge; he only felt an obscure dread growing within him, the more the features of the landscape melted into the darkness. They had to find somewhere to stay. Then again he made several attempts to do himself an injury, but was too closely guarded. The next morning, in dull, rainy weather, he arrived in Strasbourg. He seemed quite rational, talked to people; he behaved just like everyone else, but there was a hideous emptiness in him, he no longer felt any dread, any desire; his existence was a burden he had to bear. – So he lived on.

Theodor Storm

ST GEORGE'S ALMSHOUSE

Translated by G. W. McKay

Theodor Storm

STORM was a native of Holstein, born in Husum in 1817. Exiled from his native province during the years of Danish rule, he returned in 1864 and died there in 1888. The harsh, bleak landscape of the extreme north of Germany and its sea-coast form the background to many of his numerous stories. His characteristic theme is the struggle of human beings against natural forces, in particular the destructive power of time; it is reflected in the construction of the tales too, with their flashbacks, elaborate time-structures and complex perspectives. *St George's Almshouse* (*In Sankt Jürgen*) was written in 1867.

ST GEORGE'S ALMSHOUSE

IT's just a plain little town, my hometown: it lies in a treeless coastal plain and its houses are old and dark. Yet I've always thought it a pleasant place, and this feeling seems to be shared by two birds that men hold sacred: in the clear summer air storks continually hover over the town, and their nests are in the roofs beneath them; and when April comes, the first southern breezes that blow bring the swallows, and neighbour tells neighbour that the swallows have come. So it is now. In the garden beneath my windows the first violets are out and on the fence yonder the swallow too sits twittering its old song

> when I went away, when I went away ...

but the longer it sings, the more I think of one, long dead, to whom I owe many a happy hour of my childhood.

My thoughts wander up the street to the far end, where St George's Almshouse stands. For our town, like most towns of any importance in North Germany, has its almshouse. The present building was put up in the sixteenth century by one of our Dukes and has attained a certain wealth thanks to the public-spirited generosity of the townspeople, so that it is now a comfortable abode for old folk seeking peace after the toil of their life and before they enter into their long rest. One side borders St George's Kirkyard, under whose great lime-trees the first reformers preached; the other encloses an inner courtyard and next to it a narrow garden, where in my youth the almswomen picked flowers for church service on Sundays. A gateway surmounted by two heavy Gothic gables leads from the street into the courtyard, from which a number of doors lead into the interior of the house, into the spacious chapel and the almsfolk's rooms.

As a boy I often went through that gateway; for since the great Kirk of St Mary had become unsafe and had been demolished, long before I remember, the town service had for many years been held in the chapel of St George's Almshouse.

How often in summertime, before walking through the chapel door, have I stood in the sunny courtyard in the stillness of a Sabbath morning while all round me the air was filled with the scent from the near-by garden of wallflowers, pinks, and mignonette, according to season! But this was not the only reason why going to church seemed so delightful to me; often, especially if I was out and about a little earlier, I went farther into the courtyard to look up at a little window in the upper storey, lit by the morning sun, for at one side of the window a pair of swallows had built their nest. One casement was usually open; and, when my step sounded on the paving, a woman's head with grey hair parted in the middle and a snow-white bonnet would appear and nod kindly down to me. 'Good morning, Hansen!' I would call, for we children called our old friend only by her surname; we hardly knew that she bore the sweet-sounding name of Agnes, a name that must have suited her well long ago, when her blue eyes were still young and her grey hair blond. She had been many years in service with my grandmother and then, when I was about eleven, had been admitted to the Almshouse as the daughter of a burgher who had borne the burden of office in the town. With her departure the most important person for us in Grandmother's house had gone. For without our noticing it Hansen had the knack of keeping us constantly pleasantly occupied. For my sister she would cut up patterns for new doll's clothes, while it was my job to sit, pencil in hand, and practise all sorts of decorative script under her instruction, or to copy a now rare picture she owned of the Old Kirk. The one thing that later struck me about her dealings with us was that she never told us any stories about fairies or heroes, though our region is particularly rich in these; rather, if ever someone else launched forth on such stories, she seemed anxious to change the subject, as if she felt them to be useless or even harmful. Yet she was anything but cold and unimaginative by nature. But animals she adored; she particularly

loved protecting the swallows and their nests from Grandmother's broom, for Grandmother was as houseproud as a
Dutch burgher's wife and could not put up with little invaders.
And Hansen seemed to have studied the nature of these birds
closely. I remember once bringing her a swift I had found lying
apparently lifeless on the paving. 'Poor pretty creature, it
will die,' I said, sadly stroking its shining black-brown
feathers. But Hansen shook her head. 'That one?' she
said, 'It's the queen of the air, all it needs is the clear sky!
It's been knocked to the ground through fear of a hawk; its
long wings were no use to it on the ground.' Then we went
into the garden, I with the swift lying peacefully in my hand,
looking at me with its big brown eyes. 'Now throw it into
the air!' cried Hansen. And I watched amazed as the apparently
lifeless bird, thrown from my hand, quick as a flash spread its
wings and darted away twittering brightly like a feathered
arrow in the sunny space. 'The tower, that's where you should
see her flying from,' said Hansen, 'I mean the old kirk tower,
that was what you could call a real tower.'

Then sighing and stroking my cheek she went back into the
house to her usual work. 'Why does Hansen sigh like that?'
I thought. I got the answer to that question only many years
later and from the lips of one then quite unknown to me.

Now she was in her retirement, but her swallows had found
her and we children found her too. Entering the old spinster's
clean little parlour on a Sunday morning before church time,
I would find her sitting in her Sunday best with her hymn-
book before her. If she saw me about to sit down on the little
sofa beside her she would say, 'Now, you won't see the
swallows from there.' Then she would move a geranium or a
pot of pinks from the window-sill and make me sit down in
her armchair in the deep window-bay. 'But you mustn't
wave your arms about,' she would add with a smile, 'they
don't see lively lads like you every day.' And then I would sit
still, watching the slender birds as they flew to and fro in
the sunshine, building their nests or feeding their young,
while Hansen sat opposite, telling me about the good old
times – the festive occasions in my great-grandfather's house,

the parades of the old guild of marksmen or, her favourite
theme, the splendid pictures and altar in the Old Kirk in
which she had stood as godmother to the grandaughter of
the last town watchman. This went on till the last note of the
organ rolled across to us from the chapel. Then she got up
and we walked together along an endless narrow corridor,
dimly lit by curtained panes in the doors of the cells on either
side. Now and then one of the doors would open, and in the
light that for a few moments penetrated the gloom I could see
old, strangely attired men and women, most of whom had
vanished from the daily life of the town long before I was born,
shuffle out into the corridor. I would have liked to ask a
question or two; but I knew better than to expect an answer
from Hansen on the way to church, so we walked on in silence;
at the end of the corridor Hansen went with the other old folk
down a back stair to the almsfolk's pews, while I went to the
choir where I would dreamily watch the bells swinging and,
when the minister had mounted the pulpit, hear his doubtless
well-composed sermon come to me (I confess) like the distant
monotonous rolling of waves. For down on the opposite wall
hung a life-size portrait of an old priest with long black curly
hair and an oddly shaped moustache, which soon would absorb
my attention completely. The picture with those melancholy
black eyes seemed to gaze from the dim and distant world of
miracles and witches up into the modern age, and it told me
too of the town's history, that stood black upon white in the
chronicles, in full detail down to the wicked robber baron
whose last evil deed was commemorated on the funerary tablet
of his murdered victim in the Old Kirk. Of course when the
organ struck up the doxology I usually crept out and escaped
into the open air, for it was no light matter having to undergo
my old friend's cross-questioning on the sermon.

Hansen never spoke of her own past life. It was not until I
had been a few years at the university that for the first time,
during a holiday visit at home, she told me anything about it.

It was in April, on her sixty-fifth birthday. On that day as
in previous years I had delivered the traditional two ducats
from Grandmother and a few little presents from the family,

and she had treated me to a glass of Malaga, which she kept in her wall-cupboard for such occasions. After we had been chatting for a little while, I asked her to show me the great chamber which I had long wished to see, where for centuries the heads of the institution held their feasts after the annual audit. Hansen agreed, and we walked together along the long corridor, for the chamber lay beyond the chapel at the other end of the building. As I climbed down the back stairs I slipped and stumbled down the last steps, and down on the landing a door was thrown open and the ghostly bald head of a nonagenarian poked out. He murmured some half-comprehensible words of complaint and stared at us with glassy eyes till we went through the chapel door.

I knew him. The inmates called him the Spook-seer; they said he 'saw things'.

'His eyes could give you a fright,' I said to Hansen, as we walked through the chapel.

She said, 'He doesn't see you; he only looks back over his own foolish, sinful life.'

'But,' said I, jokingly, 'I expect he sees open coffins in that corner while those who lie in them still walk living among you.'

'They are only shadows, laddie; he won't do any harm now. Of course,' she added, 'he has no right to be here and only slipped in because the commissioner had a free place; for the rest of us have to prove our good character before we are admitted.'

Meantime we had procured the key from the matron and climbed up the stairs to the banqueting chamber. The room we entered was only moderately large and low-ceilinged. On one wall was an old-fashioned grandfather clock bequeathed by a departed inmate, while on the wall opposite hung a life-size portrait of a man in a plain red jerkin. There were no other ornaments in the room. 'That's the good Duke who built the almshouse,' said Hansen, 'but people enjoy his gifts and no longer think of him as he hoped they would when he was alive.'

'But you think of him, Hansen.'

She looked at me with her gentle eyes. 'Ay, laddie,' she said, 'but that's what I'm like; I don't easily forget.'

The walls facing the street and the churchyard each had a row of windows with little leaded panes; and in almost every pane, etched in black, was the name of a family – mostly respectable town families known to me; and beneath, the inscription: 'Head of the Table in this place, Anno —' with the date following.

'Look, that's your great-grandfather,' said Hansen, pointing to one of those panes, 'he's someone else I don't forget; my father learned his merchant's trade from him and afterwards often got advice and help from him; only, when things were at their worst, he was already gone.'

I read another name: 'Liborius Michael Hansen, Head of the Table Anno 1799.'

'That was my father!' said Hansen.

'Your father? How did it happen that . . .?'

'That I was in service half of my life, you mean, when I was the daughter of a man of substance?'

Hansen had sat down on one of the leather chairs. 'That was nothing out of the way, laddie,' she said. 'It was 1807, the time of the Continental blockade when rogues flourished and honest men were ruined. And my father was an honest man! – And he carried his honest name to the grave with him,' she went on after a short silence. 'I well remember how once, when we were walking together down Commerce Street, he pointed out to me an old house that has vanished long since. "Take a good look at that!" he said to me. "The good merchant Meinke Gravely lived here in the year 1549, when the great fire broke out on the third Sunday after Easter. As the flames roared on he rushed with his yardstick and his scales into the street, and prayed to God that if he had ever knowingly cheated his neighbours of a single farthing, his house should not be spared. But the flames passed over his house, while all around was burnt to ashes.

'"See, my lass," my father added, raising his hands, "I could do the same, and the Lord's punishment would pass over our house too."' Hansen looked at me. 'Men should not boast,' she said then. 'You're old enough now for me to tell you; for you must know about me when I am gone. My dear father had one weakness – he was superstitious. That weakness brought him, in a time of need, to do something that shortly afterwards broke his heart; for after that he could never again tell the story of the good merchant.

'In the house next door to ours there lived a master joiner. When he died young my father became the guardian of his orphan son. Harre – that was the lad's name, a good Frisian name – loved reading books and had got up to the fifth form in the grammar school. But there wasn't enough money for him to study, and so he stuck to his father's trade. Later, when he became a journeyman and spent two years travelling and then worked for a while with a master joiner, he got a reputation for special skill in fine work in his trade. We had grown up together; when he was still an apprentice he often read me bits from books that he had borrowed from his old schoolfriends. You know we lived in Market Square in the house with the Venetian windows opposite the town hall – there's a great box-tree still there to this day. How often we sat with our book under that tree, while over us the bees buzzed in the little blossoms! When he came back home, it was just the same, he often came to our house. So to cut a long story short, laddie, we liked each other well and didn't try to hide it.

'My mother was dead. What my father thought about the matter or whether he thought about it at all, I never knew. And it didn't get as far as a proper engagement.

'One morning in early spring I had gone out into the garden. The crocuses and the red anemones were just beginning to flower, everything around us was so young and fresh, but I felt weighed down, my father's cares lay heavily on me too. Though he had never talked to me about his affairs, I nevertheless felt that things were more and more rapidly going downhill. In the last months I had seen the town clerk again and again going into my father's writing-room. When he had gone, my father shut himself in for hours on end; many a time he got up from dinner-table without tasting a bite. In the previous week he had spent a whole evening laying cards; when I asked him, as if in fun, what he expected his oracle to tell him, he had waved me away without a word with a movement of his hand and later had gone with a gruff "Good night" to his chamber.

'All this was lying like a load upon me; I was looking into my own heart, and my eyes saw nothing of the bright sunlight that was transfiguring the world outside me. Then I heard the nightingale's song coming from the marsh beneath, and you know, laddie, when you're young your heart is so light, a little bird can lift it up as it flies. I suddenly felt I could see away beyond all the mists of worry into a sunny future – as if I need only step over into it. I remember how I knelt down by the flower-bed, and how happy it made me to look at the buds and the fresh greenery bursting forth from the earth. And I thought of Harre and in the end I was thinking of nothing but him. I heard the garden gate click open and when I looked up there he was walking towards me.

'Maybe the lark had made him happy too, for he looked the picture of hope. "Good morning, Agnes," he cried, "I've got news."

'"Good news, Harre?"

'"Of course, what do you expect? I'm going to be a master, and that very soon." You can imagine, I got quite a start. For I thought right away, goodness, now he'll need a wife.

'I suppose I looked a bit taken aback, for Harre asked, "Is there anything amiss, Agnes?"

'"With me? I don't think so, Harre," I said. "It was only the wind blowing so cold over me." Well, that wasn't true; but it's just God's good will that at such times we can't say what the other person would like to hear.

'"But there's something amiss with me!" said Harre. "The thing I love most is amiss!"

'I didn't utter a word in reply. And Harre walked beside me silent for a while, then suddenly he asked, "I wonder, Agnes, has it ever happened that a merchant's daughter married a master joiner?"

'When I looked up and he looked at me so pleadingly with

his kind brown eyes, I put my hand in his and said, "Well, this will be the first time, likely."

'"Agnes," cried Harre, "What will folk say?"

'"I don't know, Harre, but what if the merchant's daughter was poor?"

'"Poor, Agnes?" and he took both my hands, so happy, "isn't being young and pretty enough?"

'It was a happy day, that day. The spring sun shone, we walked hand in hand; and when we were silent, the larks above us in their hundreds sang joyfully. So without noticing, we came to the wall that stood opposite the house by the elder-hedge in the garden. I looked over the boarding into the water below. "See how the water glints down yonder," I said.

'Happiness makes you high-spirited and Harre wanted to tease me. "Water?" he said. "That's the gold glinting down there."

'I didn't know what he meant.

'"Don't you know there's a treasure buried in your well?" he said. "Look closely! there's a little grey man with a three-cornered hat sitting at the bottom. Maybe it's only the light burning in his hand that's glinting so eerily; for he's the guardian of your treasure."

'I suddenly thought of the straits my father was in. Harre picked up a stone and threw it down and it took a while before a dull splash came up to us. "Do you hear that, Agnes?" he said. "It struck the chest."

'"Harre, be sensible!" I cried, "What kind of nonsense is that you're speaking?"

'"I'm only saying what other folk say," he answered.

'But my curiosity was aroused, maybe too I was longing for hidden riches that would put an end to all the difficulties.

'"Where did you hear that talk?" I asked again. "I never heard of such a thing."

'Harre looked at me, laughing, "I don't know: from some-one-or-other, if I think back maybe it was from that rogue, the Goldmaker."

'"The Goldmaker?" I had mixed thoughts. The Gold-maker was a down-at-the-heel hawker; he could cast spells and tell fortunes and bewitch men and animals and knew all the other secrets that at that time could still be used to make a profit off superstitious people. He's the same man they call the Spook-seer, a name he has just about as much right to as the name he had then. In the last few days, when I happened to have work to do in the outside lobby, he had once or twice gone into my father's writing-room and without waiting for me to answer his apparently humble question "Mr Hansen at home?" he had shuffled past me with a distrustful look. Once he had been almost an hour with father. Shortly before he left I had heard the familiar sound of my father's desk being opened; then I thought I could hear the chink of money. I remembered all that now. But Harre shook me awake. "Agnes, are you dreaming?" he cried, "or are you going hunting for hidden treasure?" Oh, he didn't know the straits my father was in; he was thinking only of his golden future, and I, too, was a part of that. He took my hands and cried happily, "We don't need treasure, Agnes. Your father already has my little legacy in his keeping; that's enough to furnish our house and workshop. And", he added, smiling, "for the rest, let these hands of mine take care of that; they're not altogether unskilled!"

'I couldn't answer his hopeful words. I couldn't help thinking of the treasure and the Goldmaker. I don't know whether it was a foolish hope or the shadow of a coming disaster that passed through my mind. Maybe I had a feeling that soon my whole life's treasure would fall into that well.

'Next day I had gone out to a near-by village, where a minister's wife, a relation of ours, had asked me to help because her child was unwell. But I couldn't be at peace there; my father had been so quiet and yet so restless in the last few days. I had seen him walking quickly up and down in the garden, then standing still by the well, staring down into the depths. I was afraid he might do violence to himself. On the third day I thought I remembered that he had been oddly urgent in encouraging me to go. When the moon came up at about ten o'clock, I asked my cousin to get me back to the town, late though it was. He agreed, after trying in vain to argue me out of my worried state of mind; the horses were harnessed and, as midnight struck from the tower, the carriage stopped outside our house, the chain was taken off the gate and the apprentice, whose room was in the courtyard, opened the front door. Everything was as it had always been. "Is the master at home?" I asked.

'"The master went to bed at ten o'clock," was the answer.

'With a lighter heart I climbed up to my room, whose windows looked out on the garden. It was such a clear night outside that I didn't light the lamp but went over to the window. The moon stood over the elder-hedge whose twigs, not yet in leaf, were clearly silhouetted against the night sky; and, as I gazed, my thoughts went beyond this earth to our loving Heavenly Father, and I laid all my cares on Him. Then just as I was stepping back into the room I suddenly saw a red glow gleaming up from the pipe of the well that stood in the shadow – I saw the clumps of grass at the side of the well and then over it the twigs glinting as if in a golden fire. A superstitious fear came over me, for I thought of the candle carried by the mannikin who was supposed to sit at the bottom. But looking closer I saw a ladder against the inside of the well, though only the top of it could be seen from where I stood. At the same moment I heard a cry from the bottom of the well; then a crash and the muffled sound of human voices came to my ears. Suddenly the brightness vanished and I clearly heard someone climbing up the ladder, rung after rung.

'My fear of ghosts vanished; but in its place I was filled with vague fears for my father. With my knees shaking I went to his bedroom next to mine. When I gently pulled back the drape from his bed, the moon shone on empty pillows. I expect his poor head had long since ceased to find any rest on them, but now they were quite untouched. Frightened to death I ran downstairs to the courtyard door, but it was locked and the key was out. I went into the kitchen and lit a lamp, then into the writing-room which, like the kitchen, faced onto the garden. For a time I stood at the window, not knowing what to do, staring out. I heard footsteps among the elder-bushes but couldn't make anything out, for the wooden fence behind the bushes cast a very long shadow and hid the moon. Then I heard the courtyard door being opened from the outside, and soon the parlour door was opened too. My father came in. Old as I am, I've never forgotten it: his long grey hair was dripping with water and sweat. His clothes that he was always so particular about were dirtied all over with green mud.

'He started visibly when he saw me. "What's this? How do you come to be here?" he asked hastily.

'"My cousin brought me back, father."

'"At midnight? He might have spared himself the trouble."

'I looked at my father. He had lowered his eyes and was standing motionless. "I couldn't be at peace," I said, "I felt you needed me here, I had to come to you."

'The old man sank onto a chair and covered his face with his hands. "Go to your room," he murmured. "I want to be alone."

'But I didn't go. "Let me stay with you," I said softly. My father wasn't listening to me; he raised his head and seemed to be listening to something outside. Suddenly he jumped up. "Quiet!" he cried, "don't you hear that?" And he looked at me with wide-open eyes.

'I had gone to the window and was looking out. Everything was quiet as death; only the branches of the elder-trees were striking against each other. "I hear nothing!" I said.

'My father was still standing as if listening to something that filled him with horror. "I thought it was no sin," he muttered to himself. "There's nothing evil in it, and the well stands on my own ground, or has till now." Then he turned to me, "I know you don't believe in it, my lass," he said, "but it's sure and certain for all that. The twig jerked three times in my hand, and the information I paid only too much for all points the same way. There's a treasure in our well, buried at the time of the Swedes. Why shouldn't I bring it up? We've dammed the spring and drained off the water and tonight we've been digging."

'"Who?" I asked, "Who else do you mean?"

'"There's only one man in the town who knows about these things."

'"Surely you don't mean the Goldmaker? That's no helper for you!"

'"There's nothing evil in divining, my lass."

'"But those who do it are rogues."

'My father had sat down on the chair again, looking and seeing nothing, doubtful. Then he shook his head and said, "The spade had just struck an object; but then something happened." He broke off, then continued: "Your mother died eighteen years ago. When she saw that she'd have to leave us, she burst out crying bitterly and couldn't stop, till she fell into her last sleep. Those were the last sounds I heard from your mother's lips." He fell silent a moment, then said hesitatingly, as if he were afraid of the sound of his own voice, "Tonight, after eighteen years, when the spade struck the chest, I heard it again. It wasn't just in my ears, as it has been so often all these years; no, it came up from under the ground. You daren't speak when you're at that kind of work; but I felt as if the iron were cutting into your dead mother's heart. I cried out, the lamp went out and – you see," he added dully, "that's why it all disappeared."

'I threw myself on my knees before my father and put my arms round his neck. "I'm not a child now," I said, "We must stay together, father. I know that ill fortune has come to our house."

'He said nothing, but leaned his damp brow on my shoulder. Never before had he sought support from his own child. How long we sat like that I don't know. Then I felt my cheeks wet with the hot tears flowing from his old eyes. I clung to him.

'"Don't weep, father," I begged, "We can surely bear poverty."

'He stroked my hair with his trembling hand and said softly, so softly that I could hardly understand, "Yes, we can bear poverty, my lass, but not guilt."

'And laddie, there came a bitter hour for us; and yet an hour that even now that I'm old seems to me the most comforting hour in my life. For it was the first time that I could give my father a child's love, and from that moment it was the dearest thing he possessed and soon the last thing on earth that he could call his own. While I sat beside him, swallowing my tears to hide them, my father opened his heart to me. I learned that he was almost bankrupt, but that wasn't the worst. In a sleepless night, lying on his pillow searching in vain for a way out of his misery, he had remembered the half-forgotten tale about the treasure in our well. He couldn't put the thought from his mind ever since, neither during the day as he sat at his accounts nor at night when at last a heavy sleep came over him. In his dreams he had seen the gold glowing in the dark water, and, when he got up in the morning, he was drawn again and again out to the well to gaze down as if spellbound into its mysterious depths. Then he had taken that evil counsellor into his confidence. But he had been far from ready to help, rather had demanded first and foremost a considerable sum of money for the necessary preparations. Soon my father had no will left in him; he gave the first sum, then a second, then a third. The dream-gold ate up the real gold he still possessed. But the gold was not his own; it was the legacy of his ward that had been entrusted to him. There was no possibility of compensation. We cudgelled our brains. We had no relations to help us. Your grandfather was dead; and at last we had to face the truth that there was no hope of help from outside.

'The lamp had burnt out. I had laid my head on my father's breast, my hand lay in his; and we stayed sitting like that in the dark. What else came up between us as we talked together that night I have forgotten. But never in the past, when my father had been infallible in my eyes, like God Himself almost, never did I feel such a holy tenderness for him as in that hour, when he confessed to me an action that was a crime not only in men's eyes. Gradually the stars turned pale in the sky outside, a little bird sang in the elder-bush and the first ray of dawn came into the dim room. My father stood up and stepped to the desk on which his big account-books lay. The life-size old portrait of my grandfather with his bagwig and his leather-coloured waistcoat seemed to look sternly down upon his son. "I'll count up again," said my father. "If the total is the same," he added hesitatingly, looking up, as if begging for forgiveness, to the picture of his father, "then I have a sore task to do, and I need the mercy of God and men."

'At his request I left the room and soon the house was astir. Day had come. When I had done my chores I went into the garden and out through the little back gate onto the road. Harre always passed that way as he went in the morning to the workshop where he had been working until now.

'I didn't have long to wait; as the clock struck six, I saw him coming. "Harre, come here a minute," I said and beckoned him to come into the garden with me.

'He looked at me, taken aback; for my bad news was written on my face, I suppose; I drew him into a corner of the garden, and stood for a while holding his hand and could not utter a word. But at last I told him everything, and then I asked him, "My father is coming to see you; don't be too hard on him."

'He had become deathly pale and a look came into his eyes, maybe only a look of despair, but it frightened me.

'"Harre, Harre, what will you do to the old man?"

'He pressed his hand to his heart. "Nothing, Agnes," he said, looking at me and smiling sadly. "But I'll have to leave here now."

'I started. "Why?" I stammered.

'"I mustn't see your father again."

'"But you'll forgive him, Harre?"

'"Oh yes, Agnes. I owe him more than that. But he shan't humble his grey head to me. And then," he added as if it were just an afterthought, "I think my plan to become a master won't come to anything now." I did not answer; I could just see the happiness, that only yesterday I had stretched out to grasp, vanishing away out of sight. But nothing could be done to change that now. What Harre intended was for the best; all I said was, "When will you go, Harre?" I hardly knew what I was saying.

'"See to it that your father doesn't come to see me today," he answered. "I'll have done everything I have to see to here by tomorrow morning. Don't grieve about me, I'll easily find a place."

'After these words we parted; our hearts were too full for us to say anything more.'

She broke off her tale for a while. Then she said, 'Next morning I saw him once more, then never again since then; never again my whole life long.'

Her head sank down; she wrung her hands, that had lain still on her lap, as if to ease the pain that still made her frail old woman's body tremble, as it had made her heart tremble when she was a fair-haired girl.

But she did not stay thus bowed; giving herself a shake she rose from her chair and stepped to the window. 'Why should I complain?' she said, and pointed to the pane that bore her father's name. 'The poor man suffered more than I did. Let me tell you about that too.

'Harre had gone. He had taken leave of my father in a warm-hearted letter; they never saw each other again. Soon after that the last legal steps were taken against us and the declaration of bankruptcy was to be made very shortly.

'At that time it was the habit in our town that public announcements were not made by the minister in the kirk, as they are now, but were read out by the Town Clerk from the open window of the Council Chamber; but, before that was done, the little bell in the tower was rung for half an hour. Our house stood opposite the town hall, so I had often watched this and seen children and idle folk congregate outside the windows of the town hall and on the steps as the bell rang. The same thing happened when a bankruptcy was declared, but then people gave it an ill meaning; if anyone said, 'The bell was rung for him,' it was an insult. At such times I had listened too without thinking much about it. Now I trembled to think of the effect that this procedure would have on my father's spirit, bowed down as he was.

'He had told me that he had applied through a councillor, who was a friend of his, to the Provost to see what could be done, and the Provost, an easy-going, talkative man, had assured him that this time the announcement would be made without the bell. But I knew on good authority that this reassurance was groundless. Yet I left my father in his ignorant belief and just tried to persuade him to come on a little trip into the country to see our relatives on the day. But, as he said with a sorrowful smile, he didn't wish to leave the sinking ship before it went down. Then in my anxiety it occurred to me that I had never heard the bell ring in the innermost recess of our very deep vaulted cellars. On this I based my plan, and I managed to persuade my father to come and help me make a list of the goods in store there so that when the bailiffs came later to make their inventory that miserable business would be shortened.

'When the fatal hour came, we were already at our work underground. My father was sorting the wares while I was writing down what he dictated by the light of a lantern. Once or twice I had imagined I heard from afar the sound of a bell, and then I spoke a few words loudly till the noise of the barrels and crates as they were moved around drowned any sound from outside. Everything seemed to be going very well; my father was immersed in his work. Suddenly I heard the cellar door being thrown open above us; the old maid-servant, for some reason, was calling for me, and at the same moment the bell came at us in clear waves of sound. My father harkened and put down the crate he was carrying. "The bell of shame!" he groaned, and fell against the wall as if all the strength had gone from him. "They've spared me nothing!" But only for a moment; then he drew himself erect and before I had time to utter a word he was out of the cellar and, immediately after, I heard him mount the stairs. So I went up into the house too and looked in vain for my father in the writing-room, then found him standing, hands folded, at the open window of the living-room. At that moment the bell stopped. In the town hall opposite, that stood in the brilliant morning sun, the three windows were thrown open and I saw the beadle lay the red cushions on the window-seats. Already a whole crowd of young boys were hanging on the iron railings of the town-hall steps. My father stood motionless, watching tensely. I tried gently to persuade him to leave. "Let me be, my lass," he said, "This concerns me, and I must hear it."

'So he stayed. The old town clerk with his white-powdered head appeared at the middle window, and, while two councillors leaned on the red cushions at his side, he held a sheet of paper in both hands and with his piercing voice he read out the declaration of bankruptcy. In the clear spring air every word came across distinctly. When my father heard his full name called, across the market-place, I saw him start in pain; yet he held his ground till it was over. Then he pulled out his gold watch, that he had inherited from his father, and laid it on the table. "It must go with the estate," he said, "put it away in the chest, so it will be sealed tomorrow with the rest."

'Next day the officers came to do the sealing. But my father could not leave his bed; in the night he had had a stroke.

'When a few months later our house was sold, he was brought in a stretcher borrowed from the hospital to the little apartment we had rented at the end of town. There he lived another nine years, a broken man, paralysed. When he was well enough he did small accounts and clerical work for others, but I had to earn most of what we needed with my own hands. And then he died in my arms, firmly trusting in God's mercy. After his death I found good employers; it was your grandparents' house.'

My old friend fell silent. But, thinking about Harre, I asked, 'And didn't you ever, in all that time, hear from your lad?'

'Never, laddie,' she answered.

'D'you know, Hansen,' I said, 'I don't like that Harre of yours, he didn't keep his word!'

She laid her hand on my arm, 'You mustn't say that, laddie. I knew him, there are other things than death that force folk's will. But let's go to my room. Your hat's still lying there, and it will soon be dinner time.'

So we closed the door of the deserted room again and went back the same way. This time the Spook-seer's door did not open; but behind it we could hear his shuffling step on the sandy boards.

When we were back in Hansen's room where the last rays of the forenoon sun still shone into the windows, she opened a drawer in her chest and took out a mahogany box, brightly polished, but in an old-fashioned style. It might have been a birthday present from the young joiner when she was young.

'There's something else you must see,' said Hansen, opening the box. Inside there were bonds all in the name of Harre Jensen, "son of the late master-joiner Harre Christian Jensen of this town", but all dated ten or more years back.

'How do you come to have these bonds?' I asked.

She smiled. 'I wasn't in service for nothing.'

'But the bonds aren't in your name.'

'It's my father's debt I'm repaying. Because of that, and because all I or any one else who dies here leaves goes to the almshouse, I put the money in Mr Jensen's name right away.' For a moment, before she closed it again, she weighed the box in her hand. 'The treasure's all there again,' she said, 'but the happiness, laddie, the happiness that once was there isn't there now.'

As she spoke these words, a flight of swallows darted noisily past outside, and then two of the birds fluttered almost up to the window-panes and settled twittering on the open casements.

They were the first swallows I had seen that spring.

'Do you hear the little well-wishers, Hansen?' I cried, 'They've come home just in time for your birthday.'

Hansen just nodded. Her still beautiful blue eyes rested sadly on the little singing pair. Then she put her hand on my arm and said, affectionately, 'Off you go now, laddie, and thanks to them all for remembering me on my birthday. I'd like to be alone now.'

Several years later I was on the way back to my home town from a journey in Middle Germany. At a main station (for the Age of Steam had arrived by that time) an elderly man with white hair joined me in my compartment which till now I had

had to myself. A small trunk was handed in after him, and I helped him push it under the seat; then he sat down opposite me, saying in a friendly fashion, 'We haven't sat together before.' As he said that, there appeared round his mouth and brown eyes such a look of kindliness, even of sympathy, that willy-nilly I joined in friendly conversation with him. His tidy appearance, his brown stuff-coat and white cravat, and his well-set-up look, everything about him was reassuring and pleasant, and it wasn't long before we were deep in talk, each telling the other about his family. I learned that he was a piano-maker and was settled in a sizeable town in Swabia. One thing struck me: my companion spoke the South German dialect, yet on his trunk I had seen the name Jensen, which as far as I knew was a purely North German name.

When I remarked on this he smiled. 'Well, I've probably become quite a Swabian,' he said, 'for I've lived in that good land for forty years and more, and never left it in all those years. But my home town is in the North, and that's where my name comes from.' And he named my birthplace as his home town.

'Then we're proper compatriots,' I cried, 'I was born there too and I'm on my way back home.'

The old gentleman seized my hands and looked at me with great friendliness. 'God be praised,' he said, 'then we'll travel together, if you wish. I'm making for our home town too. I hope to meet an old friend there, God willing.'

I was happy to agree to the proposal.

On reaching what was then the railway terminus, we had another five miles to go, and soon we were seated together in the comfortable, padded seats of a well-sprung carriage whose roof we had pushed back because the autumn weather was so fine. Gradually the region grew more familiar. We left the woods behind us, then the green hedges at the side, then even the banks on which they grew, and the broad treeless plain unfolded before us. My companion looked out quietly. 'I'm so unused to all this space,' he said, 'I feel as if I were gazing into eternity wherever I look.' Then he fell silent, and I did not interrupt him.

About half way, as we came out of a village that lay on the highroad, I noticed him leaning his head forward, seemingly looking eagerly for something. Then he shaded his eyes with his hand and became visibly restless. 'My eyesight is fairly good still,' he said at last, 'but try as I may, I cannot see our tower from here, yet when I was young I always saw it from here first, when I came home from my journeyman's travels.'

'You must be making a mistake,' I replied, 'you can't possibly see that low tower from such a distance.'

'Low!' said the old man almost indignantly, 'for centuries that tower was a landmark for sailors miles out at sea!'

I understood. 'I expect', I said, 'you're still thinking of the Old Kirk tower, that was pulled down a good forty years ago.'

The old man looked at me wide-eyed, as if I were talking nonsense. 'The Kirk – pulled down? – forty years and more ago? Goodness, how long I've been away; I never heard about it!'

He clasped his hands and sat for some time, sunk in thought, looking disheartened. Then he said, 'On that handsome tower, that still existed only in my thoughts, almost fifty years ago I promised someone I'd come back, someone for whose sake I'm making this journey. If you like, I'll tell you that part of my life; maybe you can tell me what hope I have.'

I assured the old gentleman of my sympathetic interest, and, while our postillion nodded on his seat in the warm afternoon sun and the wheels ground slowly over the sand, he began his story.

'When I was young, I wanted to follow one of the learned professions; but my parents died early and there wasn't enough money for that, and so I stuck to my father's trade, I became a joiner. During my journeyman's years I was already quite eager to settle down away from home. I was not quite penniless, you see, since I was still left with a tidy sum from the sale of my father's house, enough to make a start. But I did go back home again and it was on account of a fair-haired girl. I don't think I ever saw such blue eyes as hers in my life again. A friend once said jokingly to her, "Agnes, I'll pick the violets from your eyes!" – I never forgot those words.' The old man was silent for a moment, gazing with his face transfigured, as if he saw once more those violet eyes of his youth. Then, while my mind jumped involuntarily to my old friend in St George's Almshouse, he began again. 'She was the daughter of my guardian, a merchant. We grew up together; the girl was brought up rather strictly by her father, who had early lost his wife. Maybe that's why she became more and more attached to me, her one childhood friend. Shortly after I came back home we were unofficially engaged to be married; we arranged that I should start a business in our home town, and then unexpectedly I lost the whole of my small capital. That's how it came about that I had to leave again.

'On our last day Agnes had promised to come out in the evening onto the lane behind their garden to have a last word with me. But when I got there on the stroke of the hour when we had arranged to meet, she was not there. I stood listening by the post under the overhanging branches of a limetree, but I waited in vain. At the time I daren't set foot in her father's house – not that there was strife between us, on the contrary, he thought well of me and he wasn't a proud man. There was another reason, but I don't want to rake that up. I well remember, it was a dark, stormy April evening. Several times the grating of the weather-vane on the roof made me imagine I heard the familiar sound of the courtyard gate opening, but there was no sound of steps coming down the garden path. I stayed leaning on the post, watching the black clouds scudding across the sky. At last I went away heavy-hearted.

'Next morning the church clock had just struck five when after a sleepless night I came down from my room and bade my landlord and his wife farewell. The narrow, ill-paved streets were still full of the darkness and mire of winter. The town seemed still asleep; not one known face did I see, and so I went on my way, alone and miserable. Then when I was just turning off towards the churchyard there was a sudden burst of sunlight, and the old house where the town apothecary's shop was, the lower part of which with its carved wooden ion s i gn stood in the murk of the street, suddenly seemed lbathed in spring light right up to the top of its crow-stepped gable. At the same moment, just as I was looking upwards, there sounded high in the air above me a long-drawn-out note; then again it sounded, and again, as if it were sending its call out into the wide world.

'I had stepped into the churchyard and now looked up to the top of the tower. Up on the gallery I saw the watchman standing and saw his long horn in his hand. Now I understood – the first swallows had come, and old Jacob had sounded a welcome for them, telling the whole world that spring was here. He was always rewarded with a glass of wine in the town-hall cellars and a new ducat from the Provost. I knew the man and had often been up the tower with him, both as a lad, to see my pigeon take flight from the top, and later with Agnes, for the old man had a little granddaughter who was also Agnes's goddaughter and of whom she made a great fuss. One Christmas Eve I had even helped her drag a whole Christmas tree up the tall tower. Well, now the familiar oaken door stood open; without thinking I stepped inside; in the sudden darkness I slowly mounted the stairs and the narrow, rung-like treads that followed on from them. I heard nothing but the whirring of the great tower-clock, ceaseless and solitary. I well remember how that dead thing frightened me: as I passed it I felt as if I wanted to seize the iron wheels and bring them to a stop. Then I heard old Jacob climbing down. He seemed to be talking to a child, warning it to take care. I shouted, "Good morning!" up into the darkness and asked if that was little Meta he had with him.

'"Is that you, Harre?" he called back. "Yes, it's Meta, she's coming with me to the Provost."

'At last they reached me. I had stepped aside into a louvre-window. When Jacob saw me dressed for my journey he said in surprise, "What's this, then, Harre? What brings you up my tower with your stick and your waxcloth cap? Have you got tired of us again?" "That's it, Jacob," I answered. "I hope it's not for long." "That's not what I expected of you," muttered the old man. "Ah well, what must be must be. The swallows are here again and it's the best time for setting out. And thank you for coming to say goodbye!"

'"Goodbye then, Jacob," I said, "And some day when you see me from your tower walking in through the town gate again, give me a blast on your horn to welcome me as you've welcomed your swallows!"

'The old man shook me by the hand and lifted his grand-child into his arms. "I promise, Guildmaster Harre!" he said with a smile. (He used to call me that as a joke.) But as I was about to go down with him he added, "If you want Agnes to give you a send-off, she's up there and has been since day-light. She loves seeing the birds."

'Never before did I run so fast up the last rickety steps, though my heart was pounding and I was out of breath. As I stepped out onto the platform and into the blinding light, I stopped involuntarily and looked over the iron railing. Beneath me my home town lay in the early beauty of spring; everywhere among the houses cherry-trees stood laden with blossom that the early mild spell had brought out. The gable yonder, facing the little tower of the town hall, was the gable of my guardian's house. I looked at the garden and the lane behind it, and my heart filled and maybe I cried out, overcome with homesickness, for suddenly I felt someone take my hand and when I looked up Agnes was standing by me. "Harre," she said, "You've come again!" and a happy smile flitted over her face.

'"I didn't expect to find you here," I answered. "I have to go now. Why did you keep me waiting and not come last night?"

'All the happiness drained from her face. "I couldn't come, Harre. My father needed me to stay by him. Afterwards I went out into the garden, but you had gone, so I came up the tower this morning. I thought I could watch you pass through the town gate."

'The future was unclear to me, but I had a plan for all that. Some time before, I had worked in a piano factory. Now I wanted to find the same sort of work again, and later, when I had saved my earnings, I would start a business, for pianos were already beginning to be popular. All this I told my lass, and where I intended to make for.

'She had been leaning against the railing looking as if absently into the sky. Now she slowly turned her head. "Harre," she said, "Don't go, Harre."

'When I didn't answer, but just looked at her, she said again, "No, don't listen to me! I'm a child, I don't know what I'm saying." The morning wind had loosened a few strands of her fair hair and blown them across her pale face that now looked patiently into mine.

'"We'll have to wait, Agnes," I said, "Our happiness lies far away. I'm going to try to bring it back home again. I won't write. I'll come myself when the time is right."

'She looked me full in the face a while, and then she pressed my hand. "I'll wait," she said in a firm voice. "God be with you, Harre!"

"I didn't go yet. The tower that bore us aloft stood so solitary, so high in the blue sky; only the swallows, with the sun gleaming on their steel-blue wings, wheeled about us, basking in the sea of light and air. I clung to her hand. I just couldn't leave. I felt as if we two, she and I together, were carried aloft far above all the troubles of the world. But time was pressing; beneath us the clock boomed out the quarter-hour; then, while the sound-waves were still surging round the tower, a swallow came flying, almost brushing us with its wings. It settled, quite fearless, an arm's length away from us on the edge of the railing, and, as we looked fascinated into its little shining eyes, it suddenly began to sing, sending its full-throated spring song into the air. Agnes threw herself into my arms. "Don't forget to come back," she cried. And at that the bird spread its wings and flew away.

'How I climbed down the dark tower to the ground I do not know. Once outside the town gate on the highway, I stood still and looked back. The tower stood bathed in sunlight, and on it I could clearly see her dear form: it seemed to me as if she were leaning far out over the railing, and I involuntarily cried out in fear. But the figure stayed motionless.

'And at last I turned and went, striding out along the high-way, and I didn't look back again.'

The old man fell silent a while. Then he said, 'She waited for me in vain. I never came home again. I'll tell you how that happened.

'I found my first job in Vienna, where at that time the best piano factories were. From there eighteen months later I moved to Württemberg, to the town I live in now. A fellow-journeyman had a brother there who had asked him to find him a dependable assistant. The house where I lived and worked was the home of a fairly young couple. The business was small but the owner was a friendly man and a skilled craftsman, and I quickly learned more from him than I ever had in the big factory where I had always been put onto particular jobs. I set to work with a will and had a good deal to offer as a result of my experience in Vienna, and so I soon gained the trust of these excellent people. They were especially grateful because in my spare time I gave the elder of their two sons instruction in the German language; for they liked my North German accent that I still had then and they wanted their children to learn to speak as good German as they thought I spoke. Soon the younger brother joined in our lessons, and we didn't stick to dry grammar; I got hold of books and I'd read all kinds of interesting and entertaining things to them. In that way the children became deeply attached to me. When after a year I succeeded unaided in building a piano with a particu-larly fine tone, the whole family were as delighted as if their dearest relative had produced his masterpiece. But now I began to think of returning home.

'Then the young master fell ill. A cold turned into a serious chest infection, the germ of which had probably been dormant in him. The running of the business was left almost entirely to me as a matter of course. I couldn't leave now. And I was learning more about the situation in the family, to which closer and closer bonds of friendship tied me. Harmony and industry dwelt there; but the third guest in the household was an evil thing that those two good spirits could not banish. In every corner where the sun did not penetrate the sick man saw it lodged: it was Care. "Take the broom and sweep it away!" I'd often say to my friend, "I'll help you, Martin." Then he might press my hand and a melancholy smile would flit over his face, but soon he would see its black cobwebs covering everything again.

'And, sad to say, those cobwebs did not exist only in his mind. The capital with which he had founded his business had been too small from the start. In the early years he had suffered losses from bad workmen and the sale of finished products had been slower than such circumstances required; and now on top of all that came an illness with no prospect of recovery. By the end not only the responsibility for the upkeep of the family lay on my shoulders but I had to comfort its healthy members too. The boys clung to my hand when we sat by their father's bed, which he soon was unable to leave. But his gradual loss of strength seemed only to increase the turmoil of his mind. He lay worrying on his pillow, making plans for the future. At times when he felt the icy breath of his approaching death he would suddenly sit up and cry, "I can't die, I won't die," and then say weakly with his hands clasped, "Oh God, not my will but Thine be done."

'At last the moment of his release came. We were all at his bedside. He thanked me and bade us all farewell. But then, as if he saw something he must protect them from, he pulled his wife and his sons close to him, looked at them with despair in his eyes and groaned aloud. And when I said, to give him courage, "Lay your burdens on the Lord, Martin," he cried in despair, "Harre, Harre, it's not Care now, it's Poverty. I'll lie dead in the ground, but I can't stop the poverty. Oh, my wife, my children, they won't escape from poverty!"

'There's a strange thing about a death-bed, young friend, I don't know if you know it; but at that moment I promised my dying master that I'd stand by his dear ones till the spectre that disturbed his dying hour could never again come near them. And, when I had made my promise, Death didn't tarry. Softly he came in. Martin stretched out his hand; I thought he was stretching it out to me, but it was the unseen messenger of the Lord that clasped it, for before I touched his hand, my young master's life was over.'

My companion took off his hat and laid it on his lap; his white hair was blowing in the warm afternoon air; so he sat silent, as if devoting these moments to the memory of his long-dead friend. And I could not help remembering the words that my old friend Hansen had once spoken to me: 'There are other things than death that force folk's will.' But it had been death that parted the living. For of course I was now in no doubt as to who it was that sat by my side. After some time the old man took up his story again, slowly putting his hat back on his head.

'I kept the promise I made,' he said, 'but when I made it, I broke another one; for now I could not leave. It soon became clear that things were in an even worse state than I had known. A few months after the husband's death a third child was born, a girl; as things stood, another worry to add to the rest. I did all that I could. But year after year went by and fortune still passed our door. Even though I both worked to the limits of my capacity and gave what I had saved over the years, I was still not able to win the fight against the spectre of poverty. I could not help seeing that if anyone less loyal and concerned took my place those wards of mine would fall victim to it.

'Often, I confess, in the midst of my work I would be overcome with homesickness gnawing at my heart. Many a time, unaware of the chisel lying idle in my hand, I was startled when the good wife's voice spoke to me; for my thoughts were always of my home and it was not her voice but another's that I fancied I heard. In my dreams I saw the tower of our home town – at first in bright sunshine, with an army of swallows flying around it, later, when the dream came to me again, I saw it loom black and threatening up into the empty sky; the autumn wind raged, I heard the great bells peal, but always, even then, there was Agnes leaning on the railing up yonder at the top. Still she wore the blue dress she had worn when she bade me farewell, only it was all torn and the tatters fluttered in the wind. "When will the swallows come again?"

was the cry I heard, I knew her voice, but oh how melancholy it sounded in the raging of the wind! When I woke from such dreams I would hear swallows twittering in the guttering above my window. In the first years I used to lie with my hands behind my head letting my heart fill with longing and homesickness; later I couldn't bear it and many a time when the twittering went on and on I threw the window open and chased the little birds away.

'On one such morning I declared that now I must leave, that now after so long it was time to think of my own life. But the two boys broke out into loud lamentations and their mother without speaking a word put her little daughter in my lap, where she promptly put her little arms firmly round my neck. In my heart I clung to the children, sir. I couldn't leave the children. I thought, all right, stay another year. The gulf between me and my youth grew wider; in the end, it all lay far behind me, unreachable, like dreams I mustn't think of again. I was past forty when at the wish of the grown-up children I married their mother whose only support I had so long been.

'And now a strange thing happened. I had always liked the woman and she deserved my liking. But now that she was indissolubly bound to me, a dislike, even hatred of her began to grow in me that often I could scarcely hide. Human beings are like that; in my heart I blamed her for everything, though it was only the result of my own weakness. Then God led me into temptation, and that saved me.

'It was one Sunday at the height of summer. We went on a picnic at a near-by mountain village where a relative of the family lived. The two boys and their little sister were walking well ahead of us oldsters. We were out of earshot of their chatter and laughter in the wood through which the path led. Then my wife suggested taking a short cut along a quarry that might bring us back on to the main road in front of the children. "I once went walking here with Martin before we were married," she said, as we turned off through the fir trees. "A bit further on we picked a blue flower, I'd like to know if it's still growing there."

'After a short time there were no trees on one side and the footpath ran close to the edge of the steep rocks while on the other side brambles and various bushes narrowed the path. My wife was walking briskly ahead of me. I was following slowly, lost in my old reveries. Like a happiness long lost my home lay before my mind's eye, and I was thinking unhappily and vainly how I could ever get back to it. As if through a veil I saw that where the quarry face started the ground was blue with gentians and my wife was bending down again and again to pick them. Then suddenly I heard a cry and saw her throw up her hands, and in a flash I saw the scree shift beneath her feet and fall crashing down between the crags, and ten feet further down the rock ended in a vertical chasm.

'I stood as if I were paralysed. The blood sang in my ears: don't move, let her fall, then you're free! But God helped me. Only a second passed before I was by her. Throwing myself on the ground and leaning over the edge of the rock, I got hold of her hand and pulled her up to me safe and sound. "Harre, Harre, my dear," she cried, weeping, "once again it's your hand that has saved me from the pit!"

'Her words went to my heart like drops of fire. In all those years I had uttered not a word about the past, at first out of youthful unwillingness to reveal the innermost secrets of my heart, and later, I suppose, out of an unconscious need to hide the division between us. Now suddenly I felt urged to tell everything and keep nothing back. And sitting on the edge of that chasm I poured my heart out to the woman whom shortly before I had wished to see buried in it. I told her that too. She broke out into violent weeping, weeping for me, for herself and most of all for Agnes. "Harre, Harre," she cried, with her head on my breast, "I didn't know, but it's too late now and no one can take this sin from us!"

'Now it was my turn to comfort her; and it was not till several hours later that we reached the village, where our children had long been waiting for us. But from that time on my wife with her just and kindly heart was my best friend, and there were no secrets between us. So the years passed by. Gradually she seemed to have forgotten that I had sacrificed someone else's happiness for the wellbeing of herself and the children, and I became more settled too. Only in spring when the swallows returned or later in the year when they, last of all the birds of the day, sang their song to the setting sun, the old pain came again, and still I heard that beloved young voice, still the words sang in my ears: "Don't forget to come back!"

'That's how it was one evening earlier this year. I was sitting on the bench outside the front door looking at the setting sun which was visible over the vineyards opposite through a gap in the houses. One of our younger son's little daughters had climbed on my lap and curled up, tired from playing, in Grandfather's arms. Soon her little eyes closed, and the sun sank from sight, but over our neighbour's roof a swallow perched in the dark, softly twittering a song of time past. At that moment my wife came out. She stood silent a while beside me, and when I didn't look up she asked me gently, "What is it, lad?" and when I didn't reply and only the song of the bird could be heard in the dusk she asked, "Is it the swallow again?"

'"You know how it is, Mother." I said, "You've always had patience with me."

'But how little I knew her; she had more than patience with me. She put her hands on my shoulders. "What do you think?" she said, looking at me with her kind old eyes. "We can surely manage it now. You must go to see Agnes again; if you don't you won't find peace in the grave beside me!"

'I was almost startled at this suggestion and started to object, but she said, "Put it in God's hands."

'That's what I did. And that's how I come to be returning home again. But when we drive through the town gate this time, there'll be no old Jacob to blow his horn.'

My companion fell silent. But now I could not wait longer to tell him. I was so deeply moved. 'I know you,' I said. 'I know you well, Harre Jensen. And I know Agnes too. She lived for many years in my grandmother's house, she's like a grandmother to me. I heard your whole story from her very own lips, even the part that you passed over.'

The old man clasped his hands. 'Merciful Father in Heaven,' he said, 'then she's still alive to forgive me!'

I little thought that I had kindled a hope whose fulfilment lay even then beyond the bounds of mortal life. I only answered, 'She knew the lad she loved in her young days, and she never said a word of reproach.' Now it was my turn to tell. He listened with bated breath and drank in every word eagerly.

The postillion cracked his whip. The stumpy tower of our home town had appeared on the horizon. When I pointed it out, the old man seized my hand. 'Young friend,' he said, 'I tremble at what's coming.'

It was not long before our carriage was rattling over the cobbled streets of the town. As the autumn weather was so fine there were a lot of people about and, since I had been long away, I was constantly welcomed back by passers-by. The old stranger at my side received at most a glance of surprise or curiosity. At last we stopped at the inn, where I decided to take leave of my friend for the day, for he wanted to make his first visit to St George's Almshouse alone.

A few minutes later I was at home, with my parents and family round me. 'Is everyone fine?' was my first question.

'All well here, as you see,' answered my mother, 'but there's one you won't be seeing again.'

'Hansen!' I exclaimed. Who else indeed?

My mother nodded. 'But what's upsetting you, lad? She lived her life; this morning she died peacefully in my arms.'

I told them whom I had brought back in as few words as possible, and while they stood there stunned I rushed out without taking my coat off; I daren't leave the old man alone now. I went first to the inn, and hearing that he had gone out I went straight up the street to St George's.

When I got there, I saw the Spook-seer – Death seemed to pass him by – standing in the middle of the road outside the Almshouse; with his hands at his back he was standing easily, knees bent, staring up under the broad peak of his cap at one of the gables. Following the direction of his gaze I could see on the topmost crow-steps, indeed on the bell itself

as it hung framed in the stonework of the gable, a great flock
of swallows perched, side by side, with lone birds fluttering
round them or darting up into the sky and returning with
clamorous twittering. Some of these seemed to be bringing
new recruits that then tried to find a place to settle beside the
others.

Involuntarily I stood still. I could see they were settling
ready to migrate. The northern sun was no longer warm
enough for them. The old creature beside me pulled his cap
off his head and waved it to and fro. 'Shoo!' he babbled,
'away you go, you little devils!' But the spectacle up on the
roof continued some time longer. Then suddenly, as if
wafted upwards, all the swallows together rose nearly vertic-
ally into the air, and at once vanished without trace in the
blue heavens.

The Spook-seer still stood muttering vaguely while I walked
through the dark gateway into the Almshouse courtyard. One
casement of the window in Hansen's room was open as
always; and the swallow's nest was still there. Hesitatingly I
climbed the stairs and opened the door of her room. There
lay my old Hansen, still and peaceful. The linen cloth covering
her was folded back. On the edge of the bed sat my companion,
but his eyes were fixed not on the corpse but on the bare wall.
I could see that his empty gaze was fixed on a point beyond
some enormous gulf, and on the far side stood the unattain-
able image of his youth, now fast vanishing into the misty
distance.

Apparently unnoticed by him, I had seated myself on the
armchair by the open window, looking at the empty swallow's
nest, from which straggled grass and feathers that once had
harboured safely the brood that had flown. When my gaze
returned to the room, the old man's head was directly above
that of the corpse. He seemed to be looking as if bewildered
at that sunken, aged face that lay before him in the awful
solemnity of Death. 'If only I could see her eyes again!' he
murmured. 'But God has closed them.' Then, as if to prove
to himself that it must indeed be she, he took a strand of her
shining grey hair that framed the sides of her face and flowed

on to the linen cloth, and lovingly let it slip through his fingers.

'We came too late, Harre Jensen,' I cried sorrowfully.

He looked up and nodded. 'Fifty years too late,' he said, 'and that's how life went.' Then standing up slowly, he took the shroud and folded it back over the quiet, dead face.

A sudden breeze blew on the window. I fancied I heard coming from far out yonder, from the highest current on which migrating swallows fly, the last words of their old song:

> When I came again, when I came again,
> There was nothing there.

Gottfried Keller

THE THREE JUST COMB-MAKERS

Translated by Nigel Reeves

Gottfried Keller

ONE of Switzerland's greatest writers, Gottfried Keller was born in Zürich in 1819 and died there in 1890. His youth and early manhood, his failure to become a painter, and his return to Switzerland are reflected in his semi-autobiographical novel *Green Henry*. Keller was a moralist and a humorist; his humour is sometimes whimsical, sometimes more robust as in the present story, which has a touch of Brueghel about it. It appeared in 1856 in the first volume of *The People of Seldwyla*, a collection of tales in which Keller satirizes the follies and pretensions of the inhabitants of an imaginary but typical small Swiss town.

THE THREE JUST COMB-MAKERS

THE inhabitants of Seldwyla have shown that, if need be, an entire township of unjust or frivolous citizens can survive the vicissitudes of time and commerce, whereas we see from the example of the three comb-makers that not even three just men can live for long beneath a single roof without being at loggerheads with one another. But theirs is not the justice we associate with Heaven or the natural justice of the human conscience, but that sort of anaemic justice which omits from the Lord's Prayer the petition to 'forgive us our debts, as we forgive our debtors' since they incur no debts themselves and no one is their debtor; the sort of justice that makes no one suffer but delights no one either, that is happy to work and to earn but does not wish to spend, and finds in devotion to duty self-interest alone and no pleasure. Just men such as these do not go about smashing street-lamps, but they light no lamps of their own and radiate no warmth; they take on all kinds of occupations – it seems to matter little which, provided that none involves any danger. They are happiest when living in a place where, in their view, there are many un-just men, for without them they would wear one another down like millstones that have no grist. If misfortune besets them, they are exceedingly surprised and squeal like stuck pigs, because they have never harmed anyone themselves. They regard the world as one enormous well-patrolled police sta-tion, in which no one need fear punishment, provided that he keeps his doorway well swept, looks after his window-boxes, and pours no water over the edge.

In Seldwyl there was a comb-maker's business, the owner-ship of which was usually changed every five or six years, despite the fact that it was a good business for anyone who was prepared to work hard, since the traders who frequented the local fairs bought all their combs there. In addition to staple utilities like curry-combs of all kinds, they made for the village belles and serving-maids the most wonderful

decorative combs from beautiful transparent ox-horn, on
which the apprentices – for the master comb-makers never did
a stroke of work – skilfully and imaginatively etched fine red-
brown tortoiseshell clouds. When you held the combs up
to the light you thought you could see the most magnificent
sunrises and sunsets, dappled red skies, thunderstorms and
other variegated natural phenomena. In summer when the
apprentices liked to be on the move and were scarce, they were
treated courteously and were given good wages and food,
but in winter when they were looking for a job and were in
plentiful supply, they had to knuckle under and make combs
for all they were worth in return for a pittance; the master's
wife served up bowls of sauerkraut day in and day out, and
the master called it fish. So if an apprentice dared so much as
to say, 'I'm sorry but it's sauerkraut,' he was instantly dismissed and had to set out in the winter cold. But as soon as
the meadows were green again and the paths were clear, they
said that it *was* sauerkraut and would start to pack their bags.
For even if the master's wife immediately popped some ham
on top of the sauerkraut and their master said, ''pon my soul!
I could have sworn it was fish! But this is ham all right!' the
apprentices still longed to get away, as all three of them had to
sleep in a double bed and were heartily sick of one another
after a winter of elbowings and frozen backs.

But one day there arrived from somewhere in Saxony a
respectable, mild-tempered apprentice who accepted everything, worked like a donkey, and refused to be driven out, so
that in the end he became a permanent fixture in the business
and outlasted several masters, since of late the turnover had
been far more rapid than previously. Jobst stretched out in
bed as stiffly as he could and kept his place next to the wall in
winter and summer alike; he gladly accepted sauerkraut as
fish and ate ham in spring with modest gratitude. He put aside
the low wage as carefully as the high wage, for he spent nothing and saved everything. His life was quite different from
that of other apprentices: he never drank and did not go around
with his compatriots or any other young apprentices, but
stood of an evening down by the front-door, jested with the

old women, put their water-buckets on their heads when he was in a particularly magnanimous mood, and went to bed at the same time as the hens, unless there was sufficient work for him to do in the evening, for which he would receive special remuneration. On Sundays, similarly, he worked on into the afternoon, even if it was the most beautiful weather; but one should not have the impression that he really enjoyed doing this like Johann the merry soap-boiler; throughout these hours of voluntary labour he remained depressed and constantly complained about the hardships of life. Once it was Sunday afternoon, he crossed the alley-way in his apron and floppy slippers to fetch a clean shirt, a pressed shirt-front, a wing-collar, or his best handkerchief from the laundress and, bearing these treasures before him across his outstretched arm, he marched home with the characteristically elegant gait of an apprentice. For when they are dressed in their aprons and slippers many apprentices adopt a curiously affected step, as if they were floating in higher realms – and this is particularly true of the well-read bookbinders, the merry cobblers, and those unusual and eccentric creatures, the comb-makers. But when he was back in his room, Jobst would have second thoughts about putting on his shirt or shirt-front, for despite his mildness and righteousness he was still rather a boor, and he would wonder whether he could make do with his old linen for another week or whether he would prefer to stay at home and work a little more. In this case he would set to work afresh and, sighing because the world was such a hard and laborious place, he would crossly start cutting teeth into combs or fashioning horn into tortoiseshell bowls, but in such a pedestrian and unimaginative way that he always repeated the same three tedious patterns, for unless it was specifically required of him he took no pains at all. But if he had decided to take a stroll, he would spend an hour or two dressing meticulously, would take out his walking-stick, and then strut stiffly a little way beyond the town gate, where he would stand around in a humble and bored posture, holding dull conversations with other bystanders who also had nothing better to do, such as aged Seldwylians

who could no longer go to the inn. Accompanied by people of
this sort, he loved to stop by some house that was being
built or beside a newly sown field, by an apple-tree that had
been damaged in a storm, or a new yarn factory, and would
hold the most urgent discussions, questioning the adequacy
of arrangements and the expense involved, the prospects for
the season and the state of the crops, about all of which he
understood not a jot. But that did not matter in the least: it
was the cheapest and most absorbing way he knew to kill
time, and the old folk always referred to him as that sensible,
well-bred Saxon, for they were as ignorant as he. When the
Seldwylians set up a joint-stock brewery, of which they had
the greatest expectations, and the extensive foundations were
rising above ground-level, he spent many a Sunday afternoon
there, fussing about, casting an expert eye over it and examin-
ing the progress of the work apparently with the most lively
interest, just as if he were a past master in building and the
most prodigious beer-drinker. 'My goodness!' he would
exclaim time and time again, 'that's a fine job! It's a magnificent place! But what a lot of money to spend, what a lot of
money! It's a shame that the roofing isn't that little bit higher,
and the wall ought by rights to be just a fraction stronger!'
But, as he spoke, his mind was dwelling on nothing but the
need to be home on time for supper before it was dark, for
this was the only dirty trick he played on his master's wife:
he would never miss supper on Sundays like the other apprentices, so that she would have to stay at home just for his sake
or would have to concern herself with him in some way.
Once he had made sure of his slice of joint or his piece of
sausage, he stalked around the room for a while longer, brooding, before he retired to bed; and for him that had been an
enjoyable Sunday.

But for all his modesty, decency, and gentle manners, he
did not lack a touch of inward irony, which became evident
when he surreptitiously mocked the frivolity and vanity of
this world. He seemed to have distinct doubts about the
weight and consequence of things, and to be aware of far
more profound planes of thought. Indeed he sometimes had

such a wise expression on his face, especially when delivering his expert Sunday speeches, that beneath the surface it was plain to see he had far more important matters on his mind, compared with which everything undertaken, worked on, and achieved by others was mere child's play. The great project, about which he reflected day and night, and which was his guiding star throughout the years that he spent as an apprentice in Seldwyl, was to save his wages for long enough to be able, one fine morning, to purchase the business just as it became vacant, and to make himself its owner and master. This lay behind everything he did and strove for, as it was clear to him that in these parts a hard-working and thrifty man, who went his own quiet way and knew how to reap the benefits but suffer none of the disadvantages entailed by the happy-go-lucky attitude of the others, must surely prosper. And once he was a master comb-maker, he thought he could soon earn enough to become a burgher of the city and then he intended to live more wisely and efficiently than any other citizen of Seldwyl, taking no notice of anything that did not add to his wealth, spending not a farthing, but hauling in as much as ever possible amid the carefree hustle and bustle of town life. His plan was as simple as it was logical and under-standable, especially as he persevered in following it quite effectively: he had already saved a tidy sum of money, which he stored carefully away and which, according to all calcula-tions, could not fail in time to become large enough for him to achieve his goal. But the inhuman side of this quiet, peace-able plan was surely the fact that Jobst had thought of it in the first place, for there was nothing in his heart that com-pelled him to stay in Seldwyla. He felt no particular attrac-tion to the area, or to the people, or to the country's political constitution, or to its way of life. It was all as indifferent to him as his own homeland, for which he did not long in the least. There were a hundred places on earth where he could equally well have stayed, worked hard, and lived his just life, but he had no will of his own; his empty mind was dazzled by the first chance beam of hope that fell across his path, and, he basked in it greedily. 'Where I'm best off is home to me' runs a proverb, and that is perfectly acceptable in those cases where people can really show good and vital reasons for feeling at home in their country of adoption, people who have freely decided to set out and seek their fortunes and to come back as made men; or who flee in their thousands from some cheerless land and, accepting the call of the times, join in the modern wave of emigration overseas, or men who have found more loyal friends than at home, or conditions that correspond more closely to their most profound inclinations, or have become attached by some more noble human bond. But all these people will at least have to love the new country in which they thrive so much better, no matter where it is, and if necessary they must be prepared to play their part as responsible human beings. But Jobst was hardly conscious of his whereabouts. The institutions and the traditions of the Swiss seemed incomprehensible to him, and he simply said from time to time, 'Oh well, the Swiss are politically minded. I'm sure politics are a fine thing for those that like them, but as far as I'm concerned I know nothing about them. Where I come from, it wasn't usual.' He disliked and feared the Seldwylians' customs, and, when they planned a protest or a procession, he nervously hid in the furthest recesses of the workshop, anxiously awaiting murder and assassination. And yet it was his one idea and great secret that he would remain there in Seldwyl until the end of his days. In all corners of the earth there are just men of this kind, who have settled down for no better reason than that they happened to come across some tiny source of wellbeing, which they then quietly proceeded to drain without homesickness and without any love for their new country, without an eye either for the world beyond or for the area around them, people who thus resemble not so much men with free will as those lower organisms, those strange insects and seeds that are borne by wind and water to chance locations, where they then grow and prosper.

And so he continued to live in Seldwyla year in and year out, adding to his secret hoard, which he kept concealed beneath a flagstone in his room. There was still no tailor who could pride himself on having earned a penny from him, for the Sunday coat in which he had arrived was as good as ever. There was still no cobbler who had ever taken a farthing from him, for not even the soles of the boots that had decorated the outside of his knapsack when he first came had yet worn through – the year has only fifty-two Sundays and only on half of these did he take a short stroll. No one could claim to having seen a coin, large or small, in his hand, for the moment he received his wages, they vanished on the spot in the most mysterious manner, and even when he went for a walk outside the town gate, he took not a penny with him so that it would be impossible to spend anything. Whenever women came to the workshop with cherries, plums, or pears, and the other apprentices ate their fill, his own appetite was aroused as intensely as theirs, but he stilled it by playing a most attentive part in the haggling, by stroking and touching the lovely cherries and plums, and finally, to the women's amazement, for they had thought him the keenest customer of all, by letting them go. His pleasure lay in his capacity for self-denial, and it was with a glow of contentment and a thousand tiny pieces of advice on how they ought to bake or peel the apples they had bought that he watched his fellow-apprentices eating. But if no one succeeded in getting him to hand over any money, nor did they ever hear a harsh word or an untoward remark, or see him with a long face. On the contrary, he avoided most scrupulously all intrigues, and never took any of the jokes amiss that the others made at his expense. And however curious he was to follow and assess the course of all sorts of gossip and quarrels, because these constantly provided him with a free source of entertainment in contrast to the wild drinking-bouts in which other apprentices indulged, he took great pains never to become involved or to make a fool of himself through some careless slip. In short, he was the most remarkable mixture of truly heroic wisdom and perseverance and a rather despicable lack of feeling and warmth.

There came a time when, for many weeks, he was the only apprentice in the business, and in this peaceful atmosphere he

really felt in his element. He especially enjoyed the spacious-
ness of the bed at night, and utilized this wonderful period with
the utmost economy, making up for times to come, by, as it
were, multiplying himself threefold and incessantly changing
his position, pretending that there were three of them in bed,
while two of them were beseeching the third not to put himself
out but to make himself quite at home. He was this third
person, and at their request he wrapped himself voluptuously
in the entire blanket or opened his legs wide apart, lay
obliquely across the bed or turned somersaults for sheer joy.
But one day, when he had already retired to bed at dusk, a
new apprentice was unexpectedly taken on and was shown into
the bedroom by the master's wife. Jobst had just selected a
particularly comfortable posture with his head at the foot of
the bed and his feet on the pillows, when in came the stranger,
put down his heavy knapsack, and immediately began to get
undressed, because he was tired. Jobst turned round in a
flash, lay stiffly in his original position by the wall and thought
to himself, 'He'll soon be on his way again now it's summer
and pleasant travelling!' Bearing this hope in mind, he
accepted his lot with a quiet sigh and awaited the nightly
elbowings and the contest for the blanket which would now
ensue. How amazed he was when, despite the fact that the
new arrival was a Bavarian, he politely greeted him as he got
into bed, remained on the other side as peacefully and civilly
as he did himself, and failed to disturb him in the least the
whole night long. This extraordinary state of affairs so upset
Jobst that while the Bavarian stayed fast asleep, he could not
doze off at all. The next morning he observed his odd bed-
fellow very closely and saw that he too was no longer a
young apprentice and that he inquired about local life and conditions in a courteous manner just as he would have done
himself. Noticing this, he immediately held himself in check
and kept quiet about the most basic things as if they were
part of some great secret, while attempting at the same time to
fathom out the Bavarian's own secret, for it was plain from the
first glance that he also possessed one; why should he be such
an understanding, gentle, and well-balanced man unless he was

surreptitiously planning something to his own advantage?
With the utmost care and in the most peaceable way they now
started to try and cross-examine one another by means of half-
questions and charmingly oblique remarks. Neither of them
gave a direct, sensible answer and yet within a few hours they
both knew that they were complete doubles. When, as the
day progressed, Fridolin, the Bavarian, ran up to the bedroom on a number of occasions as if he had something to do
up there, Jobst also took the opportunity to slip up while
Fridolin was working, and at one fell swoop inspected all his
companion's possessions. All he discovered were practically
the same odds and ends which he himself owned, even down
to a wooden needle-box, which, however, was in the form of a
fish while his own amusingly resembled a tiny swaddling-
child, and, instead of the tattered *Popular Introduction to French*
that Jobst occasionally thumbed through, the Bavarian
possessed a well-bound little volume entitled *The Cold
and Hot Tub. An Indispensable Manual for Dyers*. But in it he
had written in pencil, 'Kept as scurety for the three fathings
lent to the aprentice from Nassau.' From this Jobst concluded
that he was a man who held on to what he had, and he could
not help looking around the floor till he soon came across a
flagstone that looked as if it had recently been taken out, and
beneath it, sure enough, were his savings, wrapped in an old
handkerchief, bound with twine and nearly as heavy as his
own, which he kept, on the other hand, tied up in a sock.
All of a quiver, he put the stone back, shaking from excitement
and admiration for the stature of the stranger and from grief
for his own secret project. He rushed down to the workshop
at once and started working as if he had to supply the entire
world with combs – and there was the Bavarian working away
as if the very heavens had to be combed as well. The following
week entirely confirmed their first impressions of one another,
for if Jobst was industrious and easily satisfied, Fridolin was
diligent and temperate and sighed in the same thoughtful way
about the hardships entailed by such virtue. But if Jobst was
gay and wise, Fridolin was jocular and clever; if the former
was modest, the latter was humble, if Jobst was sly and ironic,

Fridolin was artful and almost satirical, and if the Saxon had a stupidly placid expression on his face when confronted with something worrying, the Bavarian looked exactly like a donkey. It was not so much the spirit of competition as the exercise of conscious mastery that inspired them, neither disdaining to take the other as his model and to imitate the most subtle features of a perfect way of life, if these were lacking in themselves. Indeed they appeared to act in such concord and with such mutual understanding that they seemed to be pursuing a common cause, and were like two valiant heroes, making a chivalrous compact and encouraging one another before throwing down the gauntlet. But barely a week later another apprentice arrived, a Swabian called Dietrich, which was a source of quiet pleasure to them both since he would be an amusing yardstick against which to measure their own silent grandeur, and they intended to place the poor Swabian, who was surely a real good-for-nothing, at the mercy of their virtue, like a monkey with which two lions are toying.

But who can describe their amazement when the Swabian behaved in just the same way as they themselves, and the act of recognition that had already taken place between them occurred again between the three of them. So not only did their relationship with the new arrival turn out to be an unexpected one, but their own situation was also quite changed.

As soon as he was in bed between them, the Swabian proved their perfect peer, lying there as straight and still as a matchstick, so that there was always a little room left between each of the apprentices and the blanket lay over them like a piece of paper on top of three herrings. The situation was now graver: as all three of them were on equal terms, like angles in an equilateral triangle, there could be no confidential arrangement, no armistice or pleasant competition between two of them, and they strove in deadly earnest to drive one another out of the bed and out of the house by dint of sheer patience. When their master realized that these three oddities put up with everything simply in order to stay, he reduced their wages and gave them less food. But they worked all the harder and enabled him to distribute large stocks of cheap goods and to meet increased orders, so that thanks to his quiet apprentices he earned a stack of money and possessed in them a veritable gold-mine. He let his belt out a few more notches and became an important figure in the town, while the foolish craftsmen slaved away day and night in the obscurity of the workshop, trying to force one another out through sheer work. Dietrich, the Swabian, who was the youngest, proved to be cast in the same mould as the others, except that he had no savings because he had not yet travelled enough. As Jobst and Fridolin already had too great a start over him, this would have been of serious consequence, had he not managed as an ingenious little Swabian to conjure up a genie who compensated for the others' advantage. As his heart was as lacking as those of his fellow apprentices in any passion apart from his fervent desire to settle down precisely there and nowhere else and then to reap the benefits, he hit on the idea of falling in love and wooing a female who possessed just about as much money as the Saxon and the Bavarian had tucked away under their flagstones. It was not the way of the Seldwylians to marry ugly or unpleasant women for the sake of financial gain. There was in any case no great temptation to do so, as the town could boast no rich heiresses whether beautiful or ugly, and they at least had the courage to turn down smaller morsels and to marry pretty, gay creatures, whom they could show off for a few years. So it was not difficult for the questing eye of the Swabian to alight upon a virtuous young lady who lived in the same street and who, he discovered through cunning conversation with old women, had in her possession securities to the value of seven hundred guldens. She was called Züs Bünzlin, a twenty-eight-year-old girl, who lived with her mother, the laundress, but had inherited directly from her father. She kept the document in a small lacquered chest together with the interest slips, her certificates of baptism and confirmation, and a painted gilt Easter egg. Then there were half a dozen silver tea-spoons, the Lord's Prayer printed in gold on a piece of transparent red material, which she called human skin, a cherry-stone, on which Christ's Passion was carved, and a pot made of pierced ivory lined with red taffeta, in which she kept a small mirror and a silver thimble; then there was a second cherry-stone, in which there rattled about a miniature game of skittles, a nut, which, when opened, revealed a tiny madonna set behind glass, a silver heart containing a smelling-pad, a sweet-tin made of lemon-peel with strawberries painted on the lid and in which there lay on a piece of cotton-wool a golden pin in the shape of a forget-me-not, a locket with a souvenir plait of hair, and a bundle of yellowing papers containing recipes and secrets, a tiny bottle of Hoffmann's drops, another of eau-de-Cologne, and a jar of musk, a further jar containing a little piece of marten's dung, a small basket woven from sweet-smelling straw, and another constructed from glass-beads and cloves, and, lastly, a small book bound in sky-blue ribbed paper with silver page-edgings, entitled *Golden Rules for Young Ladies during Engagement, Marriage, and Motherhood*, a tiny book of dreams, a manual on letter-writing, five or six love-letters, and a lancet for blood-letting, which dated from an affair with an apprentice barber or surgeon's assistant. She had intended to marry this young man, and, as she was a skilful and in every way sensible woman, she had learnt from her beloved how to open veins, apply leeches and cupping-glasses and so on, and was even able to shave him. But he had proved to be unworthy of her and had frivolously endangered her entire life's happiness, and so with sad but wise resolution she had dissolved their relationship. They returned one another's gifts with the exception of the lancet. This she retained as settlement for one gulden forty-eight kreuzer, which she had once lent him in cash, whereas the worthless fellow himself had claimed not to owe her anything, as she had given him the money on the occasion of a ball to defray expenses, and she had eaten twice as much as he had. So he kept the gulden and the forty-eight kreuzer, while she kept the lancet, which she secretly used to let the blood of all the women in her circle of acquaintances, thus earning herself quite a pretty penny. But every time she wielded the instrument she could not help reflecting painfully on the base attitude of the man who had been so close to her and had almost become her husband.

All these objects were kept in the lacquered chest, which was carefully locked and put away in an antique walnut cabinet, the key to which Züs Bünzlin always had with her in her handbag. The girl herself had thin reddish hair and pale blue eyes, which were not without charm and occasionally contrived to look gentle and wise. She possessed masses of clothes, wore but a few of the oldest ones, and was always neatly and cleanly dressed, while her room was similarly kept clean and tidy. She worked very hard and helped her mother with the laundry by ironing the more delicate articles and washing the bonnets and cuffs of the female inhabitants of Seldwyla, which earned her a great deal of money. It was probably this activity which made her adopt, week in and week out whenever they were washing, that strict mood of restraint that affects all women on laundry days, a mood that would not leave her until the ironing began, when she would become gayer, but always with a wise degree of moderation. This spirit of restraint also characterized the principal source of decoration in their home, a garland of square, meticulously cut pieces of soap, which were laid round the ledge above the pine panelling to harden and thus be more efficient in use. Züs herself always marked and cut out these pieces from the new slabs of soap with the help of a brass wire. The wire had a wooden crosspiece at each end to make it easy to hold and to slice the soft soap. But for measuring up she had a pair of compasses, made for her and given her by a toolsmith, to whom she had once been as good as betrothed. It was from him that a small shiny spice-mortar had also come, and this decorated the top of the cabinet, standing between the blue tea-pot and the painted glass vase. She had wanted a dainty little mortar like this for a long time, and so it seemed like magic when the toolsmith turned up with it on her name-day and also brought with him something to be ground – a box filled with cinnamon, sugar, cloves, and pepper. Before coming in, he dangled the mortar by one hand from his little finger and struck it sweetly with the pestle like a bell, so that it was a really festive moining. But shortly afterwards the treacherous fellow vanished from the area and never once wrote. To cap it all, his master asked for the mortar back, because the missing apprentice had taken it from his shop without paying. But Züs Bünzlin refused to hand back this valuable souvenir, and conducted courageous and vigorous legal proceedings, defending herself in court on the grounds that it served as payment for shirt-fronts she had washed for the fugitive. This period when she had to fight for her right to keep the mortar was the most important and agonizing time of her life, for, with her profound intelligence, she understood and experienced things – and particularly her appearance in court on account of such a delicate matter – far more keenly than other more superficial folk. Nevertheless she gained a victory and retained the mortar.

But if the elegant soap-gallery proclaimed her industry and precision, a small collection of diverse books, which she kept neatly in the window and which she ardently read on Sundays, was no less eloquent witness to the elevation and discipline of her mind. She still possessed all her school books from many years before, having lost not a single volume, and she still retained in her memory this whole little corpus of learning: she knew by heart the catechism, her grammar-book, her arithmetic book, her geography book, her Biblical history, and the worldly reading books. She also possessed some of those delightful stories by Christoph Schmid and his tales with the neat rhyming aphorisms at the end, at least half-a-dozen different treasuries and albums, in which she could look things up, a collection of almanacs filled with manifold fruits of experience and wisdom, some remarkable books of prophecy, a guide to reading one's fortune from cards, a book of devotion for every day of the year for educated young ladies, and an old copy of Schiller's *Robbers*, which she read whenever she felt she had forgotten enough of it, which moved her every time afresh, and of which she managed to deliver some very intelligent and shrewd accounts. She kept everything that was in these books in her head and could speak about them and many other matters in the most pleasing manner. When she was happy and not too busy, an unceasing stream of observations flowed from her lips: she could explain and judge

everything, and young and old, high born and low born,
educated and uneducated, all had to learn from her and accept
her view once she had pronounced on the nature of the problem with a smile or after a brief pause for deep reflection.
Indeed, occasionally she would say so much and with such
unction that she sounded like some blind academic who can
see nothing of the world and whose only pleasure is hearing
himself speak. Ever since her schooldays and the time when
she had been preparing for confirmation, she had kept up
with writing essays, spiritual reflections, and various aphoris-
tic sketches. Sometimes on a quiet Sunday she would compose the most extraordinary essays; taking some impressive-
sounding title she had heard or read somewhere, she would
fill sheet after sheet with the most peculiar and nonsensical
sentences, just as they sprang to mind in her strange brain.
She would write, for example, about the benefits of being
confined to one's sick-bed, about death, about the salubrity of
abstinence, the grandeur of the visible world and the mysteries
of the invisible world, life in the country and its pleasures,
about nature, dreams, love, some thoughts on Christ's work of
redemption, three points about self-righteousness, and reflections on immortality. She read these achievements to her
friends and admirers, and she would present one or two such
essays to any one whom she wished well, and that person
would then have to place them in his Bible, if he had one.
This, her intellectual side, had once attracted the profound
and honest affection of an apprentice bookbinder, who read
all the books he bound and was an ambitious, emotional, and
inexperienced young man. When he brought his bundle of
washing to Züsi's mother he felt as if he were in heaven, so
wonderful did it seem to him to hear these magnificent sentiments, sentiments which he had often thought of himself
when in an idealistic mood but had never dared to utter.
Shyly and respectfully he approached this young lady, who
alternated between severity and eloquence, and she allowed
him her company and remained a close acquaintance for a year,
but without ever concealing the obvious hopelessness of his
chances, a hopelessness for which she prepared him gently but

with ineluctable firmness. He was after all nine years younger, as poor as a church-mouse, and had no talent for business, which was not very lively in Seldwyla anyway, because people did not read much and had few books bound. So she did not deceive herself for a moment that a union might be possible, but simply tried to encourage him to follow her own philosophy of self-denial and to mummify his mind in a fog of motley phrases. He listened to her devoutly and occasionally ventured a fine phrase himself, only for her to kill it, no sooner than it had been born, with a still finer one. This was the most philosophical and noble year of her life, unsullied by the touch of anything base. In its course the young man rebound all her books and spent many evenings and holidays constructing an ingenious and costly monument to his veneration. It was a large Chinese pagoda in papier-mâché with innumerable cubby-holes and secret drawers, and it could be taken to pieces. It was covered with the finest coloured gloss paper and decorated richly with gold trimmings. Walls of mirrors and pillars featured alternately, and if you took off a piece or opened a room you saw further mirrors and tiny concealed pictures, bouquets of flowers and loving couples. From the scalloped gables hung everywhere little bells. There was a place for a lady's watch to be hung and beautifully worked hooks on the pillars, so that the gold chain could be wound backwards and forwards across the building from the case, but so far no watch-maker and no goldsmith had appeared to place either a watch or a chain on this altar. An infinite amount of energy and skill had gone into this ingenious temple, the geometric plan of which had involved no less effort than the meticulously neat work itself. When this monument to a year of beautiful memories was finished Züs Bünzlin encouraged the worthy bookbinder, with considerable self-discipline, to pull up his roots and to continue his journeyings, because the world was wide open with opportunity, and, now that his heart had been so ennobled by her company and schooling, good fortune would surely smile upon him, while she would never forget him and would commit herself to a life of solitude. He wept real tears when he was sent on

his way and left the little town. But ever since then his work
of art had been enthroned on Züsi's ancestral chest of drawers,
covered by a sea-green gauze veil, which protected it from
dust and all improper scrutiny. It was so sacred to her that
she did not use it but kept it as new, put nothing in the
cubby-holes, called its builder in retrospect Emmanuel,
though his name had been Veit, and told everyone only
Emmanuel had understood her and had had insight into her
true self. But she had only confessed that to him personally
on rare occasions, had kept a tight rein on him instead, and,
in order to spur him on to greater things, she had often shown
him that he understood her least of all just when he imagined
he did understand her. On the other hand he played a trick on
her too by concealing under a false floor in the innermost
recess of the pagoda the most wonderful, tear-stained letter,
in which he declared his inexpressible sorrow, love, veneration, and his eternal allegiance, all in a colourful, unrestrained
language which true emotion alone can find when it is trapped
in a maze. He had never given utterance to such grand sentiments because she never let him speak. But as she had no idea
of the existence of this hidden treasure, in this case fate was
just, and a false-hearted beauty never discovered what she did
not deserve to see. And again it was symbolical that it was
really she who did not understand the foolish but affectionate
and basically honest nature of the bookbinder.

She had long since praised the life led by the three comb-
makers, calling them three just and sensible men, for she had
kept a close watch on them. So once Dietrich, the Swabian,
started staying longer when he brought or fetched his shirt
and began to court her, she was friendly towards him and kept
him there for hours on end with her excellent conversation,
while Dietrich, filled with admiration, flattered her as profusely as he could. She experienced no embarrassment in
enduring hearty praise; in fact the more it was laid on the
more she enjoyed it, and when her wisdom was being extolled,
she would contain herself until her admirer had unbosomed
himself completely and then, with exalted unction, she would
take up his very words and complete the details in the picture

he had drawn of her. Dietrich had not being going out with
Züs for long before she showed him the certificate for her
securities, whereupon he was filled with good humour and
became as secretive towards his companions as if he had
invented a perpetual-motion machine. But Jobst and Fridolin
soon found out what had happened and were amazed at how
shrewd and adroit he had managed to be. Jobst in particular
literally struck himself across the forehead, for he had, after
all, frequented the house for years and it had never occurred
to him to seek anything there except his linen; indeed he
almost hated the couple, because they were the only people
to whom he had to hand over a few farthings in cash every
single week. He was not in the habit of ever thinking of
marriage, because he believed a woman could be nothing but
a creature who wanted something of him that he did not owe
her; and to want something valuable of her oneself had not
struck him either, because he only trusted himself, and his
short-sighted reflections did not go beyond the highly
restricted sphere of his own secret project. But now it was a
matter of ousting the Swabian, because if he once got hold of
those seven hundred gulden belonging to Miss Züs, his rival
could wreak havoc. And so the seven hundred gulden took on
a new, transfigured brilliance for both the Saxon and the
Bavarian. Inventive Dietrich had simply discovered a con-
tinent which at once became common property, and he shared
the harsh fate of all discoverers, for the other two immediately
followed suit and also began to woo Züs Bünzlin, who found
herself surrounded by a whole court of intelligent and honourable comb-makers. This pleased her exceptionally well. She
had never before had more than one admirer at a time, so it was
a new mental exercise for her to treat the three of them with
the utmost prudence and impartiality and to keep them all
firmly in their places, while edifying them in the meantime
with remarkable speeches on self-denial and altruism until
Heaven had reached its inexorable decision. Since each of
them had made a special point of confiding his secret and plan
to her, she resolved on the spot to marry whichever of them
reached his goal and became the owner of the business. She

excluded the Swabian, who could only achieve this through her, and decided not to marry him in any event, but because he was the youngest, cleverest, and most likeable of the apprentices she dropped a number of quiet hints that he of all of them had the best chance; and so by means of the friendliness with which she seemed to favour and charm him in particular, she spurred the others to still warmer fervour. Thus it was that the wretched Columbus who had discovered this fair country became just the joker in the pack. All three competed in displaying devotion, modesty, intelligence, and the charming art of letting this strict young lady keep them well to heel, while still admiring her with no thought for their own advantage. And so when the entire company was gathered, it resembled some strange conventicle, in which the most peculiar speeches were delivered. Yet for all their piety and humility it happened over and over again that one or other of them would suddenly stop praising their female liege and would attempt to single himself out for praise – but only to find that he would be interrupted, gently corrected, and put to shame, or that he would have to listen as she extolled the virtues of the others, which he would hastily recognize and confirm.

But this meant a hard life for the poor comb-makers. However cool their temperaments may have been, once a woman was involved, quite unwonted feelings of jealousy, anxiety, fear, and hope were aroused. In their efforts to work and to save they almost came to the point of quarrelling, and began to grow visibly thinner. They became melancholy, and while they took pains to be extremely amicable and eloquent in the presence of others, especially Züs, when they were together at work or were sitting in their bedroom they hardly exchanged a word and lay down in their common bed sighing, yet as quiet and peaceable as three pencils. One and the same dream descended on the trio every night, until it became so vivid on one occasion that Jobst, lying by the wall, threw himself round and pushed Dietrich; Dietrich recoiled and pushed Fridolin, whereupon a savage outburst of resentment broke out among the sleepy apprentices and there ensued a most terrible fight in the bed. For three minutes they pushed, kicked, and lashed out so violently with their feet that all six legs became entangled and the whole scrimmage somersaulted out of the bed with a dreadful shriek. Coming to their senses, they thought the devil had arrived to fetch them or that brigands had entered their room. With a shout they leapt to their feet. Jobst jumped on his flagstone, Fridolin flung himself onto his, and Dietrich onto the one beneath which his small savings had also begun to accumulate. There they stood in a triangle, shaking all over, waving their arms about, crying blue murder, and bellowing, 'Go away! Go away!' till the terrified master forced his way into the room and calmed them down. Quivering with fear, anger, and shame, they all finally crept back to bed together and lay silently beside one another until morning. But this nocturnal visitation was only a prelude compared with the still greater shock awaiting them when the master began breakfast by saying that he no longer needed three assistants and so two of them would have to go. They had worked so hard and produced so many combs that a number remained unsold, while the master had so spent the increased earnings that the business started to run down no sooner than it had reached its zenith, and by leading such a gay life he soon owed twice as much in debts as he received in income. Thus, however industrious and temperate his apprentices were, they suddenly became a superfluous burden. He consoled them by saying that all three were equally dear and valuable to him, and that he would leave it up to them to decide which one should stay and which should leave. But they came to no agreement and stood there as pale as death, smiling at one another, and then suddenly becoming frightfully agitated, for this was the most fateful of moments; the fact that the master had given them notice was a sure sign that he would not run the business much longer, and at long last the little comb manufactory would be for sale again. So the goal for which they had all striven was close at hand, shining like some heavenly Jerusalem, and at that moment two of them had to turn round in front of the very gates and go. Without any further ado each of them declared that he wished to stay, even if he had to work for nothing. But the master

had no use for this proposal either, and assured them that
two would still have to leave. They fell at his feet, wrung their
hands, and besought him, each imploring on his account to be
kept on two months more or even just for four weeks. But
the master was quite aware of their calculations, became
annoyed, and made fun of them by suddenly proposing an
amusing solution to the problem. 'If you are quite unable to
agree which of you are to leave,' he said, 'I shall show you how
the question can be resolved, and the result will be final!
Tomorrow is Sunday. I shall pay your wages, you will pack
your knapsacks, take your sticks, and all three of you will
set out peacefully from the gate and will walk for half an
hour in whichever direction you wish. Then you can take a
rest and can have a drink if you like, and afterwards you will
return to the town. Whoever asks me for work first will stay
on. The others must then go, wherever they wish!' Again
they fell at his feet and begged him not to carry out this
cruel plan, but all to no avail; he remained firm and immovable.
All of a sudden the Swabian leapt up and rushed out of the
house, as if possessed, to Züs Bünzlin; hardly had Jobst and
the Bavarian seen this than they broke off their lamentations
and ran after him; so the scene of desperation was immediately
transferred to the home of the frightened young lady.

She was deeply shocked and moved by this unexpected
turn of events; but she was the first to regain composure,
and, surveying the lie of the land, she determined to attach
her own destiny to the master's strange brainwave, for she
regarded it as a decision inspired from above. Filled with emotion, she produced a small treasury, and, thrusting a needle
between the leaves, hit upon a saying that spoke of the
undaunted pursuit of a good goal. She then asked the agitated
apprentices to open the book at random, and everything that
they found was concerned with zealous conduct while tread-
ing the strait and narrow path, with going forwards without
looking back, with one's course in life, or in short with walking and running of all kinds, so that the approaching race
plainly appeared to have been ordained by God. But, since
she feared that Dietrich as the youngest would easily be able

to run most quickly and so win the laurel-wreath, she decided to set out with the three suitors herself and to see what was to be done to her own advantage. She simply wanted one of the two older men to win, and it did not matter which. She therefore ordered the woeful and quarrelsome trio to be quiet and submissive, and addressed them as follows: 'You must realize, dear friends, that nothing happens which is not significant, and however remarkable and unusual your master's suggestion may be, we must regard it as an act of divine intervention, and resign ourselves to this abrupt decision with a kind of wisdom of which this impetuous fellow does not even dream. Our peaceful and harmonious life together has been too beautiful for it to continue so pleasantly for long. Alas, all that is beautiful and beneficial is transitory and ephemeral, and nothing survives for long except evil, obstinacy, and loneliness of the soul, which we may then watch and observe with pious reason. Therefore, before an evil spirit of dissension comes among us, let us rather leave and part from one another of our own free will like the sweet breezes of spring, tracing their rapid path across the heavens, before we are driven apart like the winds of the autumn storm. I shall myself accompany you on your arduous journey and shall be present when you begin your trial, so that you will be happy in mind and will be spurred on from behind as the goal of victory greets you. But just as the victor will not exalt in his good fortune, those that are defeated shall not be faint of heart and shall bear no grief or malice thence, but may expect that we shall remember them kindly. They will set out into the wide world as contented journeymen, for men have built many cities that are as lovely or even lovelier than Seldwyla: Rome is a great and remarkable city and the Holy Father lives there; and Paris is a mighty city with many souls and wonderful palaces; and in Constantinople the Sultan, who is of Turkish faith, reigns; and Lisbon, which was once ravaged by an earthquake, has been rebuilt even more beautifully. Vienna is the capital of Austria and is called the Imperial City; and London is the richest city in the world and is situated in England on a river which is called the Thames. Two million people live there! But Petersburg is the capital and royal residence of Russia, while Naples is the capital of a kingdom of the same name and has an erupting mountain, called Vesuvius, on which a damned soul once appeared to an English sea-captain, about whom I have read in a remarkable travel report, and this soul belonged to a certain John Smidt, who had been a godless man one hundred and fifty years before and who gave the said captain a message for his descendants in England, so that he would be saved – you see, the whole volcano is a refuge for the damned, as you can read in the learned Peter Hasler's tract on the supposed location of hell. There are many other towns, of which I shall only name Milan, Venice, which is built entirely in the water, Lyons, Marseilles, Strasbourg, Cologne, and Amsterdam. I have already mentioned Paris but not Nuremberg, Augsburg, and Frankfurt, Basle, Berne, and Geneva, all of which are beautiful cities, as well as beautiful Zürich, and many more which I cannot finish listing. There is a limit to all things except the inventiveness of men, who are constantly pressing forward and attempting everything that seems useful to them. If they are just, they will succeed, but the unjust shall perish like the grass in the meadow and like smoke. Many are chosen but few are called. For all these reasons and in many other respects, which impose upon us the duty and virtue of a pure conscience, let us accept the call of destiny. Therefore go forth and prepare yourselves for the journey but as just and gentle-natured men, who bear their own worth within them, wherever they may go, whose staffs will everywhere take root, and who can say, whatever opportunity they may seize: I have chosen the better path!'

But the comb-makers would have none of this and implored shrewd Züs to choose one of them and to tell him to stay, each assuming it would be himself. But she avoided making any decision and ordered them in a tone of grave authority to obey her or she would withdraw her friendship for ever. Then Jobst, the oldest, rushed out again and across to the master's house, and in a flash the others were after him, fearing that he might do something there against their own interests.

And so they hurtled backwards and forwards like shooting-stars the whole day long, and became as repulsive to one another as three spiders in a single web. Half the town watched this curious spectacle of the demented comb-makers, who had been so silent and composed hitherto, and the old folk grew anxious because they thought it might be a mysterious portent of impending doom. Towards evening they became tired and exhausted, though they had still thought of nothing better, and so with chattering teeth they climbed into the old bed. One after the other crept under the blanket, where they lay as still as death, filled with confused thoughts until soothing sleep came over them. Jobst was the first to awake at crack of dawn, and saw that a bright spring morning was shining into the room, where he had slept for six years now. However meagre its furnishings, it seemed to him like heaven, which he was being forced to leave for no just reason. He glanced around the walls and noted all the familiar traces left by the many apprentices who had lived there previously for longer or shorter periods: here was a place where one used to lean his head, leaving a dark patch, in a second place another had knocked a nail into the wall to hang his pipe from, and the red string was still there. What good men they had been! They had quietly moved on, while those lying beside him had no intention of giving way. Then his eye alighted on the area nearest his face, and he looked at the tiny objects that he had already seen a thousand times when lying in bed while it was light of a morning or evening, enjoying the benefits of a blissful and costless existence. There was a damaged place in the plaster, which looked like a country with lakes and towns, and a tiny pile of coarse sand grains represented a group of paradise islands. Then came a long hog's-hair bristle, which had fallen out of a brush and had become stuck in the blue paint – Jobst had come across the remnants of this paint last autumn, and so that it would not be wasted, he had painted a quarter of the wall, which was as far as it would go. The part he painted was the closest to where he slept. Then, beyond the hog's-hair bristle was quite a tiny bump like a diminutive blue mountain, which cast a delicate shadow across the bristle to the paradise islands. He had reflected about this mountain the whole winter, as he felt sure that it had not been there before. As he looked sadly and dreamily for it, he suddenly realized it was missing and could hardly believe his eyes when he found instead a small blank spot on the wall, while not far away there was the tiny blue mountain on the move, apparently walking along. Jobst shot up into the air in amazement, as if face to face with a miracle, and then saw that it was a bed-bug, which he had painted over last autumn without noticing it lying there dormant. But now, revived by the warm spring weather, it had awoken and at this very moment was climbing the wall, heedless of its blue back. He watched it with feeling and surprise. While it was still in the blue area, it could hardly be distinguished from the wall, but once it left the painted zone and the last odd splashes of colour, the goodly, sky-blue creature became clearly visible, forging its way across darker regions. Jobst sank back dejectedly into the pillows. However little he normally made of such things, this incident aroused the feeling in him that he too would now have to set out again, and it seemed to be a friendly sign to him that he should accept what was unalterable and should leave willingly at least. Thanks to calmer thoughts of this kind, his natural composure and wisdom returned, and on thinking the matter over more closely, he concluded that if he put a modest and resigned face on the matter and accepted this hard task, pulling himself together and behaving prudently, he would still have the best chance of victory over his rivals. Quietly he got out of bed and began putting his things in order, first and foremost taking out his savings and placing them at the bottom of his old knapsack. This woke his companions; when they saw him packing his baggage so calmly, they were extremely surprised, especially when Jobst addressed them with some conciliatory words and wished them good morning. He said nothing more, however, but continued with his work silently and peaceably. Although they did not know what he was up to, they suspected some strategy behind his actions and immediately copied him, paying the closest attention to what he did next. It was strange how, for the first time, all three openly produced their savings from under the flagstones and stowed them away in their knapsacks without counting them. They had all long known that each was aware of the others' secret, and in keeping with ancient traditions of honesty they had no fear that their property would come to harm, as they were all certain that the others would not stoop to theft – there can be no locks and bolts and no mutual suspicion in the places where apprentices, soldiers, and the like sleep.

And so, quite unexpectedly, there they were, ready to set out. Their master paid their last wages and returned their road-books in which were written the finest testimonies by the town and the master as to their constant good behaviour and excellence at work. They stood sadly in front of Züs Bünzlin's front-door, dressed in long brown overcoats with faded old dust-cloaks over the top, wearing hats which, despite their age and worn condition, were carefully covered with waxed linen. On their backs they all had little trolleys attached to their knapsacks, on which they could pull their luggage along if they had far to go; but they did not intend using them and their wheels projected high above their shoulders. Jobst leant on an honest cane, Fridolin on a mottled scarlet and black ash-staff, and Dietrich on a daring monstrosity of a stick, round which curled a wild profusion of twigs. But he was almost ashamed of this ostentatious object, because it dated from the early days of his apprenticeship, when he had not been nearly as staid and sensible as now. Many of the neighbours and their children stood round the three serious-faced men, wishing them good luck on their journey. Then Züs appeared in the doorway with an expression of solemnity on her face, and, walking ahead of the apprentices, led them with composure out of the gate. In their honour she had dressed with unusual pomp, wearing a huge hat with large yellow ribbons, a pink Indian silk dress with old-fashioned convolutions and ornamentations, a black satin sash with a tombac buckle, and red morocco shoes with fringes. She carried a large green silk reticule, which she had filled with dried pears and plums, and held an open parasol, which was crowned with a large white lyre in ivory. She had also pinned her gold forget-me-not and her locket on her dress, with the blonde plait draped round it, and was wearing white knitted gloves. She looked kind and gentle in all this splendour; she was blushing a little, and her bosom seemed to heave more markedly than usual. The departing rivals were beside themselves with melancholy and grief, for the outward appearance of things, the beautiful spring day that was shining down upon their exodus, and Züsi's costume almost added to their feeling of suspense something of what is really meant by 'love'. Outside the gate the kind young lady advised her suitors to place their knapsacks on their trolleys and to pull them along so that they would not get unnecessarily tired. They did as she bade and, as they marched up the hills behind the township, it almost looked as if an artillery unit were advancing to establish a battery on the summit. After they had walked for a good half hour, they halted on a pleasant rise, on which there was a crossroads, and sat down in a semi-circle beneath a lime-tree, from where there was a fine view across woods, lakes, and hamlets. Züs opened her bag, gave each of them a handful of pears and plums so that they could regain their strength, and there they sat for some time in grave silence, just making a quiet smacking with their tongues as they chewed the sweet fruit.

Then, throwing away a plum-stone and wiping her stained finger-tips on the young grass, Züs began to speak: 'Dear friends! Behold how beautiful and how vast the world is, full of wonderful things and everywhere inhabited by men. And yet I should be prepared to wager that at this solemn moment there are nowhere four more upright and good-natured souls gathered together than we, and none as clever and discreet in temperament, as devoted to the practice of diligence and the virtues of self-reliance, thrift, gentleness, and warm friendship. How many flowers there are around us here, flowers of all kinds brought forth by the spring, especially yellow cowslips, from which a fine-flavoured and nutritious tea can be made; but are they just and industrious, thrifty, cautious, and skilled in wise and instructive thought?

No, they are ignorant, inanimate creatures, unconsciously and senselessly wasting their time, and however beautiful they may be, they will finish up as dry hay, while we are much superior to them in our virtue and certainly are no less beautiful in physical appearance. For God has created us in His own image and has inspired us with His divine spirit. Oh, if only we could sit here for ever in such a paradise of innocence. Yes, my friends, it seems to me that we are all in a state of innocence and ennobled by sinless knowledge, for, praise be to God, we can all read and write and have all learnt a skilled trade. I have the ability and the talent for much and do not doubt I could do things that the most scholarly young woman could not, if I were to go beyond my station; but modesty and humility are the finest virtues of an honest young woman, and it suffices for me to know that my mind is not worthless and scorned when compared with a higher instance. Many men who were not worthy of me have wanted my hand, and now all at once I see three estimable bachelors gathered around me, each of whom equally deserves to possess me! Judge from this how my heart must pine amid this wonderful abundance, and, taking me as your example, think if each of you were surrounded by three equally worthy, blossoming young ladies who desired your hand, and yet, on this very account, you could incline your affections to no single one of them and could obtain none. Just imagine the scene if there were three Miss Bünzlins wooing each of you, sitting round you, dressed like me and looking like me, so that there were nine of me, so to speak, in your presence, watching you from all sides and longing for you! Can you imagine it?'

The valiant apprentices stopped chewing in sheer amazement, and, with a simple expression on their faces, attempted to carry out this curious exercise. The little Swabian was the first to try, and declared with a lascivious look, 'Well, most worthy Miss Züs! If you will kindly allow me to say so, I don't only see you threefold but a hundredfold, encircling me, looking at me with worshipping eyes, and offering me a thousand kisses!'

'No, no!' said Züs, petulantly turning down his answer,

'Not in this improper and exaggerated manner! What ever came over you, immodest Dietrich? I did not allow you to imagine me a hundredfold, offering you kisses. I said three times for each of you, and in a moral and honourable fashion that could do me no harm!'

'Yes,' Jobst finally cried, pointing round with a chewed-off pear stalk, 'I can see just three dearest Miss Bünzlins, walking round me in the most honourable way, nodding to me bene-volently and placing their hands on their hearts! Thank you, thank you, thank you very much, your most humble servant!' he said with a smirk, and bowed three times in different directions, as if he could really see these apparitions. 'That's right,' said Züs with a smile, 'if there is any difference between you, it's because you, dear Jobst, are the most talented or at least the most intelligent!' The Bavarian, Fridolin, was still not ready with his imagined scene, but when he heard Jobst praised so heartily, he was scared, and quickly shouted, 'I can see three dearest Miss Bünzlins as well! There they are walking round me in the most honour-able way, nodding to me voluptuously and placing their hands –'

'Wretched Bavarian!' screeched Züs, turning her eyes away from him, 'Not a word more! How dare you speak of me in such disgusting terms and imagine such filth? Ugh!' The poor Bavarian was thunderstruck and blushed bright scarlet without knowing why, for his mind had been a blank, and he had simply tried to imitate the words that Jobst had uttered, seeing how he had been praised. Züs turned back to Dietrich and said, 'Now, dear Dietrich, haven't you thought of a more modest way of expressing yourself?' – 'Yes, with your permission,' he replied, glad that she had addressed him again. 'Now I can see you just three times, standing round me and looking at me in a kind but proper fashion, offering me three white hands to kiss!'

'Fine!' said Züs.' And you, Fridolin? Have you left your deviation behind you? Can't your hot blood cool a little and allow a more decent account?' 'My apologies!' whispered Fridolin, 'I think I can now see three young ladies, who are offering me dried pears and appear to be not unkindly disposed towards me. None is more beautiful than the other, and to choose between them would be bitter indeed.'

'Well, now,' said Züs, 'as you are surrounded in your imaginations by nine equally worthy persons, and yet in this delightful profusion you still feel an emptiness in your hearts, judge my own situation; and seeing how I manage to compose myself wisely and modestly, take my strength as your example and vow to me and among yourselves that you will be friendly to one another in the future, and will part as lovingly as I lovingly part from you, however, the destiny that awaits you may decide! Now place all your hands together on my hand and promise!'

'Certainly, certainly,' shouted Jobst, 'I'll do so at least; I shan't be found lacking!' and the two others hastily added, 'Nor shall I, nor shall I!' and they all put their hands together thinking to themselves that whatever happened they would run as fast as they could. 'I shan't be found lacking!' repeated Jobst. 'I have had a merciful and warm-hearted character since my youth. I have never had a quarrel and could never bear to see a little creature suffer. Wherever I have been, I have got on well with people, and I have received the greatest praise on account of my peaceable conduct. For although I also understand a good deal about all sorts of things and am an intelligent young man, I have never been seen to involve myself in other people's business and have always done my duty in a reasonable manner. I can work as much as I want and it does me no harm, because I am healthy and well and in my prime! The wives of all my masters have told me I am a man in a thousand, a model apprentice, and easy to get on with! Oh, I really believe, myself, that it would be like living in heaven with you, dearest, dearest Miss Züs!'

'My goodness!' said the Bavarian eagerly. 'That doesn't take much believing! It wouldn't be difficult to find it like living in heaven with this young lady! I could do just the same! I wasn't born yesterday either! I understand my craft through and through and know how to keep things in order without losing any words in vain. I have never had any squabbles, although I've worked in big cities, and I've never hit a cat or killed a spider. I am moderate and abstinent, I like any kind of food, and I know how to get pleasure out of the tiniest things and want no more. I'm also healthy and happy and can put up with a lot; a clear conscience is the best tonic in life; all animals like me and run after me, because they can sense my clear conscience and don't want to stay with an unjust man. A poodle once followed me for three days when I was travelling from Ulm, and in the end I had to hand him over to a farmer to look after, because a humble journeyman can't feed such an animal, and when I was going through the Bohemian Woods stags and deer didn't even move at twenty yards distance and weren't afraid of me. It's wonderful how even wild animals distinguish between men and know which ones are good at heart!'

'Yes, that must be true!' chimed in the Swabian. 'Can't you see how that finch has been flying around me the whole time, trying to get closer? And that squirrel over in the fir-tree is constantly looking round at me, and here comes a little beetle crawling up my leg, refusing to be shaken off. He must surely like being with me, the dear little creature!'

But Züs was now becoming jealous, and retorted somewhat violently, 'All animals want to stay with me! I had a bird for eight years and he didn't want to die and leave me at all. Our cat is always rubbing against me, wherever I am, and the neighbour's pigeons push and squabble in front of my window when I throw them crumbs! Animals all have wonderful characteristics in their own way! The lion likes following kings and heroes, the elephant accompanies princes and brave warriors. The camel bears the merchant through the desert and keeps him fresh water in his belly, and the dog accompanies his master through all perils and would plunge into the sea for his sake! The dolphin loves music and follows ships, the eagle follows warring armies. The ape resembles the human being and does everything that he sees men doing, and the parrot understands our language and chats with us like an old man! Even snakes can be tamed, and dance on the tips of their tails. The crocodile can cry human tears and is respected and spared by the natives. The ostrich can be saddled and ridden like a horse, the wild buffalo draws man's carriages, and the horned reindeer his sleighs. The unicorn provides him with snow-white ivory, and the turtle its transparent bones –'

'Excuse me,' said all three comb-makers together, 'surely you are wrong here; ivory comes from elephants' tusks, and you make tortoiseshell combs from the shell and not the bones of the turtle!'

Züs went bright red and said, 'That's very doubtful. I'm sure you've never seen where people get it from, but just work on pieces of it. I'm rarely wrong – but be as that may – let me finish: not only animals have been given special characteristics by God but so have inanimate minerals, which are mined underground. Crystal is as transparent as glass, but marble is hard and mottled black and white; amber has electric qualities and attracts lightning but then burns and smells like incense. Magnets attract iron; you can write on slates but not on diamonds, because they are as hard as steel, and the glazier needs them for glass-cutting, because they are small and sharp. You see, dear friends, I know something about animals, too! As far as my relationship with them is concerned, let me add this: the cat is a sly and cunning creature, and is therefore only affectionate towards sly and cunning people, but the dove is a symbol of innocence and simplicity, and can only feel attracted by innocent, simple souls. Now as both cats and doves are fond of me, it follows that I am clever and simple, cunning and innocent at the same time, just as it says in the scriptures, "Be ye wise as serpents, and harmless as doves!" Indeed it is in this manner that we can appreciate animals, respect their relationship with us, and learn a great deal, provided that we know how to judge the matter aright.'

The wretched apprentices did not dare to utter another word. Züs had baulked them successfully, and went on to confuse one highfalutin matter with another till their eyes and ears refused to function any more. But they admired Züsi's mind and her eloquence, and in their admiration not one of them thought himself unworthy of such a gem, particularly since this pride and joy of any house was so inexpensive, and consisted of nothing but a tireless tongue. The question of whether they themselves deserved what they so revered and were capable of matching up to her, occurs to such simpletons last of all, if ever – they are like children who snatch at anything that shines in their eyes, who lick the paint off all bright playthings, and try to swallow bells whole instead of holding them up to their ears. So they grew more and more excited in their desire and in their vain belief that they would succeed in wooing this excellent creature, and the more crass, cruel, and conceited Züsi's nonsensical phrases became, the more deeply and miserably the comb-makers were moved. At the same time they had developed a violent thirst from the dried fruit, which they had eaten up completely in the meantime. Jobst and the Bavarian went to look for water in the wood, found a spring there, and drank cold water till they were full. The Swabian, on the other hand, had slyly brought a small flask with him, containing cherry brandy mixed with water and sugar, a delightful drink that was intended to give him strength and to guarantee a lead in the race, for he knew full well that the others were too thrifty to bring anything or to stop for a drink on the way. He now quickly took out this flask, while the others were glutting themselves with water, and offered it to Miss Züs. She drank half of it. It tasted excellent and refreshing to her, and, as she drank, she looked across to Dietrich so sweetly that the rest, which he drained himself, tasted as delicious as wine from Cyprus and greatly fortified him. He could not resist seizing Züsi's hand and tenderly kissing her fingertips. She touched him gently on the lips with her index finger, and he pretended to try and bite it, and grimaced like a smiling carp. Züs smirked at him with an expression of deceitful affection on her face; Dietrich grinned back with a sly but sloppy look, and there they sat on the ground opposite each other, touching one another occasionally with the soles of their shoes, as if their feet were substitutes for hands. Züs bent forward a little and placed her hand on his shoulder, and Dietrich was just about to reciprocate this delightful move, when the Saxon and the Bavarian got

back and looked on, pale and whimpering. All that water
which they had poured down themselves on top of the baked
pears had suddenly made them sick, and the heartfelt misery
they experienced on seeing the games the couple were playing,
combined with the empty feeling in their bellies, made them
break out in a cold sweat. But Züs did not lose her composure,
waved quite amicably to them, and called out, 'Come, my
dears, sit down with me a little more so that we may enjoy
peace and friendship together for a while longer!' Jobst and
Fridolin quickly jostled their way into the group and stretched
out their legs. Züs gave the Swabian one hand and Jobst the
other and touched the soles of Fridolin's boots with her feet,
smiling broadly at each in turn. She resembled one of those
virtuosi who can play a number of instruments at once,
shaking a set of bells on their heads, blowing a Pan's pipe
between their lips, playing a guitar with their hands, clashing
cymbals with their knees, striking a triangle with one foot,
and with their elbow beating a drum strapped to their back.

But she then got up, smoothed out her dress, which she had
carefully tucked up, and said, 'And now it is time, dear friends,
for us to set out, and for you to prepare for that serious task
which your master in his stupidity imposed on you but which
we can see to be the call of higher destiny! Set foot on this
path with zeal but without hostility or envy towards one
another, and grant the victor his crown gladly.'

The apprentices leapt to their feet, as if they had been
stung by a wasp. There they stood, about to race one another
on those trusty legs that hitherto had only strode along at a
sedate and dignified pace. Not one of them could remember
having ever run or jumped; the Swabian seemed to have the
most confidence and appeared already to be pawing the
ground gently, lifting his feet in impatience. They looked at
each other very strangely and suspiciously; their faces were
pale and they were sweating, as if they were already running at
top speed.

'Shake hands once more!' said Züs. They did so but slackly
and without enthusiasm, their hands slipping coldly past
each other and dropping down like lumps of lead. 'Are we

really going to start this absurd nonsense?' asked Jobst, drying his eyes, which were beginning to run. 'Yes,' continued the Bavarian, 'are we really going to race?' and began to weep. 'And what, dearest Miss Bünzlin,' said Jobst crying, 'are you going to do?' – 'It is my duty,' she replied, holding her handkerchief to her eyes, 'it is my duty to be silent, to watch, and to suffer!' The Swabian asked slyly, 'And what about afterwards, Miss Züs?' – 'Oh Dietrich!' she replied softly, 'surely you know it is said that one's fate is one's character?' And she threw him such a sidelong glance that he again lifted his legs and felt the urge to gallop off. While the two rivals were preparing their trolleys and Dietrich was doing the same, she several times firmly nudged his elbow and trod on his foot. She also brushed the dust off his hat but smiled across to the others at the same time, as if she were laughing at the Swabian but without his being able to notice it. Then all three puffed up their cheeks and let out great sighs. They looked round in all directions, took off their hats, wiped the sweat from their foreheads, smarmed down their sticky, lank hair, and put their hats back on again. They looked around again and gasped for breath. Züs was sorry for them, and so touched that she wept herself. 'Here are three more dry plums,' she said. 'Put one each in your mouths and keep it there to refresh you! And now depart, and turn the stupidity of evil men into the wisdom of the just! What they have thought up in mischief, transform into an edifying test of self-discipline, into the profound conclusion of many years of good conduct and of competition in the exercise of virtue!' She popped a plum into each of their mouths and they sucked at them. Jobst pressed two hands against his stomach and cried, 'If it must be so, let it happen in God's name!' and, raising his stick, he suddenly started to lift his knees high and to stride powerfully away, pulling his knapsack close behind him. Hardly had Fridolin seen this than he followed him with long steps, and, without looking round again, they hurried hastily off down the road. The Swabian was the last to set out and walked along beside Züs, apparently at his leisure, with an expression of sly content on his

face, as if he were quite confident and generously wanted his
companions to have a start. Züs praised his amicable composure and clung intimately to his arm. 'Ah, how wonderful
it is', she said with a sigh, 'to have an anchor in life! Even if
one is sufficiently gifted with intelligence and insight and leads
a virtuous life, one's route is far more pleasant on the arm of a
trusted friend!' – 'Oh, dearie me, yes, I certainly agree with
that!' replied Dietrich, pressing her elbow firmly against his
side and looking at the same time to see that his rivals were not
too far ahead. 'Don't you see, dearest lady! Is it finally coming
home to you? Now you know which side your bread is
buttered on, don't you?' – 'Oh, Dietrich, dear Dietrich!' she
said with a still greater sigh, 'I often feel really lonely!' –
'Whoops, now something's got to happen!' he cried, and
his heart leapt like a rabbit in a cabbage-field. 'Oh, Dietrich!'
she cried, and pressed herself more firmly against him. He
began to feel faint and his heart was almost bursting with artful pleasure. But at the same moment he realized that his
competitors were out of sight and had vanished around a
corner. He at once wanted to tear himself away from Züsi's
arm and run after them; but she held him so tight that he
could not do so, and she clasped herself to him as if she were
swooning. 'Oh!' she whispered, rolling her eyes. 'Don't
leave me alone now, I depend on you, support me!' – 'Damn
it all, let me go, Miss!' he cried anxiously, 'Or I'll get there
too late and it'll be goodbye to any nightcap!' – 'No, no,
you mustn't leave me, I don't feel well!' she moaned. 'Too
bad!' he screamed, and wrenched himself free, ran up on to a
rise, looked round, and saw the runners right down the hill,
going at full tilt. Then he started to run, but at the same time
glanced round at Züs just once more. He saw her sitting at the
opening to a narrow woodland path, seductively waving to
him. He could not resist this sight and, instead of rushing
down the hill, ran back to her. When she saw him coming, she
got up and went deeper into the wood, looking round to make
sure he was there, for she reckoned on preventing him at all
costs from joining in the race, fooling him, until he got back
too late and so would be unable to stay in Seldwyl.

But the ingenious Swabian changed his own mind at this point, and resolved to fight for his salvation up there on the mountain. And so it was that things turned out quite differently from the way the cunning girl had hoped. As soon as he had reached her and was alone with her in a quiet corner, he threw himself at her feet and besieged her with the fieriest declarations of love ever voiced by any comb-maker. First she tried to tell him to calm down and, without driving him away, politely attempted to keep him there as she rolled off her entire stock of wisdom and advice. But when he described heaven and hell to her in wonderful, magic words, lent him by a tense and agitated sense of enterprise, when he overwhelmed her with caresses of every kind, and tried to take possession first of her hands and then of her feet and her body and her mind, praising and extolling everything about her, till it seemed the very sky had changed colour – and all amid a setting of silent woodland beauty – Züs finally lost control like any creature, whose thoughts are, in the last analysis, no loftier than its senses: her heart began to beat wildly like a terrified and defenceless beetle lying on its back, and Dietrich was there to conquer it in every way. She had lured him into this wood with the purpose of betraying him, and in next to no time she had been vanquished by the little Swabian. This was not because she was a particularly passionate woman but, for all her imagined wisdom, she was so short-sighted that she could not see beyond the end of her own nose. They stayed for about an hour in this exciting state of solitude, embracing again and again, and exchanging a thousand kisses. In all honesty they swore eternal loyalty, and agreed to be married come what might.

Meanwhile news of the three apprentices' odd venture had spread throughout the town, and the master himself had helped to make it common knowledge for his own amusement. So the inhabitants of Seldwyl looked forward to the unexpected spectacle, and were waiting eagerly to be entertained by the just and honourable comb-makers as they came running back. A large crowd assembled in front of the gate and took up positions on either side of the road, as if a sprinter were expected. Boys clambered up into the trees, aged pensioners sat on the grass, pleasurably smoking their pipes in anticipation of a free show. Even the patricians had come out to join in the fun, and were sitting chatting in the gardens and on the terraces of the inns, backing the various runners. In those streets through which they had to pass all the windows were open, wives had put out red and white cushions in their parlours for visitors to rest their elbows on, and were receiving numerous lady-guests, so that jolly coffee parties arose quite spontaneously and the maids were run off their feet fetching cakes and biscuits. And then, outside the gate, the lads up the tallest trees saw a small cloud of dust approaching, and began to shout, 'They're coming, they're coming!' And it was not long before Fridolin and Jobst swept in like a whirlwind, kicking up a thick cloud of dust down the middle of the road. With one hand they were pulling their knapsacks, which were bouncing madly over the stones, and with the other they were holding on to their hats, which had slipped down to the backs of their necks, and their long coats were flapping and blowing about in sheer rivalry. Both were covered in sweat and dust, their mouths wide open as they gasped for breath, they saw nothing that was going on around them, and down the wretches' faces rolled big tears, which they did not have time to wipe away. They were close on one another's heels, though the Bavarian was a foot or two ahead. Dreadful shrieks of laughter rang out, rending the air as far as one could hear. Every one sprang up and pressed forwards to the road's edge, and from all sides came cries of 'That's right! That's right! Keep going, watch out Saxon! Chin up, Bavarian! One's already dropped out – there are only two of them left!' The local gentry in the inn gardens were standing on the tables, splitting their sides with laughter. Their guffaws rang out loud and clear above the confused babble from the crowd down in the street and triggered off a quite extraordinary celebration. The lads and the mob streamed along behind the two woebegone apprentices, and a wild crowd tore down the road with them towards the gate, raising a terrible cloud of dust. Even women and gutter-snipes of

girls joined in, and their squeaky, high-pitched voices added
to the screams of the boys. Now they had nearly reached the
gate, both towers of which were crammed with curious spectators, all waving their caps. Like bolting horses they galloped
along, overwhelmed by fear and pain. Then some mudlark
jumped impishly on to Jobst's knapsack trolley and took a
ride, much to the noisy delight of the crowd. Jobst turned
round and beseeched him to get off, striking at him with his
stick. But the boy ducked and grinned back. This gave Fridolin
a still greater lead and, spotting this, Jobst threw his stick
between his legs, tripping him up. But, as Jobst tried to leap
over the top of him, the Bavarian seized hold of his coat-tails
and pulled himself up on them. Jobst struck him across the
knuckles and shrieked out, 'Let go, let go!' But Fridolin did
not let go, so Jobst grabbed his coat-tails in return, and,
gripping one another tightly, they slowly waltzed through
the gate, occasionally risking a jump in the attempt to escape.
They wept, sobbed, and howled like children, shouting in
the most indescribable anguish, 'Oh God! Let go! For Jesus'
sake, let go, Jobst!' 'Let go, Fridolin! Let go, you devil!'
Between times they battered each other across the knuckles
and gradually moved forwards together. They had lost their
hats and their sticks, and two lads bore the sticks along in
front with the hats dangling on top, while behind them
advanced the raging crowd. All the windows were filled with
the ladies of the town, whose peals of laughter blended with
the ground-swell below; it was a long time since there had
been such a festive mood in Seldwyl. This uproarious pleasure
so whetted the appetite of the inhabitants that no one pointed
out to the two wretches their goal, the master's house, at
which they had finally arrived. They did not notice it themselves – they saw nothing at all – and so the crazy procession
lumbered on through the entire town and out of the gate on
the other side. The master had been standing laughing beneath
the window and, after waiting a while for the final victor,
was just about to go off and enjoy the fruits of his prank,
when Dietrich and Züs quietly and unexpectedly entered his
house.

They, in the meantime, had put their heads together and decided that, as the master comb-maker would not continue for much longer anyway, he would probably be willing to sell his business for cash. Züs would contribute her securities, and the Swabian his savings, and they would thus be in control of the situation and could just laugh at the others. They put their proposal to the amazed master, who immediately realized that he could do a deal behind the backs of his creditors before it came to a confrontation, and so quite unexpectedly obtain the cash sale-price. Everything was rapidly agreed, and before sunset Miss Bünzlin was the rightful owner of the comb-manufactory, while her fiancé was the tenant of the house in which it was situated. So thanks to the Swabian's dexterity, Züs, who had suspected nothing in the morning, had finally been caught and conquered.

Half-dead with shame, exhaustion, and anger, Jobst and Fridolin spent the night in the hostelry to which they had been taken when they had finally collapsed out in the open countryside, firmly locked together. The whole town, once aroused, had already forgotten the reason, and had an evening of merriment. They danced in many of the houses, and there was drinking and singing in the taverns, just as in the good old days of Seldwyl, for the Seldwylians need very little to produce a masterly celebration. When the two wretches saw how the courage with which they had intended to take advantage of the world's folly had only helped it to triumph and to make them objects of common scorn, they felt as though their hearts would break; not only had they lost and destroyed the fruits of several years of prudent planning, but they had also sacrificed their reputations as balanced and legitimately complacent men.

Jobst, who was the elder and had been there for seven years, was completely lost and could not come back onto an even keel. Filled with melancholy, he left the town before daybreak and hanged himself from a tree growing beside the spot where they had all sat the day before. When the Bavarian came past an hour later and saw him, he was so stricken with horror that he rushed away as if berserk; his whole character changed and he apparently became a dissolute old journeyman, who was no one's friend.

Dietrich the Swabian alone remained just and kept his reputation in the town. But he had no pleasure from it, for Züs ruled and suppressed him, and would not let him enjoy any of the glory, regarding herself as the sole source of all goodness.

Paul Heyse

L'ARRABBIATA

Translated by F. J. Lamport

Paul Heyse

PAUL HEYSE was born in 1830. He achieved considerable fame as a writer of *Novellen* and as an anthologist and theorist of the genre, in his work concentrating on, and in his theory similarly emphasizing, formal perfection and the limitation of the story to a single, striking event. Abused by the Naturalists for his lack of contemporary social relevance, his reputation later recovered somewhat and in 1910 he received the Nobel Prize for literature; but his stock has rather sunk again. He died in 1914. *L'Arrabbiata* (*The Fury*) is one of his earliest, but also one of his most perfectly achieved, tales.

L'ARRABBIATA

THE sun had not yet risen. Over Vesuvius lay a broad belt of grey mist, stretching towards Naples and casting the little towns on that part of the coast into shadow. The sea was calm and silent. But, by the *marina* that lies in a narrow inlet beneath the tall rocky cliffs of Sorrento, fishermen and their wives were already stirring, about to haul ashore on stout ropes the skiffs with their nets that had lain out all night fishing. Others were making their craft ready, preparing their sails, dragging out oars and yards from the great vaults with their iron-grilled gates, carved deep into the rock to store the sailors' gear overnight. There were no idle hands to be seen; for the old men too, who would be going out themselves no more, took their place in the long chain of fishermen hauling at the nets, and here and there an old woman stood with her spindle on one of the flat roofs or busied herself with her grandchildren, while her daughter was helping her husband.

'Look, Rachela, there's our *padre curato*,' said one grandmother to a little creature ten years old, who stood beside her with her own little spindle. 'He's just getting aboard. Antonino is taking him across to Capri. *Maria santissima*, doesn't his reverence still look sleepy!' – and with that she waved her hand to a short, friendly priest who was just making himself comfortable in the bark below, after carefully picking up his black skirts and spreading them out on to the wooden bench. The others on the shore paused in their work to watch the departure of their parish priest, who nodded friendly greetings to right and left of him.

'Why does he have to go to Capri, then, grandmama?' asked the child. 'Haven't the people there got a priest of their own, so they have to borrow ours?'

'Don't be silly,' said the old woman. 'Enough and to spare, and the finest churches and even a hermit, that's something we haven't got. But there is a lady there, a *signora*, who lived here in Sorrento for a long time and was very ill, so that the *padre* often had to go to her with the Sacrament, when they thought she wouldn't live another night. Well, the blessed Virgin was with her in her need, so that she grew fit and well again and could bathe in the sea every day. When she left here and went over to Capri, she gave the church and the poor people a great pile of ducats, and she wouldn't go, they say, until the *padre* promised to go and see her over there, so that she can confess to him. It's wonderful, what a lot she thinks of him. And we can count ourselves blessed that we have a man like that for our parish priest, a man as clever as an archbishop, that the gentry ask for. The Madonna be with him!' And she waved to the little boat below them, that was just about to cast off.

'Shall we have clear weather, son?' the little priest was asking, as he looked over towards Naples with a doubtful gaze.

'The sun's not out yet,' the youth replied. 'It'll soon clear this bit of mist.'

'Let's be on our way, then, so that we are there before it gets too hot.'

Antonino was reaching for the long oar, to drive the boat into open water, when he suddenly paused and looked up to where the steep path leads down from the little town of Sorrento to the waterfront.

The slim figure of a girl came into sight above them, hurrying down over the stony steps and waving a handkerchief. She carried a bundle under her arm, and was dressed shabbily enough; but she had an almost lordly way, only a little wild, of throwing her head back, and her long black hair braided round her head stood upon her brow like a diadem.

'Why are we waiting?' asked the priest.

'There's someone else coming for the boat, I expect they want to go to Capri too. If you don't mind, *padre* – she won't slow us down, it's only a slip of a girl, hardly eighteen.'

At this moment the girl appeared from behind the wall that encloses the twisting path. 'Laurella?' said the priest. 'What would she be doing in Capri?'

Antonino shrugged his shoulders.

The girl came towards them with quick steps, looking at the ground before her.

'Good morning, *l'Arrabbiata*!' called out some of the young sailors. They would have had more to say if the presence of the *curato* had not restrained them; for the defiant silence with which the girl received their greetings seemed to provoke the spirited lads.

'Good morning, Laurella,' the priest now called too. 'How are you? Do you want to come to Capri with us?'

'If you don't mind, *padre*!'

'Ask Antonino, he is the *padrone* aboard this ship. Every one of us is lord and master in his own place, and the good Lord God over us all.'

'Here's half a *carlino*,' said Laurella, without looking at the young sailor, 'if I can come for that.'

'You need it more than I do,' muttered the lad, and pushed aside some baskets of oranges to make room for her. He was going to sell them in Capri, for the rocky island does not bear enough fruit for the needs of all the visitors.

'I don't want to go for nothing,' answered the girl, and her black eyebrows quivered.

'Come along, my child,' said the priest. 'He is a good lad, and doesn't want to grow rich on the little you have. Here, climb in' – and he stretched out his hand to her – 'and sit down beside me. Look, he has laid his jacket there for you, to give you a softer seat. He didn't treat me so well. But that's always the way with young people. More trouble for one of the fair sex than for ten of the cloth. Now, now, no need to make excuses, Tonino, it's the way our Lord has made us; birds of a feather flock together.'

Meanwhile Laurella had come aboard and, after pushing the jacket aside without saying a word, had sat down. The young sailor let it lie where it was and muttered something between his teeth. Then he gave a powerful shove against the wall of the quayside, and the little boat sped out into the gulf.

'What have you got in your bundle?' asked the priest, as they glided across the sea lightening with the sun's first rays.

'Silk, thread, and a loaf of bread, *padre*. I have to sell the silk to a woman in Capri who makes ribbons, and the thread to another.'

'Have you spun it yourself?'

'Yes, sir.'

'If I remember rightly, you have learnt to make ribbons too.'

'Yes, sir. But mother is worse again, so I can't leave home, and we can't afford to pay for a loom of our own.'

'Worse? Really? When I called on you at Easter she was sitting up.'

'Spring is always the worst time for her. Since we have had the big storms and the earthquakes, she has had to stay lying down because of the pain.'

'Keep on praying, my child, and ask the Holy Virgin to pray for you. And be good and hard-working, so that your prayer may be heard.' After a pause: 'As you came down to the shore there, they called out "Good morning, *l'Arrabbiata*!" Why do they call you that? It's not a pleasant name for a Christian girl, who should be gentle and humble.'

The girl's sunburnt face glowed all over, and her eyes flashed.

'They make fun of me because I won't dance and sing and stand about gossiping like the others. They ought to leave me alone; I'm not hurting them.'

'But you could be friendly to people. Leave dancing and singing for others who have an easier time of it. But even one whose life is hard can spare a kind word for his neighbour.'

She cast her eyes down and knitted her brows tighter, as if to hide her coal-black eyes beneath them. For a while they sailed on in silence. The sun now stood above the mountains in splendour, the peak of Vesuvius thrust through the clouds that still gathered about its foot, and the houses on the plateau of Sorrento could be seen, sparkling white amidst the green orange-groves.

'Have you never heard anything more of that painter, Laurella, that Neapolitan, who wanted to marry you?' asked the priest.

She shook her head.

'He came that time and wanted to paint you. Why wouldn't you let him?'

'Why should he want to? There are others prettier than I am. And then, who knows what he might have done with it. He could have used it to cast a spell on me and done something to my soul, or even killed me, so mother said.'

'Don't believe such wicked things,' said the priest, seriously. 'Are you not always in God's hands, and can a hair of your head be harmed against His will? How could a man with a picture in his hand like that be stronger than the Lord Himself? – And in any case, you could see that he was fond of you. Why else would he have wanted to marry you?'

She said nothing.

'And why did you refuse him? They say he was a fine man and quite handsome, and he could have kept you and your mother better than you can yourself now, with your bit of spinning and silk-making.'

'We are poor folk,' she said, fiercely, 'and mother has been ill for a long time now. We should only have been a burden to him. And I am not fit to marry a *signore*. If his friends had come to see him, he would have been ashamed of me.'

'What a thing to say! – I tell you he was a gentleman. And what's more, he wanted to move to Sorrento as well. It will be a long time before another one like that turns up, that might have been sent from Heaven itself to help you out.'

'I'm not going to marry, never!' she said, obstinately, and as if to no one but herself.

'Have you made a vow, or do you want to enter a convent?'
She shook her head.

'People are right to hold your wilfulness against you, even if that name isn't a pretty one. Haven't you considered that you're not alone in this world, and that your stubbornness only makes your sick mother's life and her sickness the harder to bear? What sound reasons can you have for refusing every honest hand that offers you and your mother support? Answer me, Laurella!'

'I do have a reason,' she said softly and hesitantly. 'But I can't tell you what it is.'

'Can't tell? Can't tell me? Your confessor? I thought you knew that he was there to help you. Didn't you know that?'

She nodded.

'Then unburden your heart to me, my child. If you are right to do as you do, I will be the first to say so. But you are young and have seen very little of the world, and one day later you might be sorry, if you find you have thrown away your happiness for the sake of some childish notion.'

She cast a fleeting, nervous glance at the lad sitting towards the stern of the boat, rowing busily away, with his woollen cap pulled down over his forehead. He was staring sideways into the sea and seemed to be lost in his own thoughts. The priest saw her look and leant his ear closer to her.

'You didn't know my father,' she whispered, and her eyes darkened.

'Your father? He died, didn't he, when you were scarcely ten years old. What has your father – may his soul rest in paradise! – what has he to do with your wilful ways?'

'You didn't know him, *padre*. You wouldn't know it, but mother's illness was all his fault.'

'Why was it?'

'Because he ill-treated her and beat her and kicked her. I can still remember the nights when he came home in a rage. She would never say a word, and would do everything he wanted. I used to pull the blanket over my head and pretend to be asleep, but I would cry all night long. And then when he saw her lying on the floor he used to change all of a sudden and lift her up and kiss her so that she would cry out that he was stifling her. Mother told me I was never to say a word about it; but she took it badly, she has never got over it, all these years that he's been dead. And if she should die before her time, Heaven preserve us, then I know who it was who killed her.'

The little priest shook his head and seemed uncertain, after her confession, whether to approve or blame. Finally he said, 'Forgive him, as your mother forgave him. Do not keep thinking about those sad scenes, Laurella. Better days will make you forget all that.'

'I shall never forget it,' she said and shuddered. 'And let me tell you, *padre*, that's why I shall stay a maid, so I shan't have to obey anyone who ill-treated me and then made love to me. If anyone now tries to hit me or kiss me, I can defend my self. But my mother couldn't defend herself, couldn't fight the blows or the kisses, because she loved him. And I'm not going to love anyone if it's going to make me sick and wretched.'

'Now aren't you behaving like a child and talking as if you knew nothing of life on this earth? Are all men like your poor father, to give way to every whim and passion and treat their wives badly? Haven't you come across enough honest people hereabouts, and women who live in peace and harmony with their husbands?'

'Nobody knew how my father treated my mother either, for she would rather have died a thousand times over than go complaining to anyone. And all that was because she loved him. If that's what love is like, making you shut your mouth when you ought to be crying out for help, and leaving you defenceless against worse than your worst enemy could do to you, then I'll not throw my heart away to any man.'

'I tell you, you are a child and don't know what you are saying. A lot your heart will ask you about it, whether you want to love or not, when the time has come for it; then it won't be any use, any of the notions you're getting into your head now.'

After another pause: 'And that painter, did you think he was the kind of man that would ill-treat you?'

'He sometimes had the kind of look that I used to see in my father's face when he was asking my mother's forgiveness and taking her in his arms to say sweet things to her again. I know that look. A man can give you that look and find it in his heart to beat his wife when she'd never done anything against him. I was frightened when I saw that look again.'

With that she said no more, and remained silent. The priest too was silent. He thought of all kinds of fine things, to be sure, that he could have said to the girl. But the presence of the young sailor, who had seemed more agitated towards the end of her confession, sealed his lips for him.

When, after two hours' journey, they arrived in the little harbour of Capri, Antonino carried the clergyman from the boat over the last shallow waves and set him respectfully down. But Laurella hadn't wanted to wait for him to wade back again and fetch her. She tucked up her skirt, took her wooden clogs in her right hand and her bundle in her left, and paddled quickly ashore.

'I expect I shall be a long time on Capri today,' said the *padre*, 'and you don't need to wait for me. It may even be tomorrow before I come home. And you, Laurella, when you get home again, give your mother my regards. I shall be in to see you some time this week. You'll be returning before night?'

'If there's a chance,' said the girl, busying herself with her skirt.

'You know I have to go back too,' said Antonino very casually, or so he thought. 'I'll wait for you until Ave Maria. If you're not there then, I shan't mind.'

'You must be there, Laurella,' the little man spoke up. 'You must not leave your mother alone all night. Have you far to go?'

'To Anacapri, to one of the vineyards.'

'And I have to go to Capri. God bless you, child, and you, my son!'

Laurella kissed his hand and let fall a goodbye that seemed meant for the *padre* and Antonino to share, but Antonino for his part took no notice. He touched his cap to the *padre* and didn't look at Laurella.

But when they had both turned their backs on him, it was only for a short time that his eye followed the cleric, making his way with effort over the deep shingle of the beach; then he turned to look at the girl climbing the hillside to the right, shielding her eyes with her hand against the sun's glare. Before the path disappeared behind stone walls, she stopped for a moment as if to take breath, and looked around her. The sea-front lay at her feet, all around the steep cliffs rose, and the sea was azure beyond compare – it was indeed a prospect worth stopping still to view. As chance would have it, her glance skimming Antonino's boat met the glance he had cast in her direction. They made a movement, each of them, like people excusing themselves for something that they did not mean to do; then, tight-lipped, the girl continued on her way.

It was only an hour afternoon, and Antonino had already been sitting for two hours on the bench in front of the fishermen's tavern. Surely there was something on his mind, for every five minutes he would jump up, go out into the sunshine, and carefully scan the paths that lead to left and right towards the island's two townships. He didn't like the look of the weather, he told the landlady of the *osteria*. Yes, it was clear now, but he knew that tinge about the sky and the sea. It had been just like that before the last great storm, when he had only just managed to get the English family ashore. Didn't she remember?

No, the woman said.

Well, she was to think of him, if it were to change before nightfall.

'Are there many ladies and gentlemen over there?' the landlady asked, after a while.

'It's just starting. It's been bad up to now. The ones who come to bathe haven't shown up yet.'

'Spring was late. You'll have earned more than we have on Capri.'

'There wouldn't have been enough for macaroni twice a week, if the boat was all I had. Just a letter to take to Naples now and then or a *signore* to take out fishing – that's all. But you know my uncle has the big orange-groves and he's a rich man. Tonino, he says, as long as I'm alive, you'll be all right, and I'll see you're taken care of when I'm gone. So I got through the winter, with God's help.'

'Has he any children, your uncle?'

'No. He was never married. He was abroad for a long time, and made a tidy penny. Now he wants to set up a big fishing business and put me in charge of it to look after it properly.'

The young boatman shrugged his shoulders. 'Everyone has his bundle to carry,' he said. Then he jumped up and looked at the weather again to left and right, although he surely knew that it only comes from one direction at a time.

'I'll bring you another bottle. Your uncle can pay for it,' said the landlady.

'Only another glass. This wine of yours is fiery stuff. I can feel it going to my head already.'

'It won't get into your blood. You can drink as much as you like. Here's my husband just coming, you'll have to stay and talk to him for a while.'

And indeed, his net hanging over his shoulder, his red cap set on his curly hair, the *padrone* of the inn came striding down grandly from the hill. He had been taking fish to town; that fine lady had ordered it, to serve to the little priest from Sorrento. As he saw the young boatman there, he waved his hand in cordial welcome, then sat down beside him on the bench and began to talk and ask questions. His wife was just bringing another bottle of real, unadulterated Capri, when the sand rustled on the beach to their left and Laurella came along the path from Anacapri. She nodded a curt greeting and stood there, hesitant.

Antonino jumped up. 'I must go,' he said. 'It's a girl from Sorrento that came over this morning with the *signor curato* and wants to get back home to her sick mother by nightfall.'

'Well, it's a long time till nightfall,' said the fisherman. 'She'll have time for a glass of wine with us. Here, wife, bring another glass.'

'Thank you, I won't,' said Laurella and stayed at a distance.

'Pour it out, wife, pour it out! She'll change her mind.'

'Let her be,' said the lad. 'She's an obstinate one; if she doesn't want to do something, then the saints couldn't persuade her.' And with that he bade a hasty farewell, ran down to the boat, untied the painter, and stood there waiting for the girl. She turned and nodded once more to the landlord and his wife, and then walked with uncertain steps towards the boat. She looked round first in all directions, as if she expected other passengers to be coming. But the seashore was deserted. The fishermen were asleep or were at sea with rods and nets; a few women and children were sitting in the doorways, asleep or spinning, and the visitors who had come across in the morning were waiting for a cooler time of day for their return. She was not able to look round for too long, for before she could stop him Antonino had taken her up in his arms and was carrying her like a child to the skiff. Then he jumped aboard after her, and with a few strokes of the oars they were on the open sea.

She had sat down towards the bows and half turned her back to him, so that he could only see her from the side. Her features were even graver now than usual. Her hair hung low over her forehead, a wilful expression played about her finely chiselled nostrils, her full lips were tightly pursed. When they had been travelling thus in silence across the sea for a while, she began to feel the sun, took her loaf of bread out of her kerchief and bound the cloth over her braided hair. Then she began to eat from the loaf, which was her midday meal; for she had had nothing to eat while she had been on Capri.

Antonino did not simply watch for long. From one of the baskets which that morning had been full of oranges he produced two, saying, 'There's something to eat with your bread, Laurella. Don't think I've been keeping them for you. They had rolled out of the basket into the boat, and I found them when I was stowing the empty baskets on board again.'

'You eat them. My loaf is enough for me.'

'They're refreshing in the heat, and you have had a long way to walk.'

'They gave me a glass of water up there, that refreshed me.'

'As you like,' he said, and let them drop back into the basket.

Silence again. The sea was as smooth as glass, and made scarcely a ripple against the keel. And the white sea-birds too, that rest in the caves ashore, hunted their prey in soundless flight.

'You could take those two oranges to your mother,' Antonino began again.

'We have enough of them at home, and when they are all gone I can go and buy some more.'

'Go on, take them, and my compliments to her.'

'She doesn't know you.'

'Then you could tell her about me.'

'I don't know you either.'

It was not the first time that she had denied knowing him like that. A year ago, just after the painter had come to Sorrento, it happened one Sunday that Antonino and some of the other young village lads were playing *boccia* in an open space beside the high road. It was there that the painter had first seen Laurella, as she went by bearing a water-pitcher on her head, taking no notice of him. The Neapolitan, struck by the sight of her, stood gazing after her, although he was standing in the middle of their bowling-alley and with two paces could have left it clear. A ball struck his ankle, as a sharp reminder that this was not the place to lose himself in contemplation. He looked round as if expecting an apology. The young boatman whose throw it had been stood defiantly silent amid the group of his friends, and the stranger found it prudent to avoid a quarrel and withdraw. But people had talked about the little scene and began to talk about it again when the painter paid open suit to Laurella. I don't know who he is, she said crossly, when the painter asked her if it was for the sake of that rude youth that she was refusing him. And yet some of that talk had come to her ears. Later, when she had met Antonino, she had recognized him, after all.

And now there they sat in the boat like the bitterest of enemies, and both their hearts were beating like death. Antonino's usually cheerful face was flushed with anger; he dug his oars into the waves so that the spray flew over him, and his lips quivered from time to time as if he were speaking words of malice. She pretended not to notice and wore her most unconcerned expression, leant over the gunwale of the skiff, and let the waves run through her fingers. Then she untied her kerchief again and tidied her hair as if she were by herself in the boat. Only her eyebrows puckered still, and in vain she held her wet hands to her burning cheeks to cool them.

Now they were out on the open sea, and far and wide not a sail was to be seen. The island was left behind them, the coast lay far off in the haze, not even a seagull was there to break the solitude. Antonino looked about him. A thought seemed to come to his mind. Suddenly the colour drained from his cheeks, and he let fall the oars. Involuntarily Laurella looked round to see what he was doing, tense but without fear.

'I must have done,' the lad burst out. 'It's gone on far too long and it's a wonder to me that it hasn't been the death of me. You say you don't know me? Haven't you stood there watching often enough when I went by you like a madman, with my heart filled to overflowing with what I wanted to tell you? Then you would pout like that and turn your back on me.'

'What did I have to talk to you about?' she said curtly. 'I could see you wanted to start something with me. But I didn't want people gossiping about me when there was nothing in it, nothing! For I don't want you for a husband, not you nor any other man.'

'Nor any other? You won't always talk like that. Because you sent that painter packing? Pah! You were only a child then. One day you'll start feeling lonely, and then, mad as you are, you'll take the first that comes along.'

'No one knows what the future may bring. Perhaps I'll change my mind. What business is it of yours?'

'What business of mine?' he cried out, and started up from the thwart so that the whole boat rocked. 'What business of mine? And you can ask that, when you know very well how I feel? A miserable end to any man you treat better than you've treated me!'

'Did I ever make any promises to you? Can I help it if you are out of your mind? What right have you got to me?'

'Oh,' he shouted, 'it's not in writing, I admit, I haven't had a lawyer draw it up in Latin and seal it; but let me tell you this, I've as much right to you as I have to go to heaven if I've lived a good life. Do you think I am going to stand by and watch you going to church with another man, and the girls shrugging their shoulders as they pass me by? Am I going to stand for a disgrace like that?'

She drew back a little and flashed her eyes at him.

'Kill me if you dare,' she said slowly.

'No job should be left half done,' he said, and his voice was hoarse. 'There's room for us both in the sea. I can't help you, child,' – and he spoke almost with pity, as if he were dreaming – 'but we must both go under, both of us, at once, and now!' – he screamed, and seized her suddenly with both hands. But in the same moment he drew back his right hand, the blood was flowing, she had bitten him savagely.

'Must I do what you want?' she cried, and pushed him away with a quick movement. 'We shall see if I am in your power!' And with that she leapt overboard from the boat and disappeared for a moment in the depths of the water. Straight away she came up again; her skirt was clinging tightly to her, the waves had loosened her hair and it hung heavy about her throat; with vigorous strokes of her arms she swam powerfully away from the boat towards the shore, not uttering a sound. The sudden fright seemed to have robbed him of his senses. He stood in the boat bending forward, staring fixedly in her direction as if a miracle were taking place before his eyes. Then he shook himself, rushed to seize the oars, and made after her with all the strength he could muster, while the bottom of the boat turned red with the blood that flowed freely over it.

In a trice he was beside her, quickly as she swam. 'In the name of the Blessed Virgin,' he cried, 'come aboard! I must have gone mad; God knows what clouded my mind. It was like a flash of lightning from heaven in my brain, that made me blaze up so I didn't know what I was doing or saying. I'm not asking you to forgive me, Laurella, only to save your life and come aboard again.'

She swam as if she had heard nothing.

'You will never get to land, it is still two *miglie*. Think of your mother! If anything should happen to you I should die of horror.'

She measured with her glance the distance to the shore. Then, without replying, she swam up to the boat and took hold of the gunwale with her hands. He stood up to help her;

his jacket, that had been lying on the seat, slid into the water as the girl's weight tilted the skiff to one side. Deftly she hoisted herself up and climbed into her former place. When he saw that she was safely aboard, he took up the oars again. She meanwhile twisted out her dripping skirt and wrung the water from her plaits. As she did so her gaze fell upon the floor of the boat and she saw the blood. She looked quickly at his hand, pulling at its oar as if unhurt. 'Here!' she said, and held out her kerchief to him. He shook his head and rowed on. At last she stood up, went over to him and bound the cloth tightly about the deep wound. Then, despite all his resistance, she took one of the oars from his hand, sat down on the other seat, but without looking at him, fixed her eyes on the oar, stained with blood, and drove the boat on with powerful strokes. They were both pale and silent. As they came closer to the shore, they were met by fishermen, coming out to drop their nets for the night. They called out to Antonino and teased Laurella. Neither looked up or answered a word.

The sun was still fairly high over Procida when they reached the *marina*. Laurella shook out her skirt, that had almost completely dried in crossing the sea, and leapt ashore. There again, spinning on the roof, was the old woman who had watched them set out that morning. 'What have you done to your hand, Tonino?' she called down to them. 'Christ Jesus, your boat's awash with blood!'

'It's nothing, *commare*,' answered the lad. 'I cut myself on a nail that was sticking out too far. It'll be gone tomorrow. The blood comes so quickly, curse it, it makes it look worse than it is.'

'I'll come and dress it with herbs for you, *comparello*. Wait, I'm coming.'

'Don't bother, *commare*. It's all done, and tomorrow it'll be gone and forgotten. I've a sound hide, it grows quickly and heals any wounds.'

'*Addio!*' said Laurella and turned to the path that climbs the hill.

'Good night!' the lad called after her, without looking up at her. Then he carried the things out of the boat and the baskets too and climbed the few stone steps that led to his cottage.

There was no one except him in the two little rooms where he was now pacing up and down. At the small window-openings, which only had wooden shutters to cover them, the air came in in a breeze, more refreshing than out on the calm sea, and he felt better in the solitude. He stood for a long time before the little image of the Mother of God too and gazed reverently at the starry halo she wore, made of silver paper stuck on. But it did not occur to him to pray. What should he have asked for, now that he had lost all hope?

And the day seemed to stand still. He longed for it to be dark, for he was tired, and the loss of blood had affected him more than he liked to admit. He felt a violent pain in his hand, sat down on a stool, and untied the bandage. The blood that had been staunched came spurting again, and his hand was badly swollen around the wound. He washed it carefully and cooled it for a long time. When he took it out again, he could clearly see the marks of Laurella's teeth. 'She was right,' he said. 'I was like a wild beast and I don't deserve any better. I'll give Giuseppe the kerchief to take back to her tomorrow, because she won't be seeing me again.' And so he washed the kerchief carefully and spread it out in the sun, after he had bandaged up his hand again as best he could with his left hand and his teeth. Then he threw himself down on his bed and closed his eyes.

The bright moonlight woke him from a half-sleep, the pain in his hand at the same time. He was just jumping up again to calm the throbbing of his blood in some water when he heard a noise outside. 'Who is there?' he called and opened the door. Laurella stood before him.

Without stopping to ask, she came in. She threw off the kerchief that she had tied over her head, and put a little basket down on the table. Then she drew a deep breath.

'You've come for your kerchief,' he said; 'you could have saved yourself the trouble, for I would have asked Giuseppe first thing tomorrow to bring it back to you.'

'It's not about the kerchief,' she answered quickly. 'I have been on the mountain fetching herbs for you, to stop the bleeding. Here!' And she lifted the lid from the basket.

'You shouldn't bother,' he said, without any trace of bitterness, 'you shouldn't bother. It's better already, much better; and even if it was worse, it would be what I deserved. What are you doing here at this hour? Suppose someone came and found you here? You know how they gossip, even though they don't know what they are talking about.'

'I don't care about anyone,' she said fiercely. 'But I want to look at your hand, and put these herbs on it, for you won't be able to manage with your left.'

'I tell you it isn't necessary.'

'Let me see then, and I'll believe you.'

She seized his hand without further ado, as he could not stop her, and untied the strips of rag. As she saw how it had swollen, she started and cried out: 'Jesus Maria!'

'It's gathered a bit,' he said. 'That'll be gone in a day and a night.'

She shook her head: 'You won't be able to go to sea for a week like that.'

'The day after tomorrow, I hope. What does it matter, anyhow?'

Meanwhile she had fetched a basin and washed the wound anew; he endured it like a child. Then she put the healing leaves of her herbs on it, that eased the burning straight away, and bandaged his hand with strips of linen she had brought with her.

When it was done he said, 'I'm very grateful. And listen, if you want to do me another kindness, forgive me for going mad like that today, and forget all that I said and did. I don't know how it happened myself. You have never given me any cause to behave like that, you really haven't. And I'll never say anything more to offend you.'

'It's my place to ask you to forgive me,' she broke in. 'I ought to have explained everything differently and better and not made you angry, being dumb like that. And as for that wound –'

'It was self-defence, and high time I was brought to my senses again. And as I said, there's nothing to it. Don't talk about forgiving. You've been kind to me and I'm grateful. And now go home to bed, and here – is your kerchief, so you can take it with you straight away.'

He held it out to her, but she was still standing there and seemed to be struggling with herself. At last she said, 'You've lost your jacket on my account too, and I know the money for the oranges was in it. I only thought of it on the way. But I can't make it up to you, because we haven't got it, and if we had it would be mother's. But I've got this silver cross that the painter put on the table for me, the last time he was with us. I haven't looked at it since and I don't want it in my box any longer. If you can sell it – that must be worth a few piastres, mother said at the time – then it would make up for what you've lost, and what's left I'll try to earn spinning, at night when mother's gone to sleep.'

'I'm not taking anything,' he said curtly and pushed back the little shining cross that she had taken out of her pocket.

'You must take it,' she said. 'Who knows how long it will be before you can earn anything with your hand like that? There it is, and I don't ever want to set eyes on it again.'

'Then throw it into the sea.'

'It's not a present I'm giving you; it's nothing more than your right and what belongs to you.'

'Right? I've no right to anything that's yours. If you should ever meet me again, do me a kindness and don't look at me, so I shan't think you're reminding me of what I owe you. And now, good night, and let that be all between us.'

He put her kerchief in the basket and the cross with it, and shut the lid on them. But when he looked up and saw her face he was startled. Big, heavy drops were pouring down her cheeks. She let them flow.

'*Maria santissima!*' he cried, 'are you ill? You are trembling from head to toe.'

'It's nothing,' she said. 'I must go home,' and she tottered towards the door. Her tears overwhelmed her, and she pressed her forehead against the doorpost and sobbed loud and violently. But before he could reach her to hold her back, she suddenly turned and fell about his neck.

'I can't bear it,' she cried and pressed him to her as a dying man clutches at life, 'I can't bear to hear you saying kind things to me and sending me away from you with all my guilty conscience. Beat me, kick me, curse me! – or if it's true that you are fond of me, even after all the harm I have done to you, then take me and keep me and do what you want with me. But don't send me away like that!' Violent sobs interrupted her once more.

He held her for a while in his arms, speechless. 'I still love you?' he cried at last. 'Holy Mother of God! did you think I had lost all my heart's blood with that one little wound? Don't you feel it beating there in my breast, as if it wanted to leap out to you? If you are only saying it to tempt me, or because you are sorry for me, then go, and I will forget that too. You shan't think you owe me anything, because you know what I suffer for you.'

'No,' she said firmly and looked up from his shoulder and straight into his face with her tear-filled eyes, 'I love you, and I'll have to confess it, I've been afraid of it for a long time and fought against it. And now I will behave differently, for I can't bear it any longer, not to look at you when you pass me by in the street. And now I am going to kiss you,' she said, 'so you can tell yourself, if you should be in doubt again: she kissed me, and Laurella will kiss no man but the man she is going to marry.'

She kissed him three times, and then she freed herself from his embrace and said, 'Good night, darling! Go to sleep now and let your hand get better, and don't come with me because I'm not afraid, not of anyone, only of you.'

And she slipped through the door and vanished in the shadow of the wall. But he stood a long time looking through the window, out at the sea over which all the stars seemed to be wheeling.

The next time the little *padre curato* left the confessional where Laurella had been kneeling so long, it was with a quiet, private smile. Who would have thought, he said to himself, that God would so soon take pity on this strange heart? And there was I reproaching myself for not having warned her more severely against the demon obduracy. But our eyes are too short-sighted for the ways of Heaven. Well then, may the Lord bless her and let me live to be ferried over the sea by Laurella's eldest, in his father's place! Well, well, well, *l' Arrabbiata*!

Gerhart Hauptmann

THIEL THE CROSSING-KEEPER

Translated by John Bednall

Gerhart Hauptmann

ALTHOUGH it was only in 1946 that Hauptmann died, at the age of eighty-four, he is principally remembered as the leading light of the Naturalist movement of the end of the nineteenth century, and his fame rests chiefly upon his plays. The early story *Thiel the Crossing-Keeper* (1888) is also typical of Naturalism: in its pessimistic portrayal of life in a humble, even sordid setting and its deterministic view of human beings as creatures of their material environment, and also in its compassion and the symbolic concentration which raises the writing above the mere chronicling of facts.

THIEL THE CROSSING-KEEPER

I

Every Sunday Thiel the level-crossing-keeper sat in church at Neu-Zittau, except for the days when he was on duty or lay ill in bed. In ten years he had only been sick twice: once because he was struck by a lump of coal which fell from the tender of a passing locomotive and hurled him into the ditch with a shattered leg, and the other time because of a wine-bottle which flew from an express as it rushed past and hit him squarely in the chest. Apart from these two accidents, nothing had been able to keep him away from church as soon as he was off duty.

For the first five years he had had to walk the distance from Schön-Schornstein, a settlement on the river Spree, to Neu-Zittau alone. Then one fine day he had appeared in the company of a rather delicate and sickly looking female who, as people said, was ill-matched to his herculean frame. And on another fine Sunday afternoon, at the altar, he solemnly gave his hand in lifelong union to this same person. So for two years the frail-looking young woman sat by his side in the pew; for two years her sensitive, hollow-cheeked face and his brown, weather-beaten visage gazed side by side into the ancient hymn-book – and then, suddenly, the level-crossing-keeper sat there alone again as before.

On one of the days during the previous week the funeral bell had tolled; that was all there was to it.

In the level-crossing-keeper, people declared, there was scarcely any observable change. The buttons on his clean Sunday uniform were as brightly polished as before, his red hair was as well-greased, his parting as military as ever; the only difference was that he carried his hairy-naped neck a little bent, and sang hymns or listened to the sermon still more earnestly than before. The general opinion was that his wife's death had not affected him very deeply, and this opinion was confirmed when, after a year had elapsed, Thiel married again, this time a stout, strapping wench, a milkmaid from Alte-Grund.

When Thiel came to announce the wedding, even the pastor allowed himself to express a few misgivings:

'So you want to marry again already?'

'A dead woman can't keep house for me, Pastor.'

'Well, yes – but I mean – you're in a bit of a hurry.'

'I'll lose the boy, Pastor.'

Thiel's wife had died in childbed, and the son she had borne had survived and been given the name of Tobias.

'Ah, yes, the boy,' said the clergyman and made a gesture which showed clearly that he had only just remembered the baby. 'That's a different matter – where is he being looked after while you are on duty?'

Thiel described how he had handed Tobias over to the care of an old woman; once she had almost let him be burned, while on another occasion he had rolled off her lap on to the floor, fortunately coming off with nothing worse than a large bump. Things couldn't go on like that, he said, particularly since the boy, delicate as he was, needed special care. On this account and, moreover, because he had vowed, holding the dead woman's hand in his, that he would at all times take the greatest care of the boy, he had resolved upon this step.

Outwardly, people could find nothing to criticize in the new couple who now came every Sunday to church. The former milkmaid seemed as if she had been made for the level-crossing-keeper. She was scarcely half a head shorter than he, and excelled him in the massiveness of her limbs. Her features, too, were just as coarse as his, contrasting with Thiel's only in their complete lack of soul.

If it had been Thiel's wish to possess in his second wife a tireless worker and model housekeeper, then it had been astoundingly fulfilled. But with his wife he had been obliged, without knowing it, to take three other things into the bargain: a hard, domineering disposition, a love of quarrelling, and a proneness to fits of brutal passion. After six months the whole village knew who wore the trousers in the crossing-keeper's cottage. People were sorry for Thiel.

It was a slice of luck for the farm-wench that she had hooked such a docile creature as Thiel, declared the indignant husbands – there were some with whom she'd really have run into horrible trouble. Surely an animal like that could be brought to heel, they said, and if nothing else would do, there would have to be blows. A sound thrashing was what she would need, one that really hurt.

But despite his sinewy arms Thiel was not the man to thrash her. The things which other people got excited about seemed to bother him hardly at all. He submitted without a word to his wife's endless tirades, and if he did answer, the dragging tempo and cool, gentle tone of his speech made a strange contrast with his wife's screeching and scolding. The outside world seemed to have little effect upon him: it seemed as if he bore something within him which afforded ample compensation for all the evil the world did him.

Despite his unshakeably phlegmatic disposition, there were moments when he was not to be trifled with, always in matters concerning little Tobias. His soft-natured, childlike goodness then took on a firmness of hue which even Lene's intractable temperament did not dare to oppose.

However, the occasions on which he displayed this side of his character grew fewer and fewer as time passed, and finally ceased altogether. A kind of passive resistance which he had offered to Lene's domination during the first year also faded in the course of the second. After a scene with her he no longer went on duty with his earlier indifference if he had not pacified her first. Not infrequently he even descended to begging her to be friends with him again. His lonely post in the depths of the Brandenburg pine forest was no longer the favourite refuge it once had been. His quiet, devoted thoughts of his dead wife were interrupted by thoughts of the living one. No longer, as in the early days, did he set off home with reluctance, but rather with passionate haste, having frequently been counting the hours till the moment he was relieved.

He who had been bound to his first wife by a spiritualized

kind of love was now driven into the power of his second wife by the force of brute instincts, and finally became almost totally dependent upon her. At times his conscience pricked him about this change in circumstances, and he had need of a number of unusual expedients in order to overcome it. Thus he secretly declared his crossing-keeper's cabin and the section of track under his care to be holy ground, as it were, exclusively dedicated to the shade of the dead woman. By employing all manner of pretexts he had, in fact, so far managed to prevent his wife from accompanying him there.

He hoped to be able to do this in the future as well. She would not have known which direction to take in order to find his cabin; she did not even know its number.

By thus conscientiously dividing the time at his disposal between the living woman and the dead, Thiel did actually set his conscience at rest.

Frequently, of course, and in particular during moments of solitary communion when he had been fervently united with the dead woman, he saw his present condition in its true light and was filled with disgust at it.

When he was on day-duty he confined his spiritual intercourse with the dead woman to a host of pleasant memories from the period of their life together; but in the darkness, when the snowstorm howled through the pines and across the track, deep in the night, by the light of his lantern – then the crossing-keeper's little cabin became a chapel.

With a faded photograph of the dead woman before him on the table, and Bible and hymn-book open, he alternately read and sang the long night through, interrupted only by the trains which hurtled past at intervals; by so doing he worked himself into a kind of ecstasy giving rise to visions in which he saw the dead woman physically before him.

The post which the crossing-keeper had occupied uninterruptedly for ten years was certainly of a kind likely to encourage his mystical leanings.

To all four points of the compass a walk of at least three quarters of an hour separated the cabin from the nearest human habitation; it lay in the heart of the forest close

beside a level-crossing with barriers which it was Thiel's duty
to operate.

In summer, days passed by, in winter, whole weeks, without any human being apart from Thiel and his colleague
setting foot on that section of the track. The weather and the
changing seasons with their periodic cycles brought the only
variety that wilderness knew. Apart from his two accidents,
the only other occurrences to interrupt the regular course of
Thiel's duties can easily be recalled. Four years ago the
Imperial Special which carried the Emperor to Breslau had
roared past. One winter's night the express had run over a
roebuck. One hot summer's day while on line inspection Thiel
had found a corked wine-bottle which was burning hot to the
touch. He imagined the contents to be very good, since they
spurted out like a fountain when the cork was removed, and
so had obviously fermented. This bottle, which Thiel laid in
the shallow edge of a woodland pool to cool off, somehow
vanished from the spot, a loss that he still lamented years
later. A well immediately behind his cabin afforded the level-
crossing-keeper an occasional diversion. From time to time
railwaymen or telegraph engineers who were working in the
neighbourhood had a drink from it, and it was natural for
brief conversations to arise in consequence. The forester, too,
came on occasion to quench his thirst.

Tobias only developed slowly: it was not until the end of
his second year that he learned to walk and talk after a fashion.
He showed a quite especial attachment to his father. As he
became more sensible, his father's old affection reawakened
too. In proportion, as this grew, his stepmother's love for
Tobias decreased, and even changed to unmistakeable dislike
when, after a year had passed, Lene herself bore a son.

A bad time began for Tobias from then on. He was incessantly tormented, particularly in his father's absence, and
was obliged, without receiving the smallest reward for it, to
expend his feeble energies in the service of the screaming
infant, wearing himself out more and more in the process.
His head grew to an abnormal circumference; his flaming red hair with the chalk-white face beneath it made a

disagreeable impression; taken together with the rest of his puny frame, the effect was pitiful. When the backward child dragged himself thus down to the Spree with his little brother – an infant bursting with health – in his arms, imprecations were muttered behind cottage windows, but no one dared to utter them aloud. But Thiel, who was, after all, the one most directly concerned in the business, appeared quite blind to it all and was unable or unwilling to pay heed to the hints dropped by well-meaning neighbours.

2

At about seven o'clock of a June morning Thiel came off duty. No sooner had his wife finished greeting him than she started her customary grumbling. The lease on the plot of ground which till then had kept the family in potatoes had been withdrawn some weeks ago, and so far Lene had not succeeded in finding a substitute. Although the care of the plot was one of Lene's responsibilities, Thiel was obliged to hear time and again that he alone would be to blame if they had to buy ten sacks of potatoes this year at an enormous price. Thiel only mumbled and, paying scant attention to Lene's words, went over at once to the bed of his eldest, which he shared with him on nights when he was not on duty. Here he sat down and watched the sleeping child with a solicitous expression on his good-natured face. He kept the persistent flies away for a while, and then woke him. A touchingly joyful look came into the deep-set blue eyes as he awoke. He hastily grabbed at his father's hand, while the corners of his mouth were drawn back in a pathetic smile. Thiel at once helped him to put on his few bits of clothing, and whilst he was doing so a kind of shadow passed suddenly across his features when he noticed that several red and white fingermarks stood out on the slightly swollen right cheek.

Over breakfast, when Lene returned with renewed zeal to the housekeeping topic she had previously raised, he cut her off with the news that the Inspector of the Permanent Way had given him free a patch of ground close alongside the track, apparently because it was too remote for him.

At first Lene would not believe it. However, her doubts gradually faded, and then she became remarkably good-humoured. Her questions as to the size and quality of the plot, and many others as well, fairly tumbled over one another, and when she learned that, in addition, two dwarf fruit-trees were growing there, she was quite beside herself. At last there were no more questions to ask; moreover, the shop-keeper's doorbell, which, incidentally, could be heard in every single house in the village, was going continuously, so she rushed off to spread the news around.

While Lene was making her way to the shopkeeper's dark room with its bulging piles of goods, Thiel was at home devoting himself entirely to Tobias. The boy sat on his knees playing with some pine-cones which Thiel had brought with him from the forest.

'What do you want to be?' his father asked him, and the question was as stereotyped as the boy's reply: 'An Inspector of the Permanent Way.' The question was not meant as a joke, for the crossing-keeper's dreams did in fact aspire to such heights. He did in all seriousness hope and desire that Tobias might with God's help become something out of the ordinary. As soon as the child's anaemic lips uttered the reply 'An Inspector of the Permanent Way' (he did not know what it meant, of course), Thiel's face lit up until it fairly beamed with inward delight.

'Go on, Tobias, go and play,' he said shortly afterwards, lighting a pipe of tobacco with a shaving from the fire, and the child immediately slipped out through the door, shy and happy. Thiel undressed, got into bed and fell asleep after staring thoughtfully for some time at the low, cracked ceiling. He awoke towards the hour of noon and put on his clothes. While his wife was preparing their dinner in her noisy fashion, he went out into the street, where he at once snatched up Tobias, who was scratching lime out of a hole in the wall with his fingers and putting it in his mouth. The crossing-keeper took him by the hand and walked with him past the eight or so cottages in the village down to the Spree, which lay black and glassy between the sparse foliage of the poplars. Close by the water's edge lay a block of granite; on this Thiel sat down.

The whole village had got used to seeing him at this spot whenever the weather was at all suitable. The children were particularly attached to him and called him 'father Thiel' whilst he taught them many games remembered from his own youth. But his choicest memories were reserved for Tobias. He whittled arrows for him which flew higher than those of any of the other boys. He cut reed-pipes for him and even condescended to sing the appropriate invocation in his creaky bass while softly tapping the bark with the horn handle of his pocket-knife.

People took his childish tricks amiss; they couldn't imagine how he could devote so much time to snotty-nosed youngsters. But deep down they could well be quite pleased about it, for the children were safe under his care. Moreover, Thiel made them spend time on more serious matters. He heard the big ones' school-exercises, helped them learn verses from the Bible and songbooks, spelled out simple words with the little ones, and so forth.

After dinner Thiel lay down again for a short rest. When this was over, he drank his afternoon coffee and at once began to get ready for duty. He needed a great deal of time for this, as for everything he did. Each action had been fixed for years. The objects carefully laid out on the walnut chest of drawers always disappeared into his pockets in precisely the same order: knife, pocket-book, comb, a horse's tooth, the old watch in its case. A little book wrapped in red paper was always handled with particular care. During the night it lay under Thiel's pillow, and in the daytime it was always carried around in the breast pocket of his uniform. On the label under the wrapper, in clumsy but florid characters written by Thiel himself, were the words: 'Tobias Thiel's savings-book'.

The clock on the wall with its long pendulum and jaundiced face stood at a quarter to five when Thiel left. A small boat, his own property, took him across the river. On the far bank he paused several times, listening for sound from the village. Finally he turned into a broad woodland path and after a few minutes found himself in the depths of the murmuring pine-forest. Its coniferous masses surged like the waves of a dark green sea. Silently, as if on felt, he walked over the damp moss and pine-needles carpeting the forest floor. He picked his way without looking up, now passing between the rust-brown columns of the tall trees, now traversing a tangled network of young saplings, now crossing extended clearings overshadowed by slim, lofty pines which had been spared as protection for the new growth. The earth exhaled a bluish vapour, transparent and heavy with many perfumes, which caused the shapes of the trees to appear indistinct. A heavy, milky sky hung low over the treetops. Swarms of rooks appeared to bathe in the greyness of the air and uttered ceaselessly their grating cry. Black pools of water filled the hollows of the path and reflected even more dimly the dimness of the scenery round about.

Terrible weather, thought Thiel, awakening from his profound reverie and looking up.

But his thoughts suddenly took a new direction. He had a vague feeling that he must have left something at home, and in fact discovered that he was without the bread and butter which the length of his duty-period always obliged him to take with him. He stood irresolute for a time, but then turned suddenly and hurried back in the direction of the village.

He soon reached the Spree, crossed with a few powerful oar-strokes and, sweating from every pore, at once climbed the gentle incline of the village street. The shopkeeper's mangy old poodle was lying in the middle of the street. A hooded crow was sitting on the tarred fence of a crofter's cottage. It spread its feathers, shook itself, uttered an ear-splitting caw and flapped off on whistling wings, letting itself be carried by the wind in the direction of the forest.

Of the inhabitants of the little settlement, twenty odd fishermen and foresters with their families, nothing was to be seen.

The sound of a voice screeching broke the silence, so loud and shrill that the crossing-keeper paused involuntarily. A torrent of forceful and discordant sounds assailed his ears; they seemed to come from the open gable-window of a low cottage which he knew only too well.

Stepping as softly as he could, he crept closer and could now make out quite distinctly his wife's voice. A few more steps, and he could understand most of what she was saying:

'What, you cruel, heartless rascal! Has the poor mite got to scream its lungs out with hunger, eh? Just you wait, I'll teach you how to look after it! – I'll give you something to remember.' There was silence for a few moments, then a sound was heard as if someone was beating the dust out of a suit of clothes; this was immediately followed by a fresh hail of invective.

'You wretched, useless brat,' came the words, uttered at top speed, 'do you suppose I should let my own flesh and blood starve on account of a pitiful scarecrow like you? Shut your mouth,' as a soft whimpering became audible, 'or you'll get something you won't forget for a week.'

The whimpering did not cease.

Thiel felt the heavy, irregular pounding of his heart. He began to tremble slightly. His gaze was fixed absently on the floor, and his hard, clumsy hand repeatedly brushed back a lock of wet hair which kept falling across his freckled forehead.

For a moment it threatened to overwhelm him. There was a convulsion which caused his muscles to swell and his fingers to clench into fists. He relaxed, and was left dull and limp.

With uncertain step he walked into the narrow, tiled hall. Slowly and wearily he climbed the creaking wooden stairs.

'Fie! fie! fie!' the voice began again, and the words were accompanied by the sound of someone spitting three times in a paroxysm of scorn and fury. 'You low, despicable wretch! You sly, spiteful, cowardly lout!' The words followed one another with a rising emphasis, and the voice that uttered them cracked at times from sheer strain. 'So you'd strike my boy, would you? You dare to hit the poor helpless child across the mouth, miserable brat that you are, eh? eh? I wouldn't soil my hands on you, or else –'

At this moment Thiel opened the living-room door, with the result that the rest of the sentence stuck in the startled woman's throat. She was chalk-white with fury; her lips twitched malignantly; her right hand was raised; she lowered it and grabbed at the milk-jug, from which she tried to fill a baby's bottle, but the milk ran over the neck of the bottle onto the table, so she left this task half finished and, completely beside herself with agitation, picked up first one object and then another without being able to hold anything for more than a few moments at a time. Finally she regained sufficient control of herself to let fly at her husband; what did he mean by coming home at this unusual hour? surely he didn't want to eavesdrop on her? 'That would be the last straw,' she said, and followed it up by adding that she herself had a clear conscience and could look anyone in the eye.

Thiel scarcely heard what she said. He glanced briefly at Tobias, who was howling. For a moment it seemed as if he was forcibly holding down something which rose within him, then suddenly the old phlegmatic expression spread across his tense features, curiously animated by a greedy, furtive glint of the eyes. For seconds on end his gaze roved over his wife's powerful limbs. She was still fiddling around with face averted, trying to regain her composure. Her full breasts, half naked, were swelling with agitation and threatening to burst the bodice, and her hitched-up skirts made the broad hips appear still broader. The woman seemed to exude a force, indomitable and inescapable, which Thiel felt unable to match.

Something fine as a cobweb and yet strong as steel mesh settled softly upon him, binding, subduing, enervating. He would have been incapable in this condition of addressing a single word to her, least of all a hard one, and so Tobias, crouching tear-stained and frightened in a corner, had to look on while his father, without even another glance at him, took the forgotten bread from the bench by the stove, held it out to his mother by way of sole explanation and with a brief, absent-minded nod disappeared again immediately.

3

Although Thiel covered the distance to his forest solitude in all possible haste, he still did not reach his destination until fifteen minutes after the proper time.

The assistant crossing-keeper, a man who had developed consumption as a result of the rapid and unavoidable changes of temperature which his job entailed, and who worked turn and turn about with him, stood ready to leave on the small, sandy platform of the cabin; the cabin's large black number on a white background gleamed afar through the tree-trunks.

The two men shook hands, exchanged a few brief remarks, and parted. One disappeared inside the cabin, the other walked across the line, using the continuation of the path by which Thiel had come. His spasmodic cough could be heard through the tree-trunks, close at first and then further off; with him the last human sound in this solitude died away. Today as always Thiel began by making the tiny stone square of the cabin ready for the night in his own typical fashion. He did it mechanically, his mind occupied with the impressions of the last few hours. He put his supper on the narrow, brown-painted table by one of the slit-like side windows from which one could comfortably survey the track. Next he lit a fire in the little rusty stove and put a saucepan of cold water on it. When he had put the various items of equipment, the shovel, spade, spanner, and so forth, into some sort of order, he set to cleaning his lamp and filled it straight away with fresh kerosene.

When this had been done the bell gave three shrill rings, which were then repeated, announcing that a train from the direction of Breslau had been despatched from the next station. Without displaying the least hurry, Thiel remained in the cabin for quite a time before finally stepping outside with flag and detonator-pouch in his hand and walking with slow, dragging steps along the sandy path towards the level-crossing twenty-odd paces distant. Thiel always closed and opened his barrier conscientiously before and after every train, although people very seldom used the path.

He had done his job and now waited, leaning against the black and white pole of the barrier.

To right and to left the line cut dead straight through the unending green forest. On either side of it the evergreen masses were dammed back, as it were, leaving a path clear between them which was filled by the reddish-brown gravel of the permanent way. The black parallel rails together gave the effect of a huge steel netting-stitch with narrow strands which met at some point on the horizon to the extreme north and south.

A wind had sprung up which sent soft undulations down the edges of the forest into the far distance. The telegraph-poles running alongside the track hummed in chords. Dense rows of birds perched twittering on the wires which spread like the web of some giant spider from pole to pole. A woodpecker flew laughing over Thiel's head without receiving a single glance.

The sun, which was just showing below the rim of huge banks of cloud before sinking into the greenish-black sea of treetops, poured a flood of purple light over the forest. The colonnade of pine-trunks on the far side of the track seemed to ignite from within the glow like iron.

The rails, too, began to glow like fiery serpents, but they were the first to go out. And now the glow mounted slowly upwards from the ground, leaving first the shafts of the pine-trees and then the greater part of their tops bathed in a cold, putrescent light, before finally touching the highest tips with a reddish gleam. Silently, solemnly, the sublime spectacle was enacted. The crossing-keeper still stood motionless by the barrier. Finally he stepped forward a pace. A dark speck was growing on the horizon at the point where the rails met. It got larger second by second, and yet still appeared to be standing on the same spot. Suddenly it acquired movement, drew closer. A humming and vibrating passed through the rails, a rhythmical clatter, a muffled din, growing louder and louder until finally it was not unlike the hoofbeats of an onrushing cavalry squadron. From far off the sound of a spasmodic, panting roar came swelling through the air. Then, suddenly, the silence was ripped apart. A mad raving and raging filled the whole place, the rails bent, the earth shook — a sharp clap of air-pressure — a cloud of dust, smoke, and steam, and the snorting black monster was past. Just as they had grown, so now the sounds died away. The fumes dispersed. The train dwindled to a speck as it vanished into the distance, and the ancient, holy silence closed once more over that corner of the forest.

'Minna,' whispered the level-crossing-keeper as if awakening from a dream, and walked back to his cabin. After he had made himself a thin brew of coffee, he sat down and stared, taking an occasional sip, at a dirty scrap of newspaper which he had picked up somewhere on the line.

Gradually a strange restlessness came over him. He blamed it on the heat from the stove, which filled the tiny room, and tugged open his jacket and waistcoat to make himself more comfortable. When that did not help, he got up, took a spade from the corner and went out to the little plot of ground he had been given.

It was a small, sandy strip, densely overgrown with weeds. On it stood the two dwarf fruit-trees, the glory of young blossoms covering their branches like snowy froth.

Thiel grew calmer, and a sense of silent delight crept over him.

Now to work.

The spade crunched into the soil, the damp sods fell back with a thud and crumbled to pieces.

For a time he dug without stopping. Then he suddenly paused and, shaking his head, said quite loudly and distinctly: 'No, no, that won't do,' and then again: 'No, no, that won't do at all.'

It had suddenly occurred to him that Lene would now be coming out here quite often to tend the allotment, seriously upsetting his accustomed mode of existence. And suddenly his joy in the possession of the plot turned to disgust. Hastily, as if he had been on the point of doing something wrong, he ripped the spade out of the earth and carried it back to the cabin. Here he relapsed once more into his broodings. He scarcely knew why, but the prospect of having Lene with him for days on end while he was on duty grew more and more unbearable, however hard he strove to reconcile himself to it. It seemed as if he had to defend something of value to him, as if someone were trying to lay hands on what was most sacred to him, and his muscles tensed involuntarily in a mild spasm, while a short, challenging laugh escaped his lips. Startled by the echo of this laugh, he looked up and in so doing lost the thread of his musings. When he found it once more, he burrowed again, as it were, into the same subject.

And suddenly something like a thick black curtain was ripped in two pieces, and a clear prospect opened before his clouded eyes. All at once it seemed to him that he was awakening from a two years' sleep like the sleep of a dead man, and was contemplating with an unbelieving shake of the head all the hair-raising things he was supposed to have done in that condition. The sufferings of his eldest, upon which the impressions of the last few hours had only set the seal, appeared distinctly before his mind. Pity and regret gripped him, as did also a deep sense of shame that all that time he had lived on in humiliating acquiescence without doing anything for the poor, helpless little creature; without even having the strength to admit to himself how much the child suffered.

Tormenting himself with thoughts of all these sins of omission, he was overcome by a great weariness, and fell asleep with back bent, forehead on hand and hand on table.

After lying thus for some time, he called out several times in a stifled voice the name 'Minna'.

A rushing and roaring filled his ears, as if of immense masses of water. It grew dark about him, he opened his eyes and awoke. He had flushes in the limbs, nervous sweat started from every pore, his pulse was irregular, his face wet with tears.

It was pitch dark. He wanted to throw a glance towards the door, without knowing where to turn. He reeled to his feet; the anguish of fear persisted. The forest outside roared like breakers on the shore, the wind hurled rain and hail against the windows of the cabin. Thiel groped around helplessly with his hands. For a moment he felt like a drowning man – then suddenly there was a blinding bluish flash, as if drops of supernatural light were falling down into the dark atmosphere of the earth, to be immediately quenched.

This moment sufficed for Thiel to pull himself together. He grabbed at his lantern and by good luck caught hold of it; in the same instant the thunder awoke on the farthest fringe of the Brandenburg night sky. A muffled, suppressed growl at first, the thunder rolled closer in short, surging waves until finally it unleashed its mounting force in a series of giant claps, swamping the whole atmosphere, rumbling, shivering, roaring.

The panes rattled, the earth shook.

Thiel had lit the lamp. His first glance when he had regained his composure was for the clock. There were scarcely five minutes left between now and the arrival of the express. In the belief that he had missed the signal, he hurried to the barrier as fast as storm and darkness allowed. While he was still busy closing the barrier, the signal-bell rang. The wind tore the sounds to shreds and scattered them in all directions. The pines bent and rubbed their boughs together with sinister creaking and groaning noises. For an instant the moon became visible lying between the clouds like a pale golden bowl. By its light one could see the black tops of the pines thrashing in the wind. The foliage of the birches along the permanent way waved and fluttered like ghostly horse-tails. Beneath them the straight lines of the rails lay shining wet, soaking up the pale moonlight in places.

Thiel pulled his cap from his head. The rain did him good and ran down his face mixed with tears. His brain seethed; indistinct recollections of what he had seen in his dream chased one another through his mind. It had seemed to him as if Tobias was being maltreated by someone, and in such a horrible fashion that even now his heart stood still at the thought. He recalled another apparition more distinctly. He had seen his dead wife. She had come from somewhere in the distance, along one of the tracks. She had looked really ill, and had worn rags instead of clothes. She had passed by Thiel's cabin without looking round at it and finally – here the memory grew indistinct – had for some reason only moved forward with great effort, and had even collapsed several times.

Thiel reflected further, and now he knew that she had been fleeing. It was beyond all doubt, otherwise why had she cast those backward looks full of extreme fear and dragged herself on, although her feet refused to carry her? Oh, those terrible looks!

But she was carrying something with her, wrapped in cloths, something limp, pale, and bloody; and the way she looked down at it reminded him of scenes from the past.

He thought of a dying woman looking fixedly at the scarce-born child she had to leave behind, looking with an expression of most intense pain, an expression Thiel could as little forget as that he had a father and a mother.

Where had she gone to? He did not know. But one thing was absolutely clear: she had renounced him, disregarded him; she had dragged herself onward farther and farther through the storm and darkness of the night. He had called to her: 'Minna! Minna!' and this had awakened him.

Two round red lights pierced the darkness like the goggling eyes of some enormous monster. They cast a blood-red glare before them which turned the raindrops within its compass to drops of blood. It seemed as if the sky was raining blood.

Thiel had a feeling of horror; the nearer the train came, the more his fear increased. Dream and reality fused and became one. He could still see the woman walking along the rails, and his hand strayed towards his detonator-pouch as if he intended to halt the onrushing train. Luckily it was too late, for already lights were flickering in front of Thiel's eyes, and the train rushed past.

For the rest of the night Thiel's duty brought him little peace. He felt an urgent desire to be home. He longed to see little Tobias. It seemed as if he had been separated from him for years. At the end, in his growing anxiety to know how the boy was, he was several times tempted to abandon his post.

To kill time Thiel resolved, as soon as it grew light, to inspect his section. With a rod in his left hand and a long steel spanner in his right he strode off forthwith, walking on one of the rails, into the dirty grey half-light.

Now and again he tightened a bolt with the spanner or tapped one of the round iron bars connecting the rails.

The rain and wind had abated, and here and there patches of pale blue sky were visible through tattered layers of cloud.

The monotonous clatter of his soles on the hard metal, combined with the sleepy sound of dripping trees, gradually calmed Thiel.

At six in the morning he was relieved and set off home immediately.

It was a glorious Sunday morning.

The clouds had parted and receded meanwhile below the circle of the horizon. The sun rose glittering like a huge, blood-red jewel and shed a veritable flood of light over the forest.

The shafts of light shot in sharp lines through the maze of treetrunks, here breathing fire into a clump of delicate ferns with fronds like fine lace, there transforming the silver-grey lichens of the forest floor into red coral. The fiery dew flowed from treetops, boles, and grasses. A deluge of light seemed poured out over the earth. There was a freshness in the air which reached right to the heart, and inside Thiel's head, too, the visions of the night were gradually forced to fade.

But from the moment he walked into the room and saw Tobias lying more rosy-cheeked than ever in his sunlit bed they had vanished completely.

Indeed, during the course of the day Lene thought several times that she noticed something odd about him; in the pew, for example, when, instead of looking at his hymn-book, he looked at her from the side; and then again around midday, when, without saying a word, he took the baby, which Tobias had been told to carry into the street as usual, from the boy's arms and placed it on her lap. Otherwise there was nothing remarkable about him.

Thiel did not manage to lie down during the day; as he was on day-duty the following week, he crawled into bed by about nine o'clock in the evening. Just as he was about to fall asleep his wife announced her intention of going with him to the forest the next morning to dig over the ground and plant potatoes.

Thiel started; he was now fully awake, but kept his eyes tight shut.

It was high time, said Lene, if the potatoes were to come to anything; and she added that she would have to take the children with her, as they would presumably need the whole day for it. Thiel mumbled a few unintelligible words of which Lene took no notice. She had turned her back on him and was busy unlacing her bodice and dropping her skirts.

Suddenly she whipped round without herself knowing why and looked into her husband's face, which was an earthy grey and contorted with passion; he was half sitting up and staring at her with burning eyes, his hands on the edge of the bed.

'Thiel!' cried the woman, half angry and half frightened; like a sleepwalker whom one calls by name he awoke out of his stupor, stammered a few confused words, threw himself into the pillows, and pulled the quilt over his ears.

Lene was the first to get out of bed the following morning. Without making any noise she got everything ready for the outing. The baby was put in the perambulator, and then Tobias was woken and dressed. On being told where they were going, he had to smile. When all was prepared and the coffee stood ready on the table, Thiel awoke. At the sight of the preparations that had been made, his first reaction was one of unease. He would have liked to raise objections, but did not know where to begin. And what convincing reasons could he have given Lene?

Then gradually the growing radiance of Tobias's little face began to have its effect upon Thiel, so that finally, because the outing afforded the boy such pleasure, he could no longer think of saying anything against it. For all that, Thiel was not free from disquiet during the walk through the forest. He pushed the little perambulator with difficulty through the deep sand, and had all sorts of flowers lying on it which Tobias had gathered.

The boy was quite exceptionally gay. He hopped around among the ferns in his little brown plush cap and tried, albeit somewhat awkwardly, to catch the glassy-winged dragonflies that darted about over them. As soon as they had arrived Lene made an inspection of the allotment. She threw the bag of potato-pieces which she had brought for planting on to the grassy edge of a small birch-coppice, knelt down and let the rather dark-coloured sand run through her hard fingers. Thiel watched her anxiously. 'Well, how is it?'

'Certainly as good as the patch by the Spree!' A great weight was lifted from Thiel's mind. He had feared she would be dissatisfied, and he scratched his beard-stubble with relief.

After his wife had hastily consumed a thick crust of bread, she threw off her jacket and shawl and started to dig with the speed and endurance of a machine.

At fixed intervals she straightened up and drew in deep breaths of air, but only for a moment on each occasion, unless perhaps the baby needed a feed, which was given hastily with heaving, sweat-running breast.

'I must inspect my section, I'll take Tobias with me,' shouted Thiel across to her after a while from the platform of his cabin.

'Nonsense!' she shouted back, 'who is to stay with the baby? – you come here!' she added still more loudly, while Thiel, as if he could not hear her, walked off with Tobias.

For a moment she wondered whether to run after them, and only the waste of time decided her against it. Thiel walked along the section with Tobias. The boy was not a little excited; it was all strange and new to him. He could not grasp the significance of the narrow, black, sun-warmed rails. He kept asking all manner of peculiar questions. What seemed particularly curious to him was the singing of the telegraph-poles. Thiel knew the sound of each one in his section, so that even with eyes shut he would always have known in which part of it he was at any given moment.

Frequently he stopped, holding Tobias by the hand, in

order to listen to the marvellous sounds which issued from
the wood like sonorous chorales from the inside of a church.
The pole at the southern end of the section produced a particularly full and beautiful chord. There was a turmoil of tones
inside it which went on without interruption as if in one
breath, and Tobias ran round the weather-beaten wood in
order, as he fancied, to look through an opening and discover
what was producing such delightful sounds. A solemn mood
came over the crossing-keeper, just like in church. Moreover,
in time he could make out a voice which reminded him of
his late wife. He imagined to himself that it was a choir of
blessed spirits, with which she, of course, was blending her
own voice; and at this notion a longing awoke within him
and moved him almost to tears.

Tobias wanted the flowers growing further off, and Thiel,
as always, gave in to him.

It seemed as if pieces of blue sky had come down to the
floor of the wood, so marvellously dense were the little blue
flowers which grew there. The butterflies like coloured pen-
nants danced and fluttered soundlessly between the gleaming
white of the tree-trunks, whilst a soft ripple passed through
the clouds of delicate green foliage crowning the birch-
trees.

Tobias picked flowers, and his father watched him thoughtfully. At intervals the latter, too, gazed upwards through the
gaps in the leaves, searching for the sky, which gathered up
the golden light of the sun like a huge flawless blue crystal
bowl.

'Father, is that the good Lord?' asked the boy suddenly,
pointing to a red squirrel which scurried with scratching
noises up the trunk of an isolated pine.

'Little fool,' was all Thiel could reply, while torn-off pieces
of bark fell down the trunk and landed at his feet.

The mother was still digging when Thiel and Tobias came
back. Half the patch had already been turned over.

The trains followed one another at short intervals, and
each time Tobias watched them roar past open-mouthed.
Even the mother was amused by his comical expressions.

The midday meal, consisting of potatoes and the remains of some cold roast pork, was eaten in the cabin. Lene was in high spirits, and Thiel, too, seemed willing to accept the inevitable with good grace. He entertained his wife during the meal with all sorts of facts relating to his job. He asked her, for example, whether she realized that there were forty-six bolts in a single rail, and other things of that kind.

During the course of the morning Lene had finished the digging; in the afternoon the potatoes were going to be planted. She insisted that Tobias should look after the baby now, and took him with her.

'Take care –' Thiel shouted after her, suddenly gripped by alarm. 'Take care that he doesn't get too close to the lines.'

A shrug of Lene's shoulders was the reply.

The Silesian express had been signalled, and Thiel had to go to his post. Scarcely was he at his proper position by the barrier when he heard it roaring towards him.

The train became visible – it drew nearer – in innumerable rapid jets the smoke panted from the black funnel. Then: one – two – three milky-white jets of steam shot straight up, and immediately afterwards the whistling of the locomotive was borne on the air. Three times in succession, short, shrill, alarming. They're braking, thought Thiel, I wonder why? And again came the shrill shriek of the emergency whistle, awakening the echoes, this time in a long, unbroken series.

Thiel stepped forward in order to survey the whole section. Mechanically he drew the red flag from its cover and held it straight out in front of him over the line. – Jesus Christ – had he been blind? Jesus Christ – oh, Jesus, Jesus, Jesus Christ! what was that? There – there between the rails . . . 'Stop!' shouted the crossing-keeper with all his strength. Too late. A dark object had got under the train and was being tossed to and fro between the wheels like a rubber ball. A few more moments, and the grating scream of the brakes could be heard. The train stood still.

The lonely stretch of track came to life. Guards and conductors ran over the gravel towards the end of the train. Inquisitive faces peered from every window, and now – the crowd formed a knot and came forward.

Thiel was panting; he had to hold on to prevent himself collapsing like a poled ox. It was true – they were waving to him – 'No!'

A scream pierced the air from the place of the accident; a howling followed as if from the throat of some animal. Who was that? Lene! It was not her voice, yet . . .

A man came hurrying up the track.

'Crossing-keeper!'

'What's the matter?'

'An accident . . .' The messenger recoiled, for Thiel's eyes had a strange look. The cap was askew, the red hair seemed to stand up.

'He's still alive, help may still be possible.'

A gurgling sound was the only reply.

'Come quickly, quickly!'

Thiel pulled himself together with a supreme effort. His limp muscles tensed. He drew himself up to his full height; his face was dead and foolish.

He ran together with the messenger, not seeing the deathly-pale faces of the passengers at the windows. A young woman was looking out, a commercial traveller in a fez, a young couple apparently on their honeymoon-trip. What was it to him? He had never bothered his head about the contents of these noisy contraptions; Lene's howls filled his ears. Yellow spots swam before his eyes like innumerable glow-worms. He started back; he stood still. It emerged out of the dancing glow-worms: pale, limp, blood-stained. A forehead, black and blue with contusions; blue lips trickling dark blood. It was him.

Thiel did not speak. His face turned a dirty white. He smiled absent-mindedly. Finally he bent down. He felt the slack, lifeless limbs a deadweight in his arms; the red flag wound itself round them.

He went.

Where to?

'To the railway doctor, to the railway doctor,' said a jumble of voices.

'We'll take him with us,' shouted the luggage-super-intendent and made a couch of uniform jackets and books.

'Well?'

Thiel made no move to let go of the victim. People argued with him. In vain. The luggage-superintendent had a stretcher handed out of the baggage-car and ordered a man to stand by the father.

Time was precious. The guard's whistle shrilled. Coins showered from the windows.

Lene was carrying on as if she were insane. 'The poor, poor woman,' said those in the compartments, 'the poor, poor mother.'

The guard blew again. There was a whistle. The locomotive puffed white, hissing clouds of steam from its cylinders and stretched its steel sinews; a few seconds more, and the courier express was roaring through the forest with redoubled speed beneath a waving plume of smoke.

The crossing-keeper had changed his mind; he laid the half-dead boy on the stretcher. He lay there with his mis-shapen frame; now and again a long, rattling breath lifted the bony chest which was visible beneath the tattered shirt. The little arms and legs, shattered in many places, not only at the joints, adopted the most unnatural positions. The heel of one little foot was twisted to the front. The arms dangled over the sides of the stretcher.

Lene was whimpering continuously; every trace of her former defiance had left her. She kept repeating a story designed to clear her of all guilt in the accident.

Thiel seemed to take no notice of her; his gaze was fixed on the child with a horrible, frightened expression.

Silence had fallen round about, a deathly silence; the rails lay black and hot on the dazzling gravel. Noon had stifled the wind, and the forest stood motionless, as if made of stone.

The men took counsel quietly. It was necessary, in order to reach Friedrichshagen by the quickest route, to go back to the next station, which lay in the direction of Breslau, since the next train, a slow passenger, did not stop at the station nearer to Friedrichshagen.

Thiel seemed to be pondering whether to go with them. At the moment there was nobody present who knew what his duties were. A silent wave of the hand told his wife to take up the stretcher; she did not dare to object, although worried about the baby left behind. She and the strange man carried the stretcher. Thiel accompanied the procession to the end of his section, then stopped and gazed after it for a long time. Suddenly he smote his forehead with the flat of his hand; the sound was audible far and wide.

He thought he was waking himself up, 'for it must be a dream, like the one yesterday,' he said to himself. In vain. Staggering rather than running, he reached his cabin. Inside he fell upon the ground, face first. His cap rolled into the corner, his carefully cherished watch fell out of his pocket, the case split, the glass smashed. It seemed as if an iron fist were grasping him by the back of the neck, so tightly that he was unable to move, however much he attempted to free himself, groaning and moaning as he did so. His brow was cold, his eyes dry, his gullet burning.

The signal-bell woke him. Under the impact of those three repeated rings the fit passed. Thiel was able to rise and go about his duty. His feet were heavy as lead, certainly, and the track spun round him like the spoke of an enormous wheel whose hub was his head; but at least he summoned enough strength to hold himself upright for a time.

The passenger train came up. Tobias must be in it. The nearer it came, the more the images blurred before Thiel's eyes. Finally he could see nothing but the mangled boy with the blood-stained mouth. Then it was night.

After a while he awoke from a dead faint. He found himself lying by the barrier in the hot sand. He stood up, shook the grains of sand from his clothing, and spat them out of his mouth. His head grew a little clearer; he could think more calmly.

In the cabin he immediately picked his watch up from the floor and put it on the table. Despite the fall it had not stopped. For two hours he counted the seconds and minutes, imagining to himself what could have been happening to Tobias in the meantime. Now Lene was arriving with him; now she was standing in front of the doctor. The latter was looking at the boy and feeling him and shaking his head. 'Bad, very bad – but perhaps . . . who knows.' He makes a more thorough examination. 'No,' he says then, 'no, it's all over.'

'All over, all over,' groaned the crossing-keeper; but then he sat straight up and shouted, with rolling eyes fixed on the ceiling and raised hands unconsciously clenched into fists, in a voice which seemed as if it would burst the confined space: 'He must, he must live, I tell you, he must live, he must.' Already he was pushing open the cabin door again, through which the red fire of evening poured in; he ran rather than walked back to the barrier. Here he stood awhile as if perplexed, and then suddenly strode with both arms outstretched to the middle of the permanent way, as if he wanted to hold something up that was coming from the direction of the passenger train. His eyes as he did so gave an impression of blindness.

Walking backwards as if giving way before something, he forced out half-intelligible words between his teeth. 'You – do you hear – wait a moment – listen – stay – give him back – he's been beaten black and blue – yes, all right – I'll beat her black and blue in her turn – do you hear? wait a moment – give him back to me.'

It seemed as if something went past him, for he turned in the other direction as if to follow it.

'Minna' – his voice grew tearful like that of a small child. 'Minna, do you hear? – give him back – I want . . .' He groped in the air as if to hold on to someone. 'Little woman – yes – and then I'll – and then I'll hit her too – black and blue – and then with the kitchen chopper I'll – you see? kitchen chopper – I'll hit with the chopper and then she'll be done for.

'And then . . . yes, with the chopper – kitchen chopper, yes – black blood!' There was foam round his mouth, his glassy pupils moved ceaselessly.

A soft, evening breeze brushed gently persistent over the forest, and locks of burning pink clouds hung across the western sky.

He had followed the invisible something thus for about a hundred paces, when he stopped seemingly despondent; with an expression of horrible fear the man stretched out his arms, begging and imploring. He strained his eyes, shading them with his hand, as if to descry the shadowy thing once more in the far distance. Finally his hand sank, and the tense expression on his face became dull and impassive; he turned and dragged himself back the way he had come.

The sun poured its last glow over the forest, then died. The trunks of the pine-trees stretched up like pale, rotting bones between their crowns of foliage, which weighed upon them like grey-black layers of decaying matter. The hammering of a woodpecker pierced the silence. A single late rosy cloud passed through the cold steel-blue spaces of the sky. The breeze became as chilly as a vault, making the crossing-keeper shiver. Everything was new to him, everything was strange. He did not know what he was walking on, what was surrounding him. Then a squirrel scurried across the path, and Thiel remembered. He found himself thinking about the good Lord, without knowing why. 'The good Lord is leaping across the path, the good Lord is leaping across the path.' He repeated this sentence several times, as if to hit upon something connected with it. He interrupted himself; a ray of light shone into his mind: 'But good God, this is madness.' He forgot everything and turned upon this new enemy. He tried to put his thoughts in order – in vain! There was nothing there but an unstable roving and drifting. He caught himself imagining the absurdest things and shuddered in the knowledge of his own powerlessness.

From the near-by birch-wood came the sound of a child's crying. It was the signal for a complete frenzy. Almost against his will he was compelled to hurry to the spot and found the baby, which no one had taken any further notice of, lying kicking and screaming without any cover in the perambulator. What did he want to do? What had driven him here? A swirling flood of thoughts and feelings swallowed the questions up.

'The good Lord is leaping across the path' – now he knew what that meant. Tobias – she had murdered him – Lene – he had been entrusted to her – 'Stepmother, unnatural mother,' he ground out, 'and her brat lives.' A red mist shrouded his senses; a pair of child's eyes pierced him; he felt something soft and fleshy between his fingers. Gurgling, whistling noises, mingled with hoarse cries uttered by he knew not whom, assailed his ears.

Then something like drops of hot sealing-wax fell into his brain, and it was as if a kind of paralysis lifted from his mind. Coming to himself, he heard the echoes of the signal-bell quivering through the air.

Suddenly he realized what he had been wanting to do: his hand relaxed from the throat of the child, which twisted beneath his grasp. It fought for air, then began to cough and cry.

'It's alive! Thank God, it's alive!' He left it lying and hurried to the crossing. Dark smoke was rolling across the line from far off, and the wind pressed it to the ground. Behind him he heard the panting of a locomotive, which sounded like the tortured, convulsive breathing of a sick giant.

A cold half-light lay over the district.

After a time, when the smoke-clouds dispersed, Thiel recognized the gravel-train which was returning with empty trucks bringing with it the men who had been working on the line during the day.

The train ran to a generous timetable and was allowed to stop anywhere to pick up the men working at various places, or put off others. A good way from Thiel's cabin it started to brake. A lengthy screeching, rattling, clanking, and clattering rang out afar on the evening air before the train drew to a halt with a single long-drawn-out sound.

About fifty working men and women were divided up between the trucks. Nearly all of them were standing upright, some of the men with heads bared. There was a puzzling solemnity about all of them. When they caught sight of the crossing-keeper, a whispering started amongst them. The old men took their pipes from between their yellowed teeth and held them respectfully in their hands. Here and there a female turned round in order to blow her nose. The guard climbed down on to the track and walked up to Thiel. The workmen saw how he solemnly shook his hand, whereupon Thiel walked towards the last truck with slow, stiff, almost military steps.

None of the workmen dared to address him, although they all knew him.

They were just lifting little Tobias out of the last truck.

He was dead.

Lene followed him; her face was a bluish white; there were dark circles round her eyes.

Thiel did not vouchsafe her a single glance, but she was startled at the sight of her husband. His cheeks were hollow, his lashes and whiskers were stuck together, his hair, so it seemed to her, greyer than before. All over his face were the traces of dried tears, and in addition there was an unsteady light in his eyes which made her shudder. They had brought the stretcher too, in order to be able to carry the body.

For a while an uncanny silence reigned. A profound, horrible trance had taken possession of Thiel. It grew darker. A troop of deer had moved onto the track some way down. The buck stood still right in the middle of the line. He turned his supple neck curiously, then the engine whistled, and he disappeared like a flash together with his herd.

At the moment the train started to move, Thiel collapsed.

The train halted again, and a consultation developed as to what should be done now. It was decided to leave the body of the child in the crossing-keeper's cabin for the time being, and in its stead to use the stretcher to carry Thiel home; the latter could not be roused whatever they tried.

And that is what happened. Two men carried the stretcher with the unconscious Thiel, followed by Lene, who, sobbing incessantly, pushed the perambulator with the baby in it through the sand, her face bathed in tears.

The moon lay like a huge, purple, glowing ball between the shafts of the pines in the heart of the forest. The higher it rose, the smaller it seemed to get and the paler it became. Finally it hung like a lamp over the forest, piercing every chink and gap in the treetops with a feeble, luminous haze which painted the walkers' faces in corpse-like colours.

They strode ahead vigorously yet with caution, now through dense saplings, now across wide clearings surrounded by lofty trees, in which the pale light seemed to have collected as if in great dark bowls.

The unconscious man gurgled from time to time or started to ramble. Several times he clenched his fists and tried to sit up with eyes closed.

It was an effort to get him across the Spree; they had to cross a second time in order to fetch the wife and child.

As they were climbing the slight slope of the village, they met a few of the inhabitants, who at once spread the news of the accident.

The whole settlement was soon on its feet.

At the sight of her acquaintances Lene broke out into fresh lamentations.

With difficulty they got the sick man up the narrow staircase to his dwelling and put him to bed at once. The workmen turned back immediately in order to fetch the body of little Tobias.

Old and experienced folk had advised cold compresses, and Lene followed their instructions with eager circumspection. She laid towels in ice-cold well-water and renewed them as soon as the burning forehead of the unconscious man had warmed them through. Anxiously she watched the invalid's breathing, which seemed to her to grow more regular minute by minute.

The excitements of the day had, naturally enough, wearied her greatly, and she resolved to sleep a little, but could find no rest. No matter whether she had her eyes shut or open, the things that had happened passed ceaselessly before them. The baby slept; contrary to her usual habit, she had paid little heed to it. She had become a different person altogether.

There was nowhere a trace of her earlier defiance. It was true: this sick man with the face drained of colour and gleaming with sweat ruled her in his sleep.

A cloud covered the moon, it grew dark in the room, and Lene could only hear her husband's deep but regular breathing. She considered whether she should make some light. An uncanny feeling came over her in the dark. When she tried to get up, all her limbs were leaden; her eyelids closed, and she fell asleep.

Some hours later, when the men returned with the body of the child, they found the house door wide open. Surprised at this, they climbed the stairs to the upper room, the door of which was also open.

They called the woman's name several times, without receiving any answer. Finally someone struck a match on the wall, and the spurt of light revealed a scene of ghastly devastation.

'Murder! Murder!'

Lene lay there in her blood, her face unrecognizable, her skull smashed.

'He has murdered his wife! He has murdered his wife!'

People ran about aimlessly. The neighbours came; one of them bumped against the cradle. 'Great God in Heaven!' And he recoiled, his face frozen with horror. There lay the child with its throat cut.

The crossing-keeper had disappeared; a search instituted that same night was unsuccessful. The following morning the duty crossing-keeper found him sitting between the rails at the spot where little Tobias had been run over.

He was holding the little brown fur cap in his arms and caressing it as if it were a living thing.

The other crossing-keeper addressed a few words to him but received no reply and soon realized that he was dealing with a lunatic.

The man in the block signal-box, informed about this, telegraphed for help.

Then several men attempted to entice him off the track by means of friendly persuasion, but in vain.

The express which passed about this time was obliged to stop, and not until the superior strength of its crew was brought to bear could the sick man, who at once began to rave fearfully, be forcibly removed from the track.

They had to tie his hands and feet, and the gendarme who had been summoned supervised his transportation to the B rlin remand prison, whence, however, he was transferred on the same day to the mental ward of the hospital. Whilst he was being taken in he still held the little brown fur cap in his hands, guarding it with jealous care and tenderness.

Arthur Schnitzler

LIEUTENANT GUSTL

Translated by Sheila Stern

Arthur Schnitzler

SCHNITZLER (1862–1931), a Viennese Jewish doctor, was one of the leading figures of the 'Young Vienna' literary circle of the nineties. He is sometimes given the label of literary Impressionist, but one could equally well speak of psychological Naturalism in the case of many of his prose works, with their masterly, detailed analyses of his characters' mental processes, conscious and unconscious. *Lieutenant Gustl* (1901), an early example of the stream-of-consciousness technique, mercilessly exposes the ethos of the officer class of the Austro–Hungarian Empire and its supposed sense of honour.

LIEUTENANT GUSTL

How much longer is this going to go on? I shall have to look at my watch . . . probably the wrong thing to do at a serious concert like this. But who's going to notice? If anyone notices, they must be paying as little attention as I am, so I don't mind what they think . . . Only a quarter to ten? I feel as though this concert's been going on for three hours. It's just that I'm not used to it . . . What is it all anyway? I shall have to look at the programme . . . So that's what it is; an oratorio? I thought it was a Mass. Stuff like this ought to be done in church. Besides the good thing about church is that you can walk out any time – if only I had a corner seat! – Well, patience, patience! Even oratorios come to an end! Perhaps it's really very beautiful, and it's just that I'm not in the mood. How should I be in the mood? To think that I came here to forget my worries . . . I should have given the ticket to Benedek, he likes this kind of thing; plays the violin himself. But then Kopetzky would have been hurt; it was really nice of him, anyway he meant well – a good chap, Kopetzky! The only one of them you can rely on . . . His sister is singing with the others up there. At least a hundred virgins all dressed in black; how can I tell her from the others? It was because she was singing that Kopetzky had the ticket... Why didn't he go himself then? – Anyway they are singing very well. All very edifying – no doubt! Bravo! bravo! . . . Yes, let's join in the applause. The man next to me is clapping like mad. I wonder if he really likes it that much? – That girl in the box over there is very pretty. Is she looking at me or the gentleman with the fair beard? . . . Ah, a solo! Who's this? alto: Miss Walker, soprano, Miss Michalek . . . This is probably the soprano . . . It's a long time since I've been to the opera. At the opera I always enjoy myself even if it's boring. Actually I could go the day after tomorrow and see *Traviata*. Yes, but by the day after tomorrow I may be just a dead body! Oh that's rot, I don't even believe that myself!

Wait a bit, Doctor, I'll teach you to make remarks like that! I'll cut off your nose for you . . .

If only I could see that girl in the box properly! I'd like to borrow those opera-glasses from the man next to me, but he'd jump down my throat if I disturbed him at his devotions . . . I wonder where Kopetzky's sister is standing? I wonder if I'd recognize her? I've only seen her two or three times, the last time at that party in the officers' mess . . . I wonder if they're all respectable girls, the whole hundred of them? My gosh! . . . 'with the collaboration of the Choral Society!' 'Choral Society's' funny! Actually I always imagined it something rather like the Vienna Song and Dance Ensemble – well, I did know it would be a bit different! . . . Pleasant memories! That time at the 'Green Gate' . . . what was her name now? And then she sent me a picture postcard from Belgrade . . . lovely part of the world – Kopetzky's lucky, he's been sitting in the pub for ages now, smoking his cigar! . . .

Why is that fellow there looking at me all the time? I think he must have noticed I'm bored and don't belong here . . . I'd advise you to take that cheeky look off your face, otherwise I'll have a word with you afterwards in the foyer! – He's looked away pretty quick . . . It's strange how they're all afraid to meet my eyes . . . 'You have the most beautiful eyes I've ever seen!' Steffi said the other day . . . Oh Steffi, Steffi, Steffi! – It's really all Steffi's fault that I've got to sit here listening to all this caterwauling for hours on end. How these endless excuses of Steffi's are getting on my nerves! We could have had a marvellous evening. I'd like to read Steffi's note through again. I've got it here. But if I take my wallet out, this fellow'll jump down my throat! – Anyhow I know what it says . . . she can't come because she's got to go out to dinner with Him! Now that was funny last week, when she was sitting with him at the Garden Restaurant and I was sitting just opposite with Kopetzky; and she was signalling to me all the time with her eyes. He didn't notice a thing – incredible! Must be a Jew, too! Of course, he works in a bank, and that black moustache . . . Supposed to be a lieutenant in the

reserves as well! Huh, he'd better not come on exercises with
my regiment! Altogether, the way they're still giving commissions to so many Jews – all this anti-semitism they're
putting on isn't worth twopence! At that party the other day
where the business with the Doctor happened, at the Mannheimers ... the Mannheimers are supposed to be Jews as well,
converted of course ... but you'd never know it – especially
the wife ... so blonde, and a marvellous figure ... it was
really very good fun altogether. Excellent meal, splendid
cigars ... well of course, who is it's got all the money? ...

Bravo, bravo! Surely it'll be over soon now? – Yes, now
the whole company's standing up – looks very fine – impressive! – the organ too? ... I like the organ very much ...
Well, I really am enjoying this – beautiful! It's quite true, one
ought to go to concerts more often. 'It was simply beautiful,'
I shall tell Kopetzky. Shall I go and meet him afterwards at
the coffee-house? – Oh, I really don't feel like going there;
had just about enough of it yesterday! A hundred and sixty
florins lost at one sitting – too idiotic! And who won it all?
Old Ballert, of all people, the only one who doesn't need the
money anyway. It's Ballert's fault actually that I had to go to
this blasted concert. Yes, otherwise I could have played again
tonight, and maybe won something back. But it's not such a
bad thing that I've given myself my word of honour not to
touch a card for a month ... Mama will make a dreadfully
sour face again when she gets my letter! – Well, she's only
got to go to uncle, he's got tons of money; a few hundred
florins don't matter to him. If only I could get him to give me
a regular allowance! But no, one has to beg for every penny.
And then off he goes with his 'The harvest was terrible last
year!' ... I wonder if I ought to go and stay a fortnight with
uncle in the summer? Of course I'll be bored to death if I
do ... If I could find that girl again – what was her name? ...
Funny thing, I cannot remember names! Oh yes, Etelka! She
didn't understand a single word of German, but that didn't
matter in the least ... I didn't need to talk at all ... Yes, it
wouldn't be bad, fourteen days of country air and fourteen
nights of Etelka or somebody ... But I ought to spend a week

with Papa and Mama too . . . She didn't look at all well at
Christmas time . . . Oh well, by now she will have got over it.
In her place I should be glad Papa's retired. – And Clara's sure
to find a husband some day. – Uncle can give her something,
that's the least he can do. Twenty-eight isn't so old . . . Steffi
can't be any younger than that either . . . But it's a funny
thing; women like that stay young longer. When you come to
think of it: La Maretti the other day in *Madame sans Gêne* –
must be at least thirty-seven, and she looks – well, I wouldn't
say no! – Too bad she didn't ask me!

It's getting hot in here! Still not over? Ah, but I'm looking
forward to the fresh air! I shall go for a bit of a walk on the
Ringstrasse . . . The important thing tonight is – early to bed
and fresh for tomorrow afternoon! Funny how little I'm
thinking about it, shows I'm not worried! The first time it did
get me rather excited. Not that I was frightened; but I was
nervous the night before . . . It's true Lieutenant Bisanz was a
serious opponent. – And yet nothing happened to me! . . . It's
eighteen months ago now. How time flies! And if Bisanz
didn't do me any harm the Doctor certainly won't! Although
it's just these unskilled swordsmen that are sometimes the
most dangerous. Doschinsky told me he was jolly nearly run
through by a fellow who'd never had a sword in his hand
before; and Doschinsky is a fencing instructor with the
Territorials now. Of course I don't know if he was all that
good at the time . . . The main thing is – keep cool. I don't
even feel really angry any more, and yet it was such a cheek –
incredible! I'm sure he wouldn't have dared if he hadn't been
drinking champagne . . . Such a piece of cheek! Must be a
Socialist! All these rascally lawyers are Socialists nowadays.
What a gang . . . what they'd really like is to abolish the army
altogether; but then who'd stand by them when the Chinese
come and overrun them? They don't think about that!
Imbeciles! One must make an example from time to time. I
was absolutely right, I'm glad I didn't let him get away with
that remark. Just to think of it makes me furious. But I
behaved perfectly; the colonel said so too, it was exactly the
right thing to do. It won't be a bad thing for me, this affair.

I know a lot of people who would have let him get away with
it. Old Müller for instance, he would have started being
objective again or something. Being objective never did anyone any good . . . 'Lieutenant!' – even the way he said
'Lieutenant' was insulting . . . 'You will really have to admit'
. . . How on earth did we get on to it? How did I ever allow
myself to get into a conversation with that Socialist? How
did it start? I think that dark lady that I took in to supper was
there too . . . and then that young man who paints hunting-
scenes – what's his name again? Good heavens, the whole
thing was *his* fault! He began to talk about the manoeuvres;
and it was only then that this Doctor joined in and said something or other I didn't like, about playing at war or whatever
it was – but I couldn't say anything much to *that* . . . Yes, and
then we were talking of the military academies . . . Yes, that
was it – and I told them about a patriotic celebration, and
then the Doctor said – not immediately but it developed out of
the celebration – 'Lieutenant, you will really have to admit
that not all your comrades have gone into the Army solely in
order to defend the Fatherland!' What a piece of cheek! How
dare a fellow like that speak to an officer in that way! If only I
could remember what I replied? Oh yes, something about
people who meddle in things they know nothing about . . .
That's it . . . and then there was someone who tried to smooth
the thing over, an elderly gentleman with a frightful cold . . .
But I was too furious! The Doctor sounded exactly as though
he meant it for me personally. He only needed to add that I
was chucked out of high school and that that was the reason
they put me in the military academy . . . These people just
can't understand our sort, they're altogether too stupid . . .
When I think of the first time I put on my tunic, not everyone
knows what it is to feel like that . . . Last year at the manoeuvres
– I would have given a good deal if it had suddenly been
the real thing . . . And old Mirovich told me he felt exactly the
same. And then when His Highness rode past the line, and the
colonel's address – a man would have to be a regular cad if his
heart didn't beat faster. And then a bookworm like that comes
along, who's done nothing all his life but sit among his books,

and permits himself an insolent remark! Aha, just wait a bit, my friend – 'to the point where one or the other is too disabled to fight' – yes indeed, you'll be disabled when I've finished with you.

Well, what's going on? It must be over soon . . . 'Praise ye the Lord, His angels' . . . Of course, that's the final chorus . . . Marvellous, that's all one can say. Marvellous! Now I've quite forgotten that girl in the box who started flirting with me earlier. Where is she now? Gone already . . . That one looks nice too . . . How stupid that I didn't bring any opera-glasses! Old Brunnthaler has the right idea, he always leaves his opera-glasses with the cashier at the coffee-house, then you're never without them . . . If only that little one in front of me there would turn round! She's sitting there so prim and proper all the time. The one next to her must be her Mama. – I wonder if I ought not to be thinking seriously of getting married? Willy was no older than I am when he took the plunge. Not so bad to have a sweet little wife always on hand at home . . . It's too silly that Steffi can't get away tonight of all nights! If I only knew where she is I'd like to go and sit watching her again. A nice thing that would be, if *He* found out, then *I* should have her round my neck . . . To think what Fliess has to spend on his affair with that Winterfeld girl! And she deceives him right, left and centre. That's going to come to a sticky end one day . . . Bravo, bravo! So it's over! . . . Ah, it's good to stand up and stretch one's legs . . . Only I'd like to know how long it's going to take this chap to put his glasses back in their case?

'Excuse me, excuse me, are you going to let me pass?'

What a press! I'd better let some of these people go by . . . That's a well-dressed woman . . . are those real diamonds? . . . That one's nice . . . and how she's looking at me! Yes indeed, my dear, I'd like it very much! . . . Oh what a nose! – A Jewess . . . and another . . . It's quite extraordinary, half these people are Jews . . . one can't even enjoy an oratorio in peace nowadays . . . There, now I'll get into the line . . . why is this idiot pushing behind me? I'll teach him . . . Oh, an elderly gentleman! . . . Who's that greeting me over there? . . . My compliments – delighted, I'm sure! No idea who it is . . . the simplest thing to do is to go straight over and have supper at Leidinger's . . . or should I go to the Garden Restaurant? Steffi really might be there after all. Why didn't she say in her letter where they were going? She probably didn't know herself. Poor kid, it must be terrible to be so dependent on a person . . . There's the exit at last . . . Now that one really is a smasher! All alone? And she's smiling at me. That's an idea, I'll go after her! There, down the steps . . . Oh, a major from the 95th, very pleasant the way he returned my salute . . . So I wasn't the only officer here . . . Now where's that pretty girl? Ah yes, standing at the balustrade . . . Now let's get to the cloakroom for my coat . . . and I hope that girl won't slip away . . . Done for! What a dirty trick! Just waiting for that gentleman to fetch her, and now she's laughing back at me again! There isn't one of them who's any good . . . Heavens, what a crush at the cloakroom! . . . Better wait a minute. There! Now is this imbecile going to take my ticket?

'Hey, you, 224! That's it hanging up there! Are you blind? That's it there! Well at last, thank heavens! Oh, thanks *very* much!'

This fat man here is taking up all the space at the counter . . .
'Excuse me!'

'Patience, patience!'

What's the man say?

'Just a bit of patience!'

I shall have to answer him.

'Get out of the way then!'

'Don't worry, you won't miss the bus!'

What's he say? Is he speaking to *me*? That's a bit strong! I can't let that pass!

'Shut up!'

'What do you mean?'

What a tone of voice! That really is the end!

'Don't push!'

'Look here, you shut your trap!' I shouldn't have said that, it was too rude . . . Well, it's out now.

'I *beg* your pardon!'

Now he's turning round. But I know him! Heavens above, it's the master-baker who always comes to the coffee-house! And what's he doing here? I suppose he must have a daughter or something at the Academy of Music . . . But what's this? What's he doing? It's almost as though . . . Yes, good God, he's got the hilt of my sword in his hand . . . Is the man out of his mind?

'Look here, Sir . . .'

'Now, Lieutenant, you just keep very quiet.'

What did he say then? For God's sake, I hope no one heard? No, he's speaking very low . . . But why doesn't he let go of my sword? Damn and blast . . . I'll show him how absolutely livid I am. I can't get his hand off the hilt . . . only there mustn't be a scene in public! Isn't that major somewhere behind me? As long as nobody notices he's holding the hilt of my sword! He's speaking to me! What's he saying? . . .

'Lieutenant, if you make the very slightest fuss, I shall draw your sword from its sheath, break it in pieces, and send the pieces to your commanding officer. Do you understand what I say, you stupid boy?'

What's that he said? I feel as though I'm dreaming! Is he really speaking to me? I ought to reply . . . But the fellow's in earnest – he really means to pull the sword out! Oh God, he'll do it. I can feel it, he's tugging at it already. What's he saying again? For God's sake don't let us have a scene! What's he saying now?

'But I don't want to ruin your career . . . So, just be a good boy! . . . There, don't be afraid, nobody heard . . . it's all all right – there! And so that no one suspects we had words I shall pretend to be very friendly – My compliments, nice to have seen you, Lieutenant, good-evening to you.'

For God's sake, did I dream it? Did he really say that? . . . Where is he? there he goes . . . I ought to draw my sword and hack him in pieces – for God's sake, did anyone hear? . . . No, he was speaking very low, into my ear . . . Why don't I go after him and split his skull in two? . . . No, it's no good, it's no good. I ought to have done it immediately. Why didn't I do it immediately? . . . But I couldn't . . . he wouldn't let go of the hilt, and he's ten times stronger than I am. If I'd said another word he would really have broken my sword . . . I ought to be glad he didn't speak louder! If a single person had heard, I should have to shoot myself on the spot . . . But perhaps it was a dream . . . Why is that gentleman by the pillar looking at me in that way? – did he hear something after all? . . . I'll ask him . . . Ask him? . . . I must be mad! – What do I look like? – Do I look strange? – I must be quite white – where is that swine? I must kill him! He's gone . . . The whole place is empty now! Where's my coat? Oh, I've already got it on. I didn't notice . . . who helped me? . . . Ah, the attendant. I must give him something . . . There! . . . But what was all this? . . . Did it really happen? . . . Did someone really speak to me like that? . . . Did he really call me a stupid boy? . . . And I didn't cut him down there and then? . . . But I couldn't . . . Why, he had a fist like iron . . . I stood as if I were nailed to the spot. No, I must have lost my wits, otherwise with my other hand I could have . . . But then he would have pulled out my sword and broken it, and then it would have been all over – everything would have been finished! And afterwards when he was walking away it was too late . . . I couldn't have run him through with my sword from behind.

What, am I out in the street already? How did I get out here? – It's so cool . . . the wind feels good. But who's that over there? Why are they looking across at me? What if they heard something . . . No, no one can have heard . . . I know they can't, I looked round just afterwards! No one noticed me, no one was listening . . . But he said it, even if nobody heard; he said it all right. And I stood there and took it as if I'd been hit on the head! But I couldn't say anything, couldn't do anything; all I could do was stand there . . . and be very quiet, very quiet! – it's frightful, it's not to be borne; I must strike him down wherever I meet him again! . . . A man said *that* to me! A swine like that! And he knows me. God in heaven, he actually knows me, he knows who I am! He may tell anybody that he said that to me! No, no, he won't do that, otherwise he wouldn't have bothered to speak so quietly. He only wanted *me* to hear it. But who can promise me that he won't repeat it, today or tomorrow, to his wife, his daughter, his acquaintances in the coffee-house? – For God's sake, I shall be seeing him again tomorrow! When I come into the coffee-house tomorrow, there he'll be, sitting as he is every day, playing his rubber with Mr Schlesinger and the florist!... No, no, that won't do, that won't do ... When I see him, I'll cut him down ... No, I mustn't do that. I should have done it at once, at once! If only it had been possible! I shall go to the colonel and tell him the whole story ... yes, to the colonel ... the colonel is always very kind – and I shall say, 'Sir, I have to report, that he held the hilt of my sword, he wouldn't let go; I was as good as defenceless.' – What will the colonel say? I know what he'll say – Why then there's only one thing to do: leave the service in disgrace, dishonoured ... cashiered! Are those reservists over there? ... Horrible, in the dark they look like officers ... they're saluting me! – If they knew – if they only knew! ... There's the Hochleitner Café ... some of the fellows are sure to be there now ... probably one or two that I know. Supposing I told the whole thing to the first one I see, but as though it had happened to someone else? ... Really I'm practically out of my mind ... Where am I hurrying to like this? What am I doing in the street? But where am I to go anyway? Didn't I mean to go to Leidinger's? Ha, ha, to sit down among other people ... I believe anybody would see just by looking at me ... Yes, but something must be done ... What is to be done? ... Nothing, nothing – after all nobody heard a thing ... nobody knows about it ... at this moment nobody knows anything ... Suppose I went to him now in his home and begged him not to tell anyone? – Oh no, sooner than that I'd put a bullet through my head this minute! It would be the best thing to do anyway! ... The best thing? ... The best thing? – Why, there's absolutely nothing else *to* do! ... nothing else ... Whether I asked the colonel, or Kopetzky – or Blany – or Friedmair – every one of them would say: You've got no alternative! ... How about talking to Kopetzky? ... Yes, that would be the most sensible thing ... if only because of tomorrow ... Ah, of course, tomorrow ... at four o'clock in the cavalry barracks . . . I'm due to fight tomorrow at four o'clock . . . and I can't, I can't, I'm disqualified from giving him satisfaction . . . Oh, but that's all rot! Nobody knows a thing – not a soul! Lots of chaps are going about after worse things than this have happened to them. Think of all the stories they told about Deckener when he fought Rederov . . . and yet, the Council of Honour decided that the duel could take place . . . But what would the Council of Honour decide in *my* case? – Stupid boy! – Stupid boy . . . and I just stood there! – God in Heaven, it doesn't make any difference whether anybody else knows! *I* know, and that's what matters! *I* know that I'm a different person from the one I was an hour ago – I know that I'm not capable of giving satisfaction in a duel, and that's why I've got to shoot myself . . . I'd never have another minute's peace of mind . . . I should always go in fear that someone would hear of it, somehow . . . and that sooner or later someone would say it straight out to my face, all that happened this evening! – What a happy man I was an hour ago . . . Kopetzky had to make me a present of the ticket – and Steffi had to cry off for this evening, the slut! – that's the kind of thing one's fate hangs on . . . This afternoon everything was all right, everything was fine, and now I'm done for and I'll have to shoot myself . . . why on earth am I running like this? I'm not going to miss anything . . . What time is that striking? . . . one, two, three, four, five, six, seven, eight, nine, ten, eleven – eleven, eleven . . . I ought to go and have supper! After all, I must go and eat somewhere . . . I could go and sit in some little pub where nobody knows me – after all a man must eat, even if he goes and shoots himself immediately afterwards . . . Haha, death is no joke . . . who did I hear say that the other day? But it doesn't matter . . .

I wish I knew who would be most upset? . . . Mama, or Steffi? . . . Steffi . . . God, Steffi . . . she wouldn't be able to show her feelings at all, or else He would throw her out . . . Poor girl! – In the regiment – nobody would have any idea why I had done it . . . they'd all be racking their brains . . . why did Gustl kill himself? – Not a soul would ever guess that I had to shoot myself because of a wretched baker, a vulgar brute, who happens to be as strong as an ox . . . it's too stupid, too stupid! – Just for that a man like me, a young fellow full of life . . . and of course afterwards they'd all be bound to say: he shouldn't have done it, not for such a stupid reason, it's really a shame! . . . But if I asked anyone about it now, everyone would give me the same answer . . . and I too, when I ask myself . . . devil take it . . . we're completely defenceless against these civilians . . . People think we're better off, because we've got a sword . . . and when one of us does make use of his weapon, they let fly at us as if we were all born murderers . . . It would be in the papers too of course . . . 'Suicide of young officer' . . . what is it they always write? . . . 'The motives are shrouded in obscurity' . . . Haha! . . . 'He is mourned by . . .' – But it's really true . . . I keep on feeling as if I were telling myself a story . . . but it's all true . . . I shall have to kill myself, there's nothing else to do – I can't possibly let it get to the point of Kopetzky and Blany actually refusing to act as my seconds . . . and I should be a scoundrel to expect them to . . . A chap like me, who stands there and lets himself be called a stupid boy . . . by tomorrow everyone will know . . . it's too stupid to let myself imagine for a moment that a man like that won't tell anyone about it . . . he'll tell everybody he meets . . . his wife knows already . . . tomorrow the entire coffee-house will know . . . the waiters . . . Mr Schlesinger . . . the cashier – and even if he's decided not to speak of it, he'll do it the day after tomorrow . . . and if not the day after tomorrow, then in a week . . . And even if he has a stroke this very night, still *I* know it . . . I know it . . . and I am not the man to go on wearing my tunic and my sword, with such a disgrace weighing on me! . . . So there, I must do it, and that's the end of it! – What does it amount to anyway? – Tomorrow afternoon the Doctor might kill me in the duel . . . such things have happened . . . and old Bauer, poor fellow, got brain-fever and was gone in three days . . . and Brenitsch had a fall riding and broke his neck . . . but finally, once and for all – there's nothing else to do – not for me, not for me! – There are people of course who would take it more easily . . . God, what people there are! . . . Old Ringeimer got a box on the ear from a sausage-maker who caught him with his wife, and he left the service and is living in the country somewhere and got married . . . To think there should be women who will marry such a man! . . . – I swear I wouldn't shake hands with him if he came back to Vienna . . . Well, so you understand, Gustl – life is all over and done with . . . Finished and done with, that's that. That's right, so now I know, it's all quite simple . . . actually I'm perfectly calm . . . of course I've always known that when the time came I should be calm, quite calm . . . but that it should come in this way, that I never would have thought . . . to have to kill myself, because of a . . . Perhaps I didn't understand what he said . . . He really must have said something quite different . . . I was quite dazed with all that singing and the heat . . . perhaps I was out of my mind, and it's all not true? . . . Not true, haha, not true! – why I can still hear it . . . it's still ringing in my ears – and I can still feel my fingers where I tried to get his hand off the sword hilt . . . He's a professional strong man, a Mr Universe . . . Still, I'm no weakling myself . . . Franziski is the only one in the regiment who's stronger than I am . . .

Here's the Aspern bridge . . . How much further am I going to go? If I go on running like this I shall be in the open country in Kagran by midnight . . . Haha! – Heavens, how pleased we were to march in there last September. Another two hours, we said, and we'll be in Vienna . . . I was dead tired when we arrived . . . slept like a dog the whole afternoon and in the evening we were out on the town at Ronacher's . . .* Kopetzky, Ladinser, and . . . who else was with us? – Yes, of course, the volunteer, the one who told us those Jewish stories on the march – Sometimes they're quite good fellows, those Territorials . . . but they ought all to be made acting officers – because what's the point of giving them permanent commissions? We have to work hard for years and those chaps serve one year and get exactly the same rank as we do . . . it's not fair! – But what's all that got to do with me? – Why should I bother about all that stuff? – A private in the

* Music-hall. (Trans.)

Commissariat is more than I am now – I'm not in the world
at all any more – it's all over with me . . . When honour is
lost, all is lost! . . . I have nothing else to do but load my
revolver and . . . Gustl, Gustl, it seems to me you still don't
quite believe in it? Only come to your senses . . . there's
nothing else for it . . . however you rack your brains, there's
nothing else to do! – Now it's simply a question of behaving
decently at the last moment, like an officer and a gentleman,
so that the colonel will say, 'He was a brave fellow, we shall
remember him!' . . . How many companies parade for the
funeral of a lieutenant? . . . I ought to know that actually . . .
Haha! if the whole battalion parades, or the whole garrison,
and they fire twenty salvoes, it won't wake me! – I was sitting
in front of that café once last summer with Herr von Engel
after the Army Steeplechase . . . Funny thing, I've never seen
that man since . . . Why was he wearing a bandage over his
left eye? I kept wanting to ask him, but it wouldn't have been
the right thing . . . There go two artillerymen . . . they're sure
to think I'm following that woman in front . . . Let's have a
look at her anyway . . . Ugh, horrible! I just can't imagine
how a woman like that earns her living . . . I'd really rather . . .
though of course beggars can't be choosers . . . Now when I
was stationed in Southern Poland . . . afterwards I felt so
disgusted I thought I should never touch a woman again . . .
That was a hideous time up there in Galicia . . . terrific luck
that we got to Vienna actually. Old Bokorny is still sitting in
Sambor and he may sit there another ten years and get old
and grey . . . And yet if I'd stayed there, this would never
have happened to me this evening . . . and I really would
rather get old and grey in Galicia than . . . than what? than
what? – Well, what is it? what is it? – Am I mad, to keep on
forgetting it? – Yes, good heavens, I'm forgetting it every
other moment . . . has such a thing ever been heard of, that a
man about to put a bullet through his head in a few hours'
time should keep thinking of every stupid thing under the
sun when it has nothing to do with him any more? On my
soul I feel exactly as though I were drunk! Haha! a nice way
to get drunk! Dead-drunk! Suicide-drunk! – Now I'm

cracking jokes, that's just splendid! – Yes, I feel fine – I suppose that's something one's born with . . . Honestly, if I were to tell anyone I don't think they'd believe it – I think if I had the thing on me, I'd pull the trigger now . . . all over in a second – it's not everyone who's so lucky – others suffer for months – my poor cousin, she had to lie in bed for two years unable to move a muscle and in terrible pain – what misery! . . . Isn't it better to do the job oneself? Only take care, that's the thing, aim well, so that you don't have some awful accident like that cadet officer last year . . . poor devil, he didn't die but he went blind . . . What happened to him I wonder? Where's he living? – Terrible to be running around like him – that is – he's not running around, he has to be led – a young chap like that, not twenty yet . . . he took better aim at his sweetheart, she was killed instantly . . . Extraordinary the things people shoot themselves for! How can a man be jealous anyway? . . . I've never known what it is to be jealous in my life . . . There's Steffi now, sitting comfortably in the Garden Restaurant; then she'll go home afterwards with Him . . . it means nothing to me, nothing at all. She's got that place fixed up so nicely – the little bathroom with the red lamp. – The way she came in the other day in that green silk dressing-gown . . . I'll never see that green dressing-gown again – nor Steffi herself, any more – and the fine broad staircase in the Gusshausstrasse, I'll never go up it any more . . . Miss Steffi will go on amusing herself as if nothing had happened . . . she can't even tell anyone about how her dear Gustl killed himself . . . But she'll cry, I know – oh yes, she'll cry . . . Actually quite a lot of people will cry . . . Oh my God, Mama! – No, no, I mustn't think about that – no, I absolutely mustn't think about it – understand, Gustl, no thinking about home? – not even the tiniest little thought . . .

That's pretty good going, I'm actually in the Prater . . . in the middle of the night . . . I certainly never thought this morning I'd be strolling about in the Prater this evening . . . What does that policeman think? Well, let's go on . . . it's beautiful here . . . It's no good having supper, no good going to a café . . . the air's pleasant and it's calm here, very . . .

Of course it'll be very calm where I'm going, as calm as I
could possibly wish. Haha! – but goodness, I'm quite out of
breath . . . I've been running like mad . . . slower, slower,
Gustl, you won't miss anything, you've nothing more to do –
nothing, absolutely nothing more! – I believe I feel a chill? –
It must be the excitement after all . . . and then I've eaten
nothing . . . What's this strange smell here? . . . there can't
be any flowers yet? . . . What date is it? – the fourth of April
. . . of course it has been raining a lot the last few days – but
the trees are still almost all bare . . . and it's so dark, brr! it's
almost frightening . . . That was actually the only time in my
life that I've been afraid, that time in the wood when I was a
little chap . . . but I wasn't so little . . . fourteen or fifteen . . .
How long ago is that? Nine years – that's right – at eighteen I
was acting-lieutenant, at twenty lieutenant – and next year
I'll be . . . What will I be next year? What does it mean when
I say: 'next year'? Or 'next week'? What is 'the day after
tomorrow'? . . . What's this? Are my teeth chattering? Oho!
– well, let them chatter a bit . . . Lieutenant, Sir, you are alone
now and you need not put up a show for anyone . . . it's
bitter, it's bitter . . .

I'll sit down on the bench here . . . Ouf! – how far have I
come? – It's pitch dark! That must be the second Prater café
over there* . . . I was there once last summer, when our band
was giving the concert . . . with Kopetzky and Rüttner – and
a few others too . . . I'm tired out . . . I'm as tired as if I had
just finished a ten-hour march . . . A fine thing it would be if
I fell asleep here. – Haha! . . . a lieutenant of no fixed address
. . . Yes, I really ought to go home . . . but what shall I do
at home? Well, what am I doing in the Prater? – What I'd
like best would be if I didn't have to get up at all – fall asleep
here and never wake up . . . yes, that would be all right! –
No, Lieutenant, Sir, it won't be as easy as all that . . . But
how and when? – Now I have time to think the whole affair
over properly at last . . . one must think everything over of
course . . . that's how life is . . . well then, let's think it over

* There were three coffee-houses situated at intervals along the main
avenue of the Prater. (Trans.)

. . . What about it? – Heavens, how good the air is . . . one ought to go for a walk in the Prater at night more often . . . Yes, but I should have thought of that before. Now there'll be no more Prater, or fresh air, or going out for walks . . . Yes, so what about it? – Let me just take off my cap; it seems to be pressing on my brain . . . I can't think properly . . . Ah, that's better . . . Well now, Gustl, pull your thoughts together . . . make your final arrangements! Tomorrow morning, then, I'll put an end to it . . . at seven o'clock . . . seven o'clock is a fine time of day . . . Haha! and then by eight when instruction starts, it will all be over . . . but Kopetzky won't be able to take his classes because he'll be much too upset . . . but perhaps he won't know anything about it yet . . . people don't necessarily hear anything . . . Max Lippay was found only in the afternoon, and had shot himself in the early morning, and not a soul heard anything . . . But what do I care whether Kopetzky takes instruction or not? . . . Ha – so at seven o'clock then! – Yes . . . and now what else? . . . There's nothing else to decide. I shoot myself in my room and that's it! On Monday is the funeral . . . I know one man who'll be pleased, and that's the Doctor . . . the duel cannot take place owing to the suicide of one of the combatants . . . I wonder what the Mannheimers will say? – Oh, *he* won't care much one way or the other . . . but his wife, the pretty blonde . . . something could have come of that . . . Oh yes, I believe I would have had some luck there, if only I'd pulled myself together a bit . . . it would have been quite another thing from that tart Steffi . . . but of course I wouldn't have had a moment's peace . . . it would have meant paying court, sending flowers, making intelligent conversation . . . not the kind of thing where you can say . . . 'come round to my room in the barracks tomorrow afternoon!' . . . Yes, a respectable woman, that would have been an interesting experience . . . The captain's wife in Galicia, she wasn't a respectable woman either . . . I could take my oath that Libitzky and old Wermutek and that dreary little cadet-officer all had her . . . But Mrs Mannheimer . . . that would have been different, it would have been a real classy contact, perhaps I would almost

have become another person – that would have given me
some polish – I might have come to have some respect for
myself . . . But these everlasting tarts . . . and I started so
young – I was only a boy when I had that first leave and went
home to Graz . . . old Riedl was there too – it was a Czech
girl . . . must have been twice my age – I didn't come home
till early morning . . . How father looked at me . . . and Clara
. . . It was Clara who made me feel most ashamed . . . She
was engaged at the time . . . Why did nothing come of that?
I didn't bother much about it as a matter of fact . . . Poor
little mouse, she never had any luck – and now she's going to
lose her only brother . . . Yes, you'll never see me again,
Clara – it's all over! I'll bet you didn't think, little sister,
when you saw me off at the station on New Year's Day, that
you'd never see me any more – and Mama – Oh God, Mama
. . . no, I mustn't think of her . . . if I think of her, I might
turn coward . . . Oh, if only I could just go home beforehand
. . . say I've got a twenty-four-hour pass . . . to see Papa and
Mama and Clara once more, before I make an end of things. . .
Yes, I could go to Graz at seven on the first train, I'd be there
at one . . . Good day Mama, hallo Clara! Well, how are you
all? What a surprise, they'd say! . . . But they might suspect . . .
if no one else then Clara . . . Clara certainly would. Clara's
such a clever girl . . . What a nice letter she wrote me not long
ago, and I still haven't answered it – and all the good advice
she always gives me . . . such a thoroughly good creature . . .
wouldn't everything have turned out entirely different if I had
stayed at home? I would have studied agriculture, gone to
my uncle's . . . they all wanted me to when I was still a boy . . .
By now I'd be sure to have got married, some sweet good
girl . . . perhaps Anna, who was so fond of me . . . I noticed it
even last time I was at home, although she has a husband and
two children. I saw how she looked at me . . . And she still
calls me Gustl as she used to . . . It'll give her a frightful
shock when she hears what's happened to me – but her
husband will say, 'I foresaw it all along – that ne'er-do-well!' –
They'll all say I did it because I was in debt . . . and it isn't
true, everything's paid up, except for the last 160 florins, and

they'll arrive tomorrow. Yes, I must see to that, Ballert must get his 160 florins . . . I must put that on paper before I shoot myself. It's terrible, it's terrible! . . . When what I really want to do is to take the next boat to America, where no one knows me . . . In America no one knows what's happened here tonight . . . no one cares either . . . I saw something in the papers lately about a man called Count Runge, who had to leave because of some dirty business, and now he owns a hotel over there and can snap his fingers at the whole thing . . . and in a few years' time one could come back again . . . not to Vienna of course . . . not to Graz either . . . but I could go to the country place . . . and Mama and Papa and Clara would a thousand times rather I was still alive . . . And what do other people matter to me? Who else is fond of me? – Apart from Kopetzky they don't care a hang about me . . . Kopetzky is really the only one . . . And it had to be Kopetzky who gave me the ticket today . . . the ticket is to blame for the whole thing . . . but for that I wouldn't have gone to the concert, and the whole thing would never have happened . . . what was it that happened? . . . It's just as though a hundred years had passed since then, and it can't be two hours yet . . . Two hours ago a man said 'Stupid boy' to me and threatened to break my sword . . . Good God! I shall start screaming my head off here in the middle of the night! Why did it all happen? Why couldn't I wait a bit longer, till the cloakroom was empty? And why for heaven's sake did I tell him to shut his trap? How did that slip out? I'm usually a very civil person... even to my batman I don't usually speak as rudely as that . . . but naturally I was rather strung-up – everything coming at once . . . having such bad luck at cards and Steffi putting me off the whole time – and the duel tomorrow afternoon – and I haven't been getting enough sleep lately – and the grind in the barracks – you can't expect to go on like that for long! . . . Yes, sooner or later I would have become ill – would have had to apply for leave . . . Now I don't need it any more – now there's a long leave coming – with all expenses taken care of – haha!

How much longer shall I go on sitting here? It must be

after midnight . . . didn't I hear it strike earlier on? – What's that . . . a carriage going by? At this hour? Rubber tyres – I expect I can imagine . . . They're better off than I am – perhaps it's old Ballert with his Berta . . . Why should it be Ballert of all people? Drive on then! – That was a nice little turnout his Highness had in Przemysl – always drove down town in it when he went to see the Rosenberg woman . . . Very affable his Highness was – a real comrade, familiar with everyone . . . It was a good time . . . although the country round about was very bare and fearfully hot in summer . . . three men got sunstroke in one afternoon – the corporal of my platoon too – such a useful chap . . . After lunch we all used to lie on our beds with nothing on – Once old Wiesner came in to my room suddenly; I must have been having a dream and I leapt up and drew my sword that was lying beside me . . . must have looked funny . . . I thought old Wiesner would die of laughing . . . he's a cavalry captain now – Pity I didn't go into the cavalry . . . but my old man didn't want me to – would have been an expensive bit of fun – and now it's all the same anyway . . . Why though? – Yes I know, I know: I must die, that's why it doesn't matter any more . . . Well, how? – Look, Gustl, you've come down here into the Prater on purpose in the middle of the night so that no one will disturb you – now you can think it all over quietly . . . That's all nonsense about America and resigning from the service, and you're much too stupid to start on anything else – and if you live to be a hundred you'll remember that a man threatened to break your sword and called you a stupid boy and you stood there and couldn't do a thing – no, there's nothing to think over – what's done is done – and all that about Mama and Clara is nonsense too – they'll get over it all right – people get over anything. How Mama carried on when her brother died – and four weeks later she was hardly thinking of it any more . . . she used to go out to the cemetery . . . at first every week and then once a month – and now only on the anniversary of his death. Tomorrow will be the anniversary of mine – the fifth of April – Will they take me to Graz, I wonder? Haha! That will be nice for the worms in Graz! But that is none of my business, someone else can worry about that ... Well then, so what have I still to do? ... Yes, the 160 florins for Ballert – that's all – no other arrangements to make – Should I write some letters? What for? And to whom? ... to say goodbye? – Oh, devil take it, surely if a man shoots himself it's plain enough – I should think they'll notice that I've made my exit! ... If people only knew how little I care about the whole thing, they wouldn't feel sorry for me at all – *I*'m no great loss ... And what have I had out of life? – There's one thing I would have liked to experience: a war – but I might have had to wait a long time ... And I've been through everything else ... Whether the slut's name is Steffi or Lady Diana makes no difference. And I know all the best operettas – and I've been to *Lohengrin* twelve times – and this evening I even listened to an oratorio – and a baker called me a stupid boy – upon my soul, it's about enough! – And the rest doesn't interest me ... So now, let's go home, slowly, quite slowly ... No hurry. – Let's rest a few minutes in the Prater, on a bench – I won't bother to go to bed – I shall have enough time to sleep – Oh, the air! That's something I'll miss ...

What's that? – Hi, Johann, bring me a glass of cold water... What, where ... Am I dreaming? ... Oh my head ... Oh the devil ... I can't get my eyes open! – Good God, I'm fully dressed! – where am I sitting? – Holy Mother, I must have fallen asleep! How could I possibly sleep; it's already getting light! How long have I been asleep anyway? – I must look at my watch. Can't see a thing ... Where are my matches? ... Can't I get one to strike? ... Three o'clock ... and I'm supposed to fight a duel at four. – No, not a duel – I'm supposed to shoot myself! – The duel's all off; I must shoot myself because a baker called me a stupid boy ... Did it really happen though? – My head feels so funny ... my neck feels as though it were in a vice – I can't move a muscle – my right leg's gone to sleep – Get up! Get up! – Ah, that's better! – It's getting lighter ... and the air ... just like that time before dawn when I was on sentry duty, camping out in the wood ... That was a different awakening – I had quite a different day in front of me then . . . I daresay I still don't quite believe it – there's the road, grey, empty – I must be the only person in the Prater just now – I've been down here once before at four o'clock in the morning, with Pausinger – we were on horseback – I was on Captain Mirovich's horse and Pausinger was on his own old hack – that was in May last year – all the trees were in bloom – everything was green. Now it's still bare – but spring will soon be here – only a few days now. Lilies of the valley, violets – I'm sorry I shan't see anything of it – every poor beggar will have some fun out of it, and I have to die! It's so wretched! And the others will be sitting in the wine-garden having supper as though nothing had happened . . . just as we were sitting in the wine-garden the very same evening after they'd carried old Lippay out . . . And Lippay was awfully popular . . . they were fonder of him than they are of me, in the regiment – why shouldn't they sit in the wine-garden when I pop off? – It's quite warm – much warmer than yesterday – and the scent of flowers – there *must* be a tree in bloom some- where – I wonder if Steffi will bring flowers to my grave? – Of course not, it'll never even occur to her! Catch her driving out to the cemetery. If it had been Adela now . . . Adela . . . I don't suppose I've thought of her once in the last two years . . . The fuss she made when it was all over! . . . I've never in my life seen a woman cry so – I think that must have been the nicest thing that's ever happened to me . . . So modest, so un- assuming she was – she really loved me, I could swear to that – She was quite another thing from Steffi . . . I wonder why on earth I gave that girl up . . . what idiocy! It just got too dull for me, that's all it was . . . Going out every evening with the same girl . . . and then I got scared that I'd never get rid of her – always round my neck as she was – Well, Gustl, you might have waited a bit – she was the only one who cared for you after all . . . What is she doing now I wonder? Well, what should she be doing? . . . By now she's got someone else . . . of course with Steffi the whole thing is more convenient – only seeing her occasionally and someone else having all the bother while I only have the fun . . . Yes, so I really can't expect her to come trailing out to the cemetery . . . Who'd dream of going anyway, if they didn't have to! – Kopetzky perhaps, nobody else – It's sad to have nobody at all . . .

But that's nonsense! Papa and Mama and Clara . . . Well, of course, I'm their son, I'm her brother . . . but is there anything else between us? They're fond of me, yes, but what do they know about me? – That I'm a serving officer, play cards, run after tarts, yes, but what else? That I'm sometimes disgusted with myself, I've never written to them about that – in fact I don't think I really knew it myself – Oh shut up, Gustl, you're not going to start on that sort of thing. All we need now is for you to begin to cry . . . disgusting! – In step now, properly . . . yes! whether one's meeting a girl or going on guard duty or into battle . . . who was it said that? . . . Ah yes, Major Lederer in the mess when someone was talking about Wingleder, and how he went quite pale before his first duel – and threw up . . . Yes; whether one's going to meet a girl or to certain death, a true officer will never betray his feelings in his walk or his face! – So, Gustl – Major Lederer said so.

It's lighter still . . . light enough to read by . . . what's that whistling? . . . Ah yes, over there is the Northern Railway . . . There's the Tegetthoff column. I never saw it look so tall before . . . here are some carriages . . . but only sweepers on the street . . . my last road-sweepers – haha! I can't help laughing whenever I think of it . . . I just don't understand why . . . I wonder if this happens to everybody when they know it for certain? Half past three by the North Station clock . . . and at seven I shall shoot myself . . . why seven exactly? . . . As though it had to be just then . . . I'm hungry – heavens I'm hungry – no wonder . . . when did I last have anything to eat? . . . Yesterday at – at six in the coffee-house . . . yes! When Kopetzky gave me the ticket – a white coffee and two croissants. What will the baker say when he hears about it? . . . The cursed swine! – Oh, *he*'ll know why – he'll see it in a flash – then he'll understand what it means to be an officer! – A fellow like that will let himself be beaten up in the open street and there'll be no consequences, but one of our sort, even if he's insulted with not another soul present – he's as good as dead . . . If only a blackguard like that could fight – but no, *then* he'd be a bit more careful, *then* he'd think twice before he took such a risk ... And such a fellow lives on peacefully, while I – I must die! – It's he who's killed me – Yes, Gustl, do you realize? – It's that man who's killed you! But he shan't get off so lightly! – No, no, no! I shall write Kopetzky a letter and tell him everything, I'll write it all down ... or better still: I'll write to the colonel, I'll make a report to the regimental command ... just like a service report ... Yes, just you wait, you think a thing like that can be kept secret? – You're mistaken – it will be written down in black and white, to be remembered for ever, and *then* I'd like to see you come into the coffee-house – Haha! 'I'd like to see you' is pretty good! ... I'd like to see a lot of things, only unfortunately it won't be possible – it's all over! –

Now Johann will be coming into my room, now he realizes that the lieutenant hasn't slept in his bed – Well, he'll think of all sorts of reasons; but one thing that won't occur to him is that the lieutenant spent the night in the Prater ... Ah, here come the 44th! they're marching to the rifle-range – better let them go past ... I'll stand here to take the salute ... Someone's opening a window up there – pretty little thing – well, if I were you I'd put something round me before I went to the window ... So last Sunday was the last time ... I never dreamed that Steffi of all people would be the last ... God knows that's the only *real* pleasure after all ... Ah well, the colonel will come riding after them, very splendid, in about two hours' time ... those gentlemen have an easy life – yes, yes, eyes right! – Get on with it – If you knew how little I care about the lot of you! – Now there's a surprise – old Katzer ... when did he transfer to the 44th? – 'Morning, morning!' – What a face he's making? Why is he pointing to his forehead? – My dear fellow, your skull interests me very little ... Oh I see! No, old chap, you're wrong: I spent the night in the Prater ... you'll read all about it in the evening paper – 'Impossible!' he'll say, 'this very morning when we were going out to the range, I saw him in the Praterstrasse!' I wonder who'll get my platoon? – Will they give it to Walterer? That'll be a fine thing – a fellow without any style, ought to

have gone for a cobbler instead . . . Is the sun rising already? –
It will be a fine day today – a real spring day . . . The devil take
it! – that hansom-cabman will still be in the world at eight
o'clock this morning, and I . . . now what's all this? That
would be a funny thing – to lose countenance at the last
minute because of a cabdriver . . . Why has my heart begun to
beat in this stupid way? It can't be because of that . . . No, oh
no . . . it's because I've been such a long time without food –
Come on, Gustl, be honest with yourself – you're afraid –
afraid, because it's something new. But that's no earthly use,
being afraid never helped anyone, we've all got to face it
some time, one chap sooner, another chap later, and your turn
is just a bit sooner, that's all . . . You were never worth much,
so at least behave yourself decently at the last, that I do expect
of you! – Well, now I've only to think it all over – but what?
I always want to think something over . . . but the whole
business is quite simple – it's lying in the drawer of the bedside table, it's ready loaded too, I've only to press the trigger –
nothing complicated about that! – The girl over there is on
her way to work – this early . . . those poor girls! Adela was
in a shop too – I fetched her there in the evening a few times . . .
When they work in a shop they don't get to be such tarts . . .
If Steffi belonged to me alone I'd make her go into a milliner's
shop or something like that . . . How will she hear of it? From
the newspaper! . . . She'll be annoyed because I didn't write to
her about it . . . I really think I shall go off my head yet . . .
What does it matter to me if she's annoyed? . . . How long is
it anyway that I've been with her? Since January? . . . Oh no,
it must have been before Christmas . . . I know I brought her
some sweets back from Graz, and at New Year she sent me a
little note to thank me . . . That reminds me, the letters I've
got in my room – are there any I ought to burn? . . . Mm, the
one from Fallsteiner – if that letter is found . . . the chap might
get into trouble . . . As if I cared! – Still, it's no great effort . . .
but I can't be bothered to sort them all out to find that one . . .
the best thing is to burn them all together . . . who wants them
anyway? Just a lot of waste paper – And I could leave the few
books I've got to Blany. – *Through the Polar Night* – it's a pity

I'll never get to the end of it now . . . haven't got down to reading much lately . . . An organ playing – ah yes, early Mass in this church – I haven't been to Mass for a long time . . . the last time was in February when my platoon had church parade . . . but that didn't count . . . I was watching my men to see they were attending to the service and behaving properly . . . – I'd quite like to go in . . . there may be something in it after all . . . Well, by lunchtime today I'll know for sure . . . Oh, 'by lunchtime' is rather good! . . . Well so what, shall I go in? – I believe it would be a consolation to Mama if she knew I had been! . . . Clara doesn't set so much store by it . . . well, so let's go in – it can't do any harm!

Organ, choir singing – hm! – what's the matter with me? – I feel quite giddy . . . Oh God, oh God, oh God! I wish I had someone I could speak to beforehand! – That would be a fine idea – to go to confession! The priest would open his eyes, I expect, when I said at the end: Good-day your reverence; now I'm going to shoot myself! . . . I feel like lying down on the stone floor there and crying, that's what I feel like . . . No no, that's out of the question! But sometimes it does you good to cry . . . Let's sit down a moment – but no falling asleep again, like in the Prater! . . . – people who have a religion are better off . . . Oh no, now my hands are beginning to tremble! If it goes on like this I shall end up by hating myself so much that I'll kill myself in sheer disgust! – That old woman there – what's she got to pray about at her age? . . . It wouldn't be a bad idea if I said to her 'Please say a prayer for me too . . . I never learnt properly how to do it' . . . Huh! I do believe dying makes you weak in the head! – Up we get! – what does this tune remind me of? – God in heaven! Yesterday evening! – I'm getting out of here, I can't stand it . . . Sh! Not so much noise, I mustn't let my sword rattle – not to disturb the people at their prayers – that's the way! Better in the open air . . . light . . . Oh, it's coming nearer and nearer – if only it were over! – I should have done it straight away – in the Prater . . . one should never go out without a revolver . . . If only I'd had one last night! Damnation! – I could go and have breakfast at the coffee-house . . . I'm hungry . . . It always used to strike

me as peculiar when they said 'the condemned man ate a
hearty breakfast – and smoked a cigar' – Good heavens, I
haven't smoked at all! Absolutely no desire to smoke! – It's
funny: I really feel like going to my coffee-house . . . Yes, it
will be open by now, and none of our people will be there yet –
and even if they were . . . it would only be a sign of a cool head
. . . 'At six he was having breakfast in the coffee-house, and at
seven he shot himself ' . . . I'm quite calm again . . . it's pleasant
walking – and the best part of it is that nobody's forcing me –
if I wanted to, I could still chuck the whole thing up . . .
America . . . What's this: chuck the thing up? What thing? I
do believe I must have got sunstroke! . . . Oho! Perhaps I'm
feeling so calm because I'm imagining that I can get out of
it? . . . No! I must! I must! No, I want to! – Can you imagine
yourself getting out of your uniform, Gustl, and turning
away? And that cursed swine laughing himself sick – and
even Kopetzky wouldn't care to shake hands with me . . . I feel
as though I'd gone quite red in the face – The policeman is
saluting me . . . I must return his salute . . . 'Good morning!'
I actually said good morning to him! . . . It always pleases these
poor devils . . . Well, no one ever had reason to complain about
me – outside of duty I've always been civil to everybody –
When we were on manoeuvres I made a present of cigars to
my company N.C.O.s; once I heard a man behind me at rifle-
drill say something about 'damned lot of bull' and I didn't
report him – I only said, 'Look out, you there, someone else
might hear you another time and you'd be sorry for it!' . . .
Here's the Castle yard . . . Who's on guard today? – The Bos-
nians – they look fine – the colonel said the other day . . .
'When we were down there in 78, no one would have believed
that they'd turn out to be such fine soldiers!' God, I'd like to
have been in something like that – They're all standing up
from the bench – Morning, morning! – It's really too bad that
we fellows haven't had a shot at it – It would have been a lot
better to die on the field of honour, for the Fatherland, than
like this . . . Yes, my good Doctor, you're getting off lightly ! . . .
Couldn't someone else take it on for me? – By Jove, that's
what I ought to do – leave a request for Kopetzky or

Wymetal to fight the chap for me . . . Then he wouldn't get away with it! – Oh to hell with it! Can it matter, what happens afterwards? – I'll never know about it anyway! – The trees are coming into leaf . . . In the Public Gardens there I picked up a girl once – she had a red dress on – lived in the Strozzigasse – afterwards Rochlitz took her over from me . . . I believe he's still got her, but he never says anything about her – perhaps he's ashamed . . . Steffi is still asleep at this time . . . she looks so sweet when she's asleep . . . as if butter wouldn't melt in her mouth! – Oh, when they're asleep they all look like that! – I really should write her a note; why not, actually? People always do that, write a few letters beforehand – I ought to write to Clara too, tell her to comfort Mama and Papa – and the usual things people write! – and to Kopetzky as well . . . Upon my soul, I think it would be a great deal simpler if one had said goodbye to a few people . . . And the report to the regimental H.Q. – and the 160 florins for Ballert . . . still quite a lot to do, actually . . . well, nobody's forcing me to do it at seven, eight is early enough to start being dead! being dead, yes – that's what it's called – nothing to be done about it.

The Ringstrasse – now I shall soon be in my coffee-house . . . I really believe I'm looking forward to my breakfast . . . it's almost incredible. Yes, after breakfast I shall light a cigar, and then go home and write . . . First of all I'll make the report to headquarters; then comes the letter to Clara – then the one to Kopetzky – then to Steffi . . . what am I to write to the slut . . . 'Dearest girl, you probably never thought' . . . Oh rot! 'Dearest girl, thank you with all my heart' . . . 'Dearest girl, before I leave this world behind, I must not omit' . . . Yes, well, letter-writing was never my strong point . . . 'Dearest girl, a last farewell from your Gustl' – How she'll open her eyes! It's a good thing I wasn't in love with her . . . It must be sad when you're fond of someone and then . . . Now Gustl, be sensible; it's sad enough as it is . . . after Steffi there would have been lots of others, and finally one that would have been worth having – a young girl of good family with a dowry – it would have been rather nice – I must write to Clara properly, and explain that I couldn't do anything else ... 'You must forgive me, dearest sister, and please comfort our dear parents as well. I know that I have caused you all a great deal of anxiety and sorrow; but believe me, I have always loved you very much and I hope you will find happiness again one day, Clara, and not quite forget your unfortunate brother' ... Oh, I'd better not write to her at all! ... No, I shall break down ... my eyes begin to smart when I think of it ... At most I'll write to Kopetzky, a comradely farewell, and ask him to tell the others – Is it six o'clock yet? – No – half past five, a quarter to – What a sweet little face that is! ... the little thing with black eyes that I meet so often in the Florianigasse! – What will she say about it? – But she has no idea who I am – she'll only wonder why she never sees me any more ... The day before yesterday I promised myself that I'd speak to her the next time – She's been making eyes at me long enough ... she's terribly young – I shouldn't wonder if she's still innocent! ... Yes, Gustl! Never put off till tomorrow what you might do today! ... That man there certainly hasn't slept all night either. Well, now he is going to go home and lie down – and so am I! – Haha! Now it really is getting serious, Gustl! ... Well, if it weren't for having the shivers a bit, there wouldn't be much to it – And on the whole, though I say it, I'm behaving very well ... Now where do I want to go? There's my coffee-house ... they're still sweeping up ... Well, in we go ...

At the back there is the table where they always sit playing Tarok ... It's strange, I simply can't imagine that the chap who always sits there by the wall is the same one who did this to me ... Not a soul here yet ... Where's the waiter though? ... 'Hey!' Here he comes out of the kitchen ... he's hurrying to get into his tailcoat ... Well, that really isn't necessary! Oh, but he must, I suppose ... he'll have to serve other people today! –

'What can I do for you, Lieutenant, Sir?'

'Good morning!'

'You're early today, Lieutenant, Sir!'

'Oh, don't bother – I haven't much time, I can sit in my coat.'

'What would you like, Sir?'

'Coffee with cream.'

'At once, Lieutenant.'

Ah, there are the newspapers ... today's already? ...
Wonder if there's anything in them yet? ... What am I
thinking of? ... I do believe I was going to look and see if it
says in the newspaper that I've killed myself! Haha! – Why
am I still standing up? ... Let's sit down at the window ...
He's brought the coffee already ... I'll draw the curtain; I hate
it when people look in ... Although nobody is going past
anyway ... Ah, this coffee tastes good – breakfast is no vain
delusion! ... One feels quite another man – the stupid thing
was going without any supper ... What's the man standing
there again for? – Ah, he's brought the rolls ...

'Has the Lieutenant heard the news?'

'What is it?'

For God's sake, does he know about it already? ... Nonsense, that's impossible! ...

'Mr Habetswallner ...'

What? That's the baker's name ... what is he going to say?
Has the man been here already? Did he come in last night and
tell them? Why doesn't he go on speaking? But he is ...

' ... he had a stroke at twelve o'clock last night.'

'What?' I mustn't shout so ... no, I mustn't let him notice
anything ... but perhaps I'm dreaming ... I must ask him
again ... 'Who had a stroke, did you say?'

Fine, fine! – I said it absolutely calmly.

'The master-baker, Sir! ... The Lieutenant knows him, of
course ... the fat one, who plays a game of Tarok every afternoon at the next table to the officers ... with Mr Schlesinger
and Mr Wasner from the artificial-flower shop opposite!'

I'm wide awake – everything fits – though I can't really
believe it yet – I must ask him again – but quite innocently.

'He had a stroke? ... But how? And how do you know?'

'But Sir, who should know sooner than us? – the roll that
the Lieutenant is eating was baked by Mr Habetswallner. The
boy who comes round with the bread at half past four in the
morning told us all about it.'

For the love of heaven, I mustn't betray myself . . . I'd like to shout out loud . . . I'd like to laugh . . . I'd like to give Rudolf a kiss . . . but I must ask him one thing more! . . . To have a stroke doesn't mean to die . . . I must ask if he's dead . . . but quietly, because what's the baker to me – I must be looking at the newspaper while I ask the waiter . . .

'Is he dead?'

'Oh yes indeed, Lieutenant Sir; he fell dead on the spot.'

Oh marvellous, marvellous! – I'm sure it's all because I went to church . . .

'In the evening he'd been to the theatre; he fell down on the steps coming in – the porter heard the noise . . . and, well, they carried him into his flat, and the doctor came, but it was all over long before he got there.'

'Very sad. He was still in the prime of life.'

I said that really splendidly – no one could possibly have noticed anything . . . and yet it's only by an effort that I'm keeping myself from shouting or jumping on to the billiards table . . .

'Yes, Sir, it's very sad; such a pleasant gentleman he was, and he's been coming to us for twenty years – he was a close friend of our master's. And his poor wife . . .'

I don't think I've ever felt so happy in my whole life . . he's dead – he's dead! No one knows about it, and nothing has happened! – And what devilish good fortune that I came into the coffee-house . . . otherwise I would have shot myself for nothing – it's like the hand of Providence . . . Where's that Rudolf? – Oh, talking to the kitchen-boy . . . Well, and so he's dead, he's dead – I still can't believe it! I'd really like to go round there and have a look at him – I'm sure he must have had a stroke because of being in a rage, from suppressed anger . . . But it doesn't matter why. The main thing is – he's dead, and I can live, and all the world is mine again! . . . Funny how I'm sitting here crumbling the roll that Mr Habets-wallner baked for me! It tastes very good, Mr Habetswallner! Splendid! – There, now I'd like to have a little cigar . . .

'Rudolf! hey, Rudolf! Leave the kitchen-boy alone!'

'Yes, Lieutenant Sir?'

'Some cigars' . . . – I'm so happy, so happy . . . What shall I do now? . . . What shall I do? . . . I must do something, or I'll have a stroke too, from sheer joy! – In a quarter of an hour I'll go over to the barracks and get Johann to rub me down with cold water . . . at half past seven there's small-arms drill and at half past nine exercise in the parade ground – And I'll write to Steffi that she's got to be free somehow for tonight, if it's the last thing she does! And at four o'clock this afternoon . . . just you wait, my dear Doctor, just you wait! I'm in exactly the right mood . . . I'm going to make mincemeat of you!

Thomas Mann

THE INFANT PRODIGY

Translated by H. T. Lowe-Porter

Thomas Mann

THOMAS MANN was born in Lubeck in 1875. He spent the years of Nazi rule in exile and indeed never returned to live permanently in Germany; he died in Switzerland in 1955. He is celebrated for his irony and for his self-critical obsession – particularly in his early work, but recurring throughout his career – with the nature of art and the artist. For Mann, as for the German Romantics, music was the quintessence of art in its irrational, dangerous power, drawing the artist away from the solid concerns of real life. He treated the theme in many ways: tragically and comically, with passion and here (1903) with wry detachment.

THE INFANT PRODIGY

THE infant prodigy entered. The hall became quiet.

It became quiet and then the audience began to clap, because somewhere at the side a leader of mobs, a born organizer, clapped first. The audience had heard nothing yet, but they applauded; for a mighty publicity organization had heralded the prodigy and people were already hypnotized, whether they knew it or not.

The prodigy came from behind a splendid screen embroidered with Empire garlands and great conventionalized flowers, and climbed nimbly up the steps to the platform, diving into the applause as into a bath; a little chilly and shivering, but yet as though into a friendly element. He advanced to the edge of the platform and smiled as though he were about to be photographed; he made a shy, charming gesture of greeting, like a little girl.

He was dressed entirely in white silk, which the audience found enchanting. The little white jacket was fancifully cut, with a sash underneath it, and even his shoes were made of white silk. But against the white socks his bare little legs stood out quite brown, for he was a Greek boy.

He was called Bibi Saccellaphylaccas. And such indeed was his name. No one knew what Bibi was the pet name for, nobody but the impresario, and he regarded it as a trade secret. Bibi had smooth black hair reaching to his shoulders; it was parted on the side and fastened back from the narrow domed forehead by a little silk bow. His was the most harmless, childish countenance in the world, with an unfinished nose and guileless mouth. The area beneath his pitch-black, mouselike eyes was already a little tired and visibly lined. He looked as though he were nine years old but was really eight and given out for seven. It was hard to tell whether to believe this or not. Probably everybody knew better and still believed it, as happens about so many things. The average man thinks that a little falseness goes with beauty. Where should we get

any excitement out of our daily life if we were not willing to
pretend a bit? And the average man is quite right, in his
average brains!

The prodigy kept on bowing until the applause died down,
then he went up to the grand piano, and the audience cast a
last look at its programmes. First came a *Marche solennelle*, then
a *Rêverie*, and then *Le Hibou et les Moineaux* – all by Bibi
Saccellaphylaccas. The whole programme was by him, they
were all his compositions. He could not score them, of course,
but he had them all in his extraordinary little head and they
possessed real artistic significance, or so it said, seriously and
objectively, in the programme. The programme sounded as
though the impresario had wrested these concessions from his
critical nature after a hard struggle.

The prodigy sat down upon the revolving stool and felt
with his feet for the pedals, which were raised by means of a
clever device so that Bibi could reach them. It was Bibi's own
piano, he took it everywhere with him. It rested upon wooden
trestles and its polish was somewhat marred by the constant
transportation – but all that only made things more interesting.

Bibi put his silk-shod feet on the pedals; then he made
an artful little face, looked straight ahead of him, and lifted
his right hand. It was a brown, childish little hand; but the
wrist was strong and unlike a child's, with well-developed
bones.

Bibi made his face for the audience because he was aware
that he had to entertain them a little. But he had his own
private enjoyment in the thing too, an enjoyment which he
could never convey to anybody. It was that prickling delight,
that secret shudder of bliss, which ran through him every
time he sat at an open piano – it would always be with him.
And here was the keyboard again, these seven black and white
octaves, among which he had so often lost himself in abysmal
and thrilling adventures – and yet it always looked as clean
and untouched as a newly washed blackboard. This was the
realm of music that lay before him. It lay spread out like an
inviting ocean, where he might plunge in and blissfully swim,
where he might let himself be borne and carried away, where

he might go under in night and storm, yet keep the mastery; control, ordain – he held his right hand poised in the air.

A breathless stillness reigned in the room – the tense moment before the first note came . . . How would it begin? It began so. And Bibi, with his index finger, fetched the first note out of the piano, a quite unexpectedly powerful first note in the middle register, like a trumpet blast. Others followed, an introduction developed – the audience relaxed.

The concert was held in the palatial hall of a fashionable first-class hotel. The walls were covered with mirrors framed in gilded arabesques, between frescoes of the rosy and fleshly school. Ornamental columns supported a ceiling that displayed a whole universe of electric bulbs, in clusters darting a brilliance far brighter than day and filling the whole space with thin, vibrating golden light. Not a seat was unoccupied, people were standing in the side aisles and at the back. The front seats cost twelve marks; for the impresario believed that anything worth having was worth paying for. And they were occupied by the best society, for it was in the upper classes, of course, that the greatest enthusiasm was felt. There were even some children, with their legs hanging down demurely from their chairs and their shining eyes staring at their gifted little white-clad contemporary.

Down in front on the left side sat the prodigy's mother, an extremely obese woman with a powdered double chin and a feather on her head. Beside her was the impresario, a man of oriental appearance with large gold buttons on his conspicuous cuffs. The princess was in the middle of the front row – a wrinkled, shrivelled little old princess but still a patron of the arts, especially everything full of sensibility. She sat in a deep, velvet-upholstered armchair, and a Persian carpet was spread before her feet. She held her hands folded over her grey striped-silk breast, put her head on one side, and presented a picture of elegant composure as she sat looking up at the performing prodigy. Next to her sat her lady-in-waiting, in a green striped-silk gown. Being only a lady-in-waiting she had to sit up very straight in her chair.

Bibi ended in a grand climax. With what power this wee

manikin belaboured the keyboard! The audience could scarcely trust its ears. The march theme, an infectious, swinging tune, broke out once more, fully harmonized, bold and showy; with every note Bibi flung himself back from the waist as though he were marching in a triumphal procession. He ended *fortissimo*, bent over, slipped sideways off the stool, and stood with a smile awaiting the applause.

And the applause burst forth, unanimously, enthusiastically; the child made his demure little maidenly curtsy and people in the front seat thought: 'Look what slim little hips he has! Clap, clap! Hurrah, bravo, little chap, Saccophylax or whatever your name is! Wait, let me take off my gloves – what a little devil of a chap he is!'

Bibi had to come out three times from behind the screen before they would stop. Some late-comers entered the hall and moved about looking for seats. Then the concert continued. Bibi's *Rêverie* murmured its numbers, consisting almost entirely of arpeggios, above which a bar of melody rose now and then, weak-winged. Then came *Le Hibou et les Moineaux*. This piece was brilliantly successful, it made a strong impression; it was an affective childhood fantasy, remarkably well envisaged. The bass represented the owl, sitting morosely rolling his filmy eyes; while in the treble the impudent, half-frightened sparrows chirped. Bibi received an ovation when he finished, he was called out four times. A hotel page with shiny buttons carried up three great laurel wreaths on to the stage and proffered them from one side while Bibi nodded and expressed his thanks. Even the princess shared in the applause, daintily and noiselessly pressing her palms together.

Ah, the knowing little creature understood how to make people clap! He stopped behind the screen, they had to wait for him; lingered a little on the steps of the platform, admired the long streamers on the wreaths – although actually such things bored him stiff by now. He bowed with the utmost charm, he gave the audience plenty of time to rave itself out, because applause is valuable and must not be cut short. '*Le Hibou* is my drawing card,' he thought – this expression he had learned from the impresario. 'Now I will play the fantasy, it is a lot better than *Le Hibou*, of course, especially the C-sharp passage. But you idiots dote on the *Hibou*, though it is the first and the silliest thing I wrote.' He continued to bow and smile.

Next came a *Méditation* and then an *Étude* – the programme was quite comprehensive. The *Méditation* was very like the *Rêverie* – which was nothing against it – and the *Étude* displayed all of Bibi's virtuosity, which naturally fell a little short of his inventiveness. And then the *Fantaisie*. This was his favourite; he varied it a little each time, giving himself free rein and sometimes surprising even himself, on good evenings, by his own inventiveness.

He sat and played, so little, so white and shining, against the great black grand piano, elect and alone, above that confused sea of faces, above the heavy, insensitive mass soul, upon which he was labouring to work with his individual, differentiated soul. His lock of soft black hair with the white silk bow had fallen over his forehead, his trained and bony little wrists pounced away, the muscles stood out visibly on his brown childish cheeks.

Sitting there he sometimes had moments of oblivion and solitude, when the gaze of his strange little mouselike eyes with the big rings beneath them would lose itself and stare through the painted stage into space that was peopled with strange, vague life. Then out of the corner of his eye he would give a quick look back into the hall and be once more with his audience.

'Joy and pain, the heights and the depths – that is my *Fantaisie*,' he thought lovingly. 'Listen, here is the C-sharp passage.' He lingered over the approach, wondering if they would notice anything. But no, of course not, how should they? And he cast his eyes up prettily at the ceiling so that at least they might have something to look at.

All these people sat there in their regular rows, looking at the prodigy and thinking all sorts of things in their regular brains. An old gentleman with a white beard, a seal ring on his finger and a bulbous swelling on his bald spot, a growth if you like, was thinking to himself: 'Really, one ought to be shamed.' He had never got any further than 'Ah, thou dearest

Augustin' on the piano, and here he sat now, a grey old man, looking on while this little hop-o'-my-thumb performed miracles. Yes, yes, it is a gift of God, we must remember that. God grants His gifts, or He withholds them, and there is no shame in being an ordinary man. Like with the Christ Child. – Before a child one may kneel without feeling shamed. Strange that thoughts like these should be so satisfying – he would even say so sweet, if it was not too silly for a tough old man like him to use the word. That was how he felt, anyhow.

Art . . . the business man with the parrot-nose was thinking. 'Yes, it adds something cheerful to life, a little good white silk and a little tumty-ti-ti-tum. Really he does not play so badly. Fully fifty seats, twelve marks apiece, that makes six hundred marks – and everything else besides. Take off the rent of the hall, the lighting and the programmes, you must have fully a thousand marks profit. That is worth while.'

That was Chopin he was just playing, thought the piano-teacher, a lady with a pointed nose; she was of an age when the understanding sharpens as the hopes decay. 'But not very original – I will say that afterwards, it sounds well. And his hand position is entirely amateur. One must be able to lay a coin on the back of the hand – I would use a ruler on him.'

Then there was a young girl, at that self-conscious and chlorotic time of life when the most ineffable ideas come into the mind. She was thinking to herself: 'What is it he is playing? It is expressive of passion, yet he is a child. If he kissed me it would be as though my little brother kissed me – no kiss at all. Is there such a thing as passion all by itself, without any earthly object, a sort of child's-play of passion? What nonsense! If I were to say such things aloud they would just be at me with some more cod-liver oil. Such is life.'

An officer was leaning against a column. He looked on at Bibi's success and thought: 'Yes, you are something and I am something, each in his own way.' So he clapped his heels together and paid to the prodigy the respect which he felt to be due to all the powers that be.

Then there was a critic, an elderly man in a shiny black coat and turned-up trousers splashed with mud. He sat in his free seat and thought: 'Look at him, this young beggar of a Bibi. As an individual he has still to develop, but as a type he is already quite complete, the artist *par excellence*. He has in himself all the artist's exaltation and his utter worthlessness, his charlatanry and his sacred fire, his burning contempt and his secret raptures. Of course I can't write all that, it is too good. Of course, I should have been an artist myself if I had not seen through the whole business so clearly.'

Then the prodigy stopped playing and a perfect storm arose in the hall. He had to come out again and again from behind his screen. The man with the shiny buttons carried up more wreaths: four laurel wreaths, a lyre made of violets, a bouquet of roses. He had not arms enough to convey all these tributes, the impresario himself mounted the stage to help him. He hung a laurel wreath round Bibi's neck, he tenderly stroked the black hair – and suddenly as though overcome he bent down and gave the prodigy a kiss, a resounding kiss, square on the mouth. And then the storm became a hurricane. That kiss ran through the room like an electric shock, it went direct to people's marrow and made them shiver down their backs. They were carried away by a helpless compulsion of sheer noise. Loud shouts mingled with the hysterical clapping of hands. Some of Bibi's commonplace little friends down there waved their handkerchiefs. But the critic thought: 'Of course that kiss had to come – it's a good old gag. Yes, good Lord, if only one did not see through everything quite so clearly –'

And so the concert drew to a close. It began at half past seven and finished at half past eight. The platform was laden with wreaths and two little pots of flowers stood on the lamp-stands of the piano. Bibi played as his last number his *Rhapsodie grecque*, which turned into the Greek national hymn at the end. His fellow-countrymen in the audience would gladly have sung it with him if the company had not been so august. They made up for it with a powerful noise and hullabaloo, a hot-blooded national demonstration. And the ageing critic was thinking: 'Yes, the hymn had to come too. They have to exploit every vein – publicity cannot afford to neglect any means to its end. I think I'll criticize that as inartistic. But perhaps I am wrong, perhaps that is the most artistic thing of all. What is the artist? A jack-in-the-box. Criticism is on a higher plane. But I can't say that.' And away he went in his muddy trousers.

After being called out nine or ten times the prodigy did not come any more from behind the screen but went to his mother and the impresario down in the hall. The audience stood about among the chairs and applauded and pressed forward to see Bibi close at hand. Some of them wanted to see the princess too. Two dense circles formed, one round the prodigy, the other round the princess, and you could actually not tell which of them was receiving more homage. But the court lady was commanded to go over to Bibi; she smoothed down his silk jacket a bit to make it look suitable for a court function, led him by the arm to the princess, and solemnly indicated to him that he was to kiss the royal hand. 'How do you do it, child?' asked the princess. 'Does it come into your head of itself when you sit down?' '*Oui, madame*,' answered Bibi. To himself he thought: 'Oh, what a stupid old princess!' Then he turned round shyly and uncourtier-like and went back to his family.

Outside in the cloakroom there was a crowd. People held up their numbers and received with open arms furs, shawls, and galoshes. Somewhere among her acquaintances the piano-teacher stood making her critique. 'He is not very original,' she said audibly and looked about her.

In front of one of the great mirrors an elegant young lady was being arrayed in her evening cloak and fur shoes by her brothers, two lieutenants. She was exquisitely beautiful, with her steel-blue eyes and her clean-cut, well-bred face. A really noble dame. When she was ready she stood waiting for her brothers. 'Don't stand so long in front of the glass, Adolf,' she said softly to one of them, who could not tear himself away from the sight of his simple, good-looking young features. But Lieutenant Adolf thinks: What cheek! He would button his overcoat in front of the glass, just the same. Then they went out on the street where the arc-lights gleamed cloudily through the white mist. Lieutenant Adolf struck up a little nigger-dance on the frozen snow to keep warm, with his hands in his slanting overcoat pockets and his collar turned up.

A girl with untidy hair and swinging arms, accompanied by a gloomy-faced youth, came out just behind them. A child! she thought. A charming child. But in there he was an awe-inspiring . . . and aloud in a toneless voice she said: 'We are all infant prodigies, we artists.'

'Well, bless my soul!' thought the old gentleman who had never got further than Augustin on the piano, and whose boil was now concealed by a top hat. 'What does all that mean? She sounds very oracular.' But the gloomy youth understood. He nodded his head slowly.

Then they were silent and the untidy-haired girl gazed after the brothers and sister. She rather despised them, but she looked after them until they had turned the corner.

Franz Kafka

THE VILLAGE SCHOOLTEACHER
(THE GIANT MOLE)

Translated by Edwin and Willa Muir

Franz Kafka

FRANZ KAFKA was born in Prague, of Jewish parents, in 1883 and died of tuberculosis in a Vienna sanatorium in 1924. For all their lack of what commonly passes for realism, his strange tales have seized upon the imagination of modern Western European man as parables of his own estranged or alienated condition. This has rather distracted attention from the fact that they can also be very funny. It has been observed that the adjective 'Kafkaesque' is usually applied to situations rather than persons, but the protagonists of the present story are entirely characteristic. Like so much of Kafka's work, this story was published posthumously at the instance of his literary executor Max Brod. Brod gave it the title *The Giant Mole*, by which it has generally been known; it has recently been established, however, that *The Village Schoolteacher* was Kafka's intended title.

THE VILLAGE SCHOOLTEACHER
(THE GIANT MOLE)

THOSE, and I am one of them, who find even a small ordinary-sized mole disgusting, would probably have died of disgust if they had seen the great mole that a few years back was observed in the neighbourhood of one of our villages, which achieved a certain transitory celebrity on account of the incident. Today it has long since sunk back into oblivion again, and in that only shares the obscurity of the whole incident, which has remained quite inexplicable, but which people, it must be confessed, have also taken no great pains to explain; and so, as the result of an incomprehensible apathy in those very circles which should have concerned themselves with it and who in fact have shown enthusiastic interest in far more trifling matters, the affair has been forgotten without ever being adequately investigated. In any case the fact that the village could not be reached by the railroad was no excuse. Many people came from great distances out of pure curiosity, there were even foreigners among them; it was only those who should have shown something more than curiosity that refrained from coming. In fact, if a few quite simple people, people whose daily work gave them hardly a moment of leisure – if these people had not quite disinterestedly taken up the affair, the rumour of this natural phenomenon would probably have never spread beyond the locality. Indeed, rumour itself, which usually cannot be held within bounds, was actually sluggish in this case; if it had not literally been given a shove it would not have spread. But even that was no valid reason for refusing to inquire into the affair; on the contrary this second phenomenon should have been investigated as well. Instead the old village teacher was left to write the sole account of the incident in black and white, and though he was an excellent man in his own profession his abilities and his equipment alike rendered it impossible for him to produce an exhaustive description that could be used

as a foundation by others, far less, therefore, an actual explanation of the occurrence. His little pamphlet was printed,
and a good few copies were sold to visitors to the village about
that time; it also received some public recognition, but the
teacher was wise enough to perceive that his fragmentary
labours, in which no one supported him, were at bottom without value. If in spite of that he did not relax in them, and made
the question his life work, though it naturally became more
hopeless from year to year, that only shows on the one hand
how powerful an effect the appearance of the great mole was
capable of producing, and on the other how much laborious
effort and fidelity to his convictions may be found in an old
and obscure village teacher. But that he suffered deeply from
the cold attitude of the recognized authorities is proved by a
brief brochure with which he followed up his pamphlet
several years later, by which time hardly any one could
remember what it was all about. In this brochure he complained of the lack of understanding that he had encountered
in people where it was least to be expected; complaints which
carried conviction less by the skill with which they were
expressed than by their honesty. Of such people he said very
appositely: 'It is not I, but they, who talk like old village
teachers.' And among other things he adduced the pro-
nouncement of a scholar to whom he had gone expressly about
his affair. The name of the scholar was not mentioned, but
from various circumstances we could guess who it was. After
the teacher had managed with great difficulty to secure admit-
tance, he perceived at once from the very way in which he was
greeted that the savant had already acquired a rooted pre-
judice against the matter. The absence with which he listened
to the long report which the teacher, pamphlet in hand,
delivered to him, can be gauged from a remark that he let fall
after a pause for ostensible reflection: 'The soil in your neighbourhood is particularly black and rich. Consequently it
provides the moles with particularly rich nourishment, and
so they grow to an unusual size.'

'But not to such a size as that!' exclaimed the teacher, and
he measured off two yards on the wall, somewhat exag-

gerating the length of the mole in his exasperation. 'Oh, and why not?' replied the scholar, who obviously looked upon the whole affair as a great joke. With this verdict the teacher had to return to his home. He tells how his wife and six children were waiting for him by the roadside in the snow, and how he had to admit to them the final collapse of his hopes.

When I read of the scholar's attitude towards the old man I was not yet acquainted with the teacher's pamphlet. But I at once resolved myself to collect and correlate all the information I could discover regarding the case. If I could not employ physical force against the scholar, I could at least write a defence of the teacher, or more exactly, of the good intentions of an honest but uninfluential man. I admit that I rued this decision later, for I soon saw that its execution was bound to involve me in a very strange predicament. On the one hand my own influence was far from sufficient to effect a change in learned or even public opinion in the teacher's favour, while on the other the teacher was bound to notice that I was less concerned with his main object, which was to prove that the great mole had actually been seen, than to defend his honesty, which must naturally be self-evident to him and in need of no defence. Accordingly, what was bound to happen was this: I would be misunderstood by the teacher, though I wanted to collaborate with him, and instead of helping him I myself would probably require support, which was unlikely to be given. Besides, my decision would impose a great burden of work upon me. If I wanted to convince people I could not invoke the teacher, since he himself had not been able to convince them. To read his pamphlet could only have led me astray, and so I refrained from reading it until I should have finished my own labours. More, I did not even get in touch with the teacher. True, he heard of my inquiries through intermediaries, but he did not know whether I was working for him or against him. In fact he probably assumed the latter, though he denied it later on; for I have proof of the fact that he put various obstacles in my way. It was quite easy for him to do that, for of course I was compelled to undertake anew all the inquiries he had already made, and so he could always steal a march on me. But that was the only objection that could be justly made to my method, an unavoidable reproach, moreover, which the caution and self-abnegation with which I drew my conclusions palliated still more. But for the rest my pamphlet was quite influenced by the teacher, perhaps on this point, indeed, I showed all too great a scrupulosity; from my words one might have thought nobody whatever had inquired into the case before, and I was the first to interrogate those who had seen or heard of the mole, the first to correlate the evidence, the first to draw conclusions. When later I read the teacher's pamphlet – it had a very circumstantial title: 'A mole, larger in size than any ever seen before' – I found that we actually did not agree on certain important points, though we both believed we had proved our main point, namely, the existence of the mole. These differences prevented the establishment of the friendly relations with the teacher that I had been looking forward to in spite of everything. On his side there developed a feeling almost of hostility. True, he was always modest and humble in his bearing towards me, but that only made his real feelings the more obvious. In other words, he was of the opinion that I had merely damaged his credit, and that my belief that I had been or could be of assistance to him was simplicity at best, but more likely presumption or artifice. He was particularly fond of saying that all his previous enemies had shown their hostility either not at all, or in private, or at most by word of mouth, while I had considered it necessary to have my censures straightway published. Moreover, the few opponents of his who had really occupied themselves with the subject, if but superficially, had at least listened to his, the teacher's, views before they had given expression to their own; while I, on the strength of un-systematically assembled and in part misunderstood evidence, had published conclusions which, even if they were correct as regarded the main point, must evoke incredulity, and among the public no less than the educated. But the faintest hint that the existence of the mole was unworthy of credence was the worst thing that could happen in this case.

THE VILLAGE SCHOOLTEACHER

To these reproaches, veiled as they were, I could easily have
found an answer – for instance, that his own pamphlet
achieved the very summit of the incredible – it was less easy,
however, to make headway against his continual suspicion,
and that was the reason why I was very reserved in my dealings
with him. For in his heart he was convinced that I wanted to
rob him of the fame of being the first man publicly to vindicate
the mole. Now of course he really enjoyed no fame whatever,
but only an absurd notoriety that was shrinking more and
more, and for which I had certainly no desire to compete.
Besides, in the foreword to my pamphlet I had expressly
declared that the teacher must stand for all time as the discoverer of the mole – and he was not even that – and that only
my sympathy with his unfortunate fate had spurred me on to
write. 'It is the aim of this pamphlet' – so I ended up all too
melodramatically, but it corresponded with my feelings at that
time – 'to help in giving the teacher's book the wide publicity
it deserves. If I succeed in that, then may my name, which I
regard as only transiently and indirectly associated with this
question, be blotted from it at once.' Thus I disclaimed
expressly any major participation in the affair; it was almost
as if I had foreseen in some manner the teacher's unbelievable
reproaches. Nevertheless he found in that very passage a
handle against me, and I do not deny that there was a faint
show of justice in what he said or rather hinted; indeed I was
often struck by the fact that he showed almost a keener pene-
tration where I was concerned than he had done in his
pamphlet. For he maintained that my foreword was double-
faced. If I was really concerned solely to give publicity to his
pamphlet, why had I not occupied myself exclusively with him
and his pamphlet, why had I not pointed out its virtues, its
irrefutability, why had I not confined myself to insisting on
the significance of the discovery and making that clear, why
had I instead tackled the discovery itself, while completely
ignoring the pamphlet? Had not the discovery been made
already? Was there still anything left to be done in that
direction? But if I really thought that it was necessary for me
to make the discovery all over again, why had I emphasized

the original discovery so solemnly in my foreword? One
might put that down to false modesty, but it was something
worse. I was trying to belittle the discovery, I was drawing
attention to it merely for the purpose of depreciating it, while
he on the other hand had inquired into and finally established
it. Perhaps the affair had sunk somewhat into oblivion; now
I had made a noise about it again, but at the same time I had
made the teacher's position more difficult than ever. What did
he care whether his honesty was vindicated or not? All that
he was concerned with was the thing itself, and with that
alone. But I was only of disservice to it, for I did not understand it, I did not prize it at its true value, I had not real feeling
for it. It was infinitely above my intellectual capacity. He sat
before me and looked at me, his old wrinkled face quite composed, and yet this was what he was thinking. Yet it was not
true that he was only concerned with the thing itself: actually
he was very greedy for fame, and wanted to make money out
of the business too, which, however, considering his large
family, was very understandable. Nevertheless my interest in
the affair seemed so trivial compared with his own, that he
felt he could claim to be completely disinterested without
deviating very seriously from the truth. And indeed my inner
doubts refused to be quite calmed by my telling myself that
the man's reproaches were really due to the fact that he clung
to his mole, so to speak, with both hands, and was bound to
look upon anyone who laid even a finger on it as a traitor.
For that was not true; his attitude was not to be explained by
greed, or at any rate by greed alone, but rather by the touchiness which his great labours and their complete unsuccess had
bred in him. Yet even his touchiness did not explain everything. Perhaps my interest in the affair was really too trivial.
The teacher was used to lack of interest in strangers. He regarded it as a universal evil, but no longer suffered from its
individual manifestations. Now a man had appeared who,
strangely enough, took up the affair and even he did not understand it. Attacked from this side I can make no defence. I am
no zoologist; yet perhaps I would have thrown myself into the
case with my whole heart if I had discovered it; but I had not

discovered it. Such a gigantic mole is certainly a prodigy, yet one cannot expect the continuous and undivided attention of the whole world to be accorded it, particularly if its existence is not completely and irrefutably established, and in any case it cannot be produced. And I admit too that even if I had been the discoverer I would probably never have come forward so gladly and voluntarily in defence of the mole as I had in that of the teacher.

Now the misunderstanding between me and the teacher would probably have quickly cleared up if my pamphlet had achieved success. But success was not forthcoming. Perhaps the book was not well-enough written, not persuasive enough; I am a business man, it may be that the composition of such a pamphlet was still further beyond my limited powers than those of the teacher, though in the kind of knowledge required I was greatly superior to him. Besides, my unsuccess may be explicable in other ways; the time at which the pamphlet appeared may have been inauspicious. The discovery of the mole, which had failed to penetrate to a wide public at the time it took place, was not so long past on the one hand as to be completely forgotten, and thus capable of being brought alive again by my pamphlet, while on the other hand enough time had elapsed quite to exhaust the trivial interest that had originally existed. Those who took my pamphlet at all seriously told themselves, in that bored tone which from the first had characterized the debate, that now the old useless labours on this wearisome question were to begin all over again; and some even confused my pamphlet with the teacher's. In a leading agricultural journal appeared the following comment, fortunately at the very end, and in small print: 'The pamphlet on the giant mole has once more been sent to us. Years ago we remember having had a hearty laugh over it. Since then it has not become more intelligible, nor we more hard of understanding. But we simply refuse to laugh at it a second time. Instead, we would ask our teaching associations whether more useful work cannot be found for our village teachers than hunting out giant moles.' An unpardonable confusion of identity. They had read neither the first nor the second pamphlet, and the two perfunctorily scanned expressions, 'giant mole' and 'village teacher', were sufficient for these gentlemen, as representatives of publicly esteemed interests, to pronounce on the subject. Against this attack measures might have been attempted and with success, but the lack of understanding between the teacher and myself kept me from venturing upon them. I tried instead to keep the review from his knowledge as long as I could. But he very soon discovered it, as I recognized from a sentence in one of his letters, in which he announced his intention of visiting me for the Christmas holidays. He wrote: 'The world is full of malice, and people smooth the path for it,' by which he wished to convey that I was one of the malicious, but, not content with my own innate malice, wished also to make the world's path smooth for it: in other words, was acting in such a way as to arouse the general malice and help it to victory. Well, I summoned the resolution I required, and was able to await him calmly, and calmly greet him when he arrived, this time a shade less polite in his bearing than usual; he carefully drew out the journal from the breast-pocket of his old-fashioned padded overcoat, and opening it handed it to me. 'I've seen it,' I replied, handing the journal back unread. 'You've seen it,' he said with a sigh; he had the old teacher's habit of repeating unwelcome answers. 'Of course I won't take this lying down!' he went on, tapping the journal excitedly with his finger and glancing up sharply at me, as if I were of a different mind; he certainly had some idea of what I was about to say, for I think I have noticed, not so much from his words as from other indications, that he often has a genuine intuition of my wishes, though he never yields to them or lets himself be diverted from his aims. What I said to him I can set down almost word for word, for I took a note of it shortly after our interview. 'Do what you like,' I said, 'our ways part from this moment. I fancy that that is neither unexpected nor unwelcome news to you. The review in this journal is not the real reason for my decision; it has merely finally confirmed it. The real reason is this: originally I thought my intervention might be of some use to you, while now I cannot but recognize that I have damaged you in every direction. Why it has turned out so I cannot say; the causes of success and unsuccess are always ambiguous; but don't look for the sole explanation in my shortcomings. Consider; you too had the best intentions, and yet, if one regards the matter objectively, you failed. I don't intend it as a joke, for it would be a joke against myself, when I say that your connection with me must unfortunately be counted among your failures. It is neither cowardice nor treachery, if I withdraw from the affair now. Actually it involves a certain degree of self-renunciation; my pamphlet itself proves how much I respect you personally, in a certain sense you have become my teacher, and I have almost grown fond of the mole itself. Nevertheless I have decided to step aside; you are the discoverer, and all that I can do is to prevent you from gaining possible fame, while I attract failure and pass it on to you. At least that is your own opinion. Enough of that. The sole expiation that I can make is to beg your forgiveness and, should you require it, to publish openly, that is, in this journal, the admission I have just made to yourself.'

These were my words; they were not entirely sincere, but the sincerity in them was obvious enough. My explanation had the effect upon him that I had roughly anticipated. Most old people have something deceitful, something perfidious, in their dealing with people younger than themselves; you live at peace with them, imagine you are on the best of terms with them, know their ruling prejudices, receive continual assurances of amity, take the whole thing for granted; and when something decisive happens and those peaceful relations, so long nourished, should come into effective operation, suddenly these old people rise before you like strangers, show that they have deeper and stronger convictions, and now for the first time literally unfurl their banner, and with terror you read upon it the new decree. The reason for this terror lies chiefly in the fact that what the old say now is really far more just and sensible than what they said before; it is as if even the self-evident had degrees of validity, and their words now were more self-evident than ever. But the final deceit that lies in their words consists in this, that at bottom they have always said what they are saying now. I must have probed deeply into the teacher, seeing that his next words did not entirely take me by surprise. 'Child,' he said, laying his hand on mine and patting it gently, 'how did you ever take it into your head to go into this affair? – The very first I heard of it I talked it over with my wife.' He pushed his chair back from the table, got up, spread out his arms, and stared at the floor, as if his tiny little wife were standing there and he were speaking to her. 'We've struggled on alone,' he said to her, 'for many years; now, it seems, a noble protector has risen for us in the city, a fine business man, Mr So-and-so. We should congratulate ourselves, shouldn't we? A business man in the city isn't to be sniffed at; when an ignorant peasant believes us and says so it doesn't help us, for what a peasant may say or do is of no account; whether he says the old village teacher is right, or spits to show his contempt, the net result is the same. And if instead of one peasant ten thousand should stand up for us, the result, if possible, would only be still worse. A business man in the city, on the other hand, is quite a different pair of shoes; a man like that has connections, things he says in passing, as it were, are taken up and repeated, new patrons interest themselves in the question, one of them, it may be, remarks: "You can learn even from old village teachers," and next day whole crowds of people are saying it to one another, people you would never imagine saying such things, to look at them. Next, money is found to finance the business, one gentleman goes round collecting for it and the others shower subscriptions on him; they decide that the village teacher must be dragged from his obscurity; they arrive, they don't bother about his external appearance, but take him to their bosoms, and since his wife and children depend on him, they accept them too. Have you ever watched city people? They chatter without stopping. When there's a whole lot of them together you can hear their chatter running from right to left and back again, and up and down, this way and that. And so, chattering away, they push us into the coach, so that we've hardly time to bow to everybody. The gentleman on the driver's seat puts his glasses straight, flourishes his whip, and off we go. They all wave a parting greeting to the village, as if we were still there and not sitting among them. The more important city people drive out in carriages to meet us. As we approach they get up from their seats and crane their necks. The gentleman who collected the money arranges everything methodically and in order. When we drive into the city we are a long procession of carriages. We think the public welcome is over; but it really only begins when we reach our hotel. A great crowd gathers as soon as our arrival is announced. What interests one interests all the rest immediately. They take their views from one another and promptly make those views their own. All the people who haven't managed to drive out and meet us in carriages are waiting in front of the hotel; others could have driven out, but they were too self-conscious. They're waiting too. It's extraordinary, the way that the gentleman who collected the money keeps his eye on everything and directs everything.'

I had listened coolly to him, indeed I had grown cooler and cooler while he went on. On the table I had piled up all the copies of my pamphlet in my possession. Only a few were missing, for during the past week I had sent out a circular demanding the return of all the copies distributed, and had received most of them back. True, from several quarters I had got very polite notes saying that So-and-so could not remember having received such a pamphlet, and that, if it had actually arrived, he was sorry to confess that he must have lost it. Even that was gratifying; in my heart I desired nothing better. Only one reader begged me to let him keep the pamphlet as a curiosity, pledging himself, in accordance with the spirit of my circular, to show it to no one for twenty years. The village teacher had not yet seen my circular. I was glad that his words made it so easy for me to show it him. I could do that without anxiety in any case, however, as I had drawn it up very circumspectly, keeping his interests in mind the whole time. The crucial passage in the circular ran as follows: 'I do not ask for the return of the pamphlet because I retract in any way the opinions defended there or wish them to be regarded as erroneous or even undemonstrable on any point. My request has purely personal and moreover very urgent grounds; but no conclusion whatever must be drawn from it as regards my attitude to the whole matter. I beg to draw your particular attention to this, and would be glad also if you would make the fact better known.'

For the time being I kept my hand over the circular and said: 'You reproach me in your heart because things have not turned out as you hoped. Why do that? Don't let us embitter our last moments together. And do try to see that, though you've made a discovery, it isn't necessarily greater than every other discovery, and consequently the injustice you suffer under any greater than other injustices. I don't know the ways of learned societies, but I can't believe that in the most favourable circumstances you would have been given a reception even remotely resembling the one you seem to have described to your wife. While I myself still hoped that something might come of my pamphlet, the most I expected was that perhaps the attention of a professor might be drawn to our case, that he might commission some young student to inquire into it, that this student might visit you and check in his own fashion your and my inquiries once more on the spot, and that finally, if the results seemed to him worth consideration – we must not forget that all young students are full of scepticism – he might bring out a pamphlet of his own in which your discoveries would be put on a scientific basis. All the same, even if that hope had been realized nothing very much would still have been achieved. The student's pamphlet, supporting such queer opinions, would probably be held up to ridicule. If you take this agricultural journal as a sample, you can see how easily that may happen; and scientific periodicals are still more unscrupulous in such matters. And that's quite understandable; professors bear a great responsibility towards themselves, towards science, towards posterity; they can't take every new discovery to their bosoms straight away. We others have the advantage of them there. But I'll leave that out of account and assume that the student's pamphlet has found acceptance. What would happen next? You would probably receive honourable mention, the fact that you are a teacher possibly would go in your favour;

people would say: "Our village teachers have sharp eyes";
and this journal, if journals have a memory or a conscience,
would be forced to make you a public apology; also some
well-intentioned professor would be found to secure a
scholarship for you; it's possible they might even get you to
come to the city, find a post for you in some school, and so
give you a chance of using the scientific resources of a city so
as to improve yourself. But if I am to be quite frank, I think
they would content themselves with merely trying to do all
this. They would summon you and you would appear, but
only as an ordinary petitioner like hundreds of others, and not
in solemn state; they would talk to you and praise your
honest efforts, but they would see at the same time that you
were an old man, that it was hopeless for any one to begin to
study science at such an age, and moreover that you had hit
upon your discovery more by chance than by design, and had
besides no ambition to extend your labours beyond this one
case. For these reasons they would probably send you back to
your village again. Your discovery, of course, would be
carried further, for it is not so trifling that, once having
achieved recognition, it could be forgotten again. But you
would not hear much more about it, and what you heard you
would scarcely understand. Every new discovery is assumed
at once into the sum-total of knowledge, and with that
ceases in a sense to be a discovery; it dissolves into the whole
and disappears, and one must have a trained scientific eye even
to recognize it after that. For it is related to fundamental
axioms of whose existence we don't even know, and in the
debates of science it is raised on these axioms into the very
clouds. How can we expect to understand such things? Often
as we listen to some learned discussion we may be under the
impression that it is about your discovery, when it is about
something quite different, and the next time, when we think
it is about something else, and not about your discovery at all,
it may turn out to be about that and that alone.

'Don't you see that? You would remain in your village, you
would be able with the extra money to feed and clothe your
family a little better; but your discovery would be taken out of

your hands, and without your being able with any show of
justice to object; for only in the city could it be given its final
seal. And people wouldn't be altogether ungrateful to you,
they might build a little museum on the spot where the discovery was made, it would become one of the sights of the
village, you would be given the keys to keep, and, so that you
shouldn't lack some outward token of honour, they could
give you a little medal to wear on the breast of your coat, like
those worn by attendants in scientific institutions. All this
might have been possible; but was it what you wanted?'

Without stopping to consider his answer he turned on me
and said: 'And so that's what you wanted to achieve for me?'

'Probably,' I said, 'I didn't consider what I was doing carefully enough at the time to be able to answer that clearly now.
I wanted to help you, but that was a failure, and the worst
failure I have ever had. That's why I want to withdraw now
and undo what I've done as far as I'm able.'

'Well and good,' said the teacher, taking out his pipe and
beginning to fill it with the tobacco that he carried loose in all
his pockets. 'You took up this thankless business of your own
free will, and now of your own free will you withdraw. So
that's all right.'

'I'm not an obstinate man,' I said. 'Do you find anything to
object to in my proposal?'

'No, absolutely nothing,' said the teacher, and his pipe was
already going. I could not bear the stink of his tobacco, and so
I rose and began to walk up and down the room. From
previous encounters I was used to the teacher's extreme
taciturnity, and to the fact that in spite of it he never seemed to
have any desire to stir from my room once he was in it. That
had often disturbed me before. He wants something more, I
always thought at such times, and I would offer him money,
which indeed he invariably accepted. Yet he never went away
before it suited his convenience. Generally his pipe was
smoked out by that time, then he would ceremoniously and
respectfully push his chair in to the table, make a detour
round it, seize his ash-plant standing in the corner, press my
hand warmly, and go. But today his silent presence as he sat

there was an actual torture to me. When one has bidden a last
farewell to someone, as I had done, a farewell accepted in good
faith, surely the mutual formalities that remain should be got
over as quickly as possible, and one should not burden one's
host purposelessly with one's silent presence. As I contem-
plated the stubborn little old fellow from behind, while he sat
at the table, it seemed an impossible idea ever to show him the
door.

Gerd Gaiser

ANIELA

Translated by Lionel and Doris Thomas

Gerd Gaiser

GERD GAISER was born in 1908 in Oberriexingen, Württemberg. During the war he served as a fighter pilot; after the war he was a painter, art teacher, and lecturer at a teachers' training college. Two of his novels have been translated into English: *The Last Squadron* (1953), portraying a German fighter squadron during the closing stages of the war, and *The Last Dance of the Season* (1958), which depicts a small West German town through the independent but interlacing voices of a number of narrators. *Aniela*, less experimental in technique, appeared in 1956.

ANIELA

In the case of squads detailed for a particular kind of duty the regulations prescribed for all members a free period of three hours afterwards except for the individual to whom this relief could no longer be granted. In so far as it was not required for the cleaning and repair of equipment, this free time, according to the wording of the regulations, was to be devoted to resting. It was still early in the day, for executions are usually arranged for the hours around dawn. The small detachment, smothered in dust up to the waist and with strange, scared faces, was marching back past the sentries, but it did not attract attention, for the immense parade-ground was echoing and re-echoing with the tramp of units coming out on duty. Scarcely any of those who saw the section order arms and dismiss to their quarters had any idea where these men came from – or indeed gave a thought to it.

The N.C.O. Matthes propped against the wall the rifle with which he had been issued at the depot for this duty – corporals in drill squads no longer carry rifles – ripped open his tunic and stepped out of his jackboots. It was already warm, all the more so because the temperature had hardly fallen during the night; he was alone in the barrack room, where the sycamores growing in front of the windows let in a green light. The room lay far back, at the point where the town of Lavka, with its desolate boundary district only partially built over, came to a stop, and the sounds of drilling on the parade-grounds only penetrated as a confused noise. Matthes was standing in his stockings in front of his iron bedstead. He intended to go to the wash-room, but suddenly he was assailed by a weariness which he felt unable to resist. A profound sense of desolation took greedy possession of him. The room was pleasantly bare, its naked walls offering no diversion, nothing was standing on the table, the four stools were pushed underneath in their right places, the lockers closed. Like those of the other three corporals, his bed, which he had left five hours before and without waking his room-mates, had been stripped and tidied by the orderlies. Matthes let himself drop on to the bed. Although it was hot, he reached absent-mindedly for the blanket, which lay folded at the foot of the bed, and pulled it up to his neck. Soon, with an apathetic and exhausted movement, he drew the edge up still further until his face was covered too. For a few moments he lay in this way without stirring, shrouded like a dead man.

At once the impressions of the last hours came back to him, and he saw the man standing under the sparse linden-tree, which cast no shadow because the sun still seemed reluctant to appear. They had issued the man with a black, freshly washed suit of denim, working clothes for the ugly and ghastly thing that was to be done with him. The suit was wide and sack-like, and in it he looked both deeply solemn and like a straw doll, with the red patch roughly sewn on in front over the heart. Straw doll, solemn figure; solemn figure; straw doll. He knew neither the straw doll nor the solemn figure, no, no, he did not know the man, although he saw everything else so clearly. He could not make out the man's face because he dared not look at the spot where the face began. He saw it as little as one can see one's own face, which is not even one's own, in the mirror. As soon as you can see your own face, it's not yours any more; because he had not been able to see the face, he felt, when he suddenly sank for an immeasurable instant into the abyss of sleep, that he must have been the man by the tree himself.

He had been the man. He died, died and took the same path back again a second time, or had already taken it for he knew not how many times. How many times? The riding school lay out there near the Blyskanie estate and the summer sun was scorching down. The smell of the river was rising towards him; now, in the dry season, it was flowing low between banks of clay; reeds, mud in ferment, rubbish, the sweet stench of carrion rose upwards, and the gardens up the shelving slope smelt of borage and balm-mint. He was walking from Blyskanie alone, he was too fond of being alone; being alone is not a good thing for an N.C.O. who should value

comradeship. It would have been better to follow the example
of Sergeant-Major Rungenhagen with whom he had normally
gone riding – Rungenhagen who had a liking for regulations.
There was no regulation against walking alone, and this
seemed to be an omission, but if only Rungenhagen had been
with him, nothing would have happened. So he was coming
back from riding alone and had previously sat out there by the
river, in the inn from whose windows the boats could be seen
bobbing on the river and where the magpies chattered in the
poplars. A hot, dusty land, schnaps helps you in a land like
this, schnaps drunk in a water glass. Where does it come from?
Where does it go to? A magnificent land! It was not the
schnaps which made him hot, nor the sun against which he
walked and which burnt into his face. The river cast up a
mirror from below. Dreaming, and probably a bad dream at
that. The sun was flaming over the town and the silos, the
black chimneys shot up glimmering. Wires, masts, a tramline
had already been running for a while beside the path. At one
time earlier the tram had run far out of the town, now the last
stop was where the road left the town. And in the last five
minutes to the stop the girl was walking in front of him.

He had not noticed where she came from, but it must have
been from one of the gardens which stretched upwards to his
right. Anyway she had on one arm a large straw bag with its
green contents spilling over the side and in the other hand she
was carrying a hoe such as one uses for weeding. Fixed to the
shaft was a heart-shaped sheet of metal, scarcely as big as a
hand, with a glistening point. The girl was brown, thick hair
fell onto her shoulders, her shoulders too were very brown.
She was more broad than slender, she was hot and languid,
dainty and untroubled, all at the same time, and Matthes was
touched to the quick at the sight of her. But he still had not
seen her face.

Only after a while did he notice that there was a man with
the girl. Not at her side, but a little behind her, was a person
who wore a collarless shirt and had trousers and waistcoat,
both faded to grey. He himself was also grey – he looked
small, thin, and sinewy. It was obvious that the two belonged

together, although they did not speak to one another. He could scarcely be her father, if such a being had come from a father at all. It was an uncle. Somebody to watch her? Immediately Matthes began to hate him. The little man was going along, lost in thought, but still ready to turn round quickly at any moment. In the same way he seemed to be concealing a slyness of character. He came from fishing, for he was carrying his rod and tackle, on his head a straw hat and in his hand a tin bucket covered over with leaves. The bottom edges of his trousers were damp, and burrs were hanging on them.

It was a long time before the tram came, and almost to the last Matthes, the old man, and the girl were the only people waiting for it. The sun had now dipped below Lavka; far behind, the bright sand, the loop of the river at Blyskanie were still shimmering, the tram-stop was enveloped in a brooding, transparent shade. The girl had put down her bag and from time to time spoke quietly to the old man. Matthes walked up and down, he never took his eyes off her, he stared at her, his head was burning; the horses' flanks, the dry ring of the hooves, the sand rippling beneath them, the mirror of the river flashing into his face still burned in his memory. He would have liked to shout aloud to her, but the girl did not favour him with a single glance, never turned her gaze upon him. She went on speaking to the old man, and presently he noticed that they were talking in the foreign language. Aha, he thought for a moment and felt relieved, he is an old servant. It is the man who helps in the garden. And then, just as he slipped past behind the old man, she looked at him.

When the tram arrived and turned round, he was so afraid of what he had to do, that his knees hurt him. A few other passengers had climbed in and were making a din in the car. He had taken a seat, but the two did not come in. He saw that the girl and the old man were settling on the platform behind. They were close together in the corner and had arranged themselves so that the girl had her back to Matthes. He gazed into the face of the old man. When the tram jolted into motion, he went out and joined them. While the ramshackle vehicle rattled through the suburbs, his consciousness seemed to slip away from him. He stood leaning against the side and let himself be jolted. Assuming an indifferent expression and dissembling in his movements, he plucked at a leaf which was hanging out of her gardener's bag and, while he seemed to be gazing steadily and intently into the car's interior, tugged stealthily at her dress. He felt how warm she was. Perhaps she was not taking any interest in him. The heat of the day had gathered in her and was crackling in her hair; this was not surprising, she had been in the sun all day, the sun was burning on her skin. He was completely powerless, with no will to act, he did not see her face, she had her back towards him, he only saw her hand which sometimes clutched at a holding-strap, a sturdy hand with traces of garden-work still upon it. He was quite powerless; if she got out now, nothing had happened, no sign exchanged, nothing begun. His heart contracted whenever a stop drew near, and a foolish, sobbing laughter bubbled in his throat; if there was no sign that she was going to get out, he felt bliss because there was still time.

In the end he seated himself in the car and, struggling to anticipate the jolts of the tram, wrote on his writing-block, hiding it behind his left hand, 'Tomorrow opposite the Arethusa. At nine.' Then he wrote on, adding 'and the same for every day after'. The strokes were scrawled crazily, the writing of a sick or drunken man. He tore off the page and hid it in his hand.

When he stepped out onto the platform again, the two occupants had altered their position. Now the girl was standing with her face towards the car, and the old man was looking backwards, down at the rails. Although she did not look at him, Matthes had the feeling that she must have seen everything. Suddenly he was quite sure, she must have guessed his thoughts and was waiting, meeting him in his intention. Her hand was dangling, and he laid in it the note which was rolled up to look inconspicuous and no longer than a match. Immediately her fingers closed on it, and slowly, with a movement that made him tremble, she altered her position.

They went on for a long time through the whole town, and

nothing further happened, now that nothing more had to be done. He should have got out long ago, but he had forgotten that he could, now that nothing more had to be done. The car filled up while it went through the more thickly populated parts of the town and gradually emptied again, now that nothing had to be done. Outside it had grown dark and he stood trembling behind her, for nothing more had to be done now. Finally their stop was there, and first the old man got down, scraping past the door with his rods. Not until she walked past him did she look at him from beneath her dark hair. Nothing more had to be done.

At nine o'clock next day he stood by the Arethusa and waited. Nobody came. He came also on the second day and again on the third, but he waited in vain.

With a groan Matthes pulled the blanket from his face and sat up. Why, he thought, why did Rungenhagen pick on me?

Now as always when he woke, he had raised the watch close to his face; he saw that the hand had not moved on, he listened to see whether the watch had stopped, but it was ticking and had not stopped. He was bathed in sweat, the room was quiet as before, suddenly he wished that somebody would come in, perhaps Corporal Frettchen who had forgotten his cigarettes. But nobody appeared, even in the corridor there was no sound. The room lay high up on the third floor, and he looked through the window at the foot of the bed, at that spot where the horizon, pale yellow, was just visible above the edge. This was summer in yellow Lavka; their clocks did not go right, their bells did not ring; in their churches which were bolted and barred the gold stucco fell from the mouldings, a dead bat had dropped on to the steps of the altar. The land was boundless and God sided with the strong when He allowed them to enter yellow Lavka, mounted on horses or tank-tracks, decked with autumn flowers. He allowed them to march in and, because they had won, they imagined that they had been chosen to carry out His will.

Even the heaps of stone seemed to bear witness in their favour. What was it about the heaps of stone? Wherever the

units were marching across country, Sergeant-Major Rungenhagen liked to point out the neat, longish hillocks smothered
with grass and moss which rose beside the road at regular
intervals. Now hoe and shovel had bitten into these weed-
grown mounds in many places, and the gravel which they contained glittered freshly on the roads. 'Look at them,' said
Rungenhagen, 'those are the gravel heaps from the time of the
Prussians, and nobody has done anything for these roads since
that time. Even the gravel heaps here have been waiting for
us.'

So it appeared to them, and not only the gravel heaps had
been waiting, the land was boundless, it was blue with flax, it
stretched endlessly with its whispering rye-fields; in the heat
the stifling gusts of wind drove dust-clouds across the rolling
countryside. A fertile land which they had liberated, a land
full of promise, an anxious, restless land in which the troop was
now stationed long after the short campaign was over. The
hangings were no concern of theirs, and they knew little of the
people who had to do them. This was the first time, the only
time up to now, that the regiment had had to find an execution
squad.

'Why,' he thought again, 'why did Rungenhagen pick on
me for the horrible job?' He knew why, and yet he brooded
over it. The sergeant-major had been his friend, they had been
at the military training school together, until Rungenhagen
had been promoted before him. Rungenhagen was an upholder
of discipline, a clever and cold-blooded man, he was not
double-dealing, but ruthless and to be admired. Only the one
who stands by discipline, Rungenhagen said, can establish his
own law. If you stand by discipline, you must also believe in
punishment. Suddenly he hated Rungenhagen, and yet, had he
not once agreed with him in his objections to a life without
restraint? The rabble likes to live without restraint, Rungenhagen said; it must be kept in check. All the trouble begins
when you let them out. And that is true, Matthes said to himself, that is true. I couldn't have had the affair with Aniela if
the recruits hadn't gone off just then.

When the recruits were drafted, half of the permanent staff

would go on leave until the next batch came in, and in the interval that followed the next batch, it was the turn of the other half of the staff. Those who remained had very light duties, in fact nothing really, to be exact. The training staff who were chased around and chased others around for more than four months at a stretch had a quiet time then. Everyone knows what it's like, now the boozing begins, the guzzling, the wangling of extras, the unbuttoning of tunics. 'Slackness,' said Rungenhagen, 'the cushy life of the civvy, it's the beginning of the end.' On days like those Rungenhagen read or went out to Blyskanie to ride. He must have very soon noticed that Corporal Matthes was avoiding him.

So there was plenty of time, there would have even been plenty to wait near the Arethusa for a few more evenings. But there was no need, for now Aniela turned up.

Aniela. Why hadn't she come before, why had she made him wait so long, if she was willing? And again, the way she came and stood hesitantly before him, it took his breath away. He struggled foolishly, he had to make an effort to produce one of the phrases which were usual when one made a date with a girl. He had no stock of phrases, nothing suited Aniela.

'So you've come after all,' he said. 'It is good that you wanted to come. I have waited so long. But here you are at last.'

'I couldn't come before,' she said, looking calmly at him.

'Now I am glad that I didn't give up.'

'Why "give up"? You wrote "and the same for every day after".'

'Yes, but days get awfully long, if you have to wait like this.'

'How can you say "long" if you know that the waiting will lead to something?'

'I couldn't know that.'

'Yes, you could.'

She was looking at him, she had never been confused or embarrassed. Calmly she looked into his face and waited, her lips were parted a little and her breath came and went, alluring, wholesome. Nothing more had to be done.

But in spite of this he spoke in a clumsy stutter, 'Shall we go somewhere? We could go into the Rising Swan, where there is music.'

'No,' she said and looked at him brown-eyed. It was already dusk, the long evening seemed slow in coming, she was standing looking at him, and nothing more had to be done. She gave a little laugh. 'No, no,' she said, 'we don't want to go to the Rising Swan. Wouldn't we rather be alone together?'

Matthes lay back, turned on his side, and drew up his knees. He was resting on her lap, his head between her hands, she had to bend down to him, from below he looked up into her face. Or else he was holding her and she was lying on his knees. He laid his face against her and she held him firmly and pulled him down to her, she held him very firmly and did not let his head slip from her hands. She was holding him, he could not get his breath; a thrill of terror, horror, wild desire raged in him. Who was this girl, how did all this happen, why did she give herself to him without a second thought? Her name was Aniela. Who gave her this name, where did she come from? His face lay in the grass, her face opposite his. They were resting. Evening had come, the sunflowers were quite black, black stars, their points silhouetted against the feathery sky.

Footsteps in the lower part of the garden. They came up from the water, a bucket sighed. The fisherman was going to the hut; he could be heard pottering inside, then the door banged again, now it grew quiet, the fisherman must have squatted down below in the grass. Soon the smell of a cigarette, in this case an unpleasant scorching smell, penetrated the shrubs. The fisherman did not speak to him, but gave a sign of greeting whenever he, Matthes, came – he merely greeted him, nothing more. He gave no sign of what he thought, not even whether he was disgusted by Matthes's visits or indifferent to them. The fisherman always seemed to be somewhere in the garden. Whenever Matthes came in with Aniela, he could be seen pottering somewhere, or his tools lay about there and the lower gate stood ajar, because he had gone down to the river-bank. He never left the garden before them, but he didn't go with them when they left. He was sitting there now, as he

always did, noiseless, timeless, waiting. Only after they had
left did they hear him closing the gate.

'What does he think, Aniela? Is he a relative of yours?
Doesn't he mind?'

'He belongs to the house. Actually the garden is his. He
doesn't mind.'

'When I saw you for the first time, Aniela, down there with
him, I thought he was there to watch you. I made up my mind
to hate him.'

'Don't do that.'

'If you don't want me to, I won't hate him. Have you known
him since you were small?'

'Yes, we lived in the country before.'

'That's what I thought. Had you an estate out there?'

'Yes.'

'Have you had a bad time? Did they ruin you?'

'Yes, they did. But don't let's talk of it.'

He did not learn anything more from her, obviously she
didn't like talking about her affairs, and he learnt nothing by
asking. She was a mysterious being sent to him by chance, a
centauress who had no place in the ordinary scheme of things.

'Yes, yes,' he boasted, 'there's going to be a new order
now.'

This 'Order' had got hold of him, and he remembered
Sergeant-Major Rungenhagen's gravel heaps which had become overgrown with moss while the 'Order' was in abey-
ance. He paused, for scarcely had he finished speaking when
his own words did not seem quite so sincere and impressive as
they should have been. At least Aniela did not answer, perhaps
she was not so attached to the order of which he had been
speaking because her heart was filled by other things or
because she trusted the order as a matter of course.

It wasn't a good thing to have so many opportunities to go
out. An opportunity to go out and an opportunity to take the
wrong track amounted to almost the same thing, unless one
was somebody like Sergeant-Major Rungenhagen. Once,
when he visited Aniela's garden, he brought a box of pastries
with him. In doing so he had not thought of anything in par-

ticular, perhaps it had only just occurred to him as he was passing a confectioner's that the other N.C.O.s took cakes to their girls. Everybody is keen on cakes during wartime.

They were sitting under the projecting roof of the hut, for the sky was overcast and a few drops were falling through the foliage. Aniela opened his packet and pushed it towards him. It contained the sticky, sweet, brightly coloured confectionery of Lavka which people from areas where the rations were meagre fell upon avidly. People who didn't have to worry about money came up from the capital by the night trains in order to gorge themselves in Lavka for a day.

'I don't want any,' said Matthes, 'I'd rather smoke. But you have some, Aniela, perhaps there is something you like. Or don't you care much for sweet things?'

'If you bring me something, I must do honour to it.'

She helped herself, but obviously more from politeness than for any other reason, and, after throwing away his cigarette, he sat there blowing gently at her hair. The frogs were noisy in the lower garden and it already smelt fresher, although only a few drops of rain had fallen.

'Shall we go to the water?' Aniela said. 'We can go up the river and swim there.'

She had stopped eating after a few bites and was dabbing her lips with the tips of her fingers. Sweet stuff, sticky, wasn't it just like man and wife sitting together, an intimacy savoured under the roof of the hut. 'Slackness,' Sergeant-Major Rungenhagen would have said. Bathing in the river wasn't respectable either. On Sundays the rabble who had no privileges lounged about beside the river. It was expected of the victors and those who belonged to the 'New Order' that they should visit the parks which sparkled with cleanliness. But after all, Aniela came from the country, and why shouldn't he go with her now to the river where it would soon be dusk? They had already passed through the lower gate on their way there when Aniela said unexpectedly and casually, 'Oh, wait a moment, or go on a bit. I've forgotten something up there.'

'Forgotten? Tell me what it is and I'll fetch it.'

'No, no, you don't understand. Just go on.'

She jumped up quickly and disappeared amidst the greenery.
He waited and then, when she didn't come at once, he walked
thoughtlessly upwards along the fence until he stood again
almost level with the hut. Suddenly through the fence he saw
her dress move and was the involuntary witness of a curious
scene. Aniela was eating. She had rushed back to the spot
where they had been sitting and the cakes had been left. Now
he saw her standing there, quickly and greedily cramming a
piece of cake into her mouth.

The discovery alarmed him so much that he immediately
ducked down and hastily jumped to his former position as
though he himself had been caught. He even went a few steps
further down, stretched himself and behaved casually while
confused thoughts shot through his head. He listened for
Aniela's footsteps, and at the same time stared reflectively at
the garden which he had hitherto only thought of as a place
for hours of love. The garden was wild and smelt good; a
garden is a wonderful way of passing the time, and the exercise
it gives is beneficial if a peaceful home and well-stocked table
await you afterwards. Otherwise a garden can mean many
different things, and suddenly it seemed to him as though the
vegetable beds in this garden were still fresh and the seeds
planted in them with the most anxious expectations. But what
could anyone take home from this garden? For example, the
beans were still uneatable, of course they were already in
flower, but actually they were only just beginning to climb
the beanstalks. And supposing the old man's fishing was also
meant as something more than a pastime? A thought refused
to be dismissed, incomprehensible as it was, a thought that
caused him shame and horror, the thought that Aniela went
hungry.

When they parted that evening at the upper entrance, he
said casually: 'What about meeting in town for once and
spending the evening there?'

'In town?' she said, as though disappointed, and put her
arms around him. 'Whatever could you do with me in town?'

'We might dine at Hiller's Restaurant and afterwards go to
the Swan. It would make a change.'

'I see. You want a change.'

'Don't twist my words, Aniela.'

'A change. So you're already tired.'

'Aniela.'

'Very well. What's all this about going to the town? Why do you want to?'

'Suppose I would like, just for once, to show off such a beautiful girl-friend? I should like people to see you.'

'Don't do it. Let's keep all this to ourselves.'

She wouldn't change her mind, she didn't want to be invited out, but in spite of that and perhaps in order to make it up to him, she went a good part of the way with him. But he was still a little put out by her refusal, and she too was rather embarrassed, certain of herself as she normally was; she gave a sigh, played with her fingers on his arm and said, 'It's no good thinking any more about it, you won't be able to understand.'

While they had been talking, they found that they were already in the town. It would have turned out an unhappy evening in any case, Aniela had been right, it would have been better not to show her off, better for them to stay alone together. For suddenly Corporal Frettchen who shared a room with Matthes caught up with them. Frettchen too was coming back from 'the woman', as he liked to put it.

'Aha,' he said, 'at any rate I know now why we don't see you around any more, old boy. So you're courting too! May I congratulate you?

'Frettchen,' he said to Aniela and eyed her greedily. Aniela nodded and would have gladly pushed on. But Frettchen was not to be shaken off, and Matthes couldn't start a quarrel with the meddlesome fellow, for his stock among the N.C.O.s was low in any case. He was thought to be stuck-up and this provoked Frettchen.

'I'll get the tram by the Scala Palace. It is time I was going back.'

'Excellent, then we'll take you there, mademoiselle, if I shan't be intruding. After that we go the same road.'

Frettchen knew the lay-out of the town and the tram

time-table by heart. But for Frettchen they would have gone
another way, but Frettchen said, 'If we keep left and go
through the Sorana, you'll just get the 7.30 tram.'

He, Matthes, had never been through the Sorana. Soldiers
and those who worked for the 'New Order' had no cause to go
to such quarters; he scarcely went beyond the streets on high
ground where the offices and libraries were accommodated and
the new authority was created. Here in the low-lying quarter
it was cramped and gloomy; narrow-fronted, dirty houses
crowded one another, and in every basement dismal bars
seemed to have been installed. Whenever a door moved, a
light shone out, and doors were constantly banging; there
were uneasy and stealthy movements all the time. What one
noticed most was a tendency to concealment, a beggarly,
trembling kind of merry-making. One could see that the
smoky holes were stuffed full with people; some of these
oozed out and went staggering along by the walls. There was
singing. They were singing in a cellar. From an attic window
high up a voice called in a querulous and prolonged whine,
'Tadziu! Tadziu!' Time after time shadows coming towards
them moved hastily out of their path.

'What is all this?' asked Matthes, sickened. 'What's going
on?'

'Don't you know?' asked Frettchen. He was no dreamer,
he noticed things easily and without thinking too much
about them. 'It's Friday night and they're spending their
wages.'

'Who?'

'The populace, those who are allowed to work for us. As
soon as they get the dough, they go off and turn it into schnaps.
They drink on an empty stomach, they haven't much food in
their bellies now. They're allowed to keep the schnaps, then
we get some of their money back as tax.'

On the ground a man was huddled up with his back to the
wall. He didn't see them coming, and they had to step over his
legs. The back of his head was resting against the wall and he
was looking up at the sky which appeared, moonlit and
feathery, between the sooty drain-pipes. It was a feeble gaze

of animal ecstasy. 'Tadziu, Tadziu!' called the voice querulously. The gutter stank.

'Once we get that far, my dear fellow,' said Frettchen, 'they
won't even let us have schnaps. You can bet your life on that.'

'We won't.'

'Well,' said Frettchen, 'we must be careful. The world's a
slippery place.'

'You are right. But a populace is not the same as a nation.'

'What's the difference?'

'A populace lives on, a proud nation does not survive.
They're two different things.'

'I wonder. If you have the choice of living or not, you let
your pride go a bit. You try to get hold of papers, and your
wife goes out and washes the underpants of the victor.'

'Do you think so too, Aniela?'

'I can't have any opinion,' said Aniela and then fell silent.

'Tadziu!' called the voice behind them querulously.

'Let's get out of here. This is no place for a uniform.'

When they said goodbye, Aniela said: 'I have been thinking.
Perhaps it would be nice after all to do what you suggested
tonight. We will go out. Can we go tomorrow?'

'No, not tomorrow. I am duty N.C.O. then.'

'Damn it all,' said Frettchen, 'I should be pleased to act as
substitute, mademoiselle.'

'But on Sunday, Aniela. Thank you.'

'On Sunday. Very well.'

Her voice was soft. Her face glowed with a tender light.

They drew back their carbines, their hearts hammered
against their ribs for the space of a few beats, for as long as
the barrels swayed and took aim. The barrels jabbed out in the
direction they had been ordered to take and, since everything
looked the same and remained vague except for the thin
shadows which now emerged, gravel, dust, and earth in heaps,
they couldn't do otherwise, one after another they became
rooted upon the red patch, sewn on with a few rough stitches.
Badges are sewn on. Death was a badge. It all depended on
the badges, and those who had the right ones didn't need to

worry, for them the roast still turned on the spit, the corn ripened, the flax brought a joyful harvest, the sugar lay shovelled up in brownish heaps, the sand sang under their horses' hooves around the yellow town of Lavka. The 'Order' protected them, it had to be strict. Day and night the men on duty watched and prevented fraternization, for the races had been separated. There was a general, for example, who went out on patrol himself just for the fun of it. His fast, noiseless car braked close by the kerb where someone was walking on his own or a couple were on their way; he even darted about in the copses between the firs. Insignia were looked at, papers scrutinized.

Everything depended on papers. In the country and in the town there were two races, a few minorities as well and a mishmash of immigrants, and what with them all, the law had often been confused and infringed. But now violence ruled. Official papers were distributed and only these gave one the right to eat and to work, even love was now only permissible between those with rights. Houses, businesses, and pubs too had their official papers which were pasted up behind the window-panes and regulated admission. There were large, whole and half coupons, depending upon whether one belonged to the masters, those who were accepted, or those who could prove their sympathies with the regime or had learnt an indispensable trade. Many could prove nothing for themselves, or had nothing to prove, or didn't wish to prove anything. The ones without coupons were the populace. People without coupons were taboo to the soldier. He didn't see them. He had no business in their quarters.

The other side of the picture was no concern of his, and others did the hangings, as far as they were necessary. He was in the army and had kept clean; it was in the army that he had gained glory. He didn't need to be ashamed when he marched into Lavka, wreathed in flowers and cheered by those who spoke his language. He belonged to the bright side of the picture, and when off duty he had the right to associate with the daughters of the liberated people who spoke his language. For the evenings were enchanting. This evening too had stayed warm, a warm Slav evening, before the first star appeared. When the bustle had died down, when the factories were still and the trams screeched less often, the country, this immense country around the town, seemed to gain in power; it emitted a silence, a far-away smell of stables, dust, sweetish beet juice, rye only half ripe. Still, it was fun in Lavka for those with a good conscience and papers in order. The war was so far off and Lavka was watched over so securely that one could even bring back the bright lights. Voices buzzed in the streets where men of the 'New Order' were seeking relaxation. There was music coming from the garden of the Arethusa, from the Rising Swan, from the Scala Palace. The first star had still not come out, but the *papirossi* glimmered in the shadows.

Aniela came. She came just at that moment of after-glow, when the setting sun no longer shone, but here and there objects still gleamed like the dust on butterflies' wings. She came to meet him at the roundabout, where he was standing and waiting, and although he now knew her well enough, he was stirred once more to the depths of his being, as he had been before. Once more she seemed new to him; she was alien again. Outside he had grown used to her in the carefree dress she had worn in the garden, with a leaf in her tangled hair. Now she came sleek and groomed in a tight dress with white sleeves like little clouds over her brown skin. She was so cool, with no other fragrance but her own freshness, she wore no jewellery, carried no coat on her arm and hadn't even a bag, she came just as a girl leaves the house to do something, perhaps to go round the corner on an errand which will not take her long. Now she stood, nodded slowly, and put her hands together.

Meanwhile they had been interrupted while they were greeting one another, for Sergeant-Major Rungenhagen was passing and, because of their difference in rank, Matthes was obliged to show him respect even though he was on friendly terms with him. Rungenhagen did not move a muscle, he was not like Frettchen, he went past with a polite gesture of acknowledgement and had soon disappeared from view. In spite of this the meeting annoyed Matthes.

'Oh, God,' he said foolishly, his thoughts still half with Rungenhagen, 'how beautiful you are today, Aniela.'

'Why today in particular?'

'Never mind. Listen, shall we go first to the Rising Swan? There's music everywhere, but the Rising Swan is where the officers are.'

'Yes, very well. Then we'll go to the Rising Swan, where the officers are.'

In the evening the Rising Swan was overfull with visitors. Many in uniform, and also the countless people who could chalk up business trips or come to Lavka at their own expense, in order to live really well again just for a day, all those who had been transferred from their home district or were on temporary duty, the homeless who impatiently longed to make a new home, the planners, and lastly the profiteers of the 'New Order' who pocketed allowances and were taking out their secretaries while they hesitated to bring over their families to live with them. In the middle a fellow was strumming on a white grand piano brought from some Palais or other and a light shone up from below through vases filled with water. On the ceiling a rising swan of stucco, which gave the place its name, was spreading its wings. There was everything here, and thick, sweet, smoke-laden air filled the room. With great difficulty they found two seats which had just been vacated and, since several other people were squeezed in with them at the table, they couldn't talk much.

Only absent-minded words were exchanged, for the surroundings distracted them, the air lulled them to sleep, the buzzing of voices made them feel both drowsy and yet excited, it was all different from what it had been with Aniela before. At first it had been enough for him to gaze upon her, now he had his wish; she was sitting there with him, sitting quietly as she nearly always did, and yet she seemed tense to him, concentrating not on him, but on preparation for something strange, on a problem which she had to solve. Something strange, she was strange herself now, yes, she had certainly been right in thinking that he should not show her off to others. What did she mean by it? She was looking around, he gazed at her and saw many faces swimming in the smoke, in the perfumed smoke, he saw too how many faces were turned towards Aniela in the big café where the officers were, and he ordered again and went on ordering, although Aniela was not drinking with him. He drank several glasses in quick succession.

But the schnaps didn't cheer one up. Suddenly it didn't seem to him a good thing any longer that he was sitting here with Aniela. It would have been better to go first to Hiller's Restaurant and order dinner. It would have been better to start like that, he had intended something of the kind, but the meeting with Rungenhagen had distracted him. Of course, it would have been better still in Aniela's garden. He was forgetting why he had fetched her out. Of course, for dinner, he wanted to invite her out for a meal. Dinner in Hiller's Restaurant. But out there by the water the air was soft, that odd air that a river carries with it, the smell of the river was rising and a few drops of rain were falling on the branches. The old man, whom Aniela had forbidden him to hate and who never spoke a word to him, was coming up from the river with his fishing-rods, the bucket gave a sigh, a few fish lay on its bottom. Their red gills were moving.

Then the captain was standing in front of him. It was the captain in charge of a security patrol which had been in the room for some time and had been moving slowly amongst the tables. It attracted no attention, for nobody admitted here needed to be afraid of a patrol. But still the captain came to every table and saluted casually, staring through the faces before him with indifference and a trace of distaste. He remained standing while his two subordinates looked through the papers. Matthes sat erect, the regulations were that one didn't stand up in public rooms during security checks, he let them inspect his pay book and got it back. The two N.C.O.s waited, then one said impatiently: 'The lady now, please.'

But Aniela did not move, she didn't look at the N.C.O. either, but past him at the captain, who now began to show interest. He returned her glance with a look of slight surprise.

Evidently Aniela had come out without her identity card. She was not used to having to produce it. She hadn't her handbag with her either. Suddenly Aniela said without lowering her voice, so that all those sitting near by and now silent could hear it, 'I haven't an identity card.'

Even more people showed interest now, for a scandal of this kind was not to be expected in the Rising Swan. Their stares now switched from Aniela to the N.C.O. who had dared to come into the Rising Swan and let himself be caught with somebody without papers of identification. They waited. Then the stares swung back to Aniela once more.

'You haven't got one or you haven't one with you?' asked the captain.

'I haven't got one,' said Aniela.

'Stand up,' said the captain to Matthes. Matthes was standing in a flash; the N.C.O. Matthes had risen with exemplary obedience. His face was quite close to that of the captain; unthinkingly and with eyes wide open, he stared into the unknown face of a man who had burns on his cheeks, grey-eyed, lean, one who came from the front and, attached to a reserve unit, was doing a duty which bored and disgusted him. The captain said: 'You know what you have to do. Hand over your pay book again. You are to leave these premises with your companion immediately.

'Make a note of it,' he said in an unfriendly way to the N.C.O.

He asked a further question in an undertone: 'You know the standing orders. You have been instructed in the regulations?'

'Yes, sir. But I did not know –'

'That's the limit,' said the captain. 'Excuses? Leave now,' he said in a weary, contemptuous tone.

Then they were outside. They were walking up the street along which Aniela had come earlier looking so beautiful. For a while they said nothing; then Matthes stopped and said: 'What is it, then, Aniela, what is it you want, what are you aiming at?'

'I am not aiming at anything. You took me there.'

Still he did not dare to ask. 'Why have you difficulties about papers? Is something wrong?' he demanded.

Then she spoke abruptly, as though he had touched a tender spot and, as it seemed to him, full of longing that she should not lose him: 'But you must have noticed. Have you never thought about where I come from and to whom I belong? Has that really never entered your mind?'

'Honestly, I have never thought of it.'

'Is it because of the language I speak?'

'Yes, that's it.'

'Good God! Who doesn't speak several languages here.'

They went on speaking in monosyllables. What had she done to him? He had become possessed by anger and childish shame; it was stupid, ridiculous, degrading; the next patrol that stopped them would have the right to separate them. Then it occurred to him how senseless all this excitement was, she had only given way to him, he himself was to blame for everything. But why had she not spoken frankly to him, why had she not spared him such an unpleasant scene? Never, right to the bitter end, had he understood Aniela so little.

But she was now quite self-possessed again, she was no more depressed than usual, nor embarrassed, nor did she show spite.

There was not even hatred in her words when she eventually said: 'You never thought of it, you say. You never thought of it because you just couldn't believe that a man like you could be mistaken. Two different things, you said. Oh, but it is stupid to be so sure. When you said that, you began it all yourself. It was then I wanted to see how you would behave sitting at the same table with me in public.'

He never understood her completely, even after their last terrible meeting, but she obviously guessed his thoughts, for she did not want to cause him further embarrassment, so she turned quickly and climbed into the tram which had just arrived, so quickly that he couldn't even see her face any more. Only later, torn by doubts and cursing himself on the way home, did it occur to him to wonder who had helped her out in the tram, she had nothing with her, no handbag, certainly not a penny. He was ashamed.

Nothing had been decided between them when she had broken off the conversation in this way, but things shouldn't have been left unsolved like that. They should have stopped seeing one another at once. He should have gone back to Rungenhagen and forgotten the distressing incident. He should have heeded the warning in good time and been pleased that everything had been arranged with so little unpleasantness, that the report of the patrol had only led to a severe reprimand. He had a good record, clear of previous convictions. Otherwise there would have been more trouble. Now the reprimand would lengthen the period of time which had to elapse before his next promotion, which would be postponed in consequence. He could put up with that. But the other thing was far less simple: he had to give up Aniela or himself, or rather he had to give up what he had been till then and what he had believed himself to be.

Who was Aniela then? He remembered the colonel's daughter. Mother and daughter came to the barracks to see to the N.C.O.s' laundry. They went through the rooms and collected the linen, and after a few days they returned and handed it back. Their manner was humble and nervously respectable, and they did not look like members of the so-called upper classes; the wretched smell of hard-worked and poorly nourished bodies, the steam of the ironing room clung to them. Frettchen had managed to find out that they were the wife and daughter of a colonel in the defeated army. His room mates looked unconvinced, almost embarrassed, for a colonel was a colonel after all, even though he had belonged to the defeated. It is true that, if an army is annihilated and a state wiped out, titles cease to have authority, pensions are no longer paid, and then, as Frettchen observed, widows and daughters go to wash the underpants of the victors.

'She hasn't much of a figure,' said Frettchen, 'but still one shouldn't lose a chance. Do you think one can get her?' But mother and daughter always came to the rooms together, they were never apart. Only once did the thin little creature come alone; winter had come and influenza was making the rounds, so that the old woman probably had to keep to her bed. It was Sunday morning and Frettchen took the opportunity to get a little closer to her. 'I think she would play,' he said later, 'I can tell. Wait until she comes next time –' She had to come again, and Frettchen was in a good mood and made a grab at her again, the girl struggled and could not put down her laundry parcel, one could see what torture it was for her to have to go on smiling, for Frettchen did not mean any harm, he was only teasing and in any case was fussy about having his shirts well starched. – 'Let her go,' Matthes suddenly shouted at Frettchen in a fit of anger, and Frettchen did let go of her and turned around, affecting astonishment: 'What's all the fuss? I don't mean anything by it.'

No, Frettchen didn't mean anything much, in wartime one had to face up to far worse things, but still Matthes had met her later on the main stairs, as she was coming down, this lean little thing with her heavy basket, down the draughty stairs, and he saw that she was crying helplessly in her fright. To let herself be mauled about, so that the customers are not annoyed, that's not very funny, even if one can exist by it. All these things pass, he thought suddenly in terror, they pass and then lurk somewhere and find us again and come back to us. They will find us, even if they now exist in a distant misty place of which we know nothing and of which we only catch an accidental glimpse on Tuesday after Whitsun.

He thought of Tuesday after Whitsun. The detachment had marched out early for field training on the Luschin Heath; that was a popular exercise, more amusing than trudging around the parade-grounds. Matthes took the opportunity to hand over his group to the lance-corporal for a while. It was a cool morning, quite misty, and the mist grew denser, so dense that one couldn't see fifteen paces ahead. He had scarcely moved away, when all previous activity seemed swallowed up, only a distant call, or once a few reports from blank cartridges, penetrated the vapour. He went through sand and reeds, and through thin brushwood; a few birds were calling to one another. Then another, indefinite sound reached his ear, he

stood listening for a while, and finally groped towards it with
unusual caution. He had come to a section of the territory
upon which the planning authority intended to make great
physical changes, for the 'New Order' even intended to have
its own landscape, a master Order which even brought the
earth itself under regulations, it planted forests, created lakes,
and marked out parks to give the new race a fitting home.
Heaps of earth, partly scattered by trucks, rose all over the
place, and rails lay about. He stumbled. All at once the noise
was very close and almost above him and then he saw shapes.
A high mound suddenly appeared, above a few tip-trucks were
silhouetted and near them a group of men standing, leaning
or squatting on them. They moved, they sang, wildly but in a
strangely muted way, they stamped, violently but in a strangely
restrained way, they clapped, beating time sharply, but
strangely, as though they were muffled. Before them on the
rails shadows whirled in a dance of abandon. People called to
one another and shouted. The mist blotted out both faces and
colours, they were a shadowy race, the conquered who danced
here. For an hour the mist hid them and now they danced
among the rails. They got little to eat, there were no arrangements for them to support themselves, but how they danced.
A challenge, a jubilation, a terrible defiance were implied by
this dancing at half-past eight in the morning.

At that time he still looked upon history as a judgement.
The man who regards history as a judgement is to be counted
among God's band as long as he is victorious. It offends him
if the conquered do not wear ashes and the curse does not
silence them. Here suddenly, in the mist, on the ground torn
up by caterpillar tracks, amidst trucks and shovels, the condemned were dancing. He stood motionless. He did not have
to fear discovery, he could step into their midst, and very
likely they would cower and scatter quickly. Nevertheless he
drew back as though he had a bad conscience. He kept quiet
and stole back softly into the mist. The scene troubled him for
a long time. The stone heaps of Rungenhagen suddenly
seemed to him no longer such an unchallengeable guarantee
of authority. He spoke to nobody about it, but he remembered

that he left the place with a peculiar feeling, as if walking on a thin crust which threatened to break.

The walks were the cause of it. A soldier shouldn't have time for walks or else he should always go with his own kind where he would talk about the right things. Otherwise he shows himself to be soft and gives Sergeant-Major Rungenhagen a motive for detailing him to execution squads. A soft type, Corporal Matthes, thought Rungenhagen who had been his friend, the iron friend Rungenhagen. He must learn to recognize authority, thought the iron friend Rungenhagen, and must realize where he belongs. He must see what it leads to if you swerve from the path and want to leave your proper place. If you are too cowardly or too weak to stick to your proper place. If you swerve from the path, you are done for. The wheels catch up with you. The bullet finishes you.

Just a complete muddle, nothing but shameful accidents. It was just an accident that Sergeant-Major Rungenhagen was in charge of the detachment when a squad had to be detailed for the execution. It was an accident that he, Matthes, happened to pass the policeman and that the same policeman afterwards shot so swiftly and accurately and he got his pay book back so quickly. The pay book, still warm from the body of the man who lay on the ground in the clothes of Corporal Matthes, the man whom the bullet had laid low while he, Matthes, was in the clothes of this man. A madman and outcast, a half-naked man with riverweed in his hair, was wandering about among the firs and the gardens, one who only an hour before had been the trim Corporal Matthes.

The fisherman crouched amidst the currant bushes. He saw him at once when he ran up panting from the river, after he had finished with Aniela, after he had pushed her under the water. He didn't think of Aniela any more, he didn't even wonder if he could be a murderer, perhaps he was one, it was all the same, one, two, three murderers, mere murderers everywhere in the world. All thought was suffocated in him, the agony of breathing smothered all thought and his gaping mouth was dry, quite dry, madly dry, although he had

swallowed a lot of water. He saw at once that everything was
gone, clothes and boots, cap, belt, the blouse with his pay
book in the pocket, the other man had gone off fully equipped.
For a second it wasn't clear to him whether he should hurl
himself at the fisherman and strangle him, but then he rushed
towards the hut. He tore open the door; there were traces of a
man having been sheltered here, a spotted handkerchief,
breadcrumbs, a glass, then clothes, creased dirty things
thrown hastily onto the floor. He couldn't plan, he just
grabbed at them, mechanically and swift as lightning, even the
disgust with which he got into another man's clothes soon
left him. He couldn't find shoes anywhere, but while he stood
and buttoned and looked around him, the door slammed and
the key screeched in the lock.

Oh damn! Damn, he should have knocked the fisherman
down first. Now he was sitting in this fish-box, and the fisherman was lying in wait for him, and the third man, whom they
were helping to get away, was off in his things. Anyone who
wanted to could now wipe out the former Corporal Matthes
completely. A shot through the window would be enough, and
later no one would search under the loose soil of the garden,
even the police couldn't take the trouble to dig up all the gardens around Lavka. He threw himself against the door. The hut
shook, but the door held. To try to kick open a door barefoot
was senseless. Kicking a door barefoot hurts the feet, but that's
all. In such cases the usefulness of nailed marching boots be-
comes obvious; they burst a way through doors and over fron-
tiers. The windows were too small. While a man was wriggling
through one, a child could finish him off. There was only the roof.

He jumped onto the table, the table groaned under his
weight, he braced his shoulders against the rafters which gave
way and moved upwards, already the tiles were beginning to
slip, they tinkled and splashed, down into the grass outside.
At the third push the laths broke, he hauled himself up, got to
his feet and stood on the roof and, seeing nobody below him,
jumped with his feet together. There was no stir in the garden
and he hurried up to the upper garden gate in his strange
clothes. It was pulled to. No sign. Which way?

There was no point in following barefoot and in rags a man who might have gone in any direction and who now had a weapon. All the same he began to run. The gardens seemed deserted, terrified, just terrified, hostile gardens harbouring no good, everything seemed to be waiting as in a dream, and one felt the restlessness of evening among the birds in the quinces. He was running, he had already hurried past a few houses which stood far apart, the doors were closed, the ground-floor windows boarded up, not a chicken scratched, no trace of life. Then, not far off, two shots were fired, short, crisp sounds, nothing later, no other noise.

He stood still and listened, his heart beat up to his throat, as he craned forwards, hesitating; he was struck by the sight of his naked feet and the sand welling between his toes. A man in rags who had lost his insignia and been robbed of his name, how easily he is frightened; his first instinct is to jump with his naked feet and duck behind the nearest cover if there is shooting or the police appear. Then he ran more cautiously towards the noise, down between two gardens and suddenly the jeep was standing there again, but now in the middle of the road, the driver too had got out and gone to the front and the two policemen holding carbines were standing there looking down at something; they had not yet seen him, as he came up softly. At their feet lay a shabby, dust-covered figure, wearing the uniform of Corporal Matthes. It lay face downwards, and the tunic had a small hole between the shoulders.

'Your pay book, sir,' said one of the policemen who obviously knew his job and never forgot a face. 'It was lucky you passed us earlier. I had remembered your name and, of course, your face, and an hour later you come back and the pay book is in order, only the face doesn't fit it any more. He wanted to run for it, but we shot after him straightaway.'

'You've had a lucky escape,' said the policeman. 'The clothes are certainly done for. But we can take you along in our car now. How did it happen?'

Oh yes, he had certainly been lucky, even if he had become a murderer. Even if he had asked for a trial and punishment,

no court-martial will condemn a man who has acted quickly
and firmly in self-defence. As it happened Rungenhagen took
over the affair single-handed, and there had been no protocol
or entry in the penal register, especially since there were no
regulations regarding the type of punishment to be applied.
In all other respects the whole thing turned out in an in-
credibly lucky way; it was incredible luck which kept open
for him the path back to duty. The facts bore witness for
themselves; a man in bathing trunks, wearing strange clothes
over them, had been robbed while bathing in the river, this
was not even partly untrue, only a small detail was left untold
and that didn't matter. The fact that an N.C.O. intending to go
in the direction of Blyskanie suddenly changed his mind and
dived into the river to cool down, leaving his things, including
his side-arms, unguarded, that was certainly irregular conduct,
but on the other hand there were no regulations governing
cases of this kind. Thanks to the police's thorough training in
marksmanship, the culprit himself was no longer available as
a witness. The inquiry wrote itself, as it were, and the court
decided after hearing the facts not to ask for an investigation.
It left the case to be dealt with by the unit itself, in so far as any
action was necessary. The company commander expressed his
astonishment and behaved icily towards Matthes, who was
regarded as a potential officer; he decided not to award punishment, but this was the kind of irregular conduct through
which this N.C.O. attracted attention in an unpleasant way, he
would scarcely gain quick promotion now, but perhaps he
might be transferred. It would have been better to have been
transferred to some other unit where Rungenhagen would no
longer see through his weaknesses and detail him for an
execution squad. The regiment had one single deserter, a man
from a mobile unit, scarcely anyone had known him.

He hadn't known him, he didn't want to have known him
or his face, least of all the face, so that he wouldn't have to
remember the face, perhaps so that he wouldn't have to find
out that he himself had been the one out there; everything
suggested it, a growing madness drummed the idea into him,
Corporal Matthes climbed out of the water and hunted the

other one down until Corporal Matthes lay on his face with
a little hole in his tunic, and Corporal Matthes in a black denim
suit stood out there waiting until Corporal Matthes helped to
put an end to him, for this was what iron friend Rungenhagen
wanted; and now the barrels had all been lowered and were
pointing stupidly in that direction. The line of sight. The line
of sight is a straight line calculated from the eye of the marks-
man through the groove of the backsight and the tip of the
foresight. To strike the bull in the black. No, in the red. The
gradual diagonal squeezing, the delicate resistance when the
pressure point is reached, that all works on its own. The line
of sight –

They should have stopped seeing one another; immediately
after the incident in the Swan he should have broken with
her. Instead, nothing had been decided between them. Before
all that, at the time when he still used to go with Rungenhagen
to Blyskanie for riding, he had always agreed with his friend
as to what things one had to do and what not to do and what
obedience meant. Now he had suddenly become unfit for
obedience. He had despised soldiers who went out and slept
with the local girls for a loaf of bread or in winter for a bucket
of coal. These soldiers looked upon it as a joke like any other,
by which they snapped their fingers at the regulations, they
didn't know any better. Nothing went deep with them, and if
they got three days C.B., well, it was just three days; it didn't
change anything for them. But he, Matthes, had understood
obedience, and now he was spoilt for it. He had gone downhill very quickly. Four days later he was on the way to Aniela.

In the outer fields where the dismantled fort lay to the left
and the gardens began on the right, a jeep was standing, driven
sideways into the bushes. It was empty except for the driver
who was bent over a magazine. A few steps further on in the
green shadow two men, also inconspicuous, were standing
about; they wore the insignia of the field police. Round about
it was quiet, there was that strange atmosphere when something is going to happen and everyone is best advised to keep
under cover. One of the policemen took a step outside the
shadow, saluted, and said: 'Your pay book, sir. Police patrol.'

There was no official contact between the military and the organization responsible for security. Matthes saluted too and produced his pay book.

'Anything up?' he asked.

'A search. Where are you going, sir, if I may ask?'

'To Blyskanie, to the riding school.'

The policeman saluted, he too saluted and he went on his way; the road began to curve, nettles, a few more of the shoddy, unplastered houses standing there. He pulled himself together, he must force himself not to look back at the police. A little more of the road and the green footpath down to Aniela's place came into view. But, before he left the road, he looked round after all. Suddenly he had the feeling that what he was doing was disreputable and could not turn out well.

Aniela was not alone. She stood on the cinder path with another girl whom he didn't know, indolently, one hand resting on her hip, the other folded behind her, and was speaking to the girl. She stood turned towards him and although she could not see him, it seemed to him as though she were standing there on show, aware of nothing but the glorious brown of her hair and the beauty of her limbs. Something reckless seemed revealed in her, and suddenly this struck him too. He had always come in good faith, but now the desire which drove him was evil. It had begun with his breaking the law unconsciously. Now he *wanted* to break it. Then Aniela saw him and, without making a sign or breaking off her conversation, she let him approach. He went down, greedily savouring the knowledge that every step he now took was forbidden and that it couldn't turn out well and that, in spite of everything, he would take this path again.

His appearance had set in motion a series of indistinct, sometimes scarcely perceptible movements. Aniela changed her position, and the other girl scrutinized him and went through the gestures of taking leave. Further down in the garden the fisherman, who was digging for worms, had also looked up and risen, he went up towards the hut and squatted down on the threshold with his back leaning against the door.

In the hut itself there seemed also to be a slight movement.

Aniela was not alone. Why should she have been alone? The fisherman didn't count, and she couldn't have expected him to return. He had had the choice of giving up her or himself, and he had taken the second course. Or rather he had taken the risk. He had made no decision, it was simply that he was spoilt for obedience. In spite of this she perceived her triumph. When the strange girl had gone, she turned her attention to him.

The evenings, as they usually were in the summer, had been the cause of it; warm, shot through with cirrus and veils of mist. The flashes of lightning in far-off storms darted hither and thither, but no thunder was to be heard. The sun had dipped behind a bank of cloud which had gathered in the west. It was still light. He felt he had never been away.

She didn't ask any questions, or mention the incident in the Swan and he didn't broach the subject. What was there to talk about? Everything had been clarified, most of it without words, nothing had been promised. She took it for granted and did not put anxious and worried questions like: What will become of you? How will you manage? What will they do to you? He would not have known how to answer. Never had their intimacy been greater, more purposeful, more relaxed. She had an air of boldness about her, no, it was rather an expectant gaiety. Each of them showed gratitude by not keeping the other waiting.

Suddenly he said: 'You were not alone, Aniela.'

'Do you mean the girl with me just now? She is a neighbour.'

'I don't know whom I mean.'

'The fisherman is always there. Now there's no need to worry. Nobody is watching here.'

'Yes, you are right. Why should I feel like a thief? I ought to be ashamed of myself.'

'No, you shouldn't. Listen,' she said and stroked his temples, 'shall we go to the river for a swim?' She said: 'You go on ahead. You can leave your things under the elder-bush there. I'll catch you up.'

While he was undressing, the thought came to him: 'But
it's all been like this once before.' Below stretched the path
by the river-bank to Blyskanie, the disused tram-rails, then
came a meadow, the dead loops of river-bed which had no
water in the summer, finally the river itself. All in all, a little
more than a hundred yards, there was no harm in going to the
bank undressed. Between the fences nettles grew luxuriantly
and the high-grown golden-rod nodded on both sides. And it
had all been like that once before. He stood there and waited,
in the end the door opened; it had all been like this once
before, and he saw Aniela coming out in her bathing cloak. She
shouted up to the fisherman a few casual words which he did
not understand, looked round, and came slowly down. 'So
there you are,' she said, 'I thought you were waiting by the
river. We'll go up a bit, would you like that, and let ourselves
drift with the current.'

'Yes, yes,' he said. No, it had never been like this before.

Aniela left her cloak by a willow trunk and they kept to the
bank, walking up the river. The ground was sandy, often
flooded, and beards of grass dangled on the bushes and
rustled. Heat rose up from the sand, the air hung full of
midges, a cloud of midges often moved with them above their
heads, filling the air with a scarcely perceptible and yet penetrating humming. The yellow irises stood succulent on their
stems, with snails sticking all over them. Dense reeds; here,
before it entered the town, the river was still wild, it flowed
gurgling between sand-banks and patches of reed and was
calm in deep places over which bubbles slowly circled and
disappeared.

'Have you brothers or sisters?' Aniela asked.

'Yes, two sisters.'

'Younger than you?'

'I'm between them. What made you think of that?'

'I must ask *something* about you. I still know nothing. It's
strange that I still know absolutely nothing about you!'

'Do I know anything about you, Aniela?'

'Oh, goodness,' said Aniela, 'you know all about *me* now.'

'No, I don't know anything.'

'But you're satisfied with that. That's the difference. I don't
know anything, you say to yourself, and that's an end to it.'

'What do you think I ought to know?'

'Oh, we can't do it that way. But you might have asked
yourself something like that before, say.'

'Aniela, as far as I'm concerned you came out of the river or
the lilacs. One shouldn't ask a Melusina questions. But if you
like: Have you brothers and sisters too, Aniela?'

'Oh, let's drop the subject,' she said. 'I don't want to speak
of it any more now.'

She had trodden on something sharp; she was limping and
had to let him help her. – 'A reed splinter,' he said, 'they grow
here and can cut you.'

While she sat there, propped up supporting her weight on
her hands, he was holding her foot by the instep and where
the skin felt dry and parchment-like to the touch. She re-
sponded to his touch with her toes and he took her foot and
placed it against his chest. He felt her push against him and
then draw back gently. – 'Wait a minute,' he said, 'I haven't
found anything yet.' – But she withdrew her foot and stood
up quickly. – 'Can you walk again?' – 'Yes, yes,' she said, 'it's
all gone. Let's go on.'

At last they immersed themselves in the river; the water was
warm, the river-bed was not safe, and one could scarcely walk
on it, full of tangled roots, stumps, and intertwining stalks,
and thick clouds of mud were stirred up at every step. They
threw themselves in, flat on their chests, in order to get into
the current. For a while they were carried along by it side by
side, then the river grew calmer, forming a wide, deep pool.
Matthes dived, glided noiselessly beneath her, caught hold of
her by the hips and used his weight. Immediately she yielded
and came down to him, lifeless as a doll; he held her, as long
as breath lasted. They lay beside one another, while their
bodies turned, he opened his eyes and stared down at her face
beneath him, he saw her closed eyelids, her lips pressed
together in an expression of helpless, triumphant, unbearable
suffering. Now he had to release her and they both came to the
surface, breathing heavily; without a word they pushed away

from one another. They lay on their backs and drifted again, the current was flowing more evenly, occasionally they made a languid stroke, but for a while they did not speak.

They were approaching the last bend before the place they were making for, and now it began to rain. First of all it was like a sudden vapour in the air, then a downpour crashed on to the water, so that the river seemed to smoke. Immediately, however, the sun broke through a hole in the veil of mist and shot a few sickly yellow, almost horizontal beams of light towards the river-bank. In all its incredible fascination the fragment of a rainbow appeared for a second in front of the dripping garden slopes. But Matthes had no time to admire its seven colours.

For just then, a small figure, which appeared to be separated from him by the thinnest sheet of iridescent glass, went up the middle path through Aniela's garden with quick, wary steps: Corporal Matthes. The person posing as Corporal Matthes was going up the garden, he stood still for an instant, bent down, pulled at his left boot, straighted his back, adjusted his side-arms, and disappeared amidst the hedges. Then followed a harmless pause. The water was rustling, a thrush warbling in the reeds.

Matthes hurled himself against the water. Briefly, there was a void and then a flood of water shot over him, a muddy degrading flood. With a fierce stroke Aniela had approached and was holding him in a close embrace.

Aniela was holding him in her embrace. Aniela, who had not been alone, had lured him out of his clothes and was holding him firmly in the river, and the man for whom she had done it all, the bastard for whose sake she had sold him, he was getting away in his, Matthes's clothes, and with his papers. There were enemies everywhere, he had fallen into a web of trickery.

What was she after? Was she trying to drown him? She was shouting aloud in a voice which he did not recognize, an imploring voice: 'Listen!' He struck at her breast. She did not let go and they both went under immediately. As long as they wrestled breathlessly in an embrace, something inside him cried out for an end to it, a surrender to this grip, for extinction in darkness, while another feeling, a determination not to be drowned like a dog, fought on stubbornly. His head bobbed above the surface, he spat and gasped for air like a dying man. But Aniela was there again. In the end she too was struggling for breath; while they trod water and he pushed faster towards the bank, she shouted in a distorted voice: 'Listen, just listen to me –' she shouted. 'You must listen!' She shouted whenever she could get breath: 'It's Schymek. It's my brother. He – listen – !' Finally she shouted: 'If only you had asked –' She was strong, tenacious, a good swimmer, why didn't she let him go? Who was he, now, while he kicked and struck at her, struck her in the face, who had he been before? Who was she now? Who was she now? Growing weaker, she was shouting: 'Schymek. My brother. He must –' Then she couldn't say any more and he had nothing to say, he didn't need to say anything, he only needed his strength and he struck once more. Then he was free of her and dragged himself towards the bank.

What had become of her, what happened to her, who helped her, where was she now? Now it had happened, the report of the rifles sang on in his head, benumbed by the air pressure. The face of the man exterminated was no longer visible. It had sunk forward, for the body was tugging at its cords, a clumsy, feeble weight which was collapsing. The linden began to sway, just as a weak light, the first few trembling shadows sprang up. Its crown was swaying, after the lean trunk had been torn apart by the bullets which had also penetrated the body. It swayed, almost gracefully, as if caught by a gust of wind, although the air remained quite still, apart from the slow dispersal of the fumes from the spent cartridges. Then, with a drawn-out moan, the crown fell forward, farther and farther forward, until it erased the image in his mind, and nothing more could be seen but green, empty, shimmering, silent green.

Heinrich Böll

MURKE'S COLLECTED SILENCES

Translated by Leila Vennewitz

Heinrich Böll

HEINRICH BÖLL, winner of the 1973 Nobel Prize for Literature, was born in 1917 and published his first stories in 1947. Catholic, social critic, anti-materialist and anti-authoritarian, he has won an ever-increasing reputation for his personal involvement in public issues and for the record his works offer of the recent history of Germany and the various ways in which Germans have sought to come to terms with the past. This story takes an amusing look at some features of post-war 'media-dominated' culture which will be familiar to readers outside Germany as well.

MURKE'S COLLECTED SILENCES

EVERY morning, after entering Broadcasting House, Murke performed an existential exercise. Here in this building the lift was the kind known as a paternoster – open cages carried on a conveyor belt, like beads on a rosary, moving slowly and continuously from bottom to top, across the top of the lift shaft, down to the bottom again, so that passengers could step on and off at any floor. Murke would jump onto the paternoster but, instead of getting off at the second floor, where his office was, he would let himself be carried on up, past the third, fourth, fifth floors, and he was seized with panic every time the cage rose above the level of the fifth floor and ground its way up into the empty space where oily chains, greasy rods and groaning machinery pulled and pushed the lift from an upward into a downward direction, and Murke would stare in terror at the bare brick walls, and sigh with relief as the lift passed through the lock, dropped into place, and began its slow descent, past the fifth, fourth, third floors. Murke knew his fears were unfounded; obviously nothing would ever happen, nothing could ever happen, and even if it did it could be nothing worse than finding himself up there at the top when the lift stopped moving and being shut in for an hour or two at the most. He was never without a book in his pocket, and cigarettes; yet as long as the building had been standing, for three years, the lift had never once failed. On certain days it was inspected, days when Murke had to forego those four and a half seconds of panic, and on these days he was irritable and restless, like people who had gone without breakfast. He needed this panic, the way other people need their coffee, their oatmeal, or their fruit juice.

So when he stepped off the lift at the second floor, the home of the Cultural Department, he felt light-hearted and relaxed, as light-hearted and relaxed as anyone who loves and understands his work. He would unlock the door to his office, walk slowly over to his armchair, sit down, and light a cigarette. He was always first on the job. He was young, intelligent, and had a pleasant manner, and even his arrogance, which occasionally flashed out for a moment – even that was forgiven him since it was known he had majored in psychology and graduated *cum laude*.

For two days now, Murke had been obliged to go without his panic-breakfast; unusual circumstances had required him to get to Broadcasting House at eight a.m., dash off to a studio, and begin work right away, for he had been told by the Director of Broadcasting to go over the two talks on The Nature of Art which the great Bur-Malottke had taped, and to cut them according to Bur-Malottke's instructions. Bur-Malottke, who had converted to Catholicism during the religious fervour of 1945, had suddenly, 'overnight', as he put it, 'felt religious qualms', he had 'suddenly felt he might be blamed for contributing to the religious overtones in radio', and he had decided to omit God, Who occurred frequently in both his half-hour talks on The Nature of Art, and replaced Him with a formula more in keeping with the mental outlook which he had professed before 1945. Bur-Malottke had suggested to the producer that the word God be replaced by the formula 'that higher Being Whom we revere', but he had refused to retape the talks, requesting instead that God be cut out of the tapes and replaced by 'that higher Being Whom we revere'. Bur-Malottke was a friend of the Director, but this friendship was not the reason for the Director's willingness to oblige him: Bur-Malottke was a man one simply did not contradict. He was the author of numerous books of a belletristic-philosophical-religious and art-historical nature, he was on the editorial staff of three periodicals and two newspapers, and closely connected with the largest publishing house. He had agreed to come to Broadcasting House for fifteen minutes on Wednesday and tape the words 'that higher Being Whom we revere' as often as God was mentioned in his talks; the rest was up to the technical experts.

It had not been easy for the Director to find someone whom

he could ask to do the job; he thought of Murke, but the
suddenness with which he thought of Murke made him suspicious – he was a dynamic, robust individual – so he spent
five minutes going over the problem in his mind, considered
Schwendling, Humkoke, Miss Broldin, but he ended up with
Murke. The Director did not like Murke; he had, of course,
taken him on as soon as his name had been put forward, the
way a zoo director, whose real love is the rabbits and the deer,
naturally accepts wild animals too for the simple reason that a
zoo must contain wild animals – but what the Director really
loved was rabbits and deer, and for him Murke was an intellectual wild animal. In the end his dynamic personality
triumphed, and he instructed Murke to cut Bur-Malottke's
talks.

The talks were to be given on Thursday and Friday, and
Bur-Malottke's misgivings had come to him on Sunday night
– one might just as well commit suicide as contradict Bur-
Malottke, and the Director was much too dynamic to think of
suicide.

So Murke spent Monday afternoon and Tuesday morning
listening three times to the two half-hour talks on The
Nature of Art; he had cut out God, and in the short breaks
which he took, during which he silently smoked a cigarette
with the technician, reflected on the dynamic personality of
the Director and the inferior Being Whom Bur-Malottke
revered. He had never read a line of Bur-Malottke, never
heard one of his talks before. Monday night he had dreamed
of a staircase as tall and steep as the Eiffel Tower, and he had
climbed it but soon noticed that the stairs were slippery with
soap, and the Director stood down below and called out:
'Go on, Murke, go on . . . show us what you can do – go on!'
Tuesday night the dream had been similar: he had been at a
fairground, strolled casually over to the roller coaster, paid
his thirty pfennigs to a man whose face seemed familiar, and
as he got on the roller coaster he saw that it was at least ten
miles long, he knew there was no going back, and realized
that the man who had taken his thirty pfennigs had been the
Director. Both mornings after these dreams he had not needed

the harmless panic-breakfast up there in the empty space above
the paternoster.

Now it was Wednesday. He was smiling as he entered the
building, got into the paternoster, let himself be carried up as
far as the sixth floor – four and a half seconds of panic, the
grinding of the chains, the bare brick walls – he rode down as
far as the fourth floor, got out and walked towards the studio
where he had an appointment with Bur-Malottke. It was two
minutes to ten as he sat down in his green chair, waved to the
technician and lit his cigarette. His breathing was quiet, he
took a piece of paper out of his breast pocket and glanced at
the clock; Bur-Malottke was always on time, at least he had a
reputation for being punctual; and as the second hand completed the sixtieth minute of the tenth hour, the minute hand
slipped onto the twelve, the hour hand onto the ten, the door
opened, and in walked Bur-Malottke. Murke got up, and with
a pleasant smile walked over to Bur-Malottke and introduced
himself. Bur-Malottke shook hands, smiled, and said: 'Well,
let's get started!' Murke picked up the sheet of paper from the
table, put his cigarette between his lips, and, reading from the
list, said to Bur-Malottke:

'In the two talks, God occurs precisely twenty-seven times
– so I must ask you to repeat twenty-seven times the words
we are to splice. We would appreciate it if we might ask you to
repeat them thirty-five times, so as to have a certain reserve
when it comes to splicing.'

'Granted,' said Bur-Malottke with a smile, and sat down.

'There is one difficulty, however,' said Murke: 'where
God occurs in the genitive, such as "God's will", "God's
love", "God's purpose", He must be replaced by the noun in
question followed by the words "of that higher Being Whom
we revere". I must ask you, therefore, to repeat the words
"the will" twice, "the love" twice, and "the purpose" three
times, followed each time by "of that higher Being Whom we
revere", giving us a total of seven genitives. Then there is one
spot where you use the vocative and say "O God" – here I
suggest you substitute "O Thou higher Being Whom we

revere". Everywhere else only the nominative case applies.'

It was clear that Bur-Malottke had not thought of these complications; he began to sweat, the grammatical transposition bothered him. Murke went on: 'In all,' he said, in his pleasant, friendly manner, 'the twenty-seven sentences will require one minute and twenty seconds radio time, whereas the twenty-seven times "God" occurs require only twenty seconds. In other words, in order to take care of your alterations we shall have to cut half a minute from each talk.'

Bur-Malottke sweated more heavily than ever; inwardly he cursed his sudden misgivings and asked: 'I suppose you've already done the cutting, have you?'

'Yes, I have,' said Murke, pulling a flat metal box out of his pocket; he opened it and held it out to Bur-Malottke: it contained some darkish sound-tape scraps, and Murke said softly: 'God twenty-seven times, spoken by you. Would you care to have them?'

'No I would not,' said Bur-Malottke, furious. 'I'll speak to the Director about the two half-minutes. What comes after my talks in the programme?'

'Tomorrow,' said Murke, 'your talk is followed by the regular programme Neighbourly News, edited by Grehm.'

'Damn,' said Bur-Malottke, 'it's no use asking Grehm for a favour.'

'And the day after tomorrow,' said Murke, 'your talk is followed by Let's Go Dancing.'

'Oh God, that's Huglieme,' groaned Bur-Malottke, 'never yet has Light Entertainment given way to Culture by as much as a fifth of a minute.'

'No,' said Murke, 'it never has, at least –' and his youthful face took on an expression of irreproachable modesty – 'at least not since I've been working here.'

'Very well,' said Bur-Malottke and glanced at the clock, 'we'll be through here in ten minutes, I take it, and then I'll have a word with the Director about that minute. Let's go. Can you leave me your list?'

'Of course,' said Murke, 'I know the figures by heart.'

The technician put down his newspaper as Murke entered

the little glass booth. The technician was smiling. On Monday and Tuesday, during the six hours they listened to Bur-Malottke's talks and did their cutting, Murke and the technician had not exchanged a single personal word; now and again they exchanged glances, and when they stopped for a breather the technician had passed his cigarettes to Murke and the next day Murke passed his to the technician, and now when Murke saw the technician smiling he thought: If there is such a thing as friendship in this world, then this man is my friend. He laid the metal box with the snippets from Bur-Malottke's talk on the table and said quietly: 'Here we go.' He plugged into the studio and said into the microphone: 'I'm sure we can dispense with the run-through, Professor. We might as well start right away – would you please begin with the nominatives?'

Bur-Malottke nodded, Murke switched off his own microphone, pressed the button which turned on the green light in the studio, and heard Bur-Malottke's solemn, carefully articulated voice intoning: 'That higher Being Whom we revere – that higher Being . . .'

Bur-Malottke pursed his lips toward the muzzle of the mike as if he wanted to kiss it, sweat ran down his face, and through the glass Murke observed with cold detachment the agony that Bur-Malottke was going through; then he suddenly switched Bur-Malottke off, stopped the moving tape that was recording Bur-Malottke's words, and feasted his eyes on the spectacle of Bur-Malottke behind the glass, soundless, like a fat, handsome fish. He switched on his microphone and his voice came quietly into the studio: 'I'm sorry, but our tape was defective, and I must ask you to begin at the beginning with the nominatives.' Bur-Malottke swore, but his curses were silent ones which only he could hear, for Murke had disconnected him and did not switch him on again until he had begun to say 'that higher Being . . .' Murke was too young, considered himself too civilized, to approve of the word hate. But here, behind the glass pane, while Bur-Malottke repeated his genitives, he suddenly knew the meaning of hatred: he hated this great fat, handsome creature, whose books – two million, three hundred and fifty thousand copies of them – lay around in libraries, bookstores, book-shelves, and bookcases, and not for one second did he dream of suppressing this hatred. When Bur-Malottke had repeated two genitives, Murke switched on his own mike and said quietly: 'Excuse me for interrupting you; the nominatives were excellent, so was the first genitive, but would you mind doing the second genitive again? Rather gentler in tone, rather more relaxed – I'll play it back to you.' And although Bur-Malottke shook his head violently he signalled to the technician to play back the tape in the studio. They saw Bur-Malottke give a start, sweat more profusely than ever, then hold his hands over his ears until the tape came to an end. He said something, swore, but Murke and the technician could not hear him; they had disconnected him. Coldly Murke waited until he could read from Bur-Malottke's lips that he had begun again with the higher Being, he turned on the mike and the tape, and Bur-Malottke continued with the genitives.

When he was through, he screwed up Murke's list into a ball, rose from his chair, drenched in sweat and fuming, and made for the door; but Murke's quiet, pleasant young voice called him back. Murke said: 'But Professor, you've for-gotten the vocative.' Bur-Malottke looked at him, his eyes blazing with hate, and said into the mike: 'O Thou higher Being Whom we revere!'

As he turned to leave, Murke's voice called him back once more. Murke said: 'I'm sorry, Professor, but, spoken like that, the words are useless.'

'For God's sake,' whispered the technician, 'watch it!'

Bur-Malottke was standing stock-still by the door, his back to the glass booth, as if transfixed by Murke's voice.

Something had happened to him which had never hap-pened to him before: he was helpless, and this young voice, so pleasant, so remarkably intelligent, tortured him as nothing had ever tortured him before. Murke went on:

'I can, of course, paste it into the talk the way it is, but I must point out to you, Professor, that it will have the wrong effect.'

Bur-Malottke turned, walked back to the microphone, and said in low and solemn tones:

'O Thou higher Being Whom we revere.'

Without turning to look at Murke, he left the studio. It was exactly quarter past ten, and in the doorway he collided with a young, pretty woman carrying some sheet music. The girl, a vivacious redhead, walked briskly to the microphone, adjusted it, and moved the table to one side so she could stand directly in front of the mike.

In the booth Murke chatted for half a minute with Huglieme, who was in charge of Light Entertainment. Pointing to the metal container, Huglieme said: 'Do you still need that?' And Murke said, 'Yes, I do.' In the studio the redhead was singing, 'Take my lips, just as they are, they're so lovely.' Huglieme switched on his microphone and said quietly: 'D'you mind keeping your trap shut for another twenty seconds, I'm not quite ready.' The girl laughed, made a face, and said: 'O.K., pansy dear.' Murke said to the technician: 'I'll be back at eleven; we can cut it up then and splice it all together.'

'Will we have to hear it through again after that?' asked the technician. 'No,' said Murke, 'I wouldn't listen to it again for a million marks.'

The technician nodded, inserted the tape for the red-haired singer, and Murke left.

He put a cigarette between his lips, did not light it, and walked along the rear corridor towards the second pater-noster, the one on the south side leading down to the coffee-shop. The rugs, the corridors, the furniture, and the pictures, everything irritated him. The rugs were impressive, the corridors were impressive, the furniture was impressive, and the pictures were in excellent taste, but he suddenly felt a desire to take the sentimental picture of the Sacred Heart which his mother had sent him and see it somewhere here on the wall. He stopped, looked round, listened, took the picture from his pocket, and stuck it between the wallpaper and the frame of the door to the Assistant Drama Producer's office. The tawdry little print was highly coloured, and beneath the picture of the Sacred Heart were the words: *I prayed for you at St James's Church.*

Murke continued along the corridor, got into the paternoster, and was carried down. On this side of the building the Schrumsnot ashtrays, which had won a Good Design Award, had already been installed. They hung next to the illuminated red figures indicating the floor: a red four, a Schrumsnot ashtray, a red three, a Schrumsnot ashtray, a red two, a Schrumsnot ashtray. They were handsome ashtrays, scallop-shaped, made of beaten copper, the beaten copper base an exotic marine plant, nodular seaweed – and each ashtray had cost 258 marks 77 pfennigs. They were so handsome that Murke could never bring himself to soil them with cigarette ash, let alone anything as sordid as a butt. Other smokers all seemed to have had the same feeling – empty packs, butts, and ash littered the floor under the handsome ashtrays; apparently no one had the courage to use them as ashtrays; they were copper, burnished, forever empty.

Murke saw the fifth ashtray next to the illuminated red zero rising towards him, the air was getting warmer, there was a smell of food. Murke jumped off and stumbled into the coffee-shop. Three freelance colleagues were sitting at a table in the corner. The table was covered with used plates, cups, and saucers.

The three men were the joint authors of a radio series, *The Lung, A Human Organ*; they had collected their fee together, breakfasted together, were having a drink together, and were now throwing dice for the expense voucher. One of them, Wendrich, Murke knew well, but just then Wendrich shouted: 'Art!' – 'art,' he shouted again, 'art, art!' and Murke felt a spasm, like the frog when Galvani discovered electricity. The last two days Murke had heard the word *art* too often, from Bur-Malottke's lips; it occurred exactly 134 times in the two talks; and he had heard the talks three times, which meant he had heard the word *art* 402 times, too often to feel any desire to discuss it. He squeezed past the counter towards a booth in the far corner and was relieved to find it empty. He sat down, lit his cigarette, and when Wulla, the waitress, came, he said: 'Apple juice, please,' and was glad when Wulla went off again at once. He closed his eyes tight, but found himself listening willy-nilly to the conversation of the freelance writers over in the corner, who seemed to be having a heated argument about art; each time one of them shouted 'art' Murke winced. It's like being whipped, he thought.

As she brought him the apple juice Wulla looked at him in concern. She was tall and strongly built, but not fat, she had a healthy, cheerful face, and as she poured the apple juice from the jug into the glass she said: 'You ought to take a vacation, sir, and stop smoking.'

She used to call herself Wilfriede-Ulla, but later, for the sake of simplicity, she combined the names into Wulla. She especially admired the people from the Cultural Department.

'Lay off, will you?' said Murke, 'please!'

'And you ought to take some nice ordinary girl to the movies one night,' said Wulla.

'I'll do that this evening,' said Murke, 'I promise you.'

'It doesn't have to be one of those dolls,' said Wulla, 'just some nice, quiet, ordinary girl, with a kind heart. There are still some of those around.'

'Yes,' said Murke, 'I know they're still around, as a matter of fact I know one.' Well, that's fine then, thought Wulla, and went over to the freelances, one of whom had ordered three drinks and three coffees. Poor fellows, thought Wulla, art will be the death of them yet. She had a soft spot for the freelances and was always trying to persuade them to economize. The minute they have any money, she thought, they blow it; she went up to the counter and, shaking her head, passed on the order for the three drinks and the three coffees.

Murke drank some of the apple juice, stubbed out his cigarette in the ashtray, and thought with apprehension of the hours from eleven to one when he had to cut up Bur-Malottke's sentences and paste them into the right places in the talks. At two o'clock the Director wanted both talks played back to him in his studio. Murke thought about soap, about staircases, steep stairs, and roller coasters, he thought about the dynamic personality of the Director, he thought about Bur-Malottke, and was startled by the sight of Schwendling coming into the coffee-shop.

Schwendling had on a shirt of large red and black checks and made a beeline for the booth where Murke was hiding. Schwendling was humming the tune which was very popular just then: 'Take my lips, just as they are, they're so lovely . . .' He stopped short when he saw Murke, and said: 'Hullo, you here? I thought you were busy carving up that crap of Bur-Malottke's.'

'I'm going back at eleven,' said Murke.

'Wulla, let's have some beer,' shouted Schwendling over to the counter, 'a pint. Well,' he said to Murke, 'you deserve extra time off for that, it must be a filthy job. The old man told me all about it.'

Murke said nothing, and Schwendling went on:

'Have you heard the latest about Muckwitz?'

Murke, not interested, first shook his head, then for politeness' sake asked: 'What's he been up to?'

Wulla brought the beer, Schwendling swallowed some, paused for effect, and announced: 'Muckwitz is doing a feature about the Steppes.'

Murke laughed and said: 'What's Fenn doing?'

'Fenn,' said Schwendling, 'Fenn's doing a feature about the Tundra.'

'And Weggucht?'

'Weggucht is doing a feature about me, and after that I'm going to do a feature about him, you know the old saying: You feature me, I'll feature you . . .'

Just then one of the freelances jumped up and shouted across the room: 'Art – art – that's the only thing that matters!'

Murke ducked, like a soldier when he hears the mortars being fired from the enemy trenches. He swallowed another mouthful of apple juice and winced again when a voice over the loudspeaker said: 'Mr Murke is wanted in Studio Thirteen – Mr Murke is wanted in Studio Thirteen.' He looked at his watch, it was only half-past ten, but the voice went on relentlessly: 'Mr Murke is wanted in Studio Thirteen – Mr Murke is wanted in Studio Thirteen.' The loudspeaker hung above the counter, immediately below the motto the Director had had painted on the wall: *Discipline Above All.*

'Well,' said Schwendling, 'that's it, you'd better go.'

'Yes,' said Murke, 'that's it.'

He got up, put money for the apple juice on the table, pressed past the freelances' table, got into the paternoster outside and was carried up once more past the five Schrumsnot ashtrays. He saw his Sacred Heart picture still sticking in the Assistant Producer's doorframe and thought:

'Thank God, now there's at least one corny picture in this place.'

He opened the door of the studio booth, saw the technician sitting alone and relaxed in front of three cardboard boxes, and asked wearily: 'What's up?'

'They were ready sooner than expected, and we've got an extra half hour in hand,' said the technician. 'I thought you'd be glad of the extra time.'

'I certainly am,' said Murke, 'I've got an appointment at one. Let's get on with it then. What's the idea of the boxes?'

'Well,' said the technician, 'for each grammatical case I've got one box – the nominatives in the first, the genitives in the second, and in that one –' he pointed to the little box on the right with the words 'Pure Chocolate' on it, and said: 'in that one I have the two vocatives, the good one in the right-hand corner, the bad one in the left.'

'That's terrific,' said Murke, 'so you've already cut up the crap.'

'That's right,' said the technician, 'and if you've made a note of the order in which the cases have to be spliced it won't take us more than an hour. Did you write it down?'

'Yes, I did,' said Murke. He pulled a piece of paper from his pocket with the numbers one to twenty-seven; each number was followed by a grammatical case.

Murke sat down, held out his cigarette pack to the technician; they both smoked while the technician laid the cut tapes with Bur-Malottke's talks on the roll.

'In the first cut,' said Murke, 'we have to stick in a nominative.'

The technician put his hand into the first box, picked up one of the snippets and stuck it into the space.

'Next comes a genitive,' said Murke.

They worked swiftly, and Murke was relieved that it all went so fast.

'Now,' he said, 'comes the vocative; we'll take the bad one, of course.'

The technician laughed and stuck Bur-Malottke's bad vocative into the tape.

'Next,' he said, 'next!' 'Genitive,' said Murke.

The Director conscientiously read every listener's letter. The one he was reading at this particular moment went as follows:

Dear Radio,

I am sure you can have no more faithful listener than myself. I am an old woman, a little old lady of seventy-seven, and I have been listening to you every day for thirty years. I have never been sparing with my praise. Perhaps you remember my letter about the programme: 'The Seven Souls of Kaweida the Cow.' It was a lovely programme – but now I have to be angry with you! The way the canine soul is being neglected in radio is gradually becoming a disgrace. And you call that humanism. I am sure Hitler had his bad points; if one is to believe all one hears, he was a dreadful man, but one thing he did have: a real affection for dogs, and he did a lot for them. When are dogs going to come into their own again in German radio? The way you tried to do it in the programme 'Like Cat and Dog' is certainly not the right way: it was an insult to every canine soul. If my poor little Lohengrin could only talk, he'd tell you! And the way he barked, poor darling, all through your terrible programme, it almost made me die of shame. I pay my two marks a month like any other listener and stand on my rights and demand to know: When are dogs going to come into their own again in German radio?

With kind regards – in spite of my being so cross with you,

Sincerely yours,

Jadwiga Herchen (retired)

PS. In case none of those cynics of yours who run your programmes should be capable of doing justice to the canine soul, I
suggest you make use of my modest attempts, which are enclosed
herewith. I do not wish to accept any fee. You may send it direct
to the S.P.C.A. Enclosed: 35 manuscripts.
                                                    Yours,
                                                       J.H.

The Director sighed. He looked for the scripts, but his
secretary had evidently filed them away. The Director filled
his pipe, lit it, ran his tongue over his dynamic lips, lifted the
receiver and asked to be put through to Krochy. Krochy had
a tiny office with a tiny desk, although in the best of taste,
upstairs in Culture and was in charge of a section as narrow as
his desk: Animals in the World of Culture.

'Krochy speaking,' he said diffidently into the telephone.

'Say, Krochy,' said the Director, 'when was the last time
we had a programme about dogs?'

'Dogs, sir?' said Krochy. 'I don't believe we ever have, at
least not since I've been here.'

'And how long have you been here, Krochy?' And upstairs in his office Krochy trembled, because the Director's
voice was so gentle; he knew it boded no good when that
voice became gentle.

'I've been here ten years now, sir,' said Krochy.

'It's a disgrace,' said the Director, 'that you've never had
a programme about dogs; after all, that's your department.
What was the title of your last programme?'

'The title of my last programme was –' stammered Krochy.

'You don't have to repeat every sentence,' said the Director,
'we're not in the army.'

'Owls in the Ruins,' said Krochy timidly.

'Within the next three weeks,' said the Director, gentle
again now, 'I would like to hear a programme about the
canine soul.'

'Certainly, sir,' said Krochy; he heard the click as the
Director put down the receiver, sighed deeply, and said:
'Oh God!'

The Director picked up the next listener's letter.

At this moment Bur-Malottke entered the room. He was

always at liberty to enter unannounced, and he made frequent use of this liberty. He was still sweating as he sank wearily into a chair opposite the Director and said:

'Well, good morning.'

'Good morning,' said the Director, pushing the listener's letter aside. 'What can I do for you?'

'Could you give me one minute?'

'Bur-Malottke,' said the Director, with a generous, dynamic gesture, 'does not have to ask me for one minute; hours, days, are at your disposal.'

'No,' said Bur-Malottke, 'I don't mean an ordinary minute, I mean one minute of radio time. Due to the changes my talk has become one minute longer.'

The Director grew serious, like a satrap distributing provinces. 'I hope,' he said, sourly, 'it's not a political minute.'

'No,' said Bur-Malottke, 'it's half a minute of Neighbourly News and half a minute of Light Entertainment.'

'Thank God for that,' said the Director. 'I've got a credit of seventy-nine seconds with Light Entertainment and eighty-three seconds with Neighbourly News. I'll be glad to let someone like Bur-Malottke have one minute.'

'I am overcome,' said Bur-Malottke.

'Is there anything else I can do for you?' asked the Director.

'I would appreciate it,' said Bur-Malottke, 'if we could gradually start correcting all the tapes I have made since 1945. One day,' he said – he passed his hand over his forehead and gazed wistfully at the genuine Kokoschka above the Director's desk – 'one day I shall –' he faltered, for the news he was about to break to the Director was too painful for posterity '– one day I shall – die,' and he paused again, giving the Director a chance to look gravely shocked and raise his hand in protest, 'and I cannot bear the thought that after my death tapes may be run off on which I say things I no longer believe in. Particularly in some of my political utterances, during the fervour of 1945, I let myself be persuaded to make statements which today fill me with serious misgivings and which I can only account for on the basis of that spirit of youthfulness which has always distinguished my work. My written works are already in process of being corrected, and I would like to ask you to give me the opportunity of correcting my spoken works as well.'

The Director was silent, he cleared his throat slightly, and little shining beads of sweat appeared on his forehead; it occurred to him that Bur-Malottke had spoken for at least an hour every month since 1945, and he made a swift calculation while Bur-Malottke went on talking: twelve times ten hours meant 120 hours of spoken Bur-Malottke.

'Pedantry,' Bur-Malottke was saying, 'is something that only impure spirits regard as unworthy of genius; we know, of course' – and the Director felt flattered to be ranked by the We among the pure spirits – 'that the true geniuses, the great geniuses, were pedants. Himmelsheim once had a whole printed edition of his *Seelon* rebound at his own expense because he felt that three or four sentences in the central portion of the work were no longer appropriate. The idea that some of my talks might be broadcast which no longer correspond to my convictions when I depart this earthly life – I find such an idea intolerable. How do you propose we go about it?'

The beads of sweat on the Director's forehead had become larger. 'First of all,' he said in a subdued voice, 'an exact list would have to be made of all your broadcast talks, and then we would have to check in the archives to see if all the tapes were still there.'

'I should hope,' said Bur-Malottke, 'that none of the tapes has been erased without notifying me. I have not been notified, therefore no tapes have been erased.'

'I will see to everything,' said the Director.

'Please do,' said Bur-Malottke curtly, and rose from his chair. 'Goodbye.'

'Goodbye,' said the Director, as he accompanied Bur-Malottke to the door.

The freelances in the coffee-shop had decided to order lunch. They had had some more drinks, they were still talking about art, their conversation was quieter now but no less intense. They all jumped to their feet when Wanderburn suddenly came in. Wanderburn was a tall, despondent-looking writer with dark hair, an attractive face somewhat etched by the stigma of fame. On this particular morning he had not shaved, which made him look even more attractive. He walked over to the table where the three freelances were sitting, sank exhausted into a chair, and said: 'For God's sake, give me a drink. I always have the feeling in this building that I'm dying of thirst.'

They passed him a drink, a glass that was still standing on the table, and the remains of a bottle of soda water. Wanderburn swallowed the drink, put down his glass, looked at each of the three men in turn, and said: 'I must warn you about the radio business, about this pile of junk – this immaculate, shiny, slippery pile of junk. I'm warning you. It'll destroy us all.' His warning was sincere and impressed the three young men very much; but the three young men did not know that Wanderburn had just come from the accounting department where he had picked up a nice fat fee for a quick job of editing the Book of Job.

'They cut us,' said Wanderburn, 'they consume our substance, splice us together again, and it'll be more than any of us can stand.'

He finished the soda water, put the glass down on the table and, his coat flapping despondently about him, strode to the door.

On the dot of noon Murke finished the splicing. They had just stuck in the last snippet, a genitive, when Murke got up. He already had his hand on the doorknob when the technician said: 'I wish I could afford a sensitive and expensive conscience like that. What'll we do with the box?' He pointed to the flat tin lying on the shelf next to the cardboard boxes containing the new tapes.

'Just leave it there,' said Murke.

'What for?'

'We might need it again.'

'D'you think he might get pangs of conscience all over again?'

'He might,' said Murke, 'we'd better wait and see. So long.' He walked to the front paternoster, rode down to the second floor, and for the first time that day entered his office. His secretary had gone to lunch; Murke's boss, Humkoke, was sitting by the phone reading a book. He smiled at Murke, got up, and said: 'Well, I see you survived. Is this your book? Did you put it on the desk?' He held it out for Murke to read the title, and Murke said: 'Yes, that's mine.' The book had a jacket of green, grey, and orange and was called *Batley's Lyrics of the Gutter*; it was about a young English writer a hundred years ago who had drawn up a catalogue of London slang.

'It's a marvellous book,' said Murke.

'Yes,' said Humkoke, 'it is marvellous, but you never learn.'

Murke eyed him questioningly.

'You never learn that one doesn't leave marvellous books lying around when Wanderburn is liable to turn up, and Wanderburn is always liable to turn up. He saw it at once, of course, opened it, read it for five minutes, and what's the result?'

Murke said nothing.

'The result,' said Humkoke, 'is two hour-long broadcasts by Wanderburn on *Lyrics of the Gutter*. One day this fellow will do a feature about his own grandmother, and the worst of it is that one of his grandmothers was one of mine too. Please, Murke, try and remember: never leave marvellous books around when Wanderburn is liable to turn up, and, I repeat, he's always liable to turn up. That's all, you can go now, you've got the afternoon off, and I'm sure you've earned it. Is the stuff ready? Did you hear it through again?'

'It's all done,' said Murke, 'but I can't hear the talks through again, I simply can't.'

'"I simply can't" is a very childish thing to say,' said Humkoke.

'If I have to hear the word *Art* one more time today I shall become hysterical,' said Murke.

'You already are,' said Humkoke, 'and I must say you've every reason to be. Three hours of Bur-Malottke, that's too much for anybody, even the toughest of us, and you're not even tough.' He threw the book on the table, took a step towards Murke and said: 'When I was your age I once had to cut three minutes out of a four-hour speech of Hitler's, and I had to listen to the speech three times before I was considered worthy of suggesting which three minutes should be cut. When I began listening to the tape for the first time I was still a Nazi, but by the time I had heard the speech for the third time I wasn't a Nazi any more; it was a drastic cure, a terrible one, but very effective.'

'You forget,' said Murke quietly, 'that I had already been cured of Bur-Malottke before I had to listen to his tapes.'

'You really are a vicious beast!' said Humkoke with a laugh. 'That'll do for now, the Director is going to hear it through again at two. Just see that you're available in case anything goes wrong.'

'I'll be at home from two to three,' said Murke.

'One more thing,' said Humkoke, pulling out a yellow biscuit-tin from a shelf next to Murke's desk, 'what's this scrap you've got here?'

Murke coloured. 'It's –' he stammered, 'I collect a certain kind of left-overs.'

'What kind of left-overs?' asked Humkoke.

'Silences,' said Murke, 'I collect silences.'

Humkoke raised his eyebrows, and Murke went on: 'When I have to cut tapes, in the places where the speakers sometimes pause for a moment – or sigh, or take a breath, or there is absolute silence – I don't throw that away, I collect it. Incidentally, there wasn't a single second of silence in Bur-Malottke's tapes.'

Humkoke laughed: 'Of course not, he would never be silent. And what do you do with the scrap?'

'I splice it together and play back the tape when I'm at home in the evening. There's not much yet, I only have three minutes so far – but then people aren't silent very often.'

'You know, don't you, that it's against regulations to take home sections of tape?'

'Even silences?' asked Murke.

Humkoke laughed and said: 'For God's sake, get out!' And Murke left.

When the Director entered his studio a few minutes after two, the Bur-Malottke tape had just been turned on:

... and wherever, however, why ever, and whenever we begin to discuss the Nature of Art, we must first look to that higher Being Whom we revere, we must bow in awe before that higher Being Whom we revere, and we must accept Art as a gift from that higher Being Whom we revere. Art ...

No, thought the Director, I really can't ask anyone to listen to Bur-Malottke for 120 hours. No, he thought, there are some things one simply cannot do, things I wouldn't want to wish even on Murke. He returned to his office and switched on the loudspeaker just in time to hear Bur-Malottke say: 'O Thou higher Being Whom we revere ...' No, thought the Director, no, no.

Murke lay on his chesterfield at home smoking. Next to him on a chair was a cup of tea, and Murke was gazing at the white ceiling of the room. Sitting at his desk was a very pretty blonde who was staring out of the window at the street. Between Murke and the girl, on a low coffee-table, stood a tape recorder, recording. Not a word was spoken, not a sound was made. The girl was pretty and silent enough for a photographer's model.

'I can't stand it,' said the girl suddenly, 'I can't stand it, it's inhuman, what you want me to do. There are some men who expect a girl to do immoral things, but it seems to me that what you are asking me to do is even more immoral than the things other men expect a girl to do.'

Murke sighed. 'Oh hell,' he said, 'Rina dear, now I've got to cut all that out; do be sensible, be a good girl and put just five more minutes' silence on the tape.'

'Put silence,' said the girl, with what thirty years ago would have been called a pout. 'Put silence, that's another of your inventions. I wouldn't mind putting words onto a tape – but putting silence . . .'

Murke had got up and switched off the tape recorder. 'Oh Rina,' he said, 'if you only knew how precious your silence is to me. In the evening, when I'm tired, when I'm sitting here alone, I play back your silence. Do be a dear and put just three more minutes' silence on the tape for me and save me the cutting; you know how I feel about cutting.' 'Oh all right,' said the girl, 'but give me a cigarette at least.'

Murke smiled, gave her a cigarette, and said: 'This way I have your silence in the original and on tape, that's terrific.' He switched the tape on again, and they sat facing one another in silence till the telephone rang. Murke got up, shrugged helplessly, and lifted the receiver.

'Well,' said Humkoke, 'the tapes ran off smoothly, the boss couldn't find a thing wrong with them . . . You can go to the movies now. And think about snow.'

'What snow?' asked Murke, looking out onto the street, which lay basking in brilliant summer sunshine.

'Come on now,' said Humkoke, 'you know we have to start thinking about the winter programmes. I need songs about snow, stories about snow – we can't fool around for the rest of our lives with Schubert and Stifter. No one seems to have any idea how badly we need snow songs and snow stories. Just imagine if we have a long hard winter with lots of snow and freezing temperatures: where are we going to get our snow programmes from? Try and think of something snowy.'

'All right,' said Murke, 'I'll try and think of something.' Humkoke had hung up.

'Come along,' he said to the girl, 'we can go to the movies.'

'May I speak again now?' said the girl.

'Yes,' said Murke, 'speak!'

It was just at this time that the Assistant Drama Producer had finished listening again to the one-act play scheduled for that evening. He liked it, only the ending did not satisfy him. He was sitting in the glass booth in Studio Thirteen next to the technician, chewing a match and studying the script.

[*Sound-effects of a large empty church*]

ATHEIST [*in a loud clear voice*]: Who will remember me when I have become the prey of worms?

[*Silence*]

ATHEIST [*his voice a shade louder*]: Who will wait for me when I have turned into dust?

[*Silence*]

ATHEIST [*louder still*]: And who will remember me when I have turned into leaves?

[*Silence*]

There were twelve such questions called out by the atheist into the church, and each question was followed by –? Silence.

The Assistant Producer removed the chewed match from his lips, replaced it with a fresh one, and looked at the technician, a question in his eyes.

'Yes,' said the technician, 'if you ask me; I think there's a bit too much silence in it.'

'That's what I thought,' said the Assistant Producer; 'the author thinks so too and he's given me leave to change it. There should just be a voice saying: "God" – but it ought to be a voice without church sound-effects, it would have to be spoken somehow in a different acoustical environment. Have you any idea where I can get hold of a voice like that at this hour?'

The technician smiled, picked up the metal container which was still lying on the shelf. 'Here you are,' he said, 'here's a voice saying "God" without any sound-effects.'

The Assistant Producer was so surprised he almost swallowed the match, choked a little, and got it up into the front of his mouth again. 'It's quite all right,' the technician said with a smile, 'we had to cut it out of a talk, twenty-seven times.'

'I don't need it that often, just twelve times,' said the Assistant Producer.

'It's a simple matter, of course,' said the technician, 'to cut out the silence and stick in God twelve times – if you'll take the responsibility.'

'You're a godsend,' said the Assistant Producer, 'and I'll be responsible. Come on, let's get started.' He gazed happily at the tiny, lustreless tape snippets in Murke's tin box. 'You really are a godsend,' he said, 'come on, let's go!'

The technician smiled, for he was looking forward to being able to present Murke with the snippets of silence; it was a lot of silence, altogether nearly a minute; it was more silence than he had ever been able to give Murke, and he liked the young man.

'O.K.,' he said with a smile, 'here we go.'

The Assistant Producer put his hand in his jacket pocket, took out a pack of cigarettes; in doing so he touched a crumpled piece of paper, he smoothed it out and passed it to the technician: 'Funny, isn't it, the corny stuff you can come across in this place? I found this stuck in my door.'

The technician took the picture, looked at it, and said: 'Yes, it's funny,' and he read out the words under the picture: '*I prayed for you at St James's Church.*'

ALL ABOUT PENGUINS
AND PELICANS

Penguinews, which appears every month, contains details of all the new books issued by Penguins as they are published. From time to time it is supplemented by *Penguins in Print*, which is a complete list of all titles available. (There are some five thousand of these.)

A specimen copy of *Penguinews* will be sent to you free on request. For a year's issues (including the complete lists) please send 50p if you live in the British Isles, or 75p if you live elsewhere. Just write to Dept EP, Penguin Books Ltd, Harmondsworth, Middlesex, enclosing a cheque or postal order, and your name will be added to the mailing list.

In the U.S.A.: For a complete list of books available from Penguin in the United States write to Dept CS, Penguin Books Inc., 7110 Ambassador Road, Baltimore, Maryland 21207.

In Canada: For a complete list of books available from Penguin in Canada write to Penguin Books Canada Ltd, 41 Steelcase Road West, Markham, Ontario.

THE PENGUIN BOOK OF
AMERICAN SHORT STORIES

Edited by James Cochrane

This collection offers twenty-one short stories from the
literature of America, a nation which has always been particularly at home in this form, and which has produced
many of its masters. Some of the stories included – those
by Poe, James and Hemingway for example – are already
widely known. Some of the others will be less familiar to
the English reader. The collection as a whole should serve
as an introduction to the rich diversity of pleasures that
the American short story at its best can offer.

THE PENGUIN BOOK OF
ENGLISH SHORT STORIES

Edited by Christopher Dolley

Some of the stories in this collection – such as Wells's
The Country of the Blind and Joyce's *The Dead* – are classics;
others – like Dickens's *The Signalman* and Lawrence's
Fanny and Annie – are less well known. But all of them –
whether funny, tragic, wry or fantastic – show their
authors at their concise best. Which makes this representative collection, at the very least, ferociously entertaining.

NOT FOR SALE IN THE U.S.A.

FRENCH SHORT STORIES 1
NOUVELLES FRANÇAISES 1

The eight short stories in this collection, by Marcel Aymé, Alain Robbe-Grillet, Raymond Queneau and other French writers, have been selected both for their literary merit and as being representative of contemporary French writing. The English translations which are printed in a parallel text are literal rather than literary, and there are notes and biographies of the authors.

The volume is primarily intended to help English-speaking students of French, but these stories stand on their own and make excellent reading in either language.

Les huit nouvelles de ce recueil, de Marcel Aymé, Alain Robbe-Grillet, Raymond Queneau et d'autres auteurs français, ont été choisies non seulement pour leur mérite littéraire mais aussi parce qu'elles reflètent les tendances actuelles de la nouvelle française. Les traductions anglaises du texte parallèle ont visé l'exactitude plutôt que la valeur littéraire, et sont accompagnées de notes et de biographies des auteurs.

Ce livre a pour intention première d'être utile aux étudiants de langue anglaise qui étudient le français, mais, indépendamment de cela, les histoires ont un intérêt et une valeur qui permettent de les lire avec plaisir dans l'une ou l'autre langue.

ITALIAN SHORT STORIES 1
RACCONTI ITALIANI 1

The eight stories in this collection, by Moravia, Pavese, Pratolini, and other modern writers, have been selected as being representative of contemporary Italian writing. The English translations provided are literal rather than literary, and there are notes and biographies of the writers to help the student of Italian. However, the volume can also be helpful to Italians, who can improve their English by studying a strict rendering of stories with which they may already be familiar.

La scelta di scritti di Moravia, Pavese, Pratonni ed altri scrittori vuole essere rappresentativa della letteratura contemporanea italiana. Le traduzioni in inglese sono più let erali che letterarie e vi sono aggiunte note e biografie degli scrittori per aiutare lo studente di italiano. Il volume può anche essere di ausilio agli italiani che vogliano migliorare il loro inglese attraverso lo studio di una accurata traduzione di racconti a loro già noti.